# *TABLOID TERRORS EXPOSED!*

If you read the article and saw the photo, it must be true. At least that's what all those sensationalist supermarke███████████████████████ eve. But is "truth" █████████████████████████ bet it's not! At lea██████████████████████e of tabloid tales cr█████████████████naginations wriiin██████████████████eak peek at what a██████ ███.

**"The Source of It All"**—Welcome to the town that is home to all the denizens of the tabloid headlines—and wait till you find out what some of the neighbors are up to!

**"A Beak for Trends"**—He was the shrewdest bird on the stock market—until someone started lining his cage with tabloids. . . .

**"Group Phenomena"**—An ace reporter will do anything to get a story, even if it means taking a space alien to lunch. . . .

**"Unextinctions"**—When long extinct species suddenly beginning turning up, alive and well, all around the globe, does it signal the start of a wondrous new age, or something far more terrifying. . . .

# ALIEN PREGNANT BY ELVIS

## More Imagination-Clutching Anthologies
## Brought to You by DAW:

FRANKENSTEIN: THE MONSTER WAKES *Edited by Martin H. Greenberg.* From a journalist who stumbles upon a modern-day descendant of the famous doctor . . . to a mobster's physician whose innovative experiments might lead to a whole new kind of enforcer . . . to the monster's own determined search for a suitable bride . . . here are powerful new tales of creation gone awry.

JOURNEYS TO THE TWILIGHT ZONE *Edited by Carol Serling.* Sixteen unforgettable new tales—some eerie, some scary, some humorous—all with the unique *Twilight Zone* twist. Included is Rod Serling's classic, chill-provoking story, "Suggestion."

CHRISTMAS GHOSTS *Edited by Mike Resnick and Martin H. Greenberg.* Everyone knows Christmas has truly arrived when *A Christmas Carol* takes center stage in both amateur and professional productions. Now, some of the most creative minds in fantasy and science fiction tell readers exactly what those Christmas ghosts are up to when they're not scaring a stingy old man into self-reformation.

BY ANY OTHER FAME *Edited by Mike Resnick and Martin H. Greenberg.* What if Humphrey Bogart ran a detective agency? What if Groucho Marx was chosen to play Rhett Butler? What if Marilyn Monroe became a great feminist leader? Along with celebrities of stage and screen, these fanciful stories send such world-shakers as Adolf Hitler, Golda Meier, and Franklin Delano Roosevelt down entirely new pathways of destiny, transforming the world we know in ways we can't even begin to imagine.

# ALIEN PREGNANT BY ELVIS

### EDITED BY
## Esther M. Friesner and
## Martin H. Greenberg

## DAW BOOKS, INC.
### DONALD A. WOLLHEIM, FOUNDER
375 Hudson Street, New York, NY 10014

**ELIZABETH R. WOLLHEIM
SHEILA E. GILBERT
PUBLISHERS**

First Printing, June 1994
1 2 3 4 5 6 7 8 9

DAW TRADEMARK REGISTERED
U.S. PAT. OFF. AND FOREIGN COUNTRIES
—MARCA REGISTRADA
HECHO EN U.S.A.

PRINTED IN THE U.S.A.

# ACKNOWLEDGMENTS

*Introduction: Alien Pregnant by Elvis* © 1994 by Esther M. Friesner.

*The Source of It All* © 1994 by Dennis McKiernan.

*The Bride of Bigfoot* © 1994 by Lawrence Watt-Evans.

*Close-up Photos Reveal JFK Skull on Moon!* © 1994 by Barry Malzberg.

*Marilyn, Elvis, and the Reality Blues* © 1994 by James Brunet.

*Those Rowdy Royals!* © 1994 by Laura Resnick.

*My Husband Became a Zombie and It Saved Our Marriage* © 1994 by Karen Haber.

*Rock Band Conjures Satan as Manager* © 1994 by Deborah Wunder.

*2,437 UFOs Over New Hampshire* © 1994 by Allen Steele.

*Pulitzer Kills Publishing Maggot* © 1994 by Mark Tiedemann.

*Elvis at the White House* © 1994 by Kristine Kathryn Rusch.

*The Number of the Beast* © 1994 by Jeff Hecht.

*De Gustibus* © 1994 by Anthony Lewis.

*Is Your Coworker a Space Alien?* © 1994 by Eluki bes Shahar.

*A Beak for Trends* © 1994 by Laura Frankos.

*Hitler Clone in Argentina Plots Falklands Reprise* © 1994 by John DeChancie.

*Group Phenomena* © 1994 by Thomas F. Monteleone.

*Unextinctions* © 1994 by Bruce Boston and Roger Dutcher.

*How Alien He Really Was* © 1994 by Bruce Boston.

*NASA Sending Addicts to Mars!* © 1994 by Alan Dean Foster.

*Vole* © 1994 by John Gregory Betancourt.

*In Search of the Perfect Orgasm* © 1994 by Dean Wesley Smith.

*Saving Sam's Used UFOs* © 1994 by Kate Daniel.

*Danny's Excellent Adventure* © 1994 by Greg Cox.

*Royal Tiff Yields Face of Jesus!* © 1994 by Esther M. Friesner.

*Magnetic Personality Triggers Nail-Biter's Near-Death Ordeal!* © 1994 by t. Winter-Damon.

*They'd Never . . .* © 1994 by Harry Turtledove.

*Loch Ness Monster Found in the Bermuda Triangle* © 1994 by David Vierling.

*Racehorse Predicts the Future!* © 1994 by Josepha Sherman.

*Printer's Devils* © 1994 by Gregory Feeley.

*Cannibal Plants from Heck* © 1994 by David Drake.

*Psychic Bats 1000 for Accuracy* © 1994 by Jody Lynn Nye.

*Caveat Atlantis* © 1994 by Richard Gilliam.

*Frozen Hitler Found in Atlantean Love Nest* © 1994 by Rosemary Edghill.

*Those Eyes* © 1994 by David Brin.

*Stop Press* © 1994 by Mike Resnick.

*Martian Memorial to Elvis Sighted* © 1994 by George Alec Effinger.

Special thanks to
Greer Gilman
for the title.

This book is dedicated
to the Gentlefolk of the Press
and also to
Bigfoot
Nessie
Elvis
Marilyn
and all the Little People (from Mars, or wherever)
without whom the best tabloid journalism
would not be what it is today.

# Contents

# ALIEN PREGNANT BY ELVIS

### ELVIS APPEARS IN VISION,
### PREDICTS THIS BOOK!

Well, actually, it wasn't Elvis, it was a picture of a hamster. A three-foot-tall hamster that was the subject of a tabloid newspaper article describing how some guy in Godknowswhere, West Dakota, was raising these giant rodents for use as vicious guard dogs. It might have been the same issue that revealed Hitler was a 103-year-old woman when he/she/it died.

### SCIENCE FICTION LOSES
### CUTTING EDGE TO NESSIE!

So I said to myself, "I have given the best years of my fair young life to writing science fiction because I always heard that SF was the literature of *ideas*, a peephole into the dressing room of the future, the only writing that takes chances. Sure, people said to me, 'Oh, you write that *weird* stuff,' but I didn't mind. Maybe SF is weird, wild, totally gonzo, but at least it shows how far the human imagination can go!"

Now this. Three-foot-tall attack hamsters. Who'd 'a thunk it? In the race for the gonzo edge of the universe, SF has been left in the dust by the tabloids.

Dang.

### EDITOR GETS IDEA:
### THOUSANDS FLEE SCREAMING!

As I was saying to the aliens who came to take me to Planet Xax as soon as I got the chocolate chip cookies out of the oven (even Xaxians will wait for chocolate chip cookies), *"I love a challenge!"* And I was willing to bet that there were plenty of other writers out there who felt the same.

Yes, it was time to take up the gauntlet the tabloid press had flung at the feet of SF and go for the gonzo gold! *Could* science fiction writers dig deep and come up with stories even wilder than what's on the supermarket checkout newsstands?

*Would* some of the top names in the field deliver a new spin on the bizarre, the arcane, the extremely profitable News of the Weird?

*How* do you litter train a three-foot-tall attack hamster?

Even before the ink was dry on the letters of invitation, the stories came pouring in.

### SECRET BENEFITS OF READING *ALIEN PREGNANT BY ELVIS* REVEALED!
### SEX SECRETS OF THE STARS!
### AMAZING NEW DIET BREAKTHROUGH!
### THINNER THIGHS, FIRMER FANNY, FACELIFT WITHOUT SURGERY!

Yes, astounding but true, reading this book may actually help you:

*Lose unwanted pounds!* (If you don't eat anything while you're reading it.)

*Firm up that flab!* (If you put the book between your knees at least twice a day and squeeze twenty times, rest, repeat.)

*Improve your sex life!* (If you give it as a birthday gift, nicely wrapped, with maybe the keys to a new Porsche casually tied to the ribbon.)

*Remove unwanted sags and wrinkles!* (If you don't mind replacing them with laugh lines.)

*Raise your I.Q.!* (Or at least give you lots of food for thought, and that's never fattening.)

Thrill as *Martian Memorial to Elvis Sighted!*
Meet *The Bride of Bigfoot!*
Learn *The Number of the Beast!*
Confront *Cannibal Plants from Heck!*
Gasp at *2,437 UFOs Over New Hampshire!*
Discover what it is that *They'd Never . . .*
Get the scoop on *Those Rowdy Royals!*
Shudder as *Pulitzer Kills Publishing Maggot!*
See *Elvis at the White House!*
. . . and many more!

We've got tabloid tales from the past, present, and future, stories taken from the front pages and behind the scenes, sagas serious and silly. Hey, as long as you're stuck waiting in the supermarket checkout line anyway, you might as well check this out, too.

**UFO ALIENS SAY: YOU'LL BE GLAD YOU DID!**

# The Source of it All
## by Dennis McKiernan

*I can think of no better way to lead off this anthology than with a story that reveals the truth about tabloids. This week's truth, anyway.*

*The world knows Dennis McKiernan as the best-selling author of such fantasy novels as* Voyage of the Fox Rider, The Eye of the Hunter, *and the soon-to-appear story collection* Tales of Mithgar *as well as the graphic novel* The Vulgmaster.

*However, when asked to tell us a bit about himself for this book, Dennis wrote that he "was subdued and thrown in a padded cell when in a meeting of his encounter group he leaped up and confessed that every tabloid tale is in fact true, and to have found the place where all of them originate . . ."*

*Ooooooookay.*

It was right after the horse was born with the face of a boy that we found the great pyramid buried in my backyard.

"What the hell?" shouted Rikki when his shovel struck stone.

"Looks like marble," said Tikki, shoveling a bit more dirt out of the hole.

"Not just ordinary marble," muttered Tavi, squatting, taking Rikki and Tikki down with him. "Ha! I was right. This has been quarried and shaped."

"Here, let me see," I said, shoving my way in past my best friends—y'see, Rikki-Tikki-Tavi is the three-headed boy who lives next door (the man who was in labor for thirty-two hours before finally giving birth to them had been an avid reader of Kipling).

Using two shovels, all four of us dug out three more feet.

"It's sloped like the top of a pyramid," said Tavi (he was always the brightest of the three).

"Hmm," I hmmed. "Maybe we ought to get some expert advice on this before we go much deeper. I'll ask Gramps. You guys keep digging, but if you run into anything particularly special, stop."

I clambered up out of the hole and went to find Gramps. As I expected, he was in his dark room. Gramps is rather allergic to the sun. Oh, not that he's a vampire—like old Bram down the street—or anything of that sort. Instead, Gramps was out of the sunlight for so long he developed a sensitivity to it. You see, he's the survivor who spent forty-six years trapped inside the hull of the *Titanic*.

Anyway, I found Gramps in his dark room—actually, it's sort of a murky bluish color in there and not completely black.

"Gramps, we've found a pyramid buried in the backyard."

"Oh, izzat so?" he said, laying down his book and turning toward me, sloshing a bit as he always does. (In spite of his allergy, he's extremely well read—I mean, what else was there to do down there?) "Well, let me tell you, my boy, pyramids are nothing compared to what I've seen. Why, for forty-six years the *Titanic* and I drifted on currents under the ocean. Around the world we went, twice! and don't you forget it. Of course, I didn't see the usual sights—Paris and London and all of that. Oh, no, my boy, through that porthole I saw Atlantis and Mu and the statue of Rhodes and other such. And not where every so-called expert says they are, either. Instead, they're down near Bermuda. Lotsa stuff down there, let me tell you. Flight nineteen. The *Mary Deare*. More, much more. Did I ever tell you how I survived in that weed-filled air pocket? Why, who would believe that a man eats nothing but seamoss for forty-six years and lives to tell of it? Let me remind you, whippersnapper, this stuff is good for you." Sloshing as he turned, he reached one of his prune-wrinkled white hands into the ever-present bowl at his side, dredging up a fistful of slimy green weed. "Here, have some."

"Uh, no thanks, Gramps," I blurted and turned on my heel and ran. I had to get out of there before he launched into his giant-squid-saves-trapped-man story.

Well, smart as he was, Gramps had been no help.

Dejectedly, I went back to the dig. Rikki, Tikki, and Tavi had by this time recruited the giant robot to help with the excavation. In spite of his buzzing and chanking and whirring, he was a nice guy. Why the giant robot had run amok in Leningrad and killed thousands, we will probably never know. Regardless, he was doing all the digging now, while Rikki-Tikki-Tavi supervised (they always said that three heads are better than none . . . I mean, look at Arlo, the kid over on Mulberry Street, blundering around blindly as he does.).

I sat on the edge of the crater and watched as Igor (the giant robot) *zzzzzrrrppp*ed and *ckkachkkachkka*ed and *fffwwssshhh*ed, heaving great masses of dirt through the air to *wwhhhmp!* down in piles at the edge of the swamp. This wasn't going to make Beautiful Alice very happy. I mean, it looked to be blocking one of her lure paths—the one leading to the sacrificial quicksand pool. Now I ask you, would you be happy with this if you were a ghostly wraith enticing victims into a swampy quagmire?

Oh, well, we'd get that fixed later . . . once the pyramid was uncovered. And Igor was really throwing dirt now. Why, he was down about a hundred feet or so. It looked to be a massive pyramid. And speaking of pyramids, who could I turn to to help us interpret whatever we found inside? Who in the neighborhood knew about pyramids and sarcophagi and soul boats and mummies and hieroglyphs and curses and other such? Amid all the *bzzzrrp*ing and *chhnnkk*ing and *chggachggachgga*ing, Rikki and Tikki and Tavi and I talked it over. We discussed possible candidates. And no matter who was suggested, one or the other of us poo-pooed the idea.

"Mister Set? Nah! What would a guy with a dog's head know about pyramids anyway?"

"No, no! Not Mister Ghoul! He's likely to eat whatever is in there."

"That nice Mister Ripper, reincarnated and all? Not on your life. . . ."

We went through everyone we could think of. We even considered going down to the lake and asking shy Nessie, but none of us knew how to speak plesiosaur.

Sighing in dejection, we sat and watched Igor some more. And as kids all over the world do, we began talking about what we wanted to be when we grew up. Rikki wanted to be a leading man in religious movies, playing the part of the Father, the Son, and the Holy Ghost. Tikki on the other hand wanted to be a psychiatrist and work with mentally disturbed people, in particular those who hallucinate. Tavi wished to be a professional football player, a triple threat, so to speak. Then they asked me what I wanted to be.

"Oh, a writer, I think . . . that, or a newspaper reporter."

"What'll you write about?" asked Rikki.

"They say that you should write what you know," I answered.

"Hell," sneered Tikki, "you don't know much about anything other than the neighborhood."

Somewhat stung, I shot back, "Well, I'll write about that, then."

Tavi's eyes widened. "You'd write about the neighborhood? Bah, who would be interested in a bunch of ordinary homespun tales?"

"Why, lots of people, that's who," I spat.

"No-brain idiots, you mean!" shouted Rikki.

I jumped to my feet. "You leave the kid on Mulberry Street out of this!"

Rikki leaped to his feet, too, of necessity bringing Tikki and Tavi up with him. "Oh, yeah!" he shouted.

I balled my fists. "I'm gonna beat the tar out of you, Rikki," I growled, stepping forward to take a swing.

*"Oooo noooo!"* wailed Tikki and Tavi simultaneously, struggling with Rikki as to whether they would cower or fight.

*BLANG!* came a loud clang from the hole. In our heat we had completely forgotten about Igor. We spun around and peered down into the pit. Hell, he'd dug down past the foundation of the great pyramid and had struck something metallic.

*"Igor, wait!"* all four of us shouted.

Obediently, Igor straightened up and waited as we slid down into the crater, now one hundred fifty feet deep, all of us wondering what he had found. Even so, I was still burning over Rikki's remarks about me being a writer. Especially those concerning me writing about neighborhood events. One of these days I'd show him. And as to my reading public, well, we'd just see whether or not they were no-brainers.

We scrambled around to where Igor stood, and we looked down at what he'd uncovered.

Hmmm, maybe I could write about this. Yeah! This could be my first factual newspaper article—"Giant Robot Finds Alien Spaceship Beneath Great Pyramid."

Then I'd go on from there, writing about Gramps and Bram and Beautiful Alice and the kid on Mulberry Street, and all the rest of the folks and doings in the neighborhood. I don't care what Rikki says, I'm certain that there is an intelligent public out there just waiting for true-to-life, homespun, backyard tales like this.

No-brainers, ha!

# The Bride of Bigfoot
## by Lawrence Watt-Evans

*Hugo Award-winner Lawrence Watt-Evans answers the Fiction Writer's Eternal Question ("Where do you get your ideas?") by acknowledging inspiration from a genuine tabloid headline: "Bigfoot Stole My Wife!"*

*The author of numerous SF and Fantasy short stories and novels, a few of his more recent titles include* The Spell of the Black Dagger, Out of This World, *and* Split Heirs *(written in collaboration with me).*

*Lawrence adds, "My feet are 11D, which is not particularly large. I've never written for tabloids, and I've never been to Oregon."*

July, 1990·

Rodney MacWhirter had drunk a very pleasant little lunch back at the rest stop, and was feeling the aftereffects. He was of the opinion that the six-pack of Bud had not impaired his driving skills whatsoever, and would gladly argue the matter with any state cop who thought otherwise, but there was no denying the pressure in his bladder.

And the next rest stop, according to the sign, wasn't for fifteen miles.

Rodney blinked thoughtfully, then announced to no one, "Guess it's time to water the trees." He found the brake pedal on the second try, and managed to bring his battered Plymouth to a stop on the outer edge of the paved shoulder.

He was zipping his fly when someone tapped him on the shoulder.

He turned around, and the world seemed to vanish into a brown blur. Startled, Rodney stepped back, tried to focus, and found himself staring at a broad expanse of shaggy brown hair. He blinked, decided it was a coat of some kind, then raised his eyes, looking for a face.

He had to go much farther than he expected, and when he arrived he wished he hadn't.

There was a face there, as he had expected, but the face was brown and furry, with deep-set brown eyes, a broad black-tipped nose, and a wide, lipless mouth with stubby fangs protruding from the upper jaw. The heavy browridges were a good eight feet from the ground.

"Whoa!" Rodney said. "Hi, there, fella! You're a big one, ain'cha?"

The creature smiled, revealing several dozen yellow teeth, and nodded. Then it held up a stack of mismatched sheets of rather used paper in one hand, and pointed to it with the other, which clutched a handful of battered crayons.

Rodney squinted at the top sheet of paper and read, in large, shaky, red letters, I NEED RIDE TO OREGON WOODS.

"Whoa!" Rodney said again. "That's a mighty long way, friend; I can't take you that far." From the corner of his eye he saw the thing's smile vanish, and he hastily added, "But I can get you partway, I guess."

The smile returned, and together, Rodney and the creature walked to the car.

"So, you got a name?" Rodney asked.

The creature shook its head, and hair scraped audibly against the car's roof lining. A Plymouth Duster might have more headroom than the typical modern car, but it was never intended for anything the size of Rodney's passenger.

"No?" Rodney said, mildly surprised; he turned to stare, then snapped his attention back to the road at the sound of a horn blaring. A car coming the other way roared past, the driver's fist waving in Rodney's direction.

For a moment Rodney concentrated on his driving, then he suggested, "How 'bout I call you Bubba? You remind me of a fellow I useta know went by Bubba."

The creature shrugged as best it could while squeezed into the Plymouth.

"Bubba it is, then," Rodney said. For a minute or so he hummed quietly to himself.

"So where you going in Oregon, anyway?" he asked, still watching the highway unroll before him. He waited a few seconds, to give the creature time to write, then glanced over.

The beast didn't hold up a paper; instead it shrugged again.

"Just tired of Wisconsin, huh?" Rodney said, with a sympathetic smile. "I can understand that. You really need to go all the way to Oregon, though? You couldn't just check out Minneapolis?" He watched the highway, then added, "But I guess you're not the city type. Still, there's plenty of nice country in Minnesota. Or up in Maine; might be more traffic that way. Why's it got to be Oregon? Got family out there?"

The creature hesitated, then pulled a wrinkled piece of newsprint from its pile of scrap paper and held it up. Rodney glanced at it, and saw a battered fragment of tabloid—specifically, the *Midnight News* for October 1, 1987, featuring the headline, "THE BRIDE OF BIGFOOT! Scientists Report Sighting Female Creature in Oregon Woods!"

There was no photo, but a drawing captioned, "Artist's Rendition of Creature, from Scientists' Description," accompanied the article, and depicted a stooped, furry, apelike figure with ragged, waist-length head hair and immense breasts.

Rodney slowed the car slightly and looked the clipping over again.

"Bride of Bigfoot," Rodney read aloud. "That your wife, then? Mrs. Bubba?"

The creature shook his head.

"But you'd like her to be, maybe? You looking for a date out there?"

Bubba hesitated, then nodded.

"You don't like the local girls?" Rodney asked.

Bubba found one of his crayons and scrawled quickly, then held up a paper saying, CAN'T FIND ANY.

"What, *none*?"

Bubba shrugged again.

"What about guys? You got friends around here, might want help?" Rodney thought he might have a money-making idea here—a dating service for bigfoots!

Or was it bigfeet?

While Rodney was trying to puzzle out the correct plural, Bubba wrote, ALL ALONE. NO OTHERS.

Well, Rodney thought, so much for *that* idea. "Wow, tough," he said. "No family? Nothing?"

Bubba held up the same paper after underlining *ALL ALONE*.

"Jeez, no wonder you want to get out there," Rodney said. He thought for a moment.

There ought to be some way to make money off this, he told himself. He couldn't make a career out of matchmaking if Bubba and the lady in the picture were the only ones out there, but there had to be *some* way to cash in on picking up a mythical creature as a hitchhiker.

He intended to just drop Bubba off, but as he sobered up other possibilities began to occur to him. As they crossed the Minnesota state line he said, "Look, I was only going as far as St. Paul, but maybe I can . . . I mean, I might be able to take you clear to Oregon, if you're not in a hurry." He glanced over.

Bubba nodded, smiling.

Smuggling something Bubba's size in and out of motel rooms was an art Rodney had never acquired; fortunately, despite his bulk, Bubba could be amazingly stealthy. He moved in utter silence, and could hold so still that a bored motel maid might pass within a yard of him without noticing his presence.

That at least explained something of why the scientists still didn't believe in Bigfoot, or sasquatches, or whatever Bubba was.

Feeding him turned out to be simple enough—fast-food salad bars provided everything Bubba needed. Cherry tomatoes seemed to delight him no end, and Rodney made a point of getting as many of those as he could, despite the dirty looks from restaurant staffs.

Bubba had no idea what a bed was for; he was perfectly happy curling up on the motel-room carpet. He didn't understand indoor plumbing, either, but finding a few out-of-the-way bushes was usually easy enough. Rodney gathered, from a conversation that was largely grunts or nods on Bubba's side, that the creature had learned English from spying on campers, and taught himself to read and write from studying the newspapers, labels, and other scraps they left behind—a project that had occupied most of the past ten years, inspired by a discovery of a "bigfoot" photo in an old tabloid. Bubba, however, had never been inside a building before, and was not much interested in human civilization—except for picking goodies from its trash, and using it to find himself a mate.

That first night Rodney, now thoroughly sobered up, was a trifle uneasy about sleeping in the same room as this immense beast. Even though Bubba had made it clear that he preferred salads to burgers, Rodney still worried about all those teeth and claws.

When he awoke the next morning, completely intact, at first he thought he'd dreamed or imagined the whole thing; he came within inches of stepping on the still-sleeping Bubba, who had rolled over close to the bed.

By the second night they were both old hands at it.

And on the third night they made it as far as Walla Walla, Washington, just across the Oregon state line—Rodney had decided the fastest route was to leave the Interstate and take U.S. 12.

He didn't tell Bubba how close they were, for fear he'd want to go on that same night—Rodney was *tired* of driving.

When morning rolled around, though, the two of them got rolling as well, and had gone just a few miles when Rodney pointed out the WELCOME TO OREGON sign.

"We're in the right state," he said with a smile. "So where's this lady friend you're looking for?"

Bubba handed him the clipping.

Rodney glanced at it, then pulled over to the shoulder atop the next ridge and read through the clipping carefully. As he read, his smile slowly faded, to be replaced with a worried frown. "Bubba, ol' buddy," he said, "It doesn't *say* where she was anywhere in here. There's no dateline or anything, it just says 'somewhere in the Oregon woods,' and that doesn't tell us enough."

Bubba growled, and tapped a claw-tipped finger insistently on the word OREGON.

"Bubba," Rodney said, "hop out of the car for a minute, okay?"

The pair climbed out and stood by the road; Rodney waved an arm to take in the entire surrounding countryside, a broad vista of hills and forests extending seemingly forever.

"Bubba," he said, "*That's* the Oregon woods. Everything you see, and a lot more besides."

Bubba stared for a moment, then made a noise that Rodney could only liken to a strangled kitten. The huge creature turned and stared helplessly at Rodney.

Rodney thought for a moment the sasquatch was going to cry.

"Hey, don't worry, Bubba," he said, "We'll find her somehow. You just come with me."

"I tell you, Bubba, I felt really stupid buying this thing," Rodney said, as he thumbed through the latest issue of *Midnight News.* The two of them were seated in the Plymouth, parked in front of a drugstore in Milton-Freewater, Oregon. "Oh, here we go, page 6—*Midnight News,* editor, managing director, yadda yadda yadda ... telephone! Editorial, area code 407 ..." He lowered the paper. "Where the heck is area code 407?"

Bubba just stared silently at him.

Area code 407 turned out to be central Florida; the address was farther down the block of tiny print on page 6.

"Figures," Rodney said in disgust, as he dialed the motel-room phone. "The damn opposite corner of the whole damn country, is all. This call is probably gonna cost more than the damn room."

Bubba didn't answer; he sat and stared.

The phone on the other end only rang once before a female voice said, "*Midnight News.*"

"Hi," Rodney said. "Look, I need to know more about something you ran in your paper—it's very important to a friend of mine."

"What is it, exactly?" the voice asked warily.

"It's about this piece you ran in October '87, about seeing a female bigfoot in Oregon ..."

Before he could finish, the voice cut him off. " '87!" the woman exclaimed. "Mister, are you crazy? That was three years ago!"

"Yes, I know," Rodney said patiently.

"I'm sorry, but we don't keep ..." She stopped, thought better of whatever she had been about to say, and instead asked cautiously, "What did you want to know?"

"I want to know where in Oregon this bigfoot sighting was," Rodney explained. "It just says 'Oregon woods.' Oregon's a big state."

"I suppose it is," she agreed.

"So where was this sighting?"

"Mister, is there a byline on the article you've got there?"

Rodney blinked, and squinted at the yellowed clipping. "Uh ... yeah," he said. "Special correspondent Maurice Betterman, it says."

"Moe Betterman?" The voice sighed. "Well, at least I know who that is; he's a free-lancer, still writes for us sometimes. Lives in Eugene."

"Eugene, Oregon?"

"That's right."

"So, can I reach him ..."

"Listen, Mister, that's all I can tell you. It's probably more than I *should* tell you."

"But ..." Rodney began.

Then he realized he was talking to a dead phone; she had hung up.

"Eugene," he said. "That's the other end of the state." He hesitated, then dialed again.

"Directory assistance," said the voice. "What city, please?"

There was a listing for an M.C. Betterman; a few minutes and a dozen rings later Rodney finally heard someone pick up the phone—then drop it; Rodney winced at the clatter.

After assorted bumps and rattles, a bleary voice said, "'Lo?"

"Is this Maurice Betterman?" Rodney asked.

"Who wan'sa know?"

Rodney sighed. "I'm looking for the Maurice Betterman who writes for the *Midnight News*," he said.

"Why?"

"Are you him?"

"He," the voice corrected. "Are you *he*."

Rodney took that as a good sign; in his experience only teachers and writers corrected people like that. "Are you?" he asked.

"Migh' be; why?"

"We need a little more information about an article you wrote back in 1987," Rodney explained.

For a long moment there was no answer, and Rodney was beginning to wonder if he had been cut off, or if Betterman had fallen asleep, when the voice finally asked, "Who's 'we'?"

"Me'n Bubba," Rodney explained.

"Bubba."

"Well, that's what I call him."

Click. Betterman had hung up.

Rodney dialed again, and let the phone ring twenty-two times, hoping the motel operator wouldn't notice and cut him off before Betterman answered.

The motel operator didn't.

"Yeah?" Betterman's voice asked.

"It's me again," Rodney said. "Look, please don't hang up . . ."

"You'n Bubba?"

"That's right."

"Why should'n I hang up? You got three seconds to convince me."

"Money," Rodney said quickly. "Lots of money."

For another long moment the line was silent—but no one hung up. Then Betterman sighed.

"Okay," he said, "Tell me about it."

Rodney told him.

"You got a sasquatch there?" Betterman asked when Rodney had finished. "A real one?"

"That's what I said," Rodney replied. "And he wants to know where you saw that other one in '87."

"And suppose I tell you—then what?"

"Then we hang up and stop bothering you."

"Suppose I *don't* tell you?"

"Then we'll keep bothering you."

"You said there was money involved . . ."

"Well, sure—aren't pictures of a sasquatch worth money?"

"Depends how good they are."

"You can take all the pictures you want of this one."

Betterman was silent for a moment before asking, "So where are you? Where can I see this thing?"

Betterman stared at Bubba. "I didn't believe you," he said to Rodney. "I figured you'd just tell me it had got away or something."

The three of them had rendezvoused at a rest area on I-84, a few miles west of Hood River; Bubba had waited in the woods while Rodney met Betterman and escorted him over for a good long look.

"Then why'd you come?" Rodney asked.

"Oh, I figured I could get a story out of it anyway—and

besides, it seemed like the quickest way to get rid of you," Betterman explained, never taking his eyes from Bubba.

The attention seemed to make the creature uneasy, but he didn't flee.

"I call him Bubba," Rodney explained. "He doesn't have a name, really—I guess his kind don't bother with them."

"Does it . . . does it talk?" Betterman asked hesitantly.

Bubba grunted.

"No," Rodney said. "But he writes notes. You brought your camera?"

"It's in the car," Betterman answered.

"Okay. Look, here's the deal—Bubba, here, is lonely, and he saw in that article that you saw a female bigfoot, so he wants to meet her. Now, *you* tell us where she is, and *we* let you take pictures and ask questions. Fair enough?"

Betterman looked at him, startled. "*I* never saw one before!" he said.

"Okay, okay," Rodney said, "You wrote that article, but I guess it was somebody else that actually saw the critter?"

Betterman shrugged, then hesitated, then looked warily at Bubba. The creature looked nervous, and despite the size, fairly harmless.

"I made it up," he said.

Rodney and Bubba were thunderstruck. For a moment they just stared.

Then Bubba growled. Betterman, suddenly aware that he might have done something stupid, began desperately explaining, "Look, I'm being honest with you, I could've jerked you around until I got the pictures, I could've told you anything, but I figured I should be honest, I just made it all up, honest!"

"You did?" Rodney asked ominously.

"Sure!" Betterman babbled, "I make it *all* up! I mean, everything, the Elvis sightings, Hitler's clones, the UFO aliens, the three-headed babies, it's all made up! Just entertainment, just stories!"

"Nobody saw a female bigfoot?"

"Not . . . I don't . . . I don't know!" Betterman wailed, as Bubba's huge paw closed on the front of his shirt.

"You don't *know*?" Rodney demanded.

"No! I mean, I do research my stuff, I collect clippings and everything, and maybe somebody saw one and maybe that's what gave me the idea for my article, but I don't remember! It's been three years!"

Rodney looked at Bubba, and Bubba looked at Rodney. Bubba let go of Betterman's shirt and turned, reaching for his writing supplies.

"You want to go check this out?" Rodney asked. "See what he's got in his files?"

Bubba nodded. Then he scribbled quickly with a stub of purple crayon.

Betterman stared, amazed, at the sight of the huge hairy beast *writing;* when he saw what it had written, however, he let out a low moan of terror.

OR I RIP HIS HED OFF, Bubba said.


The drawer marked MYTH. BEASTS was two feet deep and full to overflowing; yellowed clippings were spilling out the sides. Betterman carefully hauled out the two fattest folders, labeled BIGFOOT and BIGFOOT (CONT.).

Bubba stared as the clippings spilled out across the rickety table. His own collection was mostly tabloids, and these were not; instead, Betterman had restricted himself to relatively respectable sources. Where Bubba's stories were mostly front-page features with screaming headlines, Betterman's were mostly tiny items clipped from the back pages of obscure local weeklies, from columns with titles like "Unexplained" and "Briefly Noted."

Rodney was impressed—until he began looking over the material at hand.

"There's nothing on here to tell where it is!" he pointed out. "Or on this one, or this . . ." He picked up a larger scrap, stared, and said, "And *this* one's from 1964!"

"I've been at this a long time," Betterman muttered.

Rodney could believe that; Betterman had to be in his fifties, at least. "Why don't you note where they're *from?*" he asked.

"Who cares?" Betterman shrugged. "This is just for ideas, I'm not writing a book or anything."

Rodney frowned.

"Well, there might be *some* we can use," he said. "I guess we better start sorting." He sat down, and began reading.


August, 1992:

"Look, Moe," the voice on the phone said, "They're *great*

pictures, I don't know how you do it, they're better than the stuff our lab here does, but we're *tired* of bigfoot stories! Two years now you've been sending us bigfoot stories! People are sick of bigfoot, Moe; give us something on Elvis, or something."

"But they're *real*," Betterman insisted desperately. "I keep telling you that!"

"If they're real," his editor answered, "Why are you sending them to *us,* and not *Scientific American?*"

"Because *Scientific American* doesn't believe me!" Betterman shouted, "and Bubba draws the line at letting anyone else see him!"

"Bubba?"

"Never mind," Betterman mumbled. "Look, I'll do an Elvis sighting, okay? I'll have it in the mail tomorrow. How about he's in a drug rehab program?"

"Well, maybe," the editor said. "But remember, people want him to look like a good guy."

"Maybe he's been held hostage?"

"Yeah, I think we could go for that. And if you could get photos . . ."

"No photos," Betterman said. "You'll have to do that part."

"Okay, no photos. And no more bigfoot." He hung up before Betterman could answer.

Betterman sighed and turned to his ancient typewriter; by the time Rodney MacWhirter came in for dinner he had a complete draft of "Elvis Escapes Terrorists!" done.

When Rodney and Bubba had first shown up, two years before, he had never expected it to turn out this way—two years spent trying to convince *somebody* that Bubba was real, when Bubba had apparently hit his limit of how many people he would allow to see him—two, Moe and Rodney.

And Rodney had gone home to Milwaukee and packed up his belongings and moved out to Eugene, trying to find some way to cash in on his friendship with Bubba, even as he continued to track down bigfoot sightings in an attempt to find Bubba a mate.

And neither of them had anything to show for it except a bunch of bylines in cheap tabloids—Moe writing the articles, Rodney providing the pictures.

And they hadn't found another sasquatch. Poor Bubba was getting depressed, frustrated, and angry.

"So how goes it?" Moe asked, when Rodney had thrown himself into the sagging armchair by the window.

"Lousy," Rodney said. "I checked out the last one of your clippings today."

"Nothing?" Moe asked sympathetically.

"Nothing," Rodney agreed.

"So now what?"

"So now we go tell Bubba the bad news. And maybe I see about finding an honest job again—my savings are just about gone."

"Ha!" Moe said. "I never *had* any savings! *Or* an honest job!"

They met at the back corner of a rest stop on I-84 again, but nowhere near Hood River this time; Bubba had been working his way eastward, searching the forests, and had gotten out past the Wallowa-Whitman National Forest, to somewhere in Baker County.

Rodney explained.

"We've tried 'em all, Bubba—everything we know to do. And we haven't found a thing." He shrugged, and turned up empty palms. "There's nothing more we can do."

Bubba frowned, and wrote.

ASK LEADING PYSCHICS, he said. He held up one of his own clippings; he had been collecting them from campsides and trash cans all across Oregon. This one's banner headline read, "Psychic Locates Child Lost In Woods For Five Years!" The subhead explained, "Boy Lived on Roots and Berries!"

"Psychics are all fakes," Moe said. "We've told you that."

Bubba wrote, ASK ELVIS, and held up a clipping headlined, "Elvis' Ghost Leads Woman to Lost Jewelry!"

"Elvis is dead," Rodney said. "Fifteen years, now."

Bubba shook his head angrily and held up "Stunning New Proof the King Still Lives!"

"But even if he does," Moe said, "How do we find *him*? He's in hiding!"

Rodney turned to argue, then thought better of it; Bubba wrote again.

ASK UFO ALIENS, he said. His exhibit this time read, "Space Aliens Reveal Pyramid Secrets!"

"There *aren't* any UFO aliens!" Moe insisted. "I keep telling you, Bubba, it's all *made up*! All that stuff in the tabloids! It's all lies!"

ALL? Bubba asked, holding a clipping of "Bigfoot Prowling Central Park!" against his chest.

"All of it," Moe insisted. "*You're* real, but the rest of it is all fiction. They just made it all up. Elvis is dead. There aren't any aliens."

NO BIGFOOT? Bubba asked.

"None except you," Moe said.

WHERE'D I COME FROM?

"I don't know," Moe said helplessly, "But you're the only one."

Bubba stared at him for a moment, then turned, and before Moe or Rodney could protest, he had vanished into the woods.

"You sure about this?" Moe asked, as Rodney forced down the trunk lid on his ancient Plymouth.

"I'm sure, all right," Rodney said. "Back in Milwaukee I've got friends and contacts; around here, I've got you, and about a thousand people who think I'm a nut who believes in bigfoot."

"You *are* a nut who believes in bigfoot," Moe pointed out.

"Yeah, but it doesn't help my job prospects," Rodney said, as he headed for the driver's seat.

"Drive safely, then," Moe said.

"I will," Rodney said, hoping Moe couldn't see the cooler of Budweiser in the shotgun seat. Driving across all that empty country was bad enough under any circumstances; he didn't want to face it sober.

One of these days, he thought, he was probably going to get himself killed by misjudging how much he drank—but right now he didn't care.

"Say hello to poor Bubba if you see him."

"I will."

And then he was gone.

The gas station was utterly nondescript except for the guy behind the counter. Rodney blinked at him in surprise.

The fellow had thick, slicked-back black hair, a heavy and oddly familiar face; he wore studded white denim and very dark sunglasses, though the light in the little mini-grocery was hardly bright. He was also grossly overweight and obviously on the wrong side of fifty, which made the hair and studs and sunglasses look very odd. Rodney had the feeling that if he could see better, and hadn't had those last few beers, he might recognize the man.

But that was silly; who would he know at a gas station outside Missoula, Montana?

"Somethin' I can help you with?" the cashier asked.

"Wish you could," Rodney said, staring at the issue of the *Midnight News* on display beside the cash register. One of his last photos of Bubba was featured on the front page.

"How's that, friend?"

Rodney pointed. "Friend of mine," he said. "Can't get a date."

The man behind the counter made a wordless noise of surprise. "The hairy fella?" he asked.

Rodney nodded, then waited for the room to steady again. "Yup. Ol' Bigfoot himself, out there in Baker County, Oregon. He's been looking for a female for years, can't find a one."

"That so?"

Rodney decided against nodding again. "Yup."

"Seems to me someone could maybe do somethin' about that," the cashier said. His voice was familiar, too, Rodney thought.

"I tried," he said. "I spent the last two years asking people all over the Northwest." It occurred to him that he must sound like a lunatic, and that he would never have been talking about it if he were sober, but the cashier didn't seem to think there was anything wrong.

"Mebbe you asked the wrong folks," the man said. His accent, Rodney realized, was from somewhere a lot farther south than Montana. "I been doin' some travelin' these past fifteen years," the cashier continued, "and I met some interestin' folks, some that was what you might call right out of this world. I'd guess that they might help us out here." He picked a copy of the *Midnight News* from the rack and studied the photo. "Seems like him and me, we got some things in common, you might say," he said, tapping the headlines.

Rodney struggled to focus on the newspaper. The photo was down at the foot of the page, captioned, "New Sightings of Mystery Beast!" Beside it, a box proclaimed, "Elvis in Iraq for Secret Negotiations!" The main headline, under the clerk's hand, read, "Space Aliens Save Sinking Ship! Bermuda Triangle Victims Rescued By UFO!"

"Poor Bubba," Rodney muttered.

"Don't you fret, son," the clerk said. "Things'll turn out jest fine. Now, you had the nachos and the bean dip; anythin' else?"

Twenty minutes later Rodney decided, as he sat in his car munching the last of the chips, that he was too tired—and, he admitted to himself, too drunk—to drive any more just then. He settled back for a quick nap.

He awoke to a loud buzzing and a bright light; blinking, trying to shield his eyes against the glare, he stared out at the gas station.

The light was coming from somewhere overhead; Rodney couldn't see its source. He *could* see the overweight clerk standing in the doorway, head tilted back, dark sunglasses protecting his eyes as he gazed upward.

He seemed to be signaling, making signs with his hands.

That was crazy, Rodney decided. He must be dreaming. He closed his eyes and went back to sleep.

When he awoke again he shook his head to clear it, blinked, and put the car into drive.

Weird dream, he thought. Some guy who looks like Elvis signaling the flying saucers. Obviously, Rodney thought, I've been reading too many tabloids.

The following night UFO sightings were reported all over Baker County, Oregon. The most peculiar feature was the story, repeated by a dozen witnesses, that a big hairy man had been standing on a hill near a campground, waving sheets of paper at the UFOs. The deputy who investigated the next day found letters burned into the grass.

They were obviously the work of pranksters; after all, why would space aliens write WE'RE ALL IN THIS TO-GETHER, BUBBA on a hillside, in plain English?

As Moe Betterman read the report his eyes widened, and then a slow smile spread across his face.

Bigfoot sightings were common enough; he had been collecting them for thirty years. People reported lone creatures most of the time, but sometimes pairs, trios, whole families, entire herds; it didn't mean much.

But when half a dozen sightings in succession, all in eastern Oregon, *all* reported *two* sasquatches, one smaller and more delicate than the other. . . .

"Congratulations, Bubba," he said quietly. "And my best to the little lady."

# Close-up Photos Reveal
# JFK Skull on Moon!
## by Barry N. Malzberg

*Lovers of fine writing will be happy to see more work by Barry Malzberg appearing of late, including many short stories, his novelette "Literary Lives," novella "Behold the Lamb of God," and novel* God of the Mountains *which he is writing with Kathleen Koja. I totally concur with his high opinion of her writing.*

*Until I saw this strange and compelling story, I thought that "gonzo" SF could only be funny. I owe Barry a special vote of thanks for thus opening the editorial eyes.*

He feels the implosion as a small and deadly shock at the base of his skull, then radiating up and down through the vertebrae and then, at last, the slow collapse, the scattering of organs, the sensation of a disaster in the blood so absolute that it is not only beyond recovery, it is what he must have sought all of his life. Dumped in the ocean, squirreling frantically with that rope between his teeth, lying on the boards in the barracks strapped against the hard, silent surfaces of his agony he had had small pieces of this disaster but nothing, nothing so complete. He embraces it willingly. Surely he had known in the tunnels and torrents of the night that this is what awaited him. He has been ready; he has always been ready. Coming out of that long and disastrous passage, then, stretched against the hard and constant surfaces of the Moon, he finds that he is lying at the bottom of a shallow crater, his eyes fixed with stunned and perceptive accuracy upon the distant swirl of Earth. He is breathing quite easily without aid of respirator or space suit, without shielding of any kind, which is an unusual experience but nonetheless one which seems unremarkable under the circumstances.

Nothing is unremarkable, JFK thinks, and comes to a seated position, finding that his organs seem to have been restored and that he is in a state of placid and flexible attention more pliant than any he has known since he was fifteen years old. The crater, scooped and brilliantly shadowed in the fading light cast by the planet, is only two feet high and he is able to scramble easily to his feet, raise himself, and emerge from the crater to place a shaky foot upon the dusty, uneven surfaces of the Moon. The Apollo project must have worked, he thinks, somehow they must have gotten there. *I* have gotten here. He cannot calculate how long it has been since the implosion, how long he lay in dreaming spaces before he was transported to the Moon, but he suspects it could not have been too long; there would have been decomposition and yet his body, neatly attired in a smock and tunic of some kind, seems to be intact. It is an extraordinary and enlightening experience, but there appear to be no others on this surface. It is desolate as far as his shadowed sight can cast, and it occurs to JFK for the first time that even though he seems to have been resurrected, his troubles may not be over. His troubles, in fact, may just be beginning. When will they come for him or do they even know he is there? In that strange and stricken light he feels the thunder of impact again, shifts his shoulders, clears his throat, reflexively grabs at the back of his head. He could not bear to go past the Depository again and yet who is to say what will happen to him? All of the known circumferences have broken,

## ELVIS AFTER PLASTIC SURGERY
## ROCKS TILL DAWN IN PARIS

Elvis, after the concert, meets the 103-year-old mother of newborn twins at the back of the bistro. She is one of his biggest fans, has followed him across the Continent, sent him messages of love and pleading, sent him photographs of the twins who, she says, are the products of a mad coupling with a descendant of Seurat on the left bank. Who could imagine that such consequence would come from the tumble of a 101-year-old woman? The realization of her pregnancy had been maddening. Nonetheless she had elected to carry the twins to term and, filled with francs and ancient mother's milk has followed Elvis in his disguise from Berlin to Munich, Lyons to this back bar of Paris. She loves him devotedly and wishes nothing more than to meet him at last and obtain his signature upon her palm. Her name is Lily and her next oldest child, Georges the grocer, is 82 and will soon be dead of heart disease, she has written him. Crazy things like this seem to happen to Elvis ever more frequently as he tries to get his career going incognito in the bistros and back saloons of a Paris he had seen only once on a 48-hour pass when he was quartered in Germany as a Private E-2.

Guitar still clasped in his hand, he meets Lily in the small backstage area they have given him. He is Renard, the American rocker, or at least that is his billing and no one except Lily herself seems to have marked him for his true identity. Standing there in a deep hunch, surely the oldest woman Elvis has ever seen, Lily seems suffused with joy and then tenderness as she reaches out to him, beckons him to give her a kiss. He does so with the utmost revulsion and delicacy, hearing her little bird's breath in his left ear. "I leave the babies with Georges," she says to him in labored English. "They are too young, *les bébés,* to be in such a place. Oh, you are so handsome. You are even more handsome here than you were way apart in the room. It is a thrill. A thrill to touch you."

"Well, yes," Elvis says. What else is there to say? The original idea had been simply to go away, go underground, get away from the drugs and the guards and the press (to say nothing of the family troubles), and it had made much sense at the time. But after a dozen years the restlessness had set in; the plastic surgery had *been* too effective. No one recognized him at all and he missed the music, if only a little. So he had taken a stab at restarting his career, not for the money really or for the attention but just to see if it could be done. And now, after five years of singing *Blue Skies* and *Prisoner of Love* in some of the dumbest, shittiest places he had ever seen outside of an army barracks, he seemed to have found only one sincere fan, the 103-year-old mother of infants and even *she* did not know who he really was, merely thought he was an *Americaine* with nice features. The encounter, some dim paradigm for what Elvis had always felt was his truest fate, to be clutched in a back room by a circumstance so horrible that it could barely be defined, let alone understood, fills him with a despair which goes beyond even the revulsion he had expected. "You must pardon me," he says, "I must prepare for the next show. I must go on the stage soon for yet another calling." He disengages from Lily, trying not to be too abrupt because if he brings her sprawling to the ground, what will happen? What can happen to him? "REN-

ARD THE FOX KILLS CENTENARIAN IN CAFE." He
would be booked, fingerprinted, seen under ultraviolet. The
whole story would come out. Oh, it is sickening, sickening!
Elvis, disengaged at last, turns from Lily, moves with desperate and clumsy haste toward that open spot in the wall
marking the demarcation of the stage. He will go out there
even now, unprepared and to empty seats, he will sing anything, say anything to be out of this. Behind he may leave
her cries of love, he does not know, this is nothing with
which he dares contend at this time.

### MARILYN AND ELVIS WERE
### SECRET LOVERS IN HOLLYWOOD LOVE NEST

"Oh, Norma Jean," she imagines him saying. "Norma
Jean, you are the most beautiful woman I have ever seen, oh
what might have been, with me and Norma Jean," his heavy
crooner's voice thickened with rhyme and love in the late afternoon. She had played with the thought of meeting him for
years, ever since he had come to make *GI Blues* in 1960 and
had rented in the Canyon only a few miles from where she
lived, but she had not done it. She was still stunned from the
divorce at that time, and there had been men, other men,
men without music or poetry in their voices, clamoring over
her, making small and insistent demands which, in her way,
she did her best to meet. But there had always been the
thought of Elvis, just Elvis and Norma Jean locked together
in long, shuddering afternoons of love after *The Prince And
The Showgirl* or *Viva Las Vegas* and she had dreamed of his
voice curling into her ear; at last she had asked Margaret to
get the number and place the call, tell him that she wanted
to speak with him. Margaret had tried and tried; she was
loyal in that way. Marilyn had used other studio contacts as
well, but somehow the connection had never been made,
there was always one reason or another why he could not be
reached and then at last the real troubles had come over her,
and so much for her dream of languid afternoons. He might
have saved her. He might have made all the difference. But
there was no way now that she could ever tell him so.

"Oh, Elvis," she dreams of saying as the Saturday night
opera begins again, the blood coursing truly, frantically through
her, carrying its own little messages of betrayal and transcen-
dence. "Oh Elvis, Elvis, love me tender, love me true, tell me

now the way you always do," and it is so palpable at this moment that she can almost feel his touch. Or indeed that *is* his splendid and desperate body covering hers now and carrying her down, carrying her down and away to the ultimate Saturday night fuck on this dawn of her aborning.

### *"IT WAS THE DUKE OF WINDSOR!" SAYS 103-YEAR-OLD MOTHER OF INFANT TWINS*

Lily knows that she would have said, would have done anything for him. Would have lied for him, would have died for him, would have placed her heart in the grasp of Elvis forever if it had been necessary. If there were a true way of proving her love and sacrifice, she would have said that the father of the twins was the Duke of Windsor, now doddering, probably homosexual, but still a believable if seedy crowned head who might have found a 101-year-old bedmate more of a sport than he could ever admit. Oh, those decadent English. But of course she could not die for him, could not lie for him; Elvis was gone. He had at last received her in his dressing room, cast his eyes over her, found her not pleasing to his sight, and had deserted. She had known in that moment of their embrace that she had horrified him, that her very touch was noxious and yet how could she have done otherwise? How could she have disengaged? He was her Prince of Song, the Renard of all of her necessity and she would have held him until the end until at last his hands had become desperate and she had been pushed from him. Now, standing in the dark, hunched in the dank alley outside the bistro, Lily hears his voice carry true into the night and hears the slow and abominable skittering of her ruined old heart. *Les bébés.* She must return to her helpless infants and yet, really, how can she leave? How can she leave this tender and terrible juxtaposition of her and her beloved Elvis, plastic-surgerized and masquerading as Renard? Her blood and brain function only thickly, only slowly, but they hammer out desperate and fixed truths. She cannot leave him.

And so Lily stands in the alley, listening to his voice cast on the night, dreaming in her old brain of Elvis and of the postures she might have assumed, feeling herself sway pendulously over the Parisian stones, knowing that she is at last now in the final months of her life and yet transfixed. She should return to *les bébés* but she cannot. She should shout for help but she cannot. She should stagger through the dust of the air and lurch onto the stage and grasp him, beg for his succor, but she cannot. Everything that she should have done lies behind her and there are only those last, intolerable moments in the dark to pace. The Duke of Windsor could not have done less for her nor treated her more rudely than her beloved Elvis.

But she does not love the Duke of Windsor nor he her.

### JFK SENDS WARNING FROM MOON
### "I WILL RETURN AND I WILL AVENGE!"

Grasping the edge of the crater, shuddering against the thin wall, the President feels that he can see for the first time the dimensions of the sin lodged against him, a sin more grievous and cunning than any of his liturgy can contain and breathing in the dust and silt which the windless Moon has laid in small deposits around him, he thinks that this, too, is ephemera, it is an aspect of the Trinity, of the Holy Ghost; against these walls of the Empyrian the spirit shall not contest in vain. He understands then or thinks he understands that reconstruction of another kind awaits him; that no less than the actress or the singer, a kind of transmogrification awaits him. Within his heart he feels a yearning so great that it cannot be codified and the President knows then with the fuming and resilient thunder of that heart that he will come back, that he will return in ways which cannot be judged. It is joy that he feels then in those leveling bursts and on the solitary landscape of the Moon, staring at the affixed and demanding Earth he knows that his time will come, his time will come again. Asking, asking, asking yet.

### ELVIS AND JFK:
### "WE'RE COMING BACK AND WE'RE GOING TO
### ROCK!"

In the hard cradle, awaiting the return of the Mom who, departed, will not return again, *les bébés* wail stiffly against the dense Continental night. The teenage nursemaid hired for a pittance for the evening while the crazy old woman living with them had hobbled into the night sullenly takes two bottles from the warmer and sticks them in *les bébés'* mouths. Greedily they suck and with a hint of knowledge. The nursemaid stares at them idly and yawns.

# Marilyn, Elvis, and the Reality Blues
## by James Brunet

*In his own words: "Prior to perpetrating this story, Jim Brunet has been guilty of work appearing in* Analog, Pulphouse, *and* Dragon, *among other places. He claims to have never sighted Elvis (even when Elvis was alive the first time) and was born in a town named Salinas, which some pronounce 'Silliness.' "*

*One hopes that wherever he lives now, he has neighbors as interesting as these.*

Henry Kizmik turned off the coffeepot and then sat down at the breakfast table of the one-room apartment he rented just off Melrose Avenue.

The *Los Angeles Times* carried the headline:

**"SURVIVORS FROM ATLANTIS CONTROL STOCK MARKET"**

Henry sighed, which was not unusual, for he sighed a lot. Idiotic. No evidence that an advanced Atlantean civilization had ever existed on the much-charted depths of the ocean floor, yet it was perfectly reasonable, at least to the mainstream press, that they were causing havoc in modern times after having remained secret for thousands of years. The only thing stupider was that having remained secret, they'd be playing the stock market and would get caught. He read the first few paragraphs; as usual, bunches of unsupported assertions, nothing that could be disproved easily on the face of it, but nothing that made any rational sense either.

Henry sighed again as he scanned the article, then turned to the comics, where the babies were still outwitting their parents, wives still outwitting their husbands, and then read the advice columns which today covered visiting mothers-in-law, teens outwitting their parents, and parents outwitting each other. Then he turned to the sports page. Chicago Cubs

14, Los Angeles Dodgers 2, he read. At least something was right with the world.

Showered and dressed, with the breakfast dishes cleared away and the beds made, Henry sat down at his word processor to continue his article entitled "The Case for Logic." Just where it would be published hadn't been determined yet. In fact, the editorial responses to his queries had been pretty lukewarm, one suggesting that ". . . it was a rather fringy kind of piece." No matter, thought Henry, as he started to write. Finish it first, then worry about where to sell it. The only way to make a living as a writer was to finish what you started.

He had been working for about an hour when a door squeaked as it opened across the hall. There was a knock at his door. Henry muttered to himself, looked at his computer screen, and called out, "Just a minute!"

When he opened the door, his neighbor stood waiting for him. A shock of platinum blonde hair swept across her forehead and she wore nothing but a red towel wrapped tightly around her body from chest to thigh, her face adorned by a smile that had once opened bank vaults and doors to high places. Actually, thought Henry, it probably still could, if people only knew that it was still around.

"Hi, Sugar," she drawled.

"Hi, Marilyn," said Henry, putting on his best face over irritation at being interrupted. "What's up?"

"Well," she said, "I was trying to whip up a little birthday cake for a dear, dear friend and I found myself a little short of ingredients. Could I borrow a cup of sugar, Sugar?" Her smile descended upon Henry like a wrestling move.

"Uh, sure, Marilyn. Just a second."

When he pressed the cup into her hands, she blew him a kiss. "Thanks, honey. Maybe I'll come by sometime and sing 'Happy Birthday' for you."

"Uh-huh." Henry's eyes followed her as she turned away, the red towel stretching with every movement, until the door to her apartment closed with a click.

Henry exhaled softly. Even in her sixties, she looked better to him than a lot of women in their twenties. But the central mystery overrode everything else. Why no one else recognized his neighbor, he couldn't imagine. It was remarkable—unbelievable, really—that the secret had lasted all these years.

He had known who she was as soon as she moved in, notwithstanding her wearing a dark wig that disguised nothing. Every week he'd expected hordes of reporters in the hallway. Now he guessed it was less likely, especially since the Secret Service detail had stopped cluttering up the building when her lover the ex-President dropped by, the one who'd supposedly been assassinated himself. Henry sighed again and shut his door to the accompaniment of clarinet notes sliding up and down the hallway. Mr. Konigsberg in 3-H again, thought Henry as he turned back to his desk.

Henry typed at the keyboard: *As Galileo wrote, "I do not feel obliged to believe that the same God who has endowed us with sense, reason, and intellect has intended us to forgo their use." Whether these qualities are bestowed by God or not is for the moment irrelevant; if they exist—and however infrequently used to good effect, we must concede they do exist—how, then, are we to apply them in processing our observations of the everyday world?*

Henry's train of thought was abruptly derailed by an eruption of guitar chords and loud, exuberant singing from overhead.

Henry looked up at the ceiling. "Yo! Elvis! How about a little less noise? There's people what's trying to work down here!"

The chords of the guitar faded away. "Yo! Hank, buddy. There's people what gots to try to work up here, too!"

But the guitar stayed silent and, near as Henry could tell, his upstairs neighbor contented himself with singing as he washed his dishes. It was somewhat quieter than with the guitar. For a man in his sixties, Elvis was remarkable. Henry sighed and turned back to his computer.

At half past noon Henry stopped to regard his progress. Not bad—three more or less smooth pages—he thought as the lines scrolled by on the screen.

*The contemporary reluctance to accept an ordered reality, with cause and effect contributing to a coherent vision—*

A key slid into the lock and turned and the door to the hallway opened. "Hi, Henry, honey. Brought some lunch."

"Hi, Tiff. Be with you in just a sec." He leaned over his keyboard to type another line.

Keys, purse, a carton of takeout and a small bottle of wine in one hand, two cartons of takeout in the other, Tiffany leaned back against the door and kicked it shut with her foot.

"I got Chinese," she said as her heels clicked across the hardwood floor and she set the food down on the kitchen counter.

"Smells good," he said, and leaned up for a kiss, brushing aside her frosted blonde bangs. "Mmmm. You, too. How goes the day of the wandering reporter?" he asked, glancing back at the computer screen as Tiffany kicked off her shoes.

"Oh, I interviewed one of those professors at USC who's studying that lost Roman colony they found living in the depths of the Brazilian rain forest," said Tiffany as she un-buttoned her blouse.

"They've gone crazy with joy as they find out how Latin was actually spoken. Of course," she said as she unbuckled her belt, unsnapped, unzipped, and stepped out of her shorts, "the Romans are a little bit shaken to find the sounds they thought were from Apollo's chariot are really jet airplanes."

"It sounds damned improbable. All the way around," said Henry with a frown. "It doesn't make sense that they could live in the Amazon for more than two millennia and have never run into an explorer or that *some* natives hadn't en-countered them and carried tales to the outside world."

Henry turned to Tiffany, who had draped her panty hose over a chair and was sliding the straps of her bra down each shoulder. "I mean, does it make sense to *you*?" he said.

"Oh, my poor little dear," she murmured as she unhooked the bra and let her breasts wiggle free. "I haven't seen you this upset since they thawed that Arctic explorer—what was his name, Hammerschmidt?—out from the ice a couple of months ago."

"Oh, sure," he said, "it's completely believable that he not only survived, but that the sound of his last words as he froze got trapped in the air pocket so people heard them when they chiseled him out."

Tiffany reached over and ran her fingers through Henry's hair. "My little logical dingbat," she said. She turned and walked toward the bed; her panties sparkled with the words "Brooklyn" and "Manhattan" high on either cheek and a scene of each, done in multicolored glitter, pictured underneath.

"Uh, Tiff . . ."

She sat down on the edge of the bed and then lay back, still looking over at Henry. "Can't you enjoy anything that doesn't meet your standards of logic?"

Henry looked at her and decided he could.

Henry and Tiffany sat at the dining table, spooning cold Chinese food directly out of the cartons into their mouths while they scanned the newspaper. "What about 'Sweet Sioux'? I haven't seen that one yet," said Tiffany.

"The one about the love affair between Custer and Sitting Bull's wife? Naah. I'd rather see a comedy, something I don't have to pretend is real, even by Hollywood standards."

Tiffany folded her section of the paper and set it down on the table; she drew the collar of Henry's faded gray terrycloth robe more closely together. "What's with you anyway?" she said.

"What do you mean, what's with me?"

"You're getting awfully hung up on this concept of everything having to be what you call rational."

"What is this, some kind of after-sex fight?"

"What do you mean, after-sex fight? You've been this way for weeks. Reading all those rags of the so-called alternative press and getting zoned in on way-out conspiracy theories like how Hitler must have *really* died in his bunker in Berlin."

"Yeah, well . . . yeah. . . ." Henry pressed his fists to his forehead. "Doesn't that make more sense than his surfacing as a ninety-year-old dee-jay for a pirate rock station in Buenos Aires?" *Of course, it makes no less sense than for Marilyn, Elvis, and God knows who to be living in my apartment building.*

Seizing the thought, Henry continued. "For instance, do you have any idea how many people in this apartment building are living here incognito? It's ridiculous. Sometimes I think I'm the only normal person living in the whole building!"

"Now, honey," said Tiffany in her most soothing voice, "there's nothing abnormal about your neighbors—at least they're no weirder than neighbors in any apartment building are."

"Tiffany, doesn't the sheer implausibility, the impossibility, of all these public figures dropping out of sight to live incognito bother you? I mean Marilyn and Elvis and quiet, broody Mr. Zimmerman and neurotic, fussy Mr. Konigsberg and Lord knows who else—why, I wouldn't be surprised if old, babbling Mr. Kopperman on the fourth floor is really the Lindbergh baby!"

Henry paused, whether for dramatic effect or to catch his breath, he wasn't sure, only to discover Tiffany looking at him sympathetically. "There, there. It's your Virgo rising that does it."

Henry opened his mouth to speak, closed it, opened it again, closed it, got up, and opened the refrigerator door. "Aw, the hell with it. You want some leftover cheesecake?"

Tiffany's face softened and she shook her head and stood up. "I've got to go," she said, walking over to stroke his hair. She dressed quickly as Henry watched her, brooding and lusting at the same time. "Don't worry about it," she said as she gathered up her purse and keys. "I'll call you later on and we can figure out something to do tonight."

She leaned over to kiss him again and he kissed her back. "Bye, Tiff," he said, and the door closed.

A light, breathy giggling floated down through the ceiling from upstairs. Henry turned on the radio to cover up the noise. After a few minutes, the blend of music and commercials was interrupted by a news bulletin about a human body being born from the womb of a sheep in Albania. Henry turned the radio off.

*We are inclined to accept the most fantastic of explanations, whether born of astrology or conspiracy or extraterrestrial design, more readily than we accept a parking ticket. We prefer reasons that sound good over sound reasoning that is good.* Henry frowned at the word processor. It was all very tight reasoning, he thought, but how to reconcile that with his own reality that included Marilyn and Elvis?

Speaking of Elvis, the giggling upstairs had given way to a *creak, creak, creak, creak* of bedsprings. Henry shook his head. He'd stopped counting the number of times a week that Elvis entertained; if only he had Elvis' stamina. He looked back at the screen of his computer.

*There are limits, of course, to the powers of sense and reason and intellect. Limits of the unknown and the unknow-*

*able, limitations which only fools or saints attempt to breach.*

The rhythm upstairs had progressed into a faster, jazzier *creak-a-crik, creak-a-crik, creak-a-crik,* acquiring in the process a lyric of "oh, baby," "oh, BAY-bee," "oh, BAY-uh-BEE!" delivered by a deep, mellow voice, harmonized by a "hunh," "hunh," "hunh" in a light, breathy voice.

Henry's arms dropped to his side; he looked up at the ceiling. *Here I am trying to be earnestly philosophical and I've got Elvis having sex ten feet over my head. Elvis, for God's sake. Elvis!*

Henry shook his head. A man whose death under a variety of lurid circumstances was widely reported, whose home had been turned into a shrine, musical career deified, and who'd been reported "discovered" any number of places except here, where he really was. How to explain it? The coroner or medical examiner, members of his family, and the friends who allegedly discovered the body would all have to be in on the conspiracy. And what possible motive could they share? And what about Elvis' motive? Why would anyone want to continue living a quiet life after staging his own death? *Well, unless he was a former vice president or something,* thought Henry.

The giggle above renewed itself as the bed gave a final solid *creak* and heavy footsteps padded first toward the bathroom, then the kitchen. "Oh, darling, you *are* such a hound dog," said the lighter voice dreamily as it carried through Henry's ceiling.

The absurdity of the world weighed upon Henry as he turned off his word processor. The first draft was finished. Tomorrow he would revise and edit, then send it off. Yet the absurd, even though it was absurd, left him with a hollow feeling, a vague discomfort, as if there was some joke that he did not understand, some secret to the world that was obvious to everyone but him. In that case, it wouldn't be a secret, would it. *Now who's falling for conspiracy theories?* Real and not real, logical or not, to believe or not believe. All his thoughts converged and tangled like a massive traffic jam on the freeway.

There was a *click* as the lock to his door opened and Tiffany walked in. "Hi, honey," she said as she closed the door behind her and put down her purse. "Are you doing okay?"

"Yeah, I guess."

Henry and Tiffany walked hand in hand past the shops and theaters of Westwood. "Now was that so bad?" she asked.

They had seen *Eternal Triangle,* the story of the love affair between a Prime Minister, a Pope, and a Hollywood starlet. He shrugged. "It doesn't matter. I love you," he said, "even if you are so grounded in improbability."

She took his hand and put it around her waist, snuggling against his shoulder as they walked past the theaters. "And I love you, even if you do live in a fantasy world."

Henry sighed and snuggled back as they walked along. So much did he bask in the glow of Tiffany's affections that he completely failed to notice the flashing lights of the flying saucer that drifted by only a couple of hundred feet overhead.

# Those Rowdy Royals
## by Laura Resnick

*Laura Resnick has lived in England, France, Sicily, Israel, and America. As a romance novelist, she was named Best New Series Writer in 1989, and was the Campbell winner for Best New Science Fiction Writer in 1993. As this book is being assembled, she is either in Mauritania, Burkina Faso, Togo, or Benin, depending.*

*Who agrees that it would be a Good Thing to send a copy of this story to the current Royal Family with the attached note reading: "So you think you've got problems?"*

### THE MEDIEVAL TIMES, ca. 1152
#### "An Annulment Is Announced"

After long and detailed negotiations, the Queen Consort and His Royal Majesty Louis VII of France have resolved to annul their marriage. The Queen Consort is expected to wed Henry, Duke of Normandy, before the end of the year—a less-than-stunning match, according to royal analysts.

For an incisive study of the effect these events are expected to have on the stability of the florin against the dinar, please turn to the financial section.

### THE NORMAN RAG
#### "Queen Claims: Those Children I Bore Weren't Mine!"

Having been caught *in flagrante delicto* with that rogue the Duke of Normandy, Eleanor of Aquitaine (rumored to be thirty years old, despite her claims to the contrary) has filed for an annulment. Can we expect His Holiness the Pope to overlook the veritable herd of children Eleanor has borne to her hapless husband, the King of France? Can the royal couple reasonably claim nonconsummation with so many of their heirs playing Crusaders 'n' Saracens in the back yard? Is the heir-apparent to the throne of France really the son of the castle chimney sweep? And will the Duke of Normandy, barely nineteen years old, really fess up and marry the Queen Consort?

### THE ANGLO-SAXON STAR
#### "Caught In The Act!"

Eleanor of Aquitaine and Henry of Normandy were caught being more than a little careless while vacationing at an exclusive seaside resort near Calais last week. Recently separated from King Louis, Eleanor was supposedly resting in seclusion while awaiting her annulment papers.

Instead, one of the *Star's* most reliable artists found the soon-to-be-former Queen of France lounging fountainside with none other than the handsome Duke of Normandy himself. As you can plainly see from the exclusive drawings below, *this* relationship is most clearly a consummated one!

### THE EVENING JESTER
#### "Palace Promises Purge!"

Sources at the French court report that King Louis suffered an uncharacteristic fit of rage upon seeing yesterday morning's edition of *The Anglo-Saxon Star*, in which exclusive drawings (whose veracity has not yet been confirmed) depict the Lady Eleanor (surely, no *lady*) and the young Duke of Normandy performing exactly the same act that Eleanor claims *not* to have performed with hubby Louis, despite the many children she bore him during their marriage.

King Louis has publicly threatened to cut off Eleanor's allowance. Will the Duke of Normandy still buzz around this aging blossom when her pollen dries up? And will the taxpayers still meekly sweat and toil in the fields of France when they realize that *they're* the ones financing these shenanigans?

### THE MEDIEVAL TIMES, ca. 1153
#### "A New Heir Is Announced"

Henry, Duke of Normandy, has been acknowledged by Stephen as heir to the throne of England.

For an analysis of how this will effect the ducat, please turn to the financial section.

## THE COURTLY CHRONICLE
"We Have A New Heir!"

Having finally made an honest woman of Eleanor of Aquitaine last year, Henry of Normandy finds himself in the headlines once again. The brash young duke has recently landed on the shores of England and forced Stephen (remember him?) to acknowledge Henry as his heir.

## THE NORMAN RAG
"Alchemist Predicted It All!"

In a late-breaking story, one of the *Rag's* top journalists has learned that Alphonse the Magnificent, formerly of "Merlin's Traveling Circus and Sideshow," predicted the succession of Henry to the throne of England, as well as his marriage to the former Queen of France.

What does this wizard see in his crystal ball regarding the royal couple's future? For an exclusive prediction of the volatile pair's destiny, clip out the attached coupon and send it with one ha'penny to the *Rag's* London offices.

Offer void where void.

## THE MEDIEVAL TIMES, ca. 1154
"Duke of Normandy Crowned King of England:
Henry II Promises Prosperity"

The stock exchange will be closed today in honor of the Royal Coronation.

For an analysis of King Henry's economic plans, please turn to the financial section.

## THE ANGLO-SAXON STAR
"Bishop Seduces Goat At Coronation Feast!"

In pursuing the tradition of first-rate journalism which our readers have learned to expect, a *Star* reporter disguised himself as the Duke of Bilberry and managed to sneak into the Royal Coronation Feast.

Our fearless *Star* journalist left no stone unturned, no

nook unsearched, no cranny uninvestigated. For an exclusive story about the bishop caught in a compromising position with a goat, please turn to Page 3.


## THE EVENING JESTER
"King Attacks Bishop, Goat Gets Away!"

In a follow-up story to this morning's *Star* headlines, a Pope who prefers not to be identified has told the *Jester* that a frightful row erupted when the King found a certain bishop with his favorite goat at the Royal Coronation festivities.

The palace has since instigated a search for the goat, which disappeared while His Grace King Henry II was throttling the bishop. *Jester* sources suggest that members of the British Union for the Rights of Beasts (B.U.R.B.) may have spirited the animal away during all the confusion.


## THE COURTLY CHRONICLE
"Coronation Climaxes in Chaos!"

Despite an auspicious beginning, the Royal Coronation was marred by a brawl between certain Church factions and a raid staged by a left-wing animal rights group.

The palace has issued a statement denying any knowledge of goat abuse.


## THE MEDIEVAL TIMES ca. 1170
"Vatican Dollar Drops Drastically"

Thomas À Becket met his death in Canterbury Cathedral yesterday. Assailants unknown. The palace denies rumors that King Henry may have used ill-considered means to end, once and for all, his on-going quarrel with the Archbishop.

All members of the financial community have gamely issued public statements in support of His Majesty, mindful of the dangers of internal political chaos so near the end of the financial quarter.

"Remember," said Lord Savile, who asked not to be quoted, "those Scots are a lot closer than you might think."

For a detailed analysis of the effect the assassination has had on the economic salubrity of the Papal States, please turn to the financial section.

### THE COURTLY CHRONICLE
#### "Murder In the Cathedral"

King Henry can rest easy at last, since his arch nemesis, the Archbishop of Canterbury, lies cold in his grave. Yes, poor Thomas is dead, killed as he knelt at prayer, slain by infidels who slipped into the country disguised as Italian sausages.

### THE ANGLO-SAXON STAR
#### "Courtly Chronicle Crushes Credibility"

The *Courtly,* known to be a mere tool of the Plantagenets ever since Henry first started bullying Stephen (remember him?), was caught printing unverified information about the identities of Thomas À Becket's assassins.

It is now known—checked and double-checked by the reliable staff of the *Star*—that Becket was slain by aliens. The same ones who built those pyramids and invented haggis.

### THE EVENING JESTER
#### "Henry Has Hemorrhoids!"

King Henry has continued to deny all rumors linking him to the murder of the Archbishop of Canterbury, claiming a chronic scatological disorder as his alibi.

Employing the responsible methods our readers have learned to expect, a *Jester* reporter disguised himself as a chamber pot to verify the King's story. We are pleased to be the first news service in Britain to report that Henry II, by the grace of God, King of England, does indeed have hemorrhoids and thus *cannot be guilty* of the Archbishop's murder!

For an exclusive account of the three days our star *Jester* journalist posed as the King's chamber pot, please turn to Page 3.

### THE NORMAN RAG
#### "Public Pressure Mobilizes Monarch!"

Despite the famous Chamber Pot Defense, the King has been unable to mitigate rumors that he ordered the assassination of Thomas Becket. Consequently, His Grace will do public penance and make a pilgrimage to Canterbury.

Now! For the first time! You, too, can *live* this historic event! Stay with us each day as, reporting live, we take you *inside* the *true* story! Get wet and muddy with Henry as he rides to Canterbury. *Feel* the sweat of the King as he approaches Becket's final resting place. *Experience* the ice cold stones of Canterbury Cathedral under your knees as the *Rag* takes you there! *Thrill* to each lash of the whip as it licks Henry's skin!

This is a once-in-a-lifetime offer, folks! The chance won't come again, so *be* there!

### THE MEDIEVAL TIMES, ca. 1173
"Civil War Threatens Britain"

At the instigation of their mother, Her Grace Queen Eleanor, King Henry's three eldest sons, Henry, Richard, and Geoffrey, have launched a full-scale rebellion against our sovereign king.

For an analysis of the effect these events have had on the ha'penny, please turn to the financial section.

### THE NORMAN RAG
"Those Rowdy Royals Are At It Again!"

As if it weren't enough that the Queen moved her own court to Poitiers on account of the King's many infidelities (including fruit of a particularly forbidden nature if the *Star* and *Jester* are to be believed!), *now* Her Grace has incited those three rowdy princes, Harry, Dickie, and Geoff, to launch a civil war against their father the King! What *will* future generations think of these royal peccadilloes?

### THE COURTLY CHRONICLE
"Peace Breaks Out!"

After unfortunate family disputes which, incidentally, cost thousands of lives and brought whole sections of the country to a standstill, the Royal family has resolved its differences.

The palace announced yesterday that the Queen has gone into seclusion to rest after the harrowing events of the past year.

### THE ANGLO-SAXON STAR
"King Throws Queen In Jail!"

Though the rebellion was a family affair, the King has responded harshly. Yesterday he locked up the Queen and threw away the key.

Posing as a chamber maid, a *Star* reporter managed to sneak into the Queen's quarters for an exclusive interview. Please turn to Page 3.

### THE EVENING JESTER
"Queen Claims: I Was Only Trying To Help!"

According to an exclusive interview printed in this morning's *Star,* Queen Eleanor claims that King Henry completely misunderstood her intentions when she and her three eldest sons raised an army and launched an attack against him.

Richard "Dickie" the Lion Heart was not available for comment, having gone off to some other country to slaughter people who never did him any harm. However, Prince Harry had this to say: "Well, um, my mom told me to do it."

Geoff was also not available for comment, as he was babysitting brother John at the time of this reporter's interviews at the palace. Too young to have participated in the war, Johnny stayed at home and pulled the wings off flies.

### THE MEDIEVAL TIMES, ca. 1189
"King Dies: Long Live the King?"

King Henry II died yesterday afternoon, and the succession remains uncertain.

Might as well turn to the financial section.

### THE COURTLY CHRONICLE
"Henry Heads Heavenward!"

His Grace King Henry II is survived by: his wife Queen Eleanor, eleven years his senior; his son Geoffrey, who is quoted as saying, "Finally! I thought the old bugger would never die!"; his mistress, the young Princess Alais who has been affianced to nearly all the king's sons at one point or another; and his sons Richard and John who could not be reached for comment at the time of the King's death, as they were busy rebelling against him again.

# My Husband Became a Zombie and it Saved Our Marriage
## by Karen Haber

*Karen Haber sent me her biographical information with an Elvis stamp on the envelope. Apart from being a woman of taste and discernment, she has had her short fiction appear in such publications as* Asimov's, Fantasy and Science Fiction, Full Spectrum, After the King, The Further Adventures of Batman, *among others. Her novels include* The Mutant Season *(co-authored with Robert Silverberg),* The Mutant Prime, Mutant Star, *and* Mutant Legacy. *With husband Robert Silverberg she edits the original SF hardcover anthology* Universe, *and is currently working on the first of an SF trilogy,* The Woman Without a Shadow, *for DAW Books.*

*She assures me that this story is not autobiographical.*


The sun broke through the morning fog and spilled down the pine-scented hills, through the spotted plate-glass window of the weekly Hillsidean's offices, across the cigarette-burned city desk, and right into the pale blue eyes of Theola Simmons, Managing Editor.

She blinked grumpily at the searing light and looked back down at the blue editing marks she had just made on the day's galleys. Theola preferred cloudy weather: she got more work done.

The swivel chair creaked beneath her as she turned away from the creeping sunlight. She had one more column to correct: Scotty Wilkins' weekly neighborhood news roundup. Theola didn't care for Wilkins' cheery airhead style but knew that if she fired him she would have to find another willing victim to do the job for less than minimum-wage or do it herself. And Wilkins was certainly at the top—or bottom—of his form today:

— Somebody's been feeding miniature poodles to our Nessy again. While that's okay, remember that Nessy's a big fish and needs a lot of protein or else she complains. Don't bother with the small stuff. She prefers large dogs, deer, or teenage boys between fifteen and eighteen years of age.

— Speaking of Nessy, Ron and Glinda Chambers are the winners of the town lottery this quarter. They get the cheery job of cleaning Nessy's pond. Congratulations, folks, and watch out for those front teeth.

— Hitler has been arrested—again—for shoplifting at McLendow's Hosiery: she's been a sucker for Hanes sales ever since her South American sex-change operation. A hundred dollar fine for Hillside's very own fuehrerette. McLendow's is threatening to prosecute next time. Hey, Adolfa, a word of advice: try support hose. They last longer.

— More on that UFO that crash-landed in Brawley's market parking lot yesterday: as we feared, the craft is a total wreck. But the passengers escaped with minor injuries and Charley Brawley hired them to collect tickets at the parking lot. So smile when you see them, folks, and remember, they're new in town.

— Calling all our maniac gardeners: Pastor Grigsby still has that pile of monster earthworms. They're big and juicy and nasty and they're free. Just bring several large pails with good lids, an electric cattle prod, and heavy gloves.

— The Neason Siamese Twins were the hit of the flaming volleyball tournament in Hillside Park: one spikes, the other doesn't, and both carry fire extinguishers. Nice going, kids. Keep that spirit smokin' in the semifinals.

— The Widow Karsh saw John Lennon's ghost again: this time he was standing in her sink lecturing her about her garbage disposal. Widow Karsh has called several repairmen and an exterminator. She would ask all you Lennon fans out there to stop putting old record albums and candles on her lawn: it scares her dog.

— Selma Roundtree reports that her husband, David, escaped from the house last night and was last seen lumbering down Main Street toward the freeway. David, as you may remember, is a zombie, and his day vision isn't too good. Selma is beside herself with worry. Anybody who happens to see David should call Selma or Dr. Nkebolo, ASAP.

Standard stuff, Theola thought as she put down the galleys. Another Lennon sighting! And the damned zombie loose for the hundredth time: Selma should buy a leash for him. Hillside was a nice town but it was so-o-o predictable sometimes.

With the relief and gratitude that only comes from finishing an odious task, she signed off on the galleys and left the pile by Senior Editor Ed Deerfield's computer terminal.

Dan Hockstader, typesetter and photo stripper, came in, swinging his take-out bag of tripe.

"Seen the aliens?" he asked.

"Not yet. They weren't on duty when I got in at six."

He blinked at her from behind faceted, triple-thickness eye glasses. "If you do, ask them what they think of the way the market's been acting. They're pretty good about that stuff."

"Thanks, but I usually get my stock tips from Pops Shorter's Siamese, Bathsheba. She hasn't led me wrong yet." Theola waved farewell but Dan was oblivious, already chowing down on his pig intestines and snorting with laughter over the sports galleys.

She tossed her thick black hair behind her neck and sashayed out the door, taking small, careful steps in her high-heeled Japanese wooden sandals.

The blast of sunshine nearly blinded her.

"Damn!" Groping for her sunglasses, she felt like a bat caught outside of its cave. It was an unseasonably bright, warm June day in the San Francisco Bay area—at least seventy-five degrees—with nary a hint of lovely, cool gray fog to make things comfortable. Theola reminded herself to reapply her sunscreen and look for her sunhat. Her glasses were at the bottom of her black velvet bag. One of the lenses came loose and she ducked, squinting, in a doorway, trying to fit it back into the frame.

No matter what Theola did, she couldn't get the lens to fit. Finally, in disgust, she flung the lens back into her purse, shoved the glasses onto her nose, and closed her exposed eye.

"Hey, Theola," called a familiar voice on her blind side. "Nice glasses. Where can I get a pair?"

She turned and saw Jamie the six-foot spider sitting at one of the picnic tables outside of Cooney's Ice House. He had a mug of root beer clutched in one feeler and waved two of his hairy multijointed legs at her. She peered at Jamie's faceted optic receptors and wondered why she had never noticed before how much he resembled Dan Hockstader. "Root beer again, Jamie?"

"I'm an arachnoid of habit. Join me?"

"Only for a minute." Theola took a seat in the shade and helped herself to one of the fried ants on the spider's plate. "Not bad," she said. "Pretty crunchy. I like that touch of hot pepper."

"I asked them to use chili oil."

Boom!

At the sound of the nearby explosion, Theola jumped in her seat.

"Must have been Fred Matthias," Jamie said. "Poor guy. Sound like he finally ran out of antacids."

"It was bound to happen, sooner or later." said Theola.

A whisper of wind raised goosebumps along her arms. The murmur grew to a shriek and an icy gust buffeted Hillside's Main Street, nearly upending the table and throwing Theola into Jamie's lap.

The light around them flickered, turned red, then green, and finally back to regular yellow. The wind died down and the summer heat returned. Two figures stood in the middle of the street. They wore medieval-style clothing and carried huge bundles wrapped in animal hide.

"Ginny, Roger, welcome back!" Jamie called.

"Hey, you guys," Theola said. "How was the thirteenth century?"

"The food was better in the 1660s, Roger said, doffing his crumpled hat. "But the bugs were worse."

Ginny shed her heavy coat. "It's great to be back. The more I travel, the more I enjoy coming home. See you all after we've bathed—it'll be the first time in weeks."

Theola waved as they receded down the street, glanced at her watch, took one more bite of fried ant, and stood up. "Jamie, let's get together for coffee sometime."

"I'll call you."

"Okay. Watch out for that root beer, now." Theola hurried

across the street and into the Brawley Market parking lot. A yellow poster on a telephone pole caught her attention.

"Wanted: single white male or female subjects for controlled experimentation . . ."

Something sharp was poking her, hard, in the back.

"Stick 'em up," said a high, piping voice.

Theola spun around and stared through her one-lens sunglasses in amazement. A group of Girl Scouts stared back at her. They were all blond, all freckled, two wore pigtails, and one of them had lost her two front teeth. The shortest Girl Scout held a huge yellow and chartreuse water cannon with its sights trained on Theola.

"Pardon me?" she said.

"Just act normal and no one will get wet."

Theola looked with horror at the cruel orange muzzle of the water cannon. "What do you want?"

"A ride to Franklin Park."

"But that's on the other side of the tunnel!"

The girls nodded. Their smiles were ugly, especially the one with missing teeth.

"I haven't eaten lunch yet," Theola said, hoping to enlist their sympathy and thereby gain time to think.

"We'll give you a hot dog once we get there," said the tallest one, who also had the most freckles.

Theola shuddered. "No, thanks." She stared in revulsion at the water cannon. These kids would soak her to the skin, ruin her dress. The only thing she disliked more than glaring sunlight was water. Everybody in her family was phobic about getting wet. "What the hell," she said. "Come on."

They marched right past the green naked alien parking lot attendant.

"Good morning," it wheezed through its membrane. "Buy low, sell high."

Help, Theola thought loudly. I'm being kidnapped by a bunch of Girl Scouts.

The alien fixed its huge moist purple eye upon Theola in what might have been a look of comprehension and encouragement, punched a ticket in the time clock, and handed it to her.

Hey, she thought, aren't you guys all telepathic? You should be reading my thoughts and calling the police.

The alien nodded. "Dow closed up 40 yesterday. Have a nice day."

"You're a big help," Theola muttered. She unlocked the door of her blue Edsel. Her stomach rumbled. "Hop in, girls."

The ride through the tunnel was dark and peaceful. But all too soon Theola had once again emerged into the merciless sunshine.

"Turn right here," the littlest Girl Scout snarled.

Obediently, Theola pulled into a driveway next to a saw-toothed wooden sign which read: "Franklin Park. Open 6 to 6. No dogs."

"We're looking for the William Howard Taft campsite."

"Can't you girls just walk from here?"

The water cannon jabbed Theola in the ribs. She winced. "No, I suppose not." She drove perhaps a half mile farther and stopped the car. There was no need to go on. The park was awash with girl scouts: a veritable sea of green uniforms, sashes, and berets. It was a frightful sight. Theola clamped her jaw and vowed to stay calm.

With nary a murmur of thanks nor even a curtsey, her captors sprang out of the car to join their friends. In a moment they were lost in the crowd, indistinguishable from the other milling girls pulling each other's hair, complaining, and eating.

Didn't your mothers teach any of you manners? Theola thought. No, of course not. Besides, there's probably a Girl Scout badge for kidnapping newspaper editors. But at least she was free again. If only she could find her way out of here and back to the familiar sights of Hillside.

The air was filled with the scent of grilling meat and the sound of prepubescent shrieks. Theola began to feel dizzy and mildly nauseated. The car was surrounded, swamped by tall, short, fat, and thin scouts. She couldn't move forward or back.

Panic clouded her thinking and she leaped from her car, gasping, trying to put as much distance as possible between her and the lunging crowd. But she was hampered by her purple sheared-velvet hobble skirt and wooden sandals, forced to take quick, mincing tiny steps. She stumbled over sticks, tripped over tree roots. An ominous crack gave her a two-second warning before the heel of her left sandal came away from the sole in two pieces. Disgusted, Theola kicked off her shoes. The carpet of pine needles and twigs pricked and bruised her feet but she had no choice. She was in the midst of a ghastly nightmare: trapped in a girl scout jamboree.

There were hot dogs, potato salad, great brimming tubs of cole slaw: it was horrible, just horrible. Plates of pink and glistening cold cuts lay, edges curling in the sun as yellow jackets nuzzled them lovingly. The rustic setting, coyly folksy, all rough-hewn picnic tables and tree stumps, nearly turned Theola's stomach. It was all so weird and repellent.

Bravely, she forged on, past the scenes of raucous merriment, the smells of a hundred outdoor grills, and into a towering grove of Monterey pines. The maddening sounds of the jamboree receded. For a moment she was blessedly alone in the park with only the whine of the mosquitoes and whisper of the tree limbs in the wind for company.

Suddenly a new and even more dreadful sound assailed her ears. Voices, male and mellifluous, rose up in lush and lifting four-part harmony.

"Sweet A—del-ine. My A—del-ine."

Theola peered out fearfully from between two pines.

Before her, the grove was filled with portly middle-aged men in red and white striped blazers and white straw boaters.

All around the grove, barbershop quartets were tuning up Men in red and white striped jackets and straw boaters leaned, shoulder to shoulder, humming. Theola wheeled in her tracks, whimpering like a cornered animal. Girl Scouts to the left of her, singing barbers on her right. Wherever she turned, alien weirdness pressed in on her. What was next, a pancake lunch with the PTA?

She hurried past the raffish singing men and found a path which seemed to lead toward the park entrance. Hurry, Theola thought. Get away before you're ill in public.

She turned left down the path, followed it for perhaps half a mile, emerged from a thicket of rhododendrons and stood, wondering which way to turn.

Behind her, something enormous roared.

Theola looked over her shoulder.

A huge black-and-yellow bus was bearing down, horns blaring. She jumped out of the way just in time but was nearly hit by a lime green Volkswagen beetle which beeped menacingly as it sped past. Theola staggered, disoriented and frightened in the hot sunlight. She blinked in disbelief.

It couldn't be true. This absolutely couldn't be happening to her.

She was standing in the middle of a busy street in a thriving suburban town. Everywhere she looked she saw car washes and supermarkets. Clean-cut cheerful young people. Dogs and cats. Little children in aerodynamically-sound, state-of-the-art strollers padded in drool-proof nonsexist colors and natural fabrics. Coffee shops where young mothers congregated over steaming cups of capuccino, oblivious to their preschool troops in rubber-bottomed toilet-training regalia gumming discarded biscotti, falling off the slatted green French bistro chairs, or chasing one another in complicated slaloms between and around the marble-topped tables.

Boys and girls in long T-shirts were wound round one another, walking down the street or sitting on benches kissing—mwah—loudly, wetly, and long.

Planters dotted the sidewalk, filled with colorful mixtures of pansies and impatiens: pink and white and orange and yellow. The sun shone brightly. Neighbors called out greetings to one another. A white truck selling ice cream drove slowly down the street ringing its bell. The scent of freshmown grass filled the air. It was all so horribly cheerful. Theola grew dizzy under the ruthless onslaught of unremitting cheerfulness.

No, she thought. Please. No. No. No. Let me find a taxi. I just want to go home. I'll never complain about good old Hillside again. I promise.

Music blared out of a speaker above the brightly-lit music store: "Good, good, good, good vibrations . . ."

Gasping, Theola plunged into the nearest doorway, desperate to get away from the upbeat euphony. She had always feared and hated the Beach Boys' music.

"And here is customer number twenty-nine," a hyperfriendly male voice boomed in her ear. "Congratulations, ma'am, you win our free makeover!"

Theola glanced right, glanced left: the speaker, a tanned, handsome, apple-cheeked blonde was grinning at her and pumping her hand. All around her were shining, happy faces and the sound of applause. She tried to back up, but somebody was standing behind her. She was trapped.

Her arms were grabbed and before she could protest she had been hustled into a back room, pushed into a hot pink chair, covered with a plastic sheet, and spun around several times until she was quite dizzy.

Attendants loomed over her.

"Let's start with her hair," said the large pink-coated one whose hair matched her smock.

"No, her face," said a skinny black girl with beaded hair.

"Her nails," said a third, a stringy white-haired woman in hot pants.

"Excuse me—" Theola said.

The hefty strawberry blonde glanced down at her as though surprised she could speak. "Don't worry, hon. You'll look gorgeous. Trust me." Then, as though Theola had suddenly turned invisible, the woman turned to her companions and said, "Good thing she was the one who won. She can really use the makeover."

All three of them began laughing.

Theola tried to think of the polite thing to do. She didn't want to offend anyone, regardless of how pink, lacquered, and well-meaning they were. She had always prided herself on her manners, hadn't she? But this was an emergency.

As she opened her mouth to explain, to say that there had been some dreadful mistake made, a booming, thumping cacophany erupted from what sounded like the very next room. A herd of elephants seemed to be marching in step to a very loud rock band.

"One and two, push it, push it!" a strident female voice commanded.

"What's that noise?" cried Theola.

"The aerobics class," the redhead said, and winked. "You'll get a free pass to that, too. Did you wash your hair today, hon?"

Distracted by the threat of exercise, Theola nodded vaguely.

"Good." The redhead held up a pink pump bottle and began to vigorously apply its contents to Theola's head. In moments she was wet and freezing.

"But—"

Her hair was being pulled, a few strands at a time, wrapped around orange plastic cylinders, and pinned in place with pointed clips.

"Ow!"

"Sorry, hon."

"I don't think—"

A hot damp cloth smelling of violets descended upon her face. Theola gagged.

"Just relax, dearie. This is our lavender refresher: it'll get you ready for your facial."

Theola managed to whip the offensive rag off her face before she choked: the scent of violets was everywhere, sweet and cloying. She just had time to draw a breath before a thick green viscous goo, redolent of pineapple, was being slapped upon her cheeks with what felt like a trowel.

Theola began to fear that she would hyperventilate and pass out right there in the chair. Grimly, she fought for consciousness. It was her only hope. If she fainted, who knew what horror the fiends would apply to her next?

"We're ready for her manicure," shouted her redheaded tormentor.

Do your worst, Theola thought defiantly.

She managed to maintain her composure through the manicure. But when they grabbed her feet and stuck them in a bucket of warm soapy water, Theola had had enough.

She stood up. The bucket went sloshing across the black-and-white linoleum.

"Where are you going?" the manicurist bleated. "Wait, we're not finished."

"That's what I was afraid of," Theola said. Before anyone could stop her, she hurried out of the room, down the hallway, and out of the shop.

Outside, the Beach Boys had moved on to "Be True To Your School."

I won't listen, Theola told herself. I don't hear anything. I am on my way to my car and I am getting out of this crazy place, right now.

An old woman pulling a two-wheeled metal shopping cart behind her stared at Theola, eyes growing wider as she got closer.

"Please, don't hurt me," cried the woman.

"Don't be ridiculous," Theola said.

"I'll do anything you say. Here, take my purse."

"Get out of my way," Theola said, her supply of good manners depleted. As she breezed past, the old woman fainted. For a moment, Theola hesitated, pondering whether she should go to her aid. If she stopped to help, she might be recaptured. She couldn't allow her compassionate nature to be used against her. With a sigh of regret, Theola redoubled her pace.

Somehow she found her way back to her car. The park was deserted, as though the Girl Scouts and all the rest had all been some terrible apparition.

Nobody would believe me, Theola thought. No one.

She gunned the Edsel's motor and raced for home.

As soon as she had reached the tunnel Theola began to feel better. It was dark and quiet in there. Her heartbeat slowed. She pulled into the Brawley's lot, turned off the car, and sat there a moment, hugging herself in utter relief.

Up the street, the Elvis triplets were walking arm-in-arm-in-arm, wearing matching white suits encrusted with rhinestones and blue suede shoes. Across the lot, a woman with two heads was being kidnapped by three of the alien parking attendants. They shoved her into a car, turned, and waved at Theola before they all disappeared in a sparkling mist. Even though they couldn't see her, Theola waved back gaily and breathed a sigh of relief. There's no place like home, she thought. She was even happy to see Scotty Wilkins walking past and gave him a dazzling smile.

"Hey, Theola," he said. "New look? I like it."

"Thanks."

Theola waited until he had ambled out of sight. Casually, she glanced into her side-view mirror. She had bright green slime dripping down her face. Orange rollers stuck in her dark hair every which way like strange Christmas lights.

She stared, transfixed. Tentatively she reached up her right index finger and spread the green ooze a bit more evenly over her cheeks. Theola smiled. She had to admit it: the green really did go awfully well with those orange rollers.

# Rock Band Conjures
# Satan As Manager—
# Group Claims "Good Business Move"
## by Deborah J. Wunder

*New writer Deborah J. Wunder has had her work appear
in anthologies such as* Aladdin: Master of the Lamp, *and*
Christmas Ghosts, *both edited by Mike Resnick and Marty
Greenberg. She tells me that one of her main concerns is
"not being mistaken for a loaf of bread or a comics character." These are things that make life interesting.*

*So is "Rock Band Conjures Satan," which confirms some-
thing we've all probably suspected at one time or another.*

In an unusually candid move, world-famous rock band,
KILL THE SMURFS, has informed *New Morning Magazine*
that their manager, Nick Nichols, is actually Satan! While
we do not advocate trafficking with Satan, we were curious
about the band's motivation, both in acquiring him and in
making this information public. We also realized this could
shed new light on the hearings of several years ago regarding the content of, and Satanic influence on, rock albums.
We therefore interviewed both the band (Dave Johnson,
Murray Levine, Steven Alben, Deirdre Lane) and their manager during their recent stop in New York to promote their
new record, READ IT AND WEEP.

NMM:   "You actually conjured up Satan to manage a rock
          and roll band?"
DJ:      "Well, it wasn't that hard to do, y'know."
SA:      "Really, what with Deirdre being a witch, Murray
          being a warlock, and all, it was quite easy."
NMM:   "Can you tell us what method you used?"

DL:     "We used a very simple ceremony, done on Bel-
        tane. Obviously, we're not going into specifics
        here."

NMM:    "Why did you do it? I mean, wasn't it dangerous?"

DL:     "Not at all! I set up the standard protections before
        invoking the spirits, so we were really quite safe."

SA:     "As for why, well, we needed a good manager. The
        managers we had before were either rip-off artists
        or lazy sods."

DJ:     "We were about to break nationally, and were afraid
        that if we didn't have powerful protection, we'd be
        prey to the same problems we've seen other
        megagroups get hit with over time."

ML:     "Yeah. I mean Old Nick, or one of his assistants,
        can count the house in the blink of an eye. Makes
        promoters and club owners think twice about rip-
        ping us off."

NMM:    "Mr. Nichols, why would you want to manage a
        rock and roll band anyway?"

NN:     "Please, my dear, call me 'Old Nick'; everybody
        else does. It seemed like an amusing idea at the
        time. Of course, since I started managing KILL
        THE SMURFS, I've learned an incredible amount
        about evil, even by my standards, which certainly
        makes it worth my while."

NMM:    "What have you learned, if that's not too personal?"

NN:     "One thing is that, while many bands still believe in
        music as a way of aspiring to some lofty ideal,
        there are a number of bands extant that pander to
        every vile human desire. Another is that, when you
        wish to spread a message to the younger generation,
        music is the best way to do it."

NMM:    "So Tipper Gore and the PMRC were right about
        Satanic influences in some records?"

SA:     "Not necessarily. Nick has no hand in our music.
        We do our own writing. I mean, Nick's a great
        manager, but he's not exactly Bruce Springsteen."

DJ:     "Besides, we don't advocate rape or racial vio-
        lence."

NMM:    "What does your band advocate, then?"

DL:     "Mostly, we'd like a return to the world's older re-
        ligions, because they really knew how to party."

NMM: "So you're trying to convert youth to a 'kinder, gentler religion'?"

ML: "Not really. After all, the old religions could get quite barbaric. Not everyone has the stomach for that sort of thing."

NMM: "What do you mean?"

DL: "Well, one advantage of having Old Nick manage us is that we get the best of everything: Accommodations, equipment, liquor, drugs, groupies, parties; all the things that make being a rock and roller worth it."

SA: "Not to mention the best deals, and major bucks for our gigs."

ML: "Really. There aren't an awful lot of people who could handle all that and keep their heads on straight."

NMM: "I suppose not."

NN: "These four have their heads on pretty straight, under the circumstances. I'd always thought that kids were pretty unreliable. Working with KILL THE SMURFS has truly been a revelation—no pun intended."

DJ: "Thanks Nick. The truth is that we want to succeed, and we're willing to pay the price."

NMM: "And just what is the price so far?"

DL: "That's between Old Nick and us but, so far, it's not unreasonable."

NMM: "We have all heard the stories about Satan requiring that clients relinquish ownership of their souls. Is that true?"

ML: "The terms of our contract with Old Nick are confidential. I mean, we don't want just any band thinking they can horn in on our deal."

NMM: "And what if Mr. Nichols wishes to add a few more select groups to his roster?"

NN: "I don't particularly seek any new clients. I prefer a minimum of human contact, if you must know the truth. One reason this situation is ideal is that I can reach many by only interacting with a few."

NMM: "When you contacted us with this information, Deirdre, we wondered why you chose to go public with it now."

DL: "Well, some rumors were starting to surface, so we had a meeting and decided that if we were up front about it, and willing to talk about it, nobody could use it against us. After all, we grew up during the Reagan administration, and can remember all the harm Tipper Gore and her friends tried to cause. Since one of the things we are fighting is that type of censorship, we decided that Nick would be a really powerful ally."

NMM: "I see that our time is almost up, so I'd like to ask what your future plans are?"

NN: "Mine are managing this band, and working on several ongoing projects, some of which are worldwide in scope."

DL: "Ours are to tour nationally to support our new album 'READ IT AND WEEP' for three months. Then we'll take a three-week break, after which we tour Europe and Japan."

ML: "Not to mention conquering the world."

SA: "Yeah, there is that."

DJ: "Then, it's back into the studio for our next album."

NMM: "Good luck with your tour and album. We hope READ IT AND WEEP burns up the charts."

# 2,437 UFOs Over New Hampshire
## by Allen Steele

*I'm not the only one who will say that Allen Steele is one of the hottest new SF writers around. He once lived in a small New Hampshire town which served as the model for the one in this story. A UFO was rumored to have crashed in a nearby lake and Allen received numerous phone calls from locals who were sure an SF writer would be interested in this. He also collected tales of UFO-related phenomena in New Hampshire, all of which resulted in the following story.*

*He now lives in St. Louis, MO, but remains mum on UFO action there.*

Giddings is a small town in the southern lakes region of New Hampshire. Located off Route 202 about halfway between Concord and Keene, it's the sort of place which typifies the adage "don't blink or you'll miss it." Indeed, most people find the town only by accident; a tourist from Massachusetts or Connecticut might briefly stop there for gas and a Coke on the way to a crafts festival in Bradford or a weekend ski trip in the White Mountains, but certainly for no other reason.

To such a visitor, Giddings appears to be just another one of the countless former milltowns scattered throughout rural New England. Near the highway is Tuck's, the Exxon convenience store that sells microwave sandwiches, lottery tickets, and vaguely obscene bumper stickers. That's as much of Giddings as most people see, but if you get off Route 202 and drive down the five miles of the two-lane Main Road toward the town center, you'll pass dense woods and ponds and dairy pastures. Dirt roads branch off Main, leading to nowhere; the woodland surrounds houses both large and small, some dating back to the last century, where beat-up old mailboxes are stuffed with free newspapers and almost every other backyard seems to have a satellite dish.

At the end of Main Road, just past the closed-down paper mill and the small stone bridge which crosses over the Contoocook River, is Giddings Center. There isn't much in the town square. Giddings Market, a grocery and general store. Zack's Pizzeria, a pizza and grinder restaurant. MovieMania, a video rental shop. The tiny U.S. post office. The town hall which is also home to the three-man police force and the volunteer fire department. At one end of the square is the stolid, windowless Congregational Church; behind it is the town graveyard whose slate tombstones date back to the Revolutionary War. Bookending the opposite end of the square is the town library, the basement of which serves as a movie theater on Friday and Saturday nights; *Batman Returns* made its Giddings premiere there last weekend, six months after its appearance on HBO. In the middle of the square is a weather-beaten bronze monument to the twelve boys from Giddings who were killed in the Civil War during the Battle of Bull Run; a flag is draped over the monument each Memorial Day, although no one remembers the names of the fallen heroes.

Nothing about Giddings suggests anything odd or unusual, at least to the incurious eye. Yet, if you look a little closer and in just the right places, you may notice a few strange details.

The magazine rack in Giddings Market has all the recent tabloid papers—the *Star,* the *Globe,* the *Sun, Weekly World News, The National Enquirer,* and so forth—as well as the current issues of *Fate, UFO Report, UFO Examiner,* and similar magazines. More copies of *Omni* are sold in Giddings than *Life, Newsweek,* and *TV Guide* combined. New periodicals are delivered each Tuesday by the regional distributor, and most of the weird-science rags are sold out by Thursday.

There's usually someone browsing in front of the shelf. Don't stare, but look a little more closely; this person is probably wearing a small plastic bracelet around his or her left wrist, its tiny blue LED pulsing once every minute.

The same newspapers and magazines are in the reading room of the town library. Two entire bookcases are devoted to (alleged) nonfiction about UFOS: *Flying Saucers Are Real, Incident At Exeter, Project Blue Book, Chariots of the*

*Gods?*, *The Bermuda Triangle*, *In Search of Extraterrestrials*, *Someone Else Is On The Moon*, *Communion*, *Missing Time*, *Out There*, the entire Time/Life "Mysteries of the Unknown" series, and much more. There's a perpetual waiting list for *Intruders* by Budd Hopkins; on the other hand, the paperback copy of *UFOs Explained* by Philip J. Klass has been defaced with a single word scrawled across its cover: "Lies!"

Over at MovieMania, there's an enormous wall of science fiction flicks, most of them about UFOs. The cinematic version of *Communion* is always rented out.

Giddings Mill appears, at first glance, to be abandoned. If you peer closer, though, you can see that the parking lot has been freshly paved. There are always cars parked near the front door; most of them are cream-colored four-wheel-drive Ford Explorers, but one of the vehicles is an ambulance. Look closer at the flat roof between the unused smokestacks and you'll spot a small grove of parabolic dishes and cellular antennae.

If you could peer through the building's smoked glass window into the high-ceilinged room where the rusted mill equipment used to stand, you would see four men and women sitting behind state-of-the-art electronic consoles, sipping coffee and murmuring into headset mikes as they watch a vast array of television monitors, LCDs, and radar screens. If you're driving down any back road in town and feel the need to pull over on the shoulder to relieve yourself by the roadside, be careful where and how you unzip your fly; the trees contain almost as many TV cameras as bird nests.

The last public place in Giddings remaining open after dark is Zack's Pizzeria, and Zack locks the doors at nine o'clock sharp. When the sun sets behind the hills and the last light of day fades upon the Civil War memorial, photosensitive timers bring to life hundreds of sodium-vapor streetlights which bathe the square and all the town roads in a bright yellowish glare. All night long, Ford Explorers from the mill prowl the streets and back roads, stopping occasionally at lonely houses in the woods where the lights stay on until dawn. When this town goes to sleep, it does so with both eyes open.

According to the 1990 federal census, Giddings has a permanent population of 157. At least two-thirds of these people claim to have been abducted by aliens from outer space.

"The last time anyone tallied how many people in this country said they were UFO abductees, it was in the mid-80s, about the time Whitley Strieber's book was on the *New York Times* bestseller list. Back then, it was around fifty or so . . . maybe a couple of hundred, if you count the obvious fruitcakes."

Paul Rucker coughs in his fist as he hands me a thick black pagebinder. Within it are 97 pages of single-spaced computer printout, row after row of names, addresses, and phone numbers. "That's the list of possible abductees we've compiled in the last three years," he says in his soft, Virginia-accented voice. "There're two thousand, four hundred and thirty-seven names in that book . . . and I haven't gotten around to adding the two hundred or so others who have contacted us in the last couple of months."

Paul Rucker doesn't look like a stereotypical UFO nut. Mid-40s, round-figured, balding, wearing horn-rimmed glasses and a navy-blue sweater over khaki trousers, he appears to be an insurance agent or a CPA rather than a former Air Force intelligence analyst. Yet as he squats on the seat of a backless isometric chair in his red brick office in the Giddings mill, he calmly talks of things you and I would consider impossible, absurd, and unbelievable.

"Look at the first name on the list," he says. I flip back to the first page; the top name has been carefully blacked out with Magic Marker, along with the address and phone number. "That's Number One," he says. "I can't tell you his name or where he lives, but he's the one who bought Giddings and made it possible for many of these people to live here."

He smiles in answer to the unspoken yet obvious next question. "If I told you his name, you'd recognize it immediately." He nods toward the list. "Besides, too many people have found out already. Why do you think the list is so long?"

Number One doesn't live in Giddings, but it's because of his wealth and influence that the town has become a sanctuary for UFO abductees. What little is known of him is that he is a millionaire who, during his salad days as a traveling salesman, was kidnapped by aliens while driving alone through Texas. After several years of experiencing the same recurrent nightmares which are symptomatic of other abductees, Number One sought psychiatric help, only to discover that there was an eight-hour gap in his memory, dating back to that roadtrip through Texas when he thought he had simply fallen asleep behind the wheel.

His quest for an explanation brought him into the small circle of people who had also experienced the "missing time" phenomena. Like Number One, most of them had repressed memories of being taken aboard flying saucers and subjected to humiliating physical examinations by extraterrestrials, horrifying memories which were later unlocked by hypnosis. They lived in constant fear of being kidnapped again, but unlike the former salesman—who, by this time, had amassed a considerable fortune and thus could afford to protect himself—they were virtually powerless against future intrusions.

Altruistic by nature, Number One decided to take matters into his own hands. Cloaking his identity behind a complex network of banks, holding companies, and real estate agencies, he searched for a town that he could transform into a fortress for his fellow abductees. When he found Giddings, it had been bankrupt for several years, rendered penniless by the demise of the local paper mill during the 70s and the wipeout of the state's economy during the recession of the 90s. Most of the houses had been foreclosed and were up for sale, and the town was inhabited by only a few farmers and die-hard oldtimers.

Number One purchased all the available private property in Giddings, including the paper mill, and turned it over to The Astra Trust, the nonprofit foundation of which Paul Rucker is the chief executive. There are precious few clues to Number One's identity; all of the Astra Trusts's property in Giddings is owned by a bank in Dallas, Texas, and the annual stipend checks are issued from the same bank. Although the leading suspect is H. Ross Perot, Perot's spokesmen have denied that he is the man behind the Astra Trust.

The Astra Trust is the McArthur Foundation for the UFO set: ninety UFO abductees and their immediate families can live in Giddings, rent-free and with a modest annual stipend, for as long as they feel the need to hide from the aliens. No strings attached; some people stay only for a year or two, others intend to remain in Giddings for the rest of their lives.

"We interview applicants, study their case histories, put them through polygraph tests and have them undergo medical examinations, including a session with our staff psychologist," Rucker says. "Obviously, with something like this, you're going to get a lot of people who are shamming, not to mention a few outright crackpots, but we've gotten pretty good at weeding out the con artists and fruitcakes. If they're let in, they're part of the community. They'll be protected for as long they want to be here."

Why doesn't Number One himself live in Giddings? Rucker shrugs. "He doesn't really need to," he says calmly. "I'm not at liberty to discuss his arrangements, but . . . well, let's just say, where he lives now, the aliens are never going to get him."

"Smile," says Dorothy Taylor. "You're on candid camera."

Dorothy—like others in this story, this is not her real name—lives with her six-year-old daughter Nancy and her two attack-trained German shepherds, Rex and Arnie, in a small cottage about a half-mile from the center of town. She is a quiet woman in her early thirties who works as a freelance artist; before she moved to Giddings, she lived in Bowling Green, Kentucky, where she had been an art instructor in the city's public school system.

We're sitting in the living room, drinking coffee as I conduct the interview. She raises her eyes toward the ceiling; I look up, and for the first time notice the fisheye camera lens positioned in the center of the ceiling, a red LED lamp glowing next to the lens. "It's on all the time," she says, "and there's one in each room except the bath. Plus the two cameras outside . . . one out front by the driveway, one in the backyard near Nancy's swingset."

Dorothy has been divorced for the past three years; like many of Giddings' abductees, her spouse wrote her off as hopelessly deranged when she began talking about aliens from space kidnapping her. She now has a boyfriend, an art student from Boston who visits her on the weekends. "When we want a little privacy," she says, smiling and blushing a little. "I tape over the lens in the bedroom. No sense in giving the guys at the mill a free show, after all."

The smile fades. "But the tape comes off after nightfall, and I don't care how Alec feels about it." She raises the front of her cotton-print smock; just below her sternum is a small vertical scar. "This is what they left behind after they took me," she says quietly. "I don't want that to happen again."

The near-total lack of privacy in her own home doesn't bother her, no more than the plastic bracelets she and her daughter wear around their wrists. The bracelets contain microtransmitters which relay, via the town's cellular radio network, their whereabouts in Giddings. When Dorothy goes shopping at the grocery, the watchers at the mill know she's there. If Nancy takes the dogs for a walk in the woods, the mill is constantly tracking her. The signals extend only as far as the town limits, but this doesn't bother Dorothy; she seldom leaves Giddings, and even then only for a few hours . . . and never overnight.

"I spent at least six hours in an alien spaceship in orbit above Earth," she says, quite seriously and without the slightest trace of dementia. "Those were the most terrifying hours of my life. They stripped me naked, took my blood, put . . . things into me." She looks away, falling silent for a few moments. "They raped me," she continues, more quietly now. "I never want to go through that again, and I want to keep my daughter safe from them. That's why we're here. Compared to what could happen . . . well, who cares about a few TV cameras?"

In a spare bedroom is her studio. Most of the incomplete paintings on easels or stacked against the walls are of New England landscapes; she sells them through an agent to hotel chains, for display in lobbies and guest rooms. Several of her oil paintings, though, depict her memories of her ordeal from her point of view. A flying saucer landing in a Kentucky farmfield. An indistinct group of bulbous-headed, wasp-waisted ETs marching down a gangway. A similar alien looming over her examination couch, a sharp surgical probe in its six-fingered hand. A view of Earth as seen through the windows of a spacecraft in high orbit above the planet.

Are these her private paintings? "No," she says. "At first they were, but when my agent saw them, she insisted that I publish them."

UFO publications? The covers of books about alien abductions? "Oh, no," Dorothy says. "Most of them are sent overseas. We've got a steady market in England for the covers of science fiction magazines." She smiles proudly. "And they love my stuff in France. I've had two gallery showings in Paris. I'm almost as big as Mickey Rourke over there."

Hidden behind the mill, encircled by a ten foot chainmesh fence topped with rolls of razorwire, is a large geodesic dome. The dome contains Giddings' SHF 15-GHz anti-aircraft radar system which constantly scans the airspace above the town; the system was procured from the U.S. Navy by the Astra Trust through Number One's defense contacts.

Not far from the edge of town is a small helicopter pad, where a French Aerospatiale SA 642 Gazelle is kept for use by the mill's security force. Two pilots and an observer live in a small house near the helipad. The mill's watchers are always watching the skies over Giddings; they've got the schedules for the commercial airliners that regularly fly over the town, so they've learned to ignore certain high-altitude blips on their screens. When they spot something on radar—particularly any erratic motion from an object that is larger than a duck or doesn't have the V-shaped profile of a flight of migrating Canadian geese— the pilots are called and whoever is on duty quickly takes the Gazelle up for a look.

"I never see anything," says Juan Torres, the former Brazilian Air Force captain who is one of the pilots for "Air Astra." He stands next to his aircraft, looking suave with his aviator shades and bandito mustache. "Small planes most times. Lots of stray goose . . . ah, geese. One time an ultralight. Scared the sheet out of him, never come back. But never any flying saucer. Not once. *Si?*"

What would he do if he ever spotted one? Juan crooks his finger toward me, then leads me to the open side door of the Gazelle. He pulls aside a canvas tarp, revealing a pintle-mounted 7.62 mm machine gun. Two outriggers on either side of the fuselage carry four SA-7 air-to-air missiles.

"Hey, you meet any leetle green hombres, you tell 'em to come this way," he says, patting the top of the gun fondly. "Me and Pedro here, we'll really fok 'em up."

Ray Bonette greets me at the door of his log cabin with a loaded Smith & Wesson .357 revolver in his hand. He stares at me with undisguised suspicion as I identify myself, then he demands that I present my credentials. Even after I do so, Ray is still wary and hostile. Before he allows me into his house, he demands that I remove my coat, shirt, and tie.

I reluctantly strip on his front porch. It's straight-up noon; songbirds warble in the dense pines surrounding his cabin, a passenger jet moans across the blue sky. When my shirt is off, Ray tells me to raise my arms above my head and slowly turn around. As I do so, he carefully studies my back and chest; he glares at the appendectomy scar near my stomach but says nothing.

"Okay, you're clean," he mutters. "Get dressed."

Ray Bonette is a heavyset man in his mid-fifties. His hair is crew-cut and is as white as his beard; he wears baggy trousers that haven't been washed in weeks and a mottled white T-shirt. He refused to tell me much about his past. He used to live in California. He was once a master electrician. He has a wife—present tense—but she's "gone now." Ditto for two kids. That's it; the only thing he wants to publically disclose is the size of his arsenal.

The cabin has four rooms, and in each room are loaded weapons. There's an Ingram MAC-10 on the coffee table in the den, a Beretta 87BB on one of the end tables next to the couch, a Colt King Cobra on the kitchen table and a Heckler and Koch HK-93 assault rifle on the counter next to the stove. Colt revolvers are on the bedside tables in both master bedroom and the guest room, each with spare rounds at ready. There's a night-sighted crossbow next to the back door, a Glock 20 beneath the pillow of his bed, and an AR-15 rifle resting in the corner next to the toilet in the bathroom.

If that's not enough, he also hints that the property line has been booby-trapped with explosives. "I got Claymores out in the bushes," he says, "so don't let me catch you out here in the middle of the night." He doesn't go into detail.

Having quickly shown me around the house, he shows me the door, still refusing to be interviewed. After he shoves me out onto the porch, though, he gives me one last pearl of wisdom.

"Tell that bitch Marilyn I'm ready for her and her little friends," he snarls at me. "Tell her that I still love God and America and Joe DiMaggio."

Then he slams the door in my face.

* * *

Charlie DuPont has been a New Hampshire resident for the past twenty-four years and has lived in Giddings for the past three. A native of South Carolina, he first came to New England as a student at Dartmouth in the 60s, but dropped out after his sophomore year to bum around the state before finally settling in Giddings, where he opened MovieMania, the latest of a long string of self-employed enterprises.

Charlie wears his hair long and lives the vegetarian, easy-vibes lifestyle of an unreformed hippie entrepreneur, yet he is one of the minority in Giddings who haven't yet been kidnapped by a UFO. "Lemme put it to you this way," he says, sipping a bottle of Evian water as he files away the videotapes which were returned to his store's overnight drop box. "I believe in Jesus. I believe in karma. I believe that Jack and Bobby Kennedy were killed by the CIA and that James Earl Ray didn't act alone. I believe that marijuana should be legalized. I believe that women are superior to men and are better in bed besides."

He sighs and shakes his head. "But I don't believe in flying saucers, and I think all these people are up to their eyeballs in donkey flop."

Charlie had opened his video shop in Giddings less than a month before he gradually became aware that most of his regular customers were heavily into UFOs He first discovered this when he began to get requests for obscure documentaries about the UFO phenomena, often for purchase despite the hefty prices such tapes commanded. It wasn't long before Charlie realized, through small talk with of the customers, that they believed that they had once gone cruising for burgers in UFOs.

"I guess, because the way I look and act, these people think I'm into all that shit," Charlie says. "What they don't know is that I've heard it all before. Yeah, when I used to drop acid, I sorta thought all that stuff was real, too, but I've been straight for a long time now, and since I got off drugs, none of that Eric von Däneken shit makes sense to me."

He cocks his thumb over his shoulder, toward the town square beyond the windows of his store. "This place, man . . . it's Weird Central Station. These people look straight, act straight. Most of 'em wouldn't know an acid tab if you put it in their hand. Y'know, half of them are Republicans. They helped keep Reagan in the White House for eight years and voted for Bush twice. Twice, for Chrissakes!"

His eyes roll up. "And they think they went for rides in flying saucers. They come in here, show me their funny-looking scars and tell me long stories about big-headed guys lurking outside the bedroom windows. Hey, I voted for Jerry Brown in the last primary and I don't believe that shit."

He pauses to open a cardboard carton of videotapes he has just received via UPS from his distributor. Not surprisingly, it contains five more copies of *Close Encounters Of The Third Kind*, all special orders from his customers. Now that the video has been marked down, everyone in Giddings wants their own copy. Meanwhile, he has copies of *Europa, Europa* and *The Player* he can't rent or sell for love or money.

"I like these people, y'know," he grumbles as he unpacks the tapes. "They're nice and polite, they always rewind their tapes and pony up the late fees ... but, shit, if I ever meet Steven Spielberg, I'm gonna rip out his lungs for making this goddamn movie."

"Tonight's quiet, least so far," Libby Reynolds says as she slowly cruises along the deserted back roads behind the wheel of one of the security trucks. "But we've got a full moon, the fog is up ... you never know."

Libby is wearing the light blue uniform of the Astra Trust's six-person private security squad. A former New York City cop, she left the city in search of a more quiet job in the country, never dreaming that she would be handling graveyard shift on what her team calls the "Spock Patrol": handling nocturnal sightings—or perhaps more accurately, "hearings"—from Giddings residents.

A thin haze has drifted off the river and into the lowlands, enveloping the road and the surrounding woods in a smoky mask. The police-band radio beneath the dashboard of the Ford Explorer chatters with crosstalk from nearby towns like Dublin and Peterborough, but Libby has it turned down low. Her job is to listen for the occasional calls sent from the mill on the cellular transceiver. This autumn night, she hasn't gotten any calls, but there's always the possibility that something might happen.

Libby slows down and stops in front of a gravel driveway. The name "G.W. Norton" is spelled in reflective tape across the mailbox; the ranchhouse at the end of the drive is clearly visible from the spotlights that surround it on all sides. Even at two o'clock in the morning, light glows from all the windows. Libby taps her car horn twice, then shifts the Explorer back into first gear and moves on.

"Once, twice, sometimes three times a week, that guy calls and tells us that aliens are in his yard." She shakes her head. "If raccoons are going through his garbage cans, they're aliens. If our own chopper flies over the house, it's a UFO. Last winter we had a nor'easter and the town lost electricity . . . happens out here now and then. He thought it was a flying saucer, and when someone from the squad came out here to calm him down, he nearly blew his butt off with a shotgun."

Libby glances at me, smiling in the wan light of her dashboard. "Why did I toot the horn? Because he stays up all night with that Remington in his lap, and I want him to know it's me and not E.T."

Nonetheless, Libby Reynolds believes in UFOs, although she has never seen one while living in Giddings. "It's crazy," she says, "but I know what fear is like. When I worked out of precinct house in the boros, I used to deal with all sorts of stuff. Crack gangs, drive-by shootings, wackos with knives in their teeth . . . hey, I once opened a garbage can and found a dismembered body stuffed inside. The people who lived on my old beat in Harlem were too scared to run out even when their building was on fire. . . ."

She stops to listen to the mill radio for a moment, then she picks up the handmike. "Ten-four, that's a twelve-fifty-six. Just went by there. Don't worry about it. Twelve Ben Gay out." She double-clicks the mike before she shoves it back into the holster. "Norton just called again. Thought we were the men in black or whatever."

Libby pauses to recollect her train of thought. "I see the same thing here," she says after a moment. "People here are scared of something, and it's not always just bears or the wind or whatever. I try to take it with a grain of salt, but. . . ."

Her voice trails off and she is quiet for a few moments. "I dunno," she finally says. "You tell me. Can all these folks be nuts or what?"

Jim and Betsy Donahue live in one of the larger houses in

town, a two-hundred-year-old farmhouse on thirty acres of land near a bend in the Contoocook River. Even before he left his position as a municipal stock analyst for a Chicago brokerage at age 65, they had considered retirement in New England; in fact, they had previously looked at places elsewhere in the Hillsborough and Chesire counties not far from Giddings. Their relocation to rural New England, therefore, was not wholly unanticipated; only the circumstances are different.

The Donahues' retirement home is a big, sprawling house with oak beams across the downstairs ceilings and Indian shutters on the windows. The rooms are furnished with antiques, the four-poster bed is covered with a handmade quilt, the kitchen walls are decorated with old iron skillets and cat's tails. The mantel over the fieldstone fireplace holds framed photos of their children and grandchildren, and the shelves in the basement are stocked with Ball jars containing Betsy's homemade preserves. And there's a spaceship out in the backyard.

Jim Donahue's flying saucer is a full-scale replica of the UFO which he and Betsy visited in 1981, while they were driving back to Chicago from a vacation in Minnesota. Unlike most abductees, however, neither he nor Betsy experienced the "missing time" syndrome, nor did the aliens who unforcibly took them aboard their spacecraft subject them to painful physical examinations. As a result, both have vivid recollections of the encounter which later enabled Jim to rebuild the shapeship in precise detail.

The UFO is about thirty feet tall and nearly sixty feet in diameter. It's shaped like an upside-down bowl with a round pillbox on top, and it stands on six wide flanges which fold down from the flat bottom of the hull. There are no windows in the hull. Five red-tinted glass hemispheres arranged along the bottom of the ship between the landing gear hint at the mysterious antigravity drive which enabled the vessel to silently land on the lonely highway in front of their car almost thirteen years ago.

The pseudo-UFO looks as if it is made of burnished aluminum, but that's an illusion produced by Jim and Betsy's skillful use of silver enamel paint. Their reproduction is constructed almost entirely out of particle board, with various pieces of scrap metal salvaged from junkyards and electronics purchased from the Radio Shack in Peterborough. Electrical lines snake across the yard to a small port beneath the hull. Jim belonged to the U.S. Army Corps of Engineers during World War II and built his first house after the war; his carpentry talents have lent themselves to making a do-it-yourself UFO.

"I did this to convince people what Betsy and I saw was real," Jim says as he leads me up a recessed ladder in one of the flanges to a trapdoor beneath the saucer. "We were fortunate in that we were invited aboard, not kidnapped like most of the others here in town. Because of this, we figure that the aliens wanted us to spread the word of their presence."

The trapdoor leads to a small anteroom in the center of the ship. After Jim clicks a couple of toggle switches next to the trapdoor which turn on the ceiling fluorescents—"They weren't there, I just put 'em in so you could see everything"—he points out the hatches on each of the four walls. Although in the real saucer they slid open automatically, he has been unable to reproduce the same effect. He has to push open the hatch which leads into the main control room: the cockpit, as he calls it.

The room is wedge-shaped, with a single wingbacked chair positioned in front of a wraparound console. "Notice the chair," he says. "It's short, isn't it? That's because the tallest of them was only four feet in height . . . but they were still humanoid in shape."

Jim gently settles down in it; the chair creaks under his weight. "See? The armrests are right where they're supposed to be."

The chair isn't what immediately attracts my attention. The console controls are evenly laid out and consist mainly of large round buttons, spaced apart from each other in unlabeled rows; I count no more than sixty in all. There are three nonfunctional TV monitors on the wall above the console, a panel of lights near the ceiling, and enough empty floor space behind the command chair to contain a pool table.

Contrast this with the flight deck of a NASA space shuttle—four seats, myriad control panels with dozens of tiny toggle switches jammed into every available space, two computer keyboards, and a half-dozen CRT displays, and in a craft capable of only flying to low-Earth orbit—and one comes to the realization that the aliens must have very advanced technology indeed.

Jim stands up and leads me through another hatch into the adjacent compartment. "This is the monitor room," he says. "It's where Betsy and I were shown Earth. By now, of course, we were in orbit above the Moon."

This compartment has a wall-sized TV screen, a couple of big-buttoned control panels on the walls, and little more. I press one of the buttons experimentally; nothing happens, but Jim is quick to give me an all-encompassing explanation. "They only had four fingers on each hand," he says. He holds up his right hand, his little finger crooked into his palm. "Like this. So they couldn't handle things the same as we do."

The next hatch leads to what he calls the "hibernation chamber." There are few more panels in this compartment, but the floor is dominated by three daises, each surrounded by Plexiglass tubes. Jim launches into a long-winded treatise on how the tubes each contained the bodies of aliens who were being held in suspended animation, but by now a small memory which has been tugging at the back of my mind comes to focus.

"Excuse me, Mr. Donahue," I say softly, and he instantly falls silent, awaiting my next question. I pause reluctantly, shuffling my notebook in my hands. "But . . . did you ever see an old TV show called *The Invaders?*"

Jim stares as me, not saying anything. "A show back in the 60s? With Roy Thinnes?" I add, and his face darkens. He slowly shakes his head. "About alien invaders from space?"

His hands are clenched into small, tight fists as his body begins to tremble. "I don't mean to imply anything," I continue, "but everything you've shown me . . . this entire ship . . . looks like the flying saucers they used in . . ."

"Get out," he rasps, glaring at me.

"Umm . . . excuse me?"

"You heard me." He speaks in a low, barely controlled voice as he wrestles with his suppressed rage. "You son of a bitch, get out of here. Right now."

There's little more to be said between us. I leave him alone in his UFO, finding my way through another hatch into the central anteroom. As I climb down the ladder and start to walk away from the UFO, Betsy is walking into the backyard, carrying a pewter tray laden with a pitcher of iced tea and three tall glasses. She looks confused as I make a lame excuse for my hasty exit, then her face falls into a disapproving look.

"Oh, no," she says. "You didn't mention Quinn Martin Productions, did you?"

"Ummm . . . no, ma'am. All I did was mention an old TV show called . . ."

"*The Invaders.* Oh, dear. You didn't know." She tsks. "They swiped the whole idea from us. We didn't earn a dime from them. Didn't Jim tell you about that?"

I gently remind her that *The Invaders* was a show on ABC in the mid-sixties; by their own account, the Donahues didn't encounter a UFO until almost fifteen years later. Betsy Donahue brushes this aside with a motherly look of condescension. "Young man," she says sternly, "time means nothing where we're concerned."

She gazes up at the perfect blue sky over Giddings, her face becoming placid as she contemplates eternity itself. "Black holes," she murmurs. "Don't you know about them already? They bend everything, even time itself. The aliens told us this."

For a few moments Betsy Donahue is caught in transcendental rapture, remembering alien voices which spoke to her long ago and far away. Through the open hatch of the UFO, I can hear her husband shouting curses, hurling things about. Something crashes as if it has been thrown against a bulkhead, but this doesn't seem to register upon her beatitude.

She looks back down from the sky, gradually focusing on me again, her smile as sweet as the sugar cubes on her pewter platter.

"Now," she says. "Are you sure you won't stay for tea?"

# Pulitzer Kills Publishing Maggot
## by Mark W. Tiedemann

*A 1988 Clarion Workshop graduate, Mark Tiedemann has sold stories to Jane Yolen,* Asimov's, Fantasy and Science Fiction, Universe 2 *and* Tomorrow SF.

*He writes: ". . . I have never seen a UFO, been abducted by one, encountered Sasquatch, Nessie, or Elvis . . . and I feel pretty damn cheated!"*

*He does not say whether the following story in any way reflects his personal opinion of your humble and ob't editor.*

"Rizzel!"

Rizzel looked up from his work station, across the bull pen, to the editor. Orber hulked in his doorway, his eyes yellowish slits. Pale blue smoke drifted around the old worm's rings. Rizzel had rarely seen him so angry. A few others looked up and gave Rizzel sympathetic looks.

He scooped up the piece he had prepared two weeks earlier, giving the unsavory mess in his tray a dirty look. Orber had been pushing him hard for that one, but it simply would not gel. He dropped the other button into his pouch and headed for the editor's cage.

Trella scooted across the floor from the other side of bull pen and met Rizzel at Orber's door.

"Come in!" Orber boomed.

Trella gave Rizzel a brief unreadable look, then entered the glass cage and hustled up to Orber. Rizzel slid in and moved to the window.

He looked out on the hive. Beneath the thick shelf of the ancient volcano, thousands of burrow holes led into the heart of the city. *His* city, Rizzel considered, the city he intended—*had* intended—to claim someday as one of the hottest reporters in tablet news. Unfortunately, he was stuck under Orber, the oldest, most venerable purveyor in the medium, stout, astute, and showing no signs of becoming fodder for his own consumers.

"Finished the bit on the giant moss eaters, Chief," Trella said and dropped three pieces on the desk. "And Burif says he'll have the material on Council Leader Shtrulles' affair with the barbarian arachnids from Fus-Fus Island first thing in the morning."

"About time," Orber grumbled. "I wanted that for the headliner. How about that delectable morsel on the three-tailed hatchling in Zez Province? You know, that same brood that gave us the hatchling that looked just like Mount Ghisz last year?"

"Oh, Prons is on that. Looks like all the ingredients by the end of the week. Headliner for the weekend."

A deep, satisfied vibration filled the office. Trella smiled at Rizzel.

"That's all for now, Trella," Orber said.

She quickly slid from the office, leaving the door open a crack. Rizzel felt a bubble of resentment float up and he closed the door all the way.

"Now *she's* a reporter, Rizzel."

Orber fondled the three morsels Trella had left. Each was a different shade of green. Suddenly he opened his wide mouth and popped them all in.

His eyes slammed shut, his mouth compressed until his entire pasty face was sucked into a huge pucker. One by one Rizzel heard each piece slide down Orber's gullet and impact his stomach.

Orber's color changed to a mild minty green. Slowly the smoke around him also altered, becoming wispier, bluer. His immense, many-ringed bulk shook gently, like a mound of jelly lightly tapped. Rizzel felt rather than heard the deep sound. He glanced out at Trella in her cubicle and felt a twinge of envy. Trella *was* good. Always a master epicurean of tablet news, she was all but Orber's pet. At least, Rizzel thought, she isn't twining with the old worm. He hoped not anyway.

A definitive belch brought Rizzel's attention back. Orber's eyes were pleasant slits.

"Now *that's* news," he said.

Orber closed his eyes once more and strained. A bubbling noise came from behind his desk. A tray on the floor beside it received a smooth dollop of brighter green. Orber sighed and pressed his intercom button.

"Copy!"

A few moments later old Kaso entered the office and, stooped and patient, scooped up the fresh material.

"Second tier," Orber said, "right after the headliner."

Kaso nodded and left.

"Now, then, Rizzel. What's happening with the vanity vendors' strike?"

"Well, I haven't finished that piece yet."

"*What?* How long does it take?" Orber slithered up to the window and tapped it. "This is a difficult business, Rizzel. Business hell, it's a mudpit! Journalism. Bad stuff. Our job is to take the unpalatable and churn out something the public can accept, something unique, new, but not so different they can't chew it. What do we get to work with? Vanity vendor's on strike. Tasteless. Citizens going around with their rings unadorned because there's nowhere to go to cover it all up." He grunted. "Might even be good for them to go around facing each other honestly for a change, showing their fellow creatures their true natures. I might even believe that myself," He turned on Rizzel. "But it doesn't *matter* what I *believe!* It's my *job* to deliver regular helpings, to see to it they *get* what they *want!* How am I supposed to *do* that if my reporters don't cough up the material on schedule?"

Rizzel backed away, wincing. "I just want to make sure my work is done right."

"That's *my* job! The day I let a reporter prepare his own work for public consumption is the day I roll over and die!" He eased back behind his desk. "I suppose you have an explanation?"

"I don't have a good handle on it yet. There are parts of this that just don't ring true."

"*Truth!* I don't care about truth, Rizzel! I want flavor, I want texture, I want calories! We're looking for consumable, Rizzel, not verity!"

Rizzel pulled the piece from his pouch and dropped it on the desk.

"What's this?" Orber asked.

"Something else I've been working on."

"Spec work?"

"Sort of, sure—"

"It is or it isn't."

"Spec work."

"Hm." He picked up the piece. It was blue with lavender swirls. "What kind of spec is this?"

"I talked to Honorable Fanal at the Three P Institute."

Orber's mouth wrinkled.

"Not more of that crap. The third planet is *not* newsworthy, Rizzel, how many times do I have to tell you that?"

"But—"

"They can't do anything right there and our public is impatient with them! Hell, they finally got around to sending an envoy and when the damn thing arrived *there wasn't anybody on it!* How *dumb* can you get? They forgot to put the ambassador on board what *must* have been a *damned* expensive ship!"

"But, sir, you heard what Three P said about that. It was never intended as an envoy, it was just—"

"Yeah, yeah, I *heard* but I didn't *swallow.* That's the difference between you and me, you'll take in anything, indiscriminately."

"I admit I have a lot to learn, but . . ."

"Of course you do. That's why you're here. You know, Rizzel, you could be good. *Damn* good. You've got the potential." Orber flexed his mouth into a brief, caustic grin. "In a lot of ways you remind me of me. You know how I got my start, Rizzel? I uncovered the Joyride Plot."

Rizzel started, surprised. "You're kidding. You did that?"

Orber settled back, self-satisfied and proud. "That was me. All those privileged spindleshafts enjoying the pleasures of terrorizing all those creatures on the third planet. Going down, scaring them with sudden appearances, sometimes abducting memories—not completely blocked, just enough to make them crazy after a while."

He heaved forward, an angry slant to his eyes. "And they were *hoarding* it! Keeping it to themselves!" He chuckled. "Not after I finished my piece. Their monopoly crumbled. For a while there was a hell of an increase in joyriding, but it's slacked off now. Thing is, the third planet's just too damn boring. Those people have never caught on. And they call themselves intelligent."

"They may be, only they're preaware . . ."

"*Pah!* Preaware. That's one of those trendy poplogisms you get from hanging around the Three P Institute. Meaningless." He rolled Rizzel's piece around on the desk. "So what exactly *is* this one about?"

Rizzel almost smiled. "Well . . . Honorable Fanal has been monitoring some of their media and discovered something interesting about them." Rizzel waited till Orber grunted. "They give awards for it."

Orber's eyes slitted skeptically. "They do what?"

"They give awards. For the best in a given year. All kinds of awards. And they name them. Oscars, Emmys, Tonys—"

"Sound like people. Sort of."

"Well, some of them *are* named after people. Dead people."

"Oh? They have an award called an Elvis?"

"No, they still aren't sure he's dead."

Orber chuckled. The glass rumbled sympathetically. Then he sobered. "Sounds absurd. If it's good product, why award it? The award is in the reception by the public."

"True, but the awards themselves become part of the media, a new form, and are consumed the same way the media being awarded is consumed."

"Conspicuous."

"I thought so."

"So they recycle?"

"Seems so."

Orber toyed with the little button on the desk before him. "Hard to swallow, Rizzel."

Rizzel waited. Suddenly Orber popped the button into his mouth. Rizzel straightened anxiously. He couldn't believe it. Now he just had to ride it out.

"Hmm," Orber intoned. He frowned. "Interesting." He closed his eyes for a few seconds, then they snapped open. Wide. Rizzel's pulse raced. "My—oh, now wait—Rizzel!"

Orber's tail swung up to arc over his head. It twitched for a moment, then slammed back into the floor. Rizzel almost fell over from the shaking. Orber's eyes were squeezed shut. He opened his mouth. Dark, blue-black smoke began to envelop his head.

"Ah! Ah! Ah!" He slammed his tail again. Rizzel made for the door.

"Sucksilt! How could you—"

Rizzel stopped and looked around. Orber's eyes were wide and full of wonder. They were a vivid pink now and his skin was violet. Smoke filled the office.

The door opened. Trella peered in cautiously.

"What is it?"

Before Rizzel could answer, Orber leaned against his desk.

"It's true," he said quietly. "It's true. It must be true." He looked around at Rizzel. "Pulitzers. . . ? To the reporters. . . ?" He scowled, baffled. "No . . ."

Then his entire, huge body quivered. The tail began slamming in earnest, repeatedly, and Orber grunted painfully. The story was lodged in him, unwilling to come out either way, and it was poisoning his whole system. Rizzel watched the death throes with a twinge of regret.

A thick, wet sound followed the last beat of Orber's tail. Rizzel glanced down at the tray behind the desk and saw an ooze of brilliant cobalt blue.

Then Orber keeled over and lay still.

"What did you feed him?" Trella asked, awed.

"Something he just couldn't handle." He moved around to the pallet. "But it looks like his last act was productive. What an editor."

"Your story?" Trella asked. Others were crowding the door behind her, staring at Orber's corpse.

Rizzel nodded.

"I guess that means you're the new editor," she said. "By tradition—"

"I know. I wish there was another way. But. . ." He looked up and frowned. "Okay, back to work. We've got a hungry public to feed!"

"Congratulations," Trella said. "And if there's anything I can do for you . . ."

Rizzel smiled. "We'll talk about it later. Thank you."

Trella closed the door behind her. Rizzel pushed Orber's body aside and pulled the desk back into place. He made a note to contact Honorable Fanal at Three P later. The material he had gotten from him was just right. It might, with the proper preparation, really make his career. All it required was—what did they call it on the third planet?—the proper spin.

He picked up the pallet containing the last effort of a once great editor. Orber deserved some memorialization. This would have to do. Rizzel stabbed the button on the intercom.

"Copy!"

# Elvis at the White House
## by Kristine Kathryn Rusch

*When I asked Kristine Kathryn Rusch the loaded question,
"Tell me a little about yourself," she went and gone and did:
"Kristine Kathryn Rusch was assigned three names as a
penance for smarting off one too many times in class. She
also had to write on the blackboard lots which translated
into a writing career, with ten novels sold to date (the most
recent, Facade, features dead birds, actors, and cocaine).
She has never seen Elvis, although she did have a ticket for
his final concert in 1977."*

*See where smarting off in class can get you, kiddies?*

The gray Atlanta skyline had traces of red, left over from the
unrest started by those short-sighted jurors in Simi Valley,
California. I leaned against my office window, feet aching in
my new low pumps, cup of coffee in my left hand. The digital clock on the bank across the street read 10:30 a.m., and
eighty degrees. The first truly hot day of the season was
upon us.

I never did understand how my momma could drink coffee in the heat, with the humidity dripping out of the air like
a live thing. But I started with the coffee habit during those
last few months in Louisiana, and it wasn't one I was going
to break.

A mound of paperwork waited on my mahogany desk, and
three messages blinked red on my answering machine. I
wasn't up to clients that morning, especially the wackos a
psychic investigations office could attract. I had come to Atlanta a few weeks before, figuring I would be safe here. The
riots reassured me, unlike the rest of the country, that I was
in a big modern city with big modern concerns. My business
would drop off to the kind of business it should have been:
a few difficult police cases, and a few true believers. I had

no stomach for the nutcases, which was why I left Louisiana in the first place.

Atlanta, now. Atlanta's ghosts were buried under steel and concrete, laid to rest by CNN, Coca Cola, and the most conference-friendly hotels in the entire country. Business heaven, where no one had the time to reflect on those niggly nightmares, those awful feelings.

No one but me.

A knock on the door almost made me spill the coffee on the blouse of my new tailored blue business suit. I slid behind my desk. I pushed some papers aside, and said, "Come on in," with the most demure voice I could manage.

The door opened, revealing the sexiest six-foot hunk of male I'd seen since I'd left the bayous. "Chelsea LaFronde?" he said with an accent as soft and lilting as my own.

Right then I knew I was in trouble. The problem with these Southern boys was that they *believed.* Even if they never saw a spirit on their own, even if they never dreamed, even if no one in the family ever had a feeling that came true, these boys knew such things were possible. And they wanted results.

Problem was, the last time I encountered one of these boys, he claimed he was the reincarnation of John F. Kennedy, and he had a secret to impart. That so? I said. Yep, he replied and leaned forward with the secret.

*I was murdered,* he said with all seriousness.

*Tell me something I don't know,* I replied, and lost the commission right there.

"You Chelsea LaFronde?" the hunk repeated. I had no idea how long he had waited while I was lost in the memory of the murdered JFK clone.

"Yessir," I said, resisting the urge to stand up to my full height. Not that it would have done any good. Five-two in low slung pumps is no match for six foot any day. "You were expecting someone different?"

He grinned and shook his head, a lock of black hair falling along his forehead. My heart started pounding—and not with fear. He reminded me of someone. "My Granny had a bit of the touch, too," he said. "So I was trying not to expect anything at all."

The touch. That put him right in the Alabama, Tennessee, Louisiana circle. I suppressed a sigh. I had a bit of the touch, too. Not enough to read someone on sight, like my Momma did, and too much to ignore it all together. *We got a service to perform,* Momma always said. *It's our duty so we can keep the gift.*

I always wanted to give it back, but then, that was me.

"What can I do for you, Mr—?"

"Neville," he said, as if the name didn't come out of his mouth that often. "Vernon Neville."

"What name do you usually use?"

He looked down. A blush stained those high cheekbones. "Presley," he mumbled. "I'm an impersonator."

That was when it all fell into place. The cocky walk, the come-hither smile, those luscious eyes, and that unruly shock of black hair. Elvis. Not the old fat one who couldn't remember lyrics on stage, but the gorgeous one—the one that caused me to subsidize the United States Post Office to the tune of $285, so that my fifteen hundred votes would guarantee his picture on the all-important Elvis stamp. I owed him. That sexy voice oozing out of my family's black-and-white TV screen during a rerun of *Love Me Tender* made me cream my jeans for the very first time.

"Looks like you do pretty well, Mr. Neville," I said, trying to remain professional. That young Elvis was my secret vice. I had all his movies on tape. Whenever the world got too much, I watched them in a darkened living room while I shoved chocolates in my face. I always thought I could forgo the chocolates. "What can I do for you?"

The flush still tinged his cheeks red. "My granny's been dead going on ten years," he said. "Last night, she came to me in a dream and said I'd better get some help with this."

I sighed. When someone with the touch spoke through a dream, it was usually worth listening to. "Help with what, Mr. Neville?"

"A murder." He was examining his hands as if he had never seen them before. "You see, Elvis's been telling me—"

I stood up. I had heard enough. I thought I would get away from these kinds of crazies in Atlanta. "Elvis Presley was not murdered. I investigated it for the Elvis Presley Fan Club from St. Louis, Missouri, and all the reports are in order. He was fat, he was a drug addict, and he died facedown in his own puke in one of the ritziest bathrooms I've ever seen. Now, get out of my office."

He put his hands up and slid his chair back as if he thought I was going to launch myself across the desk at him. "I know how he died—"

I slipped off my shoes to prepare myself before I used some of those fako karate moves I had learned in my women's self-defense class.

"—and I know it was his own fault—"

I placed my hands on my desk to steady myself. The adrenaline was reaching an all-time high.

"—but that's not why I'm here."

"Glory Hallelujah, Mr. Neville, because if it was, you wouldn't last another five minutes in this office." I sat down, trying to retain some of my dignity. I had written three books on psychic investigation, and ever since my successful solution to the Bayou Bomber case two years before, I could be choosy about my clients.

"I thought you believed in this stuff," he said.

"Elvis has been appearing to too many people lately."

"Elvis has been with me since I was seven years old, Ms. LaFronde." He got up and turned his back on me, as if the conversation was becoming too much to bear. "I'll never forget that day in August, 1977. The rest of the country wore black, and I was happy because this guy said he would stay with me for the rest of my life if I wanted, and make me rich and famous. My Granny said he just walked right in, and took over, but he didn't really. He always advises, never acts. I just listen to him a lot. He says he made too many mistakes to be entrusted with another life."

The problem with having a bit of the touch was that I could tell when people believed what they were saying. And Vernon Neville, handsome hunk of human male that he was, believed every word.

"So what is Elvis telling you these days?"

He threw me a dark, hurt look over his shoulder. "No need to be snide, Ms. LaFronde."

"Sorry," I said. Too many wackos came to me about Elvis. I couldn't take him seriously any more. I took a deep breath and kept my shoes off. If he mentioned Marilyn Monroe, John F. Kennedy, or Adolf Hitler, I would show him to the door. "Why are you here?"

"There's a little boy in Dallas, Texas. Elvis says he's going to be murdered."

\* \* \*

He found the best way to yank my heartstrings: talk about kids and death. Maybe it had to do with that day almost a decade before when I was living in Southern Louisiana and doing fortunes out of my home because Jesse was too little to carry on cases. The day my precious baby boy turned blue and stopped breathing just like the visions warned me he would do. And nothing the doctors did ever got that breathing started again. Of course, my husband blamed me, and so did the family, and so did I, more than a little. I vowed to pay attention to that touch and use it in all seriousness right then and there. Which was why the crazies bothered me more than most. They didn't understand just how important all of this could be.

"Where in Dallas?" I asked.

"Don't know," he said.

"How?"

"Don't know that either."

"When?"

"Ma'am, if I knew the answers to all those questions, I wouldn't need you, now would I?"

He had a point, one I wasn't sure I wanted to investigate. "How does Elvis know about this?"

He shrugged. "I guess the kid's grandma was a big fan. He gets special knowledge about fans sometimes." He gripped the back of the chair, and gave me the sultry I-could-seduce-you-in-a-minute look. "Usually Elvis tells me where to perform, what to wear, and how much pelvis to shake. He stays away from my business affairs, and he never talks about family. This is the first time anything like this has happened."

To him, maybe, but not to me. A little old lady in Manhattan came to me one afternoon, all embarrassed because her upscale religion didn't prepare her for visions of her dead husband in his underwear, warning her that some teenage hooker in Chicago was going to die, and it was in her best interest to stop the murder. We did, and she paid me a king's ransom for keeping her name out of the papers when the hooker spilled all she knew about the local mob boss who had been trying to kill her. The hooker went away rich, I made a nice commission, the papers took a heavy bribe, and no one connected that mob boss to the husband's business fronts all up and down Second Avenue.

"All right," I said, finally getting serious. "You need to tell me everything you know."

Dallas was a lot like Atlanta, only worse. The concrete stretched for miles over land that looked like it didn't have a history, even though it did. I didn't like it. The psychic vibrations were powerful and bad. I wagered the number of crazies who came here on a pilgrimage to JFK's death site made the number of crazies in New York look like a meeting of Shakers.

I brought Vernon with me. He had the room next to mine in a big corporate hotel that had rooms twice the size of those in Atlanta. Dallas amazed me the more I drove in it. Somehow, I never expected Ross Perot country to be Strip Mall Ville U.S.A.

Vernon thought he was along to see if Elvis would give us any more guidance. I figured he was along to protect me from embarrassment. If the press got wind of this, and it turned out to be wrong, I had no qualms about throwing Vernon to the wolves.

What are Elvis impersonators for, anyway, except to take up all that loathing that humanity had lying around, and bear it like a cross on the road to Calgary?

Once we got there, though, I found I spent more of my time trying not to think about the lock on the door separating our rooms. Vernon imparted flashes of wisdom about the boy, wisdom Elvis would suddenly "remember."

The boy lived out near the airport, in a part of Dallas I never could keep straight. Was it Dallas, Fort Worth, or one of those odd little towns that blended into other little towns that made up the concrete megalopolis that stretched as far as the eye could see? It didn't really matter since we weren't going to mail the kid anything. We hadn't even decided on a plan. Vernon's information was that vague.

And Elvis wouldn't give, unless he thought I really needed to know.

Vernon said that was because Elvis didn't like me. What a blow to my teenage soul! He said Elvis thought I was too loud and too rude to be a lady. I wondered if he'd seen Priscilla in *Naked Gun,* but decided silence was the better part of valor.

Besides, he probably would have blamed her transformation on that tennis pro or yoga instructor or whoever it was she ran off with.

All we knew was that by the first of June, that kid would be toast. The kind I make. Burnt and smoking.

Vernon just wanted to knock on the door, and inform the kid. I could imagine it. *Excuse us, but we're from LaFronde Psychic Investigations, and Elvis told us you're going to die by June unless you listen to everything we have to say.* That would go over big. I'm sure he'd march right out of that house, into our car, and off to protective custody.

Elvis would dish out information like pennies on allowance day. He finally told us that the kid's name was E.P. White, and he lived with his grandmother in a two-bedroom house that had stood on that spot since the mid-1950s. I did the rest of the legwork. E.P. was a good student who played six instruments and sang too loudly for his choir teacher's satisfaction. ("And he has a jukebox slide," the teacher told me later as if it were original sin. "Just kinda falls into the notes. No discipline at all.")

No discipline, and no enemies. Most of the kids he went to class with had no idea he was there. Only a few of the girls noticed him—and they didn't look at his face. Seems that twelve-year-old E.P. White was unusually well endowed. Puberty came early to boys living beneath the fumes of 747s.

Vernon was doing a number on Granny. They met in a bar, and he said he could have brought her home the first night. I didn't like her irresponsibility—imagine leaving a kid who was about to be murdered home alone—but Vernon said she couldn't be expected to know everything.

I hated the way he was defending her, and I hadn't even met her yet.

At that point, we hit a dead end. I was beginning to wonder why I took the case—I hated Dallas and the lock on the door between our rooms remained bolted tight. Vernon spent most of his evenings with Granny, and I spent too many alone in my car, watching E.P. make peanut butter mash for dinner, study six dull sitcoms, and crawl into bed.

At least Vernon would drop Granny off at a reasonable hour. I would have hated to watch a dark house past midnight, especially when I might miss the sound of squeaking bedsprings from the room next to mine.

Vernon had said there were perks to being an Elvis impersonator. I just didn't expect humping grandmas to be one of them.

It all changed the night of the concert. It was like the Lord stepped down from Heaven and gave me a vision, a sign—or maybe Elvis was speaking to me, and I just didn't know it.

E.P. was performing in the all-school year-end concert. Granny had asked Vernon to go with her, and I trailed along like a dutiful bodyguard, three paces behind and five rows up.

The concert was in a big gymnasium that smelled like dirty sweatsocks and was filled with oversized people hunching on bleachers built for children. A good handful of the men looked like overage Elvises. I shook my head. This case was getting to me.

Sam Hill Elementary had quite a music program. Each kid had the chance to perform in at least one choir, one orchestra, and one band. Most students, deserving or not, were given solos. The concert started at six-thirty, and about an hour-and-a-half into it, I realized my eardrums would never be the same. I was beginning to like the discordant sound of youthful voices warbling one-quarter step off-key.

Then the school's pride and joy came out. The big kids. The sixth graders, all muscle and toughness, filled with knowledge that they were the best.

Which, in this group, was not saying much.

They climbed on the risers and the teacher ducked behind the piano, playing a rousing medley of late fifties–early sixties hits, and directing with her head. A few kids bounced off the bleachers to attempt solos: One boy did a lousy "Rock Around the Clock"—he couldn't decide if he was supposed to be Bill Haley or Richie Cunningham. A little blonde girl, wearing too much makeup, pouted her way through "It's My Party," and then the pièce de résistance:

E.P., singing "You Ain't Nothing But A Hound Dog."

And I knew why Elvis, the old dog, had been interested all along.

He hadn't lied when he told Vernon he shouldn't be entrusted with another life. He had a bunch of other lives, and he was manipulating them all to become the King again.

Either that, or E.P. White was one hell of a natural at pelvis grinding.

The kid finished, and the whole crowd was on its feet, shouting "El-vis! El-vis!" Even Vernon was standing, but he wasn't clapping. He knew, same as I did, that E.P. didn't stand for Ernest Paul, and that that kid was more of an Elvis clone at twelve than most impersonators were at twenty-nine.

I ran down the bleachers and grabbed Vernon's hand. "We got to go," I said.

Granny looked over at me, spots of pleasure on both cheeks slowly fading. Jane Fonda had taught too many women that fifty didn't mean the end of beauty, and this woman had taken it all to heart.

I wanted to rip the red bow from the back of her long, silver-blonde hair.

"Where?" Vernon said.

"Backstage!" I shouted over the din. "Come on."

He let me yank him up the bleachers, past the rows of shouting parents, and through the back door into the hallway. The air was cool here and smelled of dust. It was refreshing after smelling dirty sweat socks for the better part of the evening.

I scanned. The hallway was empty. To my left, stairs ran down to the first floor. "We've got to get backstage," I said.

I started down the stairs. Vernon followed, his feet clumping on the tile. "Why?"

"Because tonight's the night E.P.'s going to bite it."

We had reached the main floor. Some parents in the hallway were smoking cigarettes. I ran around them to the huge double doors which had to lead to the back of the gymnasium.

"How do you know?" Vernon asked as I pulled open the door.

"See them?" I pointed to the men working their way down the bleachers to the wooden floor. None of them were wearing white lamé jumpsuits, but none of them had to. The resemblance to Elvis hadn't been coincidental. "The kid's too talented. They're going to kill him."

"I was thinking of that myself," Vernon mumbled.

I shot him a dirty look.

He held up his hands. "Just kidding."

"You better be." We crossed the wooden floor behind the performance shell. Granny saw us, got to her feet, and started waving. "Yoo-hoo!" she shouted. "Vernon!"

I grabbed his arm and yanked him through the wooden doors on the other end of the gymnasium. Kids milled in the back. E.P. stood near the outer doors, a cigarette dangling from his long thin fingers. I took the cigarette and stomped on it, then put my arm around his shoulders and pulled him outside.

"Hasn't Elvis been warning you?" Vernon said as he followed us onto the concrete steps. In the flickering fluorescent light, I saw E.P.'s face go red. So Elvis *was* talking to him, the creep.

"I—I don't know what you're talking about, Mister."

"You're just about the greatest Elvis impersonator who ever lived, you got the King inside you, and he's been telling you you're gonna die. Don't you get it, boy? You're not going to *live* if you don't listen to him."

"Jesus," E.P. said to me. "You go out with this nutcase?"

"Actually," I said, "Your grandmother does."

Then the inside doors burst open and a horde of Elvis impersonators flooded the halls. Vernon picked up E.P. and we ran across the dew-covered grass. This was the point in all my other cases that I turned things over to the cops. I had no plan. I didn't even know what a plan was.

"The car," Vernon hissed.

Something zinged by us, then I heard a pop. "Jesus," E.P. said. "They've got guns."

"You threaten someone's livelihood, they get a little pissed," I said. Well, I actually didn't say. I huffed each word as my breath got shorter and shorter.

We could have parked in a nearby parking lot, but no. We had to choose one clear across the street. Bullets pinged off the concrete beside us.

"Wish I had me a gun," Vernon said in a deep, sexy voice that didn't belong to him.

"Shut up, Elvis," I snapped. "This isn't a movie."

We finally reached the car. A bullet smacked into the windshield, shattering the glass. Vernon threw E.P. in the back and I sat up front, a sitting duck, as I fumbled for my keys.

"Start the damn car," Vernon said.

"You got the keys?"

"This isn't the time to lose your keys."

"Well, I didn't plan on it."

"How old is the car?" E.P. piped.

"It's a rental. It's new."

"Damn. New ones are almost impossible to hot-wire."

More bullets pinged against the sides. Good thing Elvis impersonators only killed people with song. If they had had any practice with those guns, we'd have been dead a long time ago.

I turned my pockets inside out and finally found the keys. I jammed them in the lock, put my foot on the accelerator, and started the car. It hopped over the parking bump like a little bird.

"Jesus, Chelsea, drive it. Don't smash it up." Vernon had peeked his head over the back seat.

"It's a car chase, isn't it? Aren't cars supposed to get smashed up?" My hands were shaking. The impersonators were crossing the street. They were leaving me no choice but to mow them down.

Then the cavalry arrived. We heard them before we saw them, sirens echoing off in the distance, blue and red lights changing the pictures of the landscapes. The Elvises didn't stop. They were too intent on us. They fired again, just as the first cop cars zoomed around the corner.

Sometimes the luck is with you.

Of course we didn't tell the cops everything. They didn't need to know about my touch or Vernon's Elvis voice. We told them that Vernon had heard about this kid in Dallas who was really good from another impersonator who made it clear that the kid would die. Vernon called me and we came down together, to see how good the kid really was. And found ourselves in a nest of impersonator vipers.

Granny thought Vernon was the biggest hero she had ever seen. I thought I was going to puke.

The case ended when we went back to the White house. Granny went back to her bedroom to look for some Elvis memorabilia. Vernon started to join her when E.P. grabbed his arm.

"Elvis really talk to you?" E.P. said.

"He sure does, kid."

"And he told you I was going to die."

"Yep."

"Doesn't it seem kinda strange to you that he would have all that foreknowledge? Do you think he's working with some of those impersonators that were there tonight?"

Vernon looked at me. I shrugged. "He never said a kind word to me," I said. "How would I know?" Vernon sat at the table, a frown creasing his beautiful forehead. "I wonder how many people he's suckering into this kind of life."

E.P. nodded. "He's been telling me it's great, but I keep having visions of myself singing in smoky nightclubs for women who make my grandmother look old."

"Your grandmother isn't old, kid," Vernon said.

I hit his shoulder. He wasn't supposed to say that.

He glanced at me as if he hadn't understood. "Well," he said. "Sometimes it's better than that. Sometimes you get to go to Vegas."

"Great," I said. "Where you can lose all the money you earn."

"Sometimes," Vernon said.

E.P. leaned back in the chair, tapping his finger against his lips. "You mean it's not teenage girls screaming and fainting? Lots of sex and all the food you want?"

"Vernon!" Granny's voice floated from the bedroom. She was doing girlish and cute. "I got something here you might like."

"There's sex," I said.

Vernon blushed. He pushed away from the table and hurried down the hall.

*"With Grandma?!?"* E.P.'s mouth fell open. "Gross."

"My take on it, E.P., is that if you want girls swooning over you, you've got to do it your way. Pretending to be someone else isn't going to cut it for you."

He got up and peered down the hall. A series of girlish giggles had ended in a moan. "No shit," he said. "Come on, let's get out of here."

We left a note saying we'd be gone for a while. Good thing, too, since, over double fudge chocolate sundaes, E.P. convinced me to find an exorcist for him. The only one I knew was my Great-aunt Louisa in Louisiana, so we drove there, and she worked on him for two days. She finally got the chunk of Elvis out, bottled it, and sold it to the Elvis Presley Museum in Nashville for a hefty chunk of change. Seems some people will pay a fortune for even a whiff of Elvis.

I took E.P. back home to find that Granny and Vernon hadn't even missed him. They had gone to Vegas to get married. E.P. assured me he'd be fine—seems Granny had done this before—and I caught the earliest flight back to Atlanta.

Where I sit now, behind my big mahogany desk, shoes off, feet sliding on the polish. Five lights blink on my machine, and I'm cradling a cup of coffee against my chest.

I really didn't want Vernon. Permanently anyway. But it would have been kinda nice if he had snuck into my room at least once. I could have pretended he was Elvis and well, you know.

Except Elvis hated me. Elvis was probably the one who talked him out of it. When I got back to Atlanta, I immediately went to my apartment and threw out all those old Elvis movies. Chocolate would have to do. I was getting too old for that teenybopper stuff anyway. I had seen the future and it was Granny.

There's a knock on my door. I take my feet off the desk, sit up, and invite the caller in. A slender, well made man in his early twenties shuffles through the door. "Ms. LaFronde?" he asks. If he had a hat, he would be twisting it between his fingers.

"That's me," I say.

"I got a problem," he says. "And I want you to tell me if I'm crazy."

I suppress a sigh. Half the nuts in the world think I can diagnose better than their psychiatrist. "I'll do what I can." I lean forward sympathetically and indicate the chair.

He folds into it, still twisting that imaginary hat. "It's Elvis," he says. "I—I know you won't believe this, but he ain't dead. I know him personally."

"So do I," I say as I lean back. A psychic investigator never escapes her fate. "And isn't he a disappointment? Those big stars are just never quite what they're cracked up to be."

# The Number of the Beast
## by Jeff Hecht

*This one came in over the transom (which is a neat trick in a transomless suburban Colonial house) and I'm glad it did.*

*Jeff Hecht is the author of ten nonfiction books, numerous nonfiction articles, and has had about a dozen stories appear in places including* Twilight Zone, Analog, *and Robert Silverberg's* New Dimensions. *He was also once misquoted in the* Sunday Sport, *a real British tabloid. He says he in fact does get calls from people with strange theories about bar codes. He'd better be ready to get more.*

Run a laser magazine, and you get all kinds of crazy calls. The one that started it was from some guy in God-Knows-Where, Vermont. He'd seen something in my Raw Rumors & Random Data column about bar-coding jail inmates. Not with old-fashioned striped prison uniforms, but with little plastic bracelets with striped symbols like you see in the supermarket. They wanted to keep track of the inmates, just like a supermarket keeps track of its inventory. Makes sense.

This guy wanted to talk about another idea. Some hotshot security outfit was going to put the bar codes right on people, and use them for identification. None of this futuristic automatic reading of retinal patterns or fingerprints. If you wanted to get into a controlled area, you'd stick your right hand into the scanner, and it would read the bar code. If you were on the list, it would open the door and let you in. If you weren't . . . well, he didn't say what happened then.

Sounded interesting, so I took some notes. He said the technology came from Entrance Control Systems, a start-up out in Silicon Valley. I asked him if he knew how it worked.

"It's all in your Bible, you know," he assured me.

"What?" We publish an annual industry guide, but I'd never heard anybody take it that seriously before.

"The Book of Revelation. Where it says that people shall wear the number of the beast."

"What?" This time a bit louder. He must have thought I was pretty dense.

"The bar codes. They'd all be wearing bar codes. And you know what's hidden in the bar codes, don't you?" He didn't wait for me to reply. "Remember the blocking digits? The ones that aren't printed as numbers, but define the start, the middle, and the end?"

"Yeah?" Clearly this guy knew something about bar codes. If you look very carefully at your typical can of soup, you'll see that most bar codes have two groups of five numbers printed under them. On each end and between the two groups of digits are bars that are longer than the rest. Those are the blocking codes, which help the scanner orient itself, but don't contain any data. Or so the techies tell me, anyway.

"Each one of those digits is a six!" he concluded, pouncing verbally. "So everyone with the code would be wearing Satan's mark!"

The number of the beast, 666. I groaned to myself. Was this crackpot being visited upon me for my one venture into horror fiction? "Radio 666" had netted me a check for $23.36, which bounced, and two copies of what turned out to be a poorly printed amateur magazine. I wound the call down. I am always polite; the publisher regularly reminds us that anyone might someday become a potential advertiser.

At least the crackpot's news tip panned out. Information found me the phone number for Entrance Control Systems in San Jose. Not only was the company real, but they were working on bar-code identification systems. Four bright young engineers had started the company about a year ago, after they were laid off from the nuclear weapons program when the Cold War fizzled out.

"We weren't about to sell our souls to some third-world dictator who wanted to build bombs," said one engineer, when the conference call was set up.

"It's a good thing we didn't. We had to sell them to the venture capitalists to get the company going," added a second voice.

"That's why they called them vulture capitalists," I kidded them.

As I listened, I could see those guys had some good ideas. Nobody wanted to use permanent visible tattoos; it looked too much like Nazi concentration camps. So they had developed special permanent infrared inks. They left the skin looking perfectly normal in visible light, but in infrared light the inks looked bright and shiny, while ordinary skin is dark. "At four microns, you couldn't tell the grand dragon of the Ku Klux Klan from Bill Cosby," one engineer said. Our eyes don't work at four microns, he added, so nobody would care if they stamped infrared bar codes right on people's foreheads.

They gave me a pretty damn impressive sales pitch. I took notes furiously. They had a solvent which carried the ink so deep into the skin that the bar code would never wash or wear off. It could be painted on the right hand or the forehead in a minute, and no one would ever notice it. Once people were coded, all they had to do was wave their hand by a scanner, or show it their forehead, and the computer automatically identified them. No need to worry about leaving a badge in the wrong suit, forgetting a password, or losing a key.

They had lined up contracts with the feds and some big security companies. They had a prototype working at the government weapons lab which had laid them off. Everybody going into the lab was being coded. A computer kept track of who was authorized to be inside, and what areas they could enter. Monitors checked people going in and out. "Total security, based on infallible hard-coded symbols," they boasted.

And they had more plans, all outlined in a five-year business strategy. They would sell bar-code readers for household security systems. Stick your hand into the reader, and it would identify you instantly. It would tell the homeowner if the guy in the gas company uniform really was the meter reader. The venture capitalists had a scheme to use bar-code readers for verification of checks and credit cards. They wanted to go big time; in five years, they told me, you would have to be bar-coded if you wanted to buy anything with a check or credit card.

They also mentioned that they would be looking for a manager of marketing communications in a couple of months. It was clear they were talking big bucks that you don't get in the trade magazine business. Believe me, it was mighty tempting.

I was mighty proud of that story. We don't do much reporting; we usually crib our new stories from press releases or the daily papers. But we had this before anybody else. I wrote a full-page story, to open the news section, with a full-color photo. And, just for laughs, I closed my Rumors column with the crackpot's tale about the number of the beast. I turned the issue over to the production department and got on with the next one.

When you're in the monthly magazine business, anything that's in print on your desk is ancient history. So my mind was a million miles from bar codes when "John mumble, from a British newspaper" called early one morning, a couple of weeks after the issue came out. If I had been about two cups of coffee further into the morning, I would have asked him what newspaper, but I was too busy trying to cope with the morning and the mountain of mail in my *IN* basket.

He had seen my articles on bar codes. Turns out they clip just about every magazine that's printed, looking for interesting stories. Mine were sitting in front of him. Could I tell him a bit more?

Sure, I talk faster than I think. Don't we all? I went over the whole thing with him. Bar codes on the hands and forehead, and lasers reading the symbols for the security computers. Great for paranoid suburbanites with a few thousand to drop on home security systems, I told him. And great for the government security establishment, too.

Then he asked me about the rumor column and the number of the beast.

"Just some crackpot," I laughed. "We get them all the time. Not many of them quote the Bible, though."

He tried again, asking what I knew about the numbers coded in the extra bars.

"The bars are real; you can see them yourself. But I don't know what the hell they mean." I offered to look up a phone number for an outfit that would know what the codes were, but he told me not to bother.

By this time, the coffee was kicking in, and I realized I didn't know where he was from.

"The *Sunday Sport,*" he said. "It's an entertainment weekly."

"Oh!" Our British sales rep once told me that the tabloids of his native land make ours look like *The New York Times.* As I put the phone down, I had visions of my head grafted onto an alien body on page 1. I couldn't remember if I had spelled my name for the reporter; I hoped he got it wrong in print. I told myself that no one I knew would ever see it.

Ten days later, I arrived at the office to find a fax taped to my door. 'LASERS READ SATAN'S SIGN' heralded the front-page headline. "YANK CALLS BIBLE 'CRACKPOT'" it said below. "VICAR WARNS OF EVIL CODE." My bleary eyes opened wider as I read. I couldn't remember exactly what I'd said, but I could tell it wasn't what John Mumble had written. He had me reciting Chapter 13, Verses 16-18 from the King James Bible, which I'd never even read. I know I hadn't told him that the United States government was going to make every citizen wear a bar code that included 666. John Mumble had made up more quotes from me in his first three paragraphs than I'd made up in the last issue of *Laser News.*

"It's an utter fabrication," I told the publisher, waving the fax in my hands. "I didn't say any of this!"

She read it and looked at me, and read it again, and looked again, and finally she laughed. "I can't imagine anyone believing this," she sighed, and handed it back to me. "But next time be careful who you talk with."

Relieved, if not totally reassured, I walked back to my office, tossed the fax onto the pile of papers to be filed, and sat down to dig into the mail. The phone buzzed urgently. A panicked-sounding receptionist announced, "it's Senator Hokum, and he says he has to talk with you immediately."

I remembered the name, but I couldn't quite place it. I asked her to bring me a cup of strong black coffee, and punched the button. "What do you know about this Satanic scheme?" bellowed the senator, prompting my memory. He was the one who thought God had created digital technology to help the senator play rock music backward to hunt for Satanic messages.

"It's all a fabrication . . ."

"It's nothing of the sort, and you know it. You'd better come clean, or I'll have you hauled before my committee."

I tried to explain. I told him I didn't know what digits

were in the blocking codes. I told him I'd call and check, but he told me not to bother. I told him about the identification system, and he said that was right straight out of the Bible, which said specifically that no man might buy or sell unless he wore the mark of the beast on his right hand or forehead. "We can never allow that to happen to law-abiding, God-fearing citizens," he thundered, and pledged to stop it in its tracks.

Sure enough, he did. That night he was on every television news program, warning of hellfire, brimstone, and bar codes. He stood shaking hands with someone from the American Civil Liberties Union, who denounced the identification scheme as un-American, and said he was pleased to find something on which he and Senator Hokum could agree. The senator stood with various other dignitaries who nodded their heads while he thundered. He stood beside a very pale young woman with very thick glasses who pronounced that the blocking digits on the bar codes were indeed sixes. He boasted to the camera that he had single handedly uncovered this devilish scheme. I was not about to challenge him. I was just glad he didn't mention my name.

I still haven't sorted it all out. The angry call I had expected from Entrance Control Systems never came. When I tried to call them, nobody answered their phone. The people at the Bar Code Institute won't talk to me, so I still don't know if those are really sixes, or if the senator's assistant needs new glasses. But I've got other things to worry about now. Somebody is projecting a full-color life-size hologram outside my window. It's light-years beyond the state of the art, with real-time motion and lifelike color. It shows this guy all dressed in white, hovering in the air with some kind of big fake wings, and he's raising this golden trumpet to his mouth.

# De Gustibus . . .
## by Anthony R. Lewis

*Anthony Lewis is another of the newer writers represented in this book. His work has appeared in other publications, including* Aladdin: Master of the Lamp.

*Anyone familiar with the workings of Wall Street may argue that this is not a work of fiction.*

Lily Blak bowed her head as Schuyler Hamish Arcot, the oldest senior partner in Arcot, Wade & Morey: Brokers recited the blessing from the book of Tao Jhonj. However serene she appeared to the others at the banquet table, she was gamboling inside her mind. Here she was—a success at 27, on her way to greater successes in the financial world. She was now an Associate in the firm. It had been close, both she and Freddie Mack had been in contention and, had her startling projections of the Azeri truffle harvest not proved out, Freddie would be in her seat and she would be in the kitchen.

The kitchen . . . the kitchen of Uomani's, the best restaurant in the Manhattan Financial District, possibly the best restaurant in the world. Certainly, it was one of the most exclusive. It never advertised; it did not need to. It was never reviewed; its patrons had sufficient influence to keep it private. Price would keep out most undesirables, but there was new money and such people did not understand. Only one cover was turned each night, but that was enough. And she and her colleagues were in the private dining room, the inner sanctum, the holy of holies, das Urspeisenzimmer. Lily was happy to be in this room; she never wanted to go into the kitchen.

"We welcome our new Associate, Miss (they were very traditional) Lily Blak, into the firm," Mr. Arcot said. "It was a fair contest, and to the victors, go the victuals, if I may be permitted to utter such a pleasantry." He looked about; however, no one was going to tell him he couldn't utter whatever he pleased. Aging, balding men, with six billion (or so) dollars have a rare form of charisma. "They both played the game. No smoking—not for aspiring Associates, no drugs, but," and here he smiled, "a little drink now and then is not amiss. I have always thought of it as a marinade." All smiled. "Mr. Mack made no fuss when I told him that Miss Blak would be the new Associate. He understood that there must be penalties for failure, or our firm would be no different from those parvenus whose antics have so disgraced our profession." Cries of "hear, hear" were heard. "His family will not suffer for this. As we have done for six centuries and more, the recoverables have been converted to solid investments in trust for his children." He looked at the serving door, "now to the meal," and he sat down.

The first course was a fine clear consomme; Lily had never tasted anything so delicate. It coyly hinted at rather than declaring it possessed a taste. This was followed by a liver pâté with those marvelous rye wafers that only the Finns can make properly.

With the main course, rump steak swimming in gravy, a red wine was served. No wine tasting ceremony was ever held in Uomani's, since all the restaurant's wines were of an excellence, and no diner would presume to refuse a wine selected by the proprietor. The meal continued in a companionable silence, only the occasional clinking of silverware against china was to be heard. Even this slowed as the food disappeared.

"Freddie was a man of good taste," Eliot Rensselaer Morey IV remarked to no one in particular, as he carefully chewed his meat the requisite amount before swallowing (his parents had been very strict in all his training). Only "the Eel," as he was known to his subordinates, would joke at such a solemn occasion. Like the rest of the Associates, Lily responded with a twisted half smile, letting the others know that while she respected Morey for his position, she did not think such levity was appropriate. There were college stories about Morey—one involved a pair of Jehovah's Witnesses as the main course at a fraternity house dinner. Adam's representative had been served with an apple in his mouth; Eve's stuffing had been of a more ophidian nature. Lily didn't believe it. That sort of prank would not be tolerated at Harvard, not with the Commonwealth's strict health codes. Yale? Possibly. Dartmouth? Certainly. But not Harvard (who knew what went on down the Charles at MIT. It upset her digestion to think of such things).

Now, as she had been warned, he would tell his one joke. "You know," said Morey, "ours is a dog eat dog profession." The obligatory chuckles rose and fell as the waiters wheeled in the dessert carts. Lily chose a chocolate mousse. Now that she would not be served, she was exempt from the code and need not keep her cholesterol and fat level to a minimum. She ate slowly, savoring the sensation as the rich dark substance embraced her taste buds. It was true that the sex act was only a poor substitute for eating chocolate.

The meal was ending. Replete with the failed competitor, the diners leaned back in their seats. As she sipped her tokay essenzia, Lily knew that as a junior partner, she no longer need fear being eaten; it was as if she had tenure at a university. When she retired or died, her body would be cremated. No one, not even the worms of the earth, got to eat the winners, the partners in the Wall Street brokerage house of Arcot, Wade & Morey. Tomorrow, she would write to her parents back in Highmore, South Dakota, and tell them her mother's fears had been groundless. "Don't go to Wall Street, honey," her mother had sobbed. "They'll eat you alive." Nonsense! No one had done that since the 1930s. Life was truly full and good.

# Is Your Coworker a Space Alien?
## by "Bob" bes Shahar

*eluki bes shahar informs me that she "was raised by great apes in the ruins of Fort Zinderneuf. The last descendant of the once-numerous Rassendyll family, she bears the purple pimpernel birthmark entitling her to rule the small Graustarkian country of her choice. Her hobbies are ranching dust* lepusae *and getting her own way."*

*That said, who are we to doubt it? But do read her wonderful SF novels* Hellflower, Darktraders, *and* Archangel Blues.

Not that it actually matters, but this is a true story. Some of the best full-roleplaying, live-action SF of our age occurs in the tabloids, y'know. Space-alien baby born to gorilla, three-hundred pound Argentinian grandmother by age 4, Australia found to be lost continent of Atlantis. That sort of thing. Real Philip K. Dick country.

Space aliens. Right. I remember back when they were called just plain aliens. There's some truth to the theory that the language is being devalued as a medium of communications by excessive modifiers. If the salt shall lose its savor, wherewith shall it be salted? Which is okay, since nobody talks to anybody anymore anyway.

Which is, in *its* way, the lead-in to my wail of toe (to quote Wallace Tripp).

I'm a writer, (which is what I'm doing here, of course. Where do you think books come from, typesetters?) which you would think would be the reason I had a bizarre, dead-end job about ten years ago in a place called Houston Graphics. Pronounce that "How-ston," because this is a New York story. It's also about space aliens, honest.

Anyway, Houston Graphics was a design and mechanicals studio that did book design, layout and pasteup, and me-

chanicals (which are the things they use to make the dies
that stamp the actual covers of the books which no one looks
at any more since the invention of the dust jacket). Once you
read between the lines (or know something about publishing) you'll know that Houston Graphics was a dead-end job
on the way to dying, since all that stuff is done nowadays by
computers. The only way the place survived was by under-
bidding machines, which gives you an idea what Mikey the
owner paid *us.*

And I was not there as a writer looking for quaint employment to put on my resume. (That came later, when I could
truthfully boast that I had once killed vampires for a living)
What you called me in those days was recently-divorced-
with-no-job-skills—except, of course, for a long-standing
fannish publishing habit that made for damn sure I knew
layout, pasteup, and design. Also where to go to steal the
parts to repair an obsolete-model Gestetner, but that's another long story.

So with one thing and another—and the help of someone
whose real life was as Magus of a White Lodge I can't mention by name because in addition to being old established
and English they've got real good lawyers—I was there at
Houston, razor-blade in hand, trying to make sense of my
life.

If you've ever been divorced, Gentle Reader, you'll know
that space aliens could have *landed* during the next year and
I wouldn't have noticed. I came from New Jersey—yeah,
like in the old joke: "Hey, you're from Jersey? What exit?".
In this case Exit 19 off the Garden State Parkway, I mean,
I'd *heard* of New York . . .

So when I got here, New York was a summer festival and
Rodger-my-in-the-process-of-becoming-ex was being a pain
(the man who thought *I* was too strange for his projected
lifestyle had moved to L.A. and taken up historical cross-
dressing, but not before trashing my *complete* collection of
*X-Men* and my nude Darth Vader poster).

Anyway, then it was a year later, I was still working at
Houston Graphics, and I'd sort of gotten to know my fellow inmates—at least a little—which is actually where the
trouble started.

Houston, as has been previously intimated, was the universal Day Job. Everyone there was something else—
actresses, painters, magicians, slumming preppies . . . If I'd

been conscious when I took the job I would probably have run screaming into the street, but by a year later familiarity had bred inertia. Everybody there was weird, and I fit right in, which tells you something about me, I guess, but what the hell?

Anyway. Factoids. Working at Houston with me was a guy named Royce whose serious ambition was to achieve a vision of the Holy Grail (and he did, but that, too, is another story), a Neo-Pagan private detective (I never asked what kind of cases she specialized in), a Thai-citizen fine-artist who had regular exhibitions of his abstracts in Germany and who was exactly as Chinese as Leslie Charteris, and a French nurse who supplemented her income working at Houston which made sense until you realized she was making six dollars an hour at Houston and private duty nursing in Manhattan paid a minimum of $27.50 an hour.

I swear I am not making any of this up.

There were others, too, since the turn-over rate for the kind of scutwok and abuse that Houston Graphics provided was high. There was also the strange fact that some people actually didn't like Mikey Pontifex, which is about on a level with having a personal opinion of the Black Death, but that is a volume in itself. Anyway, at the time of my tale there were about eight of us regulars (people there over a year; I was the newest) plus four more spearcarriers who lasted on the average about six months each, max. One of them never did bring back my hat.

The point. I swear I'm getting to the point, okay? Here it is.

I don't remember now where the story came from. I can't imagine it was the cover story, and I don't know why I would have bought the thing. It was an honest-to-Buddha supermarket press newspaper—I forget which one—which is not the sort of thing I read anyway, simply because there's nothing better on the inside than the cover headlines on the outside, which you can get for free, and since Carol Burnett won that libel suit most of the news is about television-series-reported-as-real-news.

This particular story was, on the surface, pretty harmless: *Is Your Co-worker A Space Alien* (it wanted to know)? It then went on to give you a nice little checklist of Ways To Tell.

The main thing I remember is is all stuff that could apply

to anyone; a masterpiece of supermarket press writing. There were warning signs like about space aliens among us not knowing how to eat Earth Food—trying to drink Jell-O, that sort of thing, just like the *National Pit* to try to give millions of Americans paranoia over their table manners— wearing inappropriate clothes (like what, for God's sake? Looked at *Women's Wear Daily* lately?), having inadequate knowledge of language and local customs (in *New York?*).

And then there was my favorite, which was "trying to pump coworkers for strategic information on Earth's defenses". Yeah, just what we worried about down below 14th Street, all right.

But it was sort of apposite, since all of us at Houston dressed like mudlarks and navigated like zombies, so I cut it out of the paper and blew it up to about 11x17 on the studio stat-camera, and waxed the back and stuck it up on the wall along with the rest of the local color. It got a few giggles, and Mikey didn't take it down, but that was about it.

And that was where the trouble started, because about a week after that Mikey hired Clifford.

It was 9:30 of a Wednesday morning and I was sitting crouched over my light-table in company of my fellow sufferers when an Apparition walked through the door.

I could tell he was an Apparition because he was wearing a suit—and not any of those wussy colors like charcoal or navy, either. The suit was black, the shirt was white, there was a one-inch-wide knitted tie (black) with a plain gold tie clasp (yellow-metal tie clasp, as our friends the police like to say) making sure it wouldn't get away. The Apparition was wearing real shoes (black), not sandals or sneakers, and he was carrying a cheap black briefcase that had been shipped Air Express from Nerd Central.

But Apparition sightings weren't what I was getting paid for, so I went back to work.

Mistake. Now was when I actually should have run screaming into the night, even if it was mid-morning. Well, that's what they always say, but I guess They (giant ants?) don't have to make the rent. And besides, everything looked as normal as it usually gets below 14th Street (Chester Anderson joke). There's a story about the toad in the crockpot that's germane to this argument, by the way, but if I told it I'd probably be picketed by PETA. Isn't freedom of speech wonderful?

Well, back to Clifford—a.k.a. The Apparition. It turned out he wasn't a passing fancy. No, Clifford was our newest employee.

"This is Clifford," Mikey said, as Clifford set down his briefcase in the carrel next to mine. Mikey P. being the owner and operator of Houston Graphics, condign cash cow, he got to make intellectual policy statements like that. And Clifford must have been working here, or he wouldn't be taking his lunch out of his briefcase in a series of neat brown-wrapped parcels and piling them next to the box of razor blades and technical pen humidifier with which Houston was wont to provide its new employees (those things never work, by the way. Fill your ink reservoir with ammonia instead when your pen's not in use).

I looked at Clifford. Clifford looked at me. Then Clifford uttered the statement that would forever set the tone of our relationship.

"*Gentleman's Quarterly* says that the new narrower silhouette is the menswear look for fall," quoth Clifford.

I know what you're thinking, right? After a five-page buildup of great subtlety I will reveal that the Cliff-man is a space alien. Sure I will. And then I'll jump into my temporal rheosimulator and bop off to sell this to *Planet Stories* circa 1950, right?

Not. Trust me; I'm a starving writer.

Fact: Clifford *swore* he wasn't a space alien. Okay? Satisfied? I even asked him.

It went like this:

Here was me, and here was this Official White Boy From Hell poster child. Clifford looked like an FBI agent gone to seed. He looked like he was from Oklahoma. Clifford just didn't fit the sub-14th-Street ethnic blend. Blue eyes, light brown hair, skinny, no beard or mustache or earring. Or visible tattoo. Clifford looked, as I have said anon, like a White Boy From Hell. Transparent in a strong light.

And he was weird, make few mistakes about it, because when was the last time you ever saw someone wear a suit to work? Even *executives* don't wear suits to work any more, or if they do they wear them over stupid little polo shirts—or (yig) over T-shirts—and *Miami Vice* has been off the air for years.

Clifford wore suits. With cute white shirts with the regulation number of white fake mother of pearl plastic buttons. Always.

But what the hell—Royce wore *dresses* (very nice ones; antique rayon, but then Royce was into retro as well as Grailology, and besides he didn't do it all the time). Seiko wore black leather and studs—*all* the time. Even in the summer, when the temperature in the studio hit one hundred broken air conditioner degrees, and powdered herself down with alum and cornstarch so she wouldn't sweat (never let them see you sweat). Seiko looked like a constipated vampire or a refugee from a canceled British TV series. And Angela—well, the less said about what Angela wore the better. I hope it was because she was into performance art. I did not ask. Ever. I am not precisely a coward, but blue-eyed women have a lot of problems to deal with in this life, as I shall explain in a few paragraphs. Meanwhile I did my best to remain in ignorance.

So yes, Clifford was weird. For weirdness' sake he fit right in. We were all weird, in those thrilling days of yesteryear. Even me (I guess), if we're being fair, and listening to Rodger-my-ex's opinion but how much credence can you put in the words of a man who's in the process of leaving you for a Tudor corset?

But this is about space aliens. Remember that checklist? The one that, actually, most of my fellow inmates came up one hundred percent positive on?

Clifford came up negative right down the line. Like he'd studied for it.

Like the first day. Obviously a place like Houston Graphics didn't have a lunchroom, and eating at your desk was not encouraged, as mayo and repro don't mix. But sometimes you did anyway, and Mikey didn't make too much trouble about it as long as you were discreet.

So here's Clifford, putting his sandwich on an actual china plate and pouring his soda into a real silica glass and doing the knife and fork bit and *everything*.

It was strange. And he never stopped doing it, every time he ate at his desk. China plate, silica glass. Stainless steel tableware. That was what the briefcase was for.

Don't you see where this is going—at least, where it was going, back in the days when I was young and foolish and looking for distraction? Back before I sold my first book and went to my first science fiction convention and developed all the distraction a body was ever going to need in life?

Allow me to lay it all out for you. Clifford knew everything there was to know about about how to eat Earth food appropriately. He knew exactly how to wear Earth clothes, and never did anything like come to work wearing a torn lampshade and some Hefty bags (or a tea-dress in cabbage rose rayon. Or—).

And he never asked questions. In fact, if you wanted to know more than you ever wanted to know about anything, get stuck in Clifford's idea of a conversation. Which I did, having the misfortune to sit right next to him and own a face that has *always* convinced people I want to start a conversation. Or probably, like I said, it's the blue eyes. I have thought of getting colored contacts, but with my correction I'd have to wear glasses, *too*, and I can't deal with that. Maybe mirrorshades (prescription mirrorshades? How *déclassé.*) but that would only make things worse. It's the curse of the blue-eyed woman. Trust me.

And what it meant in this context was that at the end of a week I knew how many stories tall the Empire State Building was. I knew how many people rode the subways (on the average) every day. I knew how many professional baseball teams there had been in the five boroughs since 1906, how long they were there, how many games they won, and against who. I even knew who *hadn't* patented the automatic typesetter (Mark Twain. It's in his autobiography, and a salutary lesson on the necessity of financial management for writers. Go look it up.).

In short, not only was Clifford very weird, Clifford was very weird in a focused, disciplined fashion that none of the rest of us could possibly beat even on a good day.

So naturally, less than six months after Clifford was hired, it occurred to me that if there *were* space aliens, and if they *had* seen the article in the *National Midnight Astronomical Object,* they would be very careful to make sure that none of the checklist could possibly apply to them.

In short, what convinced me that Clifford was a space alien was that he had absolutely none of the qualifying requirements to be one. He hadn't even asked me about Earth's defenses.

Yeah, I know, I've already told you that Clifford wasn't a space alien—or at least that he said he wasn't, and I promise

I haven't got any contrary factoids that I'm going to reveal at the end of this story. This is, nevertheless, a weird, starkly unbelievable pulse-pounding true story. Promise.

Besides, would it actually be exciting if Clifford really-o truly-o was a space alien? I doubt it. Probably it would be depressing and New Wave, because here would be all these strange visitors from another planet living clandestinely among us, and what would it have done to the quality of life on Earth or the free market economy? I personally predict that when we do dance the whole "klaatu burada nikto" riff it will get 72 hours of coverage on CNN and have no other impact on life as we know it. And anyway, I can't do a 'No Contact' story as funny and depressing as Terry Bisson's "They're Made Out of Meat."

Yeah, yeah, yeah—the *story*. My story. One (Blue-eyed) Woman's Encounter with the Cutting Edge of Reality.

I really think I could have had a normal life if I'd been born with brown eyes.

Onward. Lecture time on the nature of experiential reality. When weird things happen, your memory tends (in retrospect) to drop the setting of the events from the information it files (which explains why witnesses make such lousy witnesses). Case in point (Rod Serling *homage* alert): the last conversation I had with Clifford. I remember everything he said. I remember everything I thought. I even remember when—and a couple of isolated window-dressing details (I'll put them in when I get to the events)—but as far as I can visualize it, it could have been a radio program being broadcast to an empty soundstage.

Which is where being a writer and an amateur of deductive reasoning comes in. I'll tell you the way it probably was and how everything probably looked and what everyone probably did. But except for what Clifford said, think of it as a Best Guess; which is a sort of frightening take on the nature of reality, if our projections of it depend on our memories and our memories are like that.

Okay, here we go. It's winter—I think it was November, because I remember the studio was always dead in December and Mikey always laid people off just before Thanksgiving. It's dark, because it's after six. Everybody's gone for the day but me and Clifford. This is okay by Mikey, since I've been there a year and I have my own keys to the inside door so I can get into the studio whenever the building is open—

which also means I can lock up. I remember I worked late a lot when there was work because freelance artists are paid by the hour and the more hours you worked the more money you had. I was also trying to rack up bucks while there was work because money will get you through times of no work better than work will get you through times of no money. To coin an aphorism.

And Clifford was there, too, but not for the same reason. Clifford was okay at layout and pasteup, but he was also slow, which meant that Mikey was looking to let him go, and I'd told Clifford that one way of delaying this was to work extra time and not bill for it, so it looked like you got through your piecework in less time than you actually did. That was why Clifford was there.

In six months I'd never found out what his last name was.

I finished up for the night—I know this, because I would not start a potentially stupid conversation in the middle of working—and put everything away, and turned off my table so it was just my tensor lamp and Clifford's and the light over the stat-camera lighting up the big studio space. And I said:

"Clifford, are you a space alien?"

"There are no confirmed reports of UFO sightings," said Clifford, who never—now that I came to think of it—asked questions requiring answers.

"Yeah, but Clifford, are you a space alien?" I said, or something similarly witty and persistent.

Clifford looked at me. "Don't you think that's a suspicious sort of question?" Which was a rhetorical question, so it didn't count. Behind him I could see my old stat of the "Is Your Coworker A Space Alien" article stuck up on the wall of Clifford's carrel, having migrated there from the wall beside the door.

"You are so a space alien," I said with the immense maturity that characterized my actions in those days.

Clifford sighed. "I am not a space alien."

Which you would think would end the conversation, but you know how it is when you start asking stupid questions—it's just like potato chips.

"So if you're not a space alien, Cliffie, what are you?" I riposted.

Clifford sighed again.

"My name is Clifford Mutton-Jones. I'm an ethnographer."

Now as we have all learned in later years, an ethnographer is someone who studies ethnogs. But at the time I must have looked like somebody who thought "ethnographer" was another word for space alien.

It's the blue eyes.

"I'm an ethnographer from Aphasia State College," Clifford expanded patiently. "I study cultures. Earth cultures. I'm not a space alien studying Earth cultures. I'm studying *space aliens.*"

It wasn't really Aphasia State College, but I can't remember the name and I don't want to get sued if I get it wrong. Some place in Pennsyltucky, anyway. But at the time I gave Clifford's statement all the serious consideration you would give to E-mail from the *Twilight Zone* delivered by someone who was between you and the door.

You may wonder why it was okay for Clifford to be a space alien and not okay for him to be a soon-to-be professor from Boombatz University. The answer to this is that academics are weird desperate sophonts capable of bizarre irrational behavior and space aliens aren't any weirder than New Yorkers.

"And, um, where do you study space aliens, Clifford?" I asked. I reached for my purse and that changed my angle of vision enough that the Austrian crystal snowflake that Royce had hung on his tensor lamp hit the light by the stat-camera and made a gorgeous eight-pointed star prism against my glasses. I mention this specially because that's the one thing I actually definitely remember seeing.

"Here," said Clifford morosely.

Here.

The Cliff-man studied space aliens *here.*

Clifford was studying *us.*

*We* were space aliens?

Not since eighth grade, when I caused riots at the June M. Triplett Elementary School by proclaiming that I was an exchange student from Mars had I seriously considered the possibility that I was from another planet. It was an interesting thought. I did a severe brain-cudgel for corroboratory evidence, but actually I have never had any performance anxiety ingesting gelatin desserts of any kind and gave it up as wishful thinking.

Meanwhile, secure in my undivided attention, Clifford was expounding.

"You see," said Clifford, "when I decided I wanted to do my doctoral dissertation on disenfranchised cultures—aliens living on Earth—I realized right off that the most important thing to do was to gain your trust. Paradoxically, this could best be achieved not by emulating your own culture patterns, but by maintaining an explicit ethnographic distance between interviewer and subject through the use of universal culture markers."

This was the longest nonstatistical speech I ever heard Clifford make. I wanted to explain that he hadn't interviewed anybody, much less gained their trust, and that he was in the wrong place besides if what he wanted was space aliens.

On the other hand, who was I to stand in the way of someone becoming a Doctor of Ethnography for the University of Gibberish? I said something mordant and witty like:

"Yeah, Cliffie, I see how that works. Absolutely."

Which must have satisfied him because I honestly don't remember any more of the conversation and if I could make anything up I would. I left (which means that someone else with keys showed up or else Clifford left with me), Clifford went back to work (or else left when I did), and if this were fiction I would never have seen him again, but since it isn't, Clifford Mutton-Jones worked at Houston Graphics another two weeks (or so) and was fired as part of Mikey Pontifex's Great Thanksgiving Massacre. (I was not. In fact, I worked at Houston for four more years, trivia fans.)

We did not, as far as I remember, discuss ethnography again. I didn't mention it to anybody else, either, but I looked it up in one of the encyclopedias we had around the studio and there really is such a thing—it's where sociologists or anthropologists or some damn kind of academic go out and study weird alien *(Earth* alien) microcultures, like Trekkies or tattooists.

Or space aliens.

I admit I gave the matter more than a little thought on some of those bleak January lunchtimes after Clifford's departure when I could scope the studio and see Royce in a mauve faille tea gown with a copy of *Avalon of the Heart* negotiating a peanut butter and anchovy sandwich, Seiko looking like a later-stage Terminator and eating Jell-O with her fingers (one-handed!) while she worked at her board. Tyrell carefully spreading canned chocolate frosting on lettuce, leaf by leaf, before eating it, Angela wearing—well, never mind, and carefully mixing instant coffee with her Diet Pepsi until it reached the consistancy of Filboid Studge, after which she drank it. (I was on a tunafish and hard boiled egg fast, myself.)

These were my people. Perfectly normal.

Space aliens? Us?

"Hey, Chantal? What do you know about Earth's defenses?" I asked the moonlighting nurse.

"Earth?" said Chantal vaguely.

Never mind.

So I spent about six months wondering if I was a space alien or if anyone I knew was. I then realized that the Secret Fundamental Truth of the Universe was that *it didn't matter.* And by then I'd actually finished my first book and had lots of other problems.

So I freely admit that I have not given Clifford and his ethnography much brain time over the years, but now that I think about it, what you've got to wonder is why a nice white boy after eight years in college would believe that there were space aliens living among us and working in a design studio in New York City?

Of course, you could also wonder about why *I* thought there were space aliens living among us and working in a design studio in New York City.

Or how long it took Clifford to memorize all those statistics to lull his space aliens into a false sense of security. I do hope it worked wherever he went next. There's nothing crankier than a cheesed-off space alien. This is the voice of experience, probably.

Because the real kicker is that what you don't get to wonder about (topspin time) was whether Clifford was telling me the truth. The whole reason I remember him after ten years is that he *was.* Clifford *was* an ethnographer, and he *was* studying space aliens. He even wrote his book—I saw it remaindered in the *Scholar's Bookshelf* catalog last year. At least he wrote *a* book (you don't forget a name like Clifford Mutton-Jones that easily) and from the title it *could* have been about space aliens living among us. Of course, it could also have been about exiled South American poets. Or Lucius Sheppard.

Does this not fill you with wonder and terror? Do you realize that not only Clifford Mutton-Jones but about a dozen college professors of legal age and sound mind had to agree that this was a *reasonable* topic for a dissertation? That hundreds of technically-sane standup breathers are all out there believing in space aliens among us with their hearts and minds and souls at this very nanosecond?

Who was it that said reality is not only stranger than we imagine, it's stranger than we *can* imagine? I, personally, don't have all that much time for imagining things. But good old Clifford sort of grips the sensawunder right by the sweetbreads, don't he? Maybe he commuted from a parallel universe.

Or what if the National Pit *is* telling the absolute truth about everything, and its just some kind of intellectual snobbery that keeps us all from noticing? In the year fifteen hundred something, Pope Urban II (I think it was) promulgated a famous bull that said, more or less, not that there *weren't* elves and fairies and creatures of wonder, but that it was a sin to *see* them. So everybody should stop at once—no matter what their senses told them—and move into a rationalist age, right? You can't change reality with things like papal bulls—only the consensus about reality (theme music here please).

Because if you can change consensus reality one way with one piece of paper, it only follows that you can change it the other way again with another piece of paper. Or a book.

Like Clifford's book.

I bet there are space aliens among us *now*. I bet they work in design studios in New York City. Probably they wear Hefty bags to work and eat Jell-O with their fingers and don't know who the President of the United States is.

Yes, your coworker *is* a space alien. And there are more of them every day. Reality modified while you wait. The only thing that really bugs me any more is that I never got a chance to ask Clifford all about Earth's defenses. I'm sure he knew what they were.

He might even have told me.

# A Beak for Trends
## by Laura Frankos

*Laura Frankos is a native Californian and graduate of UCLA. Her work has been published in* Analog *and she is the author of* St. Oswald's Niche, *an academic mystery. She is currently at work on her third mystery novel. She has collaborated with husband Harry Turtledove on three lovely children, Alison, Rebecca, and Rachel.*

*This story is for all of you who believe that the only thing tabloids are good for is lining birdcages.*

Benjamin Hatcher was not surprised when his grandmother's attorney sent him a letter soon after her death. As her favorite grandchild and her stockbroker, he knew Grandma Gladys had a sizable estate to distribute. He opened the envelope, pausing for a moment to look at his grandmother's handwriting. He would never see her again, he thought sadly.

*Dearest Benjamin,*

*If you are reading this, I am no longer among the living. Don't mourn for me, dear boy, I've had a long and happy life. I must now reveal to you a secret. It concerns my beloved pet, Ptolemy III.*

Ptolemy was an enormous scarlet macaw. As a boy, Ben loved helping care for him whenever the family visited Boston. It was always the highlight of his vacation.

*You will find this difficult to believe, but it is the complete truth: years ago, I taught Ptolemy how to read using the same flash cards my first-graders used. He especially enjoys the sports and financial sections of the newspapers. The news section, however, confuses him. Although intelligent, he lacks the background needed to make sense of it.*

Ben shook his head. He'd never realized Grandma was losing her marbles.

*But now I shall let you in on Ptolemy's other secret. Not only can he read the financial section, he is the one who chose all my stocks. He is, as you may have noticed, very good at it.*

Ben sat back in his desk chair, thinking hard. Around ten years ago, after her brother left her some money, his grandmother had called him with a peculiar list of small stocks she wanted to buy. Ben had tried to talk her into a more conservative program of government securities, but she insisted. The bizarre little portfolio took off, but when Ben asked Grandma how she did it, she'd just chuckled and said, "A little birdie told me."

After that, she'd called several times a year, with similarly unusual but successful instructions. She couldn't possibly mean the parrot was advising her. Could she?

*Considering his skill at picking stocks, I am sure that caring for him will prove profitable. But to ease your way, I have made arrangements to provide for him. My estate shall be divided into four parts: one-quarter each directly to you, your sister, and your cousin, with the remaining fourth placed in a trust fund for Ptolemy's care. As long as you care for him properly including regular check-ups you may draw upon the fund for his care. It will provide a monthly allowance, and after Ptolemy's death, the remaining money shall be divided among my three grandchildren.*

*Care for the old bird well, Ben, for my sake. I've included a little list describing his diet and schedule. Above all, give him fresh newspapers daily and keep things regular for him. He gets upset when his world is chaotic.*

*With everlasting love,*

*Grandma*

"A little list!" Ben dug out four pages detailing diets, bathing, cage-cleaning, and other unpleasant things. Then came copies of the will and the trust. Ben scrutinized them. Then he whistled. "A generous allowance indeed! Thirteen hundred a month! But he'll have to stay in the office; Barbara's allergic. Oh, Grandma, what have you gotten me into?"

Though he didn't believe a word of his grandmother's fantasy, Ben wouldn't let her down. That weekend, he drove to Boston to pick up his new dependent.

\* \* \*

Ptolemy was not happy. He missed Gladys. He liked Dr. Moore, but the vet's assistant was slow about changing papers. Worse, she'd given him the classifieds, which confused him. What did "87 Prelude Si 70M,auto,snrf,$5995" mean? Oh, well, whenever he ran into a perplexing bit, he always remembered Gladys' adage: "Don't believe everything you read in the papers!" She'd taught him that not long after he learned to read the flash cards.

He did not complain when Dr. Moore and a dark-haired man put him in a box. Perhaps, he hoped, there would be fresh papers whenever he was released and put in a new cage. He wondered how the Celtics were doing.

The trip seemed endless. Ptolemy fell asleep in the dark box, lulled by rumbling vibrations. He awoke when the box was lifted and carried someplace. The lid came off suddenly; Ptolemy blinked. There was the dark-haired man, looking disgruntled.

"Okay, Ptolemy," he said. "Welcome to your new home. I'm Ben, your new owner. We've met, not that you'd remember." He extended his arm to Ptolemy, who hopped on it, looking all around.

Ben had a spacious office on the fifteenth floor, with windows on two sides offering views of other skyscrapers. To Ptolemy's joy, he spotted his own cage among the office furniture. Nearby, on a low table, was his t-stand. He shrieked with happiness at the sight of the old familiar things.

"Jesus! If you keep that racket up, they'll never let me keep you here! Why don't I put you on your stand, and I'll fix your lunch." He brought Ptolemy a dish of treats, carefully prepared according to Gladys' instructions. Ptolemy ate and drank heartily, then looked pointedly at his cage.

"Cage?" he asked. He could see papers spread invitingly on the bottom.

"By God, you do still talk," said Ben. "Okay, go in."

Ptolemy climbed in and settled near the bottom, on what Gladys called his reading perch. He was a little disappointed that it wasn't the sports page, but only for a moment. He'd never seen *Investor's Daily* before. He lowered his head, scrutinizing the Dow Jones industrial average, catching up on days he had missed. He riffled the pages with his toes, checking for Gladys' stocks. Completely absorbed, he didn't realize that Ben was watching him closely.

Ptolemy noticed a downward trend in two of Gladys'

companies. One of them, his instinct told him, was going to take a big nosedive. What should he do?

He glanced up. Ben was sitting on the edge of his desk, arms folded, face puzzled.

"WedgeTech," Ptolemy said clearly. "Sell WedgeTech."

Ben started at the parrot's voice, then checked to make sure the door to his secretary's anteroom was shut. "What did you say, Ptolemy?" he crooned. "Say that again."

Ptolemy wondered what kind of a dope Ben was. "Sell WedgeTech," he repeated.

Ben came closer, speaking low. "Can you show me where it says WedgeTech on the paper, Ptolemy?"

He *was* a dope, Ptolemy decided. Couldn't he even read? Ptolemy jabbed a toe at the agate type under the W's. "WedgeTech down."

"It could be an accident," Ben muttered. He tried another angle. "Do you know all Gladys' stocks, Ptolemy? Can you tell me her stocks?"

"WedgeTech. HyperVectors, Unlimited. Aussie Springs Sodas. Kilgore Chemical Industries. Briarton Aeronautic Enterprises. N-N-T Airlines. Electr—"

Ben waved his hands. "Enough, Ptolemy, enough. My God, you *can* read. And you know her stocks. And you're right about WedgeTech; I've been thinking the same thing about them. Was Grandma telling the truth all along?"

Ptolemy clambered up to the top and hung upside down. "Sell WedgeTech!"

"Okay, okay. But don't tell everybody what you can do. God only knows what would happen to me if they find out. A parrot stockbroker! Now that's a story for the birds!" He snorted at his own joke.

That reminded Ptolemy he hadn't seen a sports page for days. He was worried about his favorite player, Larry Bird, who had an injured back. "Celtics!" he squawked.

Ben, who had gone to his desk and was playing with the gray box, was puzzled. "Sell Tix? Ticketron? Ticketmaster?"

The man was a complete dope. Ptolemy needed twenty minutes to make Ben understand.

Once Ben figured out Ptolemy was indeed a Wall Street wizard, he did everything he could to make the bird comfortable. He got to the office early, to give Ptolemy his bath and play with him before checking the morning newswire and going over his bond inventory. He bought special treats; Ptolemy loved dog biscuits. Ben even began seeing clients from one until three, not three until five as before, all because that was Ptolemy's quiet time. Barbara, who didn't know about Ptolemy's talent, complained that Ben left earlier and came home later. He also began visiting the office on the weekends. She accused him of having an affair, which he denied. His secretary quit, saying Ben had changed since his grandmother's death a year ago. "He never used to mind if I came in his office to discuss things. He's secretive, paranoid."

But Ben's boss and clients didn't mind his behavior because Ben, long known for coming up with a few successful stocks every quarter, now piled up several dozen. "Ptolemy, old boy," he said one morning, "you definitely have a beak for trends. The second quarter reports are in, and even in this stinking recession we're sitting pretty. I don't know how you do it."

Ptolemy was happy. Ben changed his papers several times a day, giving him not only those fascinating copies of *Investors Daily,* but the *New York Times* sports pages (though he still preferred reading about the Boston teams). He sat on his t-stand, playing with a rawhide strip. Ben was cutting up a hard boiled egg.

"Hey, Ptolemy, what do you think of Hippocrates Pharmaceuticals? They had a big lawsuit against them a few years ago, but I hear they're working on a promising new AIDS drug. Any good?"

Ptolemy tugged at the rawhide with his beak, then dropped it. "No good."

Ben's face fell. "Damn. Thought we could get in on the bottom floor, so to speak. Okay, pal, here's your snack." Ben shared the egg with Ptolemy, sprinkling his slices with salt and pepper. Even after a year, Ptolemy found this a strange ritual.

Ben misunderstood the parrot's glance. "Yeah, I know. I need all this cholesterol and sodium like a hole in the head. Everybody's always telling me what to do; don't you start, bird!" Ben stuffed the rest of his egg into his mouth, then went back to his desk to wolf down his lunch. Ptolemy played with his other favorite toy, an old key chain. Ben, who was long accustomed to the racket, didn't like it today. "Too loud, Ptolemy. Knock it off."

An hour later, Ben expected the first of his afternoon appointments. He grumbled as he went to greet his client. "Damn job. Damn rotten food. Damn indigestion." Ptolemy, now back in his cage preening, ignored Ben's complaints.

He did look up, startled, a short time later when the client shouted, "Ben! Are you all right?" The client slapped at the intercom: "We need some help in here! Ben's passed out." Ben sat slumped in his chair, holding his left arm, his chubby face sickly gray. Ptolemy had a bad feeling, the same kind of queasiness that shook his insides before the '87 crash and when Gladys never got up from her couch, no matter how he called her. More people flooded into the office, crowding around the desk. One man was yelling into the telephone. Two more moved Ben to the floor where Ptolemy couldn't see him.

Later, other men ran in, carrying a metal bed with wheels. Ptolemy hooked himself up to the very top of his cage, but still couldn't see anything except Ben's legs. Then the men put Ben on the bed and wheeled him away.

It was the last time Ptolemy ever saw him.

Ptolemy, as Gladys had noticed, did not like disorder. Unfortunately, Ben's death turned his life upside down. After a temporary stay at his vet's, he went on a horribly scary voyage in a box, shut up for what seemed like an eternity. Eventually, the box reached its destination: Cicero, Illinois, the suburban home of Gladys Hatcher's middle-aged granddaughter, Cindy Ledbetter.

"Jesus, what a stink," were the first words of his new owner. She was forty-three, overweight, with hair colored a peculiar orange. Ptolemy stared at the hair.

"For thirteen hundred bucks a month, I'll put up with a skunk," said another female. Ptolemy's head swiveled around. The other woman was also pudgy, with blonde hair in loose curls. She laughed. "He's checking us out, Cindy. Did your grandma's trust fund say if he could talk? Hey, Polly! Hello, pretty boy! Polly want a cracker?"

Ptolemy was thirsty. "Water?" he croaked.

Cindy jumped backward. "God, he does talk. Grandma sent a letter with him. She said he's special, but that I'd never believe how special. All I know is that he never said much when we visited Boston."

"Boston," Ptolemy said wistfully.

Curly-hair said, "What fun! He repeats everything. Don't let Ed teach him swear words. Let's feed him and make him feel at home."

Cindy looked cautiously at Ptolemy. "But Kathy, how am I supposed to get him in his cage? Do I pick him up? What if he bites?"

"Don't be chicken, Cin. That trust said if you don't take good care of this bird, he goes to your cousin Linda and you lose that money. Just give him your arm. I don't think he'll bite. Go on." Kathy pushed her friend.

Cindy nervously extended her arm. Ptolemy obediently climbed up. "Easy, bird, easy, Ptolemy, nice and easy, here's your cage."

Magic words to homesick Ptolemy. He hopped gracefully from Cindy's arm to his waiting cage. He climbed over to the water cup and drank, then dug into the plentiful helping of parrot mix.

The women watched him. Kathy slapped Cindy on her hefty shoulder. "There! He's settled. You've done everything right so far, just like those papers said. "He's got his cage, his food, his exercise stand—"

Cindy frowned. "Yeah, I had to move Ed's gun rack to fit that in. Ed wasn't happy, but wait till we get that first check—"

"You can make the kids give him his baths and play with him," Kathy continued. "What more can a parrot need?"

Ptolemy, having satisfied his stomach, knew: he needed to find out how the Dream Team was doing, if the proposed takeover of Save-Big Retail had gone through. He nibbled one last pumpkin seed, then slowly made his way to the printed sheets below.

Immediately, Ptolemy knew something was different. The typeface was not that of *ID* or the *Times* or the *Globe*. It was bigger, and had less copy on the sheet than he was used to. Half the page was a garish photo of a baby with four arms. Around the margins ran little squares—advertisements for hair tonics and fortune tellers. Ptolemy lowered his head and began to read: "Pedro Sanchez is like any other toddler. He lives in a rural section of Mexico, adores his mother's home-made tortillas, and plays with his big sister. But little Pedro has four arms!"

Ptolemy shook his head. He'd seen lots of people in his life, but none of them had four arms. An image of Gladys came to his mind, smiling sweetly, spreading fresh papers for him. "Now, Ptolemy, don't believe everything you read in the papers!"

Ptolemy certainly didn't believe this silliness. He turned another page with his long toes. "Unusual markings in a Nebraska wheatfield were discovered following a terrifying night of bizarre lights in the sky. Residents of Martinsville huddled in their homes during the onslaught, believed to be the result of alien invaders. Hildy Fitzwarren says: 'It began at midnight. You could see the lights blinking off and on over the wheatfields.' "

Ptolemy uncurled his toe, letting the paper drop. What was this drivel? Maybe the other side was better. He expertly flipped the section over, revealing the front page of *The Nation's Eye*. ELVIS, JIM MORRISON, JIMI HENDRIX ALL ALIVE AND JAMMING ON REMOTE SOUTH PACIFIC ISLAND screamed the headline. SHOCKING MIX-UP: MAN MARRIES HIS DAUGHTER AFTER DIVORCING HIS SISTER! BABY BORN WITH FOUR ARMS—see page sixteen! Too late; he'd already seen page sixteen.

Ptolemy didn't know what to make of *The Nation's Eye*. He'd certainly never seen anything like it before. Reading it gave him that uneasy feeling, the one he got when he'd read about a failing corporation. Something in this newspaper was not quite right. But he was starved for reading material, so he doggedly went through the whole issue, though he kept worrying about how much of it was true.

Matters did not improve for Ptolemy. For one thing, he was used to going to sleep at eight-thirty, but the Ledbetter family sat in front of the television long past then. Ptolemy couldn't sleep because of the lights and noise. Cindy began by dutifully cleaning his cage every day, but that slipped to every week before long. The two kids were supposed to bathe him regularly, but they kept putting it off, too, especially after ten-year-old Mitch pulled Ptolemy's tail and the parrot bit the brat.

The food was adequate, though Cindy did not lavish treats as Ben and Gladys had. But worst of all, in Ptolemy's view, was the weekly supply of *The Nation's Eye*. The more he read, the worse he felt. Nearly every paragraph gave his stomach flip-flops.

The alien stories made him feel worst. Ptolemy was continually amazed at the variety of "aliens": green faces, strange appendages, glowing bodies, weird helmets; all the details, but no substance at all. His inner sense quivered at each UFO sighting. He much preferred stories about talking codfish in Newfoundland or ghostly pirate ships.

Three months of *The Nation's Eye* convinced him it was shit, and he felt a certain satisfaction in defecating on it. But even though Ptolemy didn't believe a word of it, that didn't stop him from reading it front page to back. He was, after all, a confirmed print junkie.

"Thanks for taking him, Kathy," said Cindy. She handed Ptolemy to her neighbor. Ptolemy perched on Kathy's shoulder, nibbling at the frame of her glasses. He was glad they weren't nervous around him any more, but he wondered why the Ledbetter brat was taking his cage outside.

"We'll be back next Friday," Cindy continued. "Mitch will bring over all Ptolemy's food and toys. I hope he won't be a bother."

"No, it's no trouble," Kathy said. "We're old friends now, huh, bird?"

She took Ptolemy into the house next door where Mitch was setting up the cage. "Here, Ptolemy, you'll be staying with me for a while."

Ptolemy looked around. The living room was similar to the Ledbetters', but he noticed one difference right away: two bookshelves! Gladys and Ben had had lots of those. He perked up, feeling better than he had before. He tried reading the names on the spines: Stephen King, Sidney Sheldon, Danielle Steel. They didn't jog Ptolemy's memory, but they didn't upset his tummy, either.

He felt happier still when Kathy's daughter, a kindhearted seventeen-year-old, came home and offered to play with him and bathe him. She did it very well, to Ptolemy's surprise. Kathy looked on with pride. "You'll be a great vet, kid. Why don't you change his papers, too?"

"Okay, Mom." She put Ptolemy on his t-stand. He watched her disappear, then return with several sheets of newspapers. His eyes widened. *Real* newspapers!

When the girl put him back, he hopped down faster than he had in months, indulging himself in the *Chicago Tribune*.

Even learning the Red Sox were in fifth didn't dampen his joy at reading true stories, not lies that made him ill.

"Hey, Mom, that parrot's reading the paper!"

"No, he's not. Cindy says he likes to look at the pictures. Does it all the time. It just looks like he's reading it. Can you feed him tomorrow morning?"

"Uh-uh. I'm sleeping over at Michelle's; won't be back till lunch."

Kathy sighed. "Okay, I'll do it. The things we do for our friends. . . ."

Kathy Plotkin was trying a new facial mask—avocado oatmeal—when the parrot squawked early Saturday morning.

Her husband, still in bed, grumbled, "Shut that damn bird up, or we're having Thanksgiving dinner early!"

"I'm going, I'm going." She pulled on her slippers and hurried out into the living room.

Ptolemy had to squawk with happiness. The *Tribune* was still there. He'd feared it might have been a pleasant dream. He looked up when he heard a scuffling sound. What he saw in the doorway paralyzed him with fright.

Toward him came a humanlike being with a green face, strange pink devices on its scalp, and huge, fuzzy, blue feet.

Ptolemy stared, then fluttered his wings in horror and panic. The stories in *The Nation's Eye* were true! There *were* aliens! One was coming right up to his cage—and if there *were* aliens, then all those other stories Ptolemy never believed must also be true. His universe crumbled around him.

The alien reached out a hand with long red claws. It touched the door of the cage. Ptolemy shrieked and fell from his perch. He landed on the box scores, thrashed once, lay still.

Kathy stared at the dead bird in dismay. "Oh, Christ. What am I going to tell Cindy?"

# Hitler Clone in Argentina
# Plots Falklands Reprise
# or
# Death and Transfiguration
## by John DeChancie

*John DeChancie writes some very funny fantasy books, such as* Castle Perilous *and others in the* Castle *series. However, that's not all there is to the man, who has also written such critically acclaimed SF novels as* Starrigger *and* Paradox Alley, *as well as this haunting, poignant tale.*

*In a funny vein again, he claims he wrote it because "I was ordered to . . . by Friesner, who, in concert with hamsteroid aliens, has established mind control over key cultural figures in the Earth's population . . ." Sorry, John, but you're not going to blame* Madonna's Truth or Dare *on me.*

A sunny calm lay over the South Atlantic that afternoon. The water sparkled and shimmered, a lacework of silvery light playing across it. The sea had taken on a strange color, the artificial blue-green of a swimming pool. The sky, almost the same hue, though of a deeper shade and having less green, was mostly clear, a few lonely clouds drifting close to the horizon like cotton sailboats.

A frost-haired, rime-bearded old man in a wheel chair sat on a veranda high above the sea, meditating, his wrinkled skin waxlike, almost translucent in the bright sunlight. The face was set sternly, defiantly, its lines forming a perpetual pout. The eyes were pale brown. His jaw muscles worked, as though he were chewing over what was on his mind. He seemed on the verge of making an important decision.

The villa stood on a steep hill overlooking the sea. From the edge of the veranda, stone steps zigzagged through the rocks to the beach, where a few bathers waded in the surf or lounged under umbrellas.

From close above came the cry of a gull, like a question. The old man did not look up. The same cry, the same question sounded again. Then again; and once more. At length, tired of hovering and entreating, the gull stooped toward the beach and crossed the old man's field of vision. The old man took no notice.

At long last he said to himself, *"Ja."* He nodded his hoary head; the hair atop it was as thick as the beard. He still groomed it, as was his long habit, slicked down with oil. *"Ja, ich muss."*

Slowly, painfully, he turned the chair around and wheeled himself through tall French doors and into the library.

It was a spacious room, lined with glassed shelves holding thousands of books, many bound in leather. Some looked of antiquarian interest. In one corner stood an ancient Victrola playing a scratchy old recording of *Tod und Verklärung*, by Strauss. He wheeled himself to the far wall and reached for the bell pull. He yanked once, twice. Then he moved toward the farther of two oaken library tables. The nearer was covered with a maritime map on which were arranged a number of tiny model ships—cruisers, aircraft carriers, and such like. Red and blue plastic markers picked out the positions of land units on the group of islands represented in the middle of the map. Dust covered everything on the table.

On the far table sat heaps of yellowing magazines and newspapers. He took a haphazard stack and began to sort through it, searching. Not finding much to his liking, he dumped the papers back on the table, took another stack, and searched again. This time he turned up the newspaper he wanted. He scanned the headlines, opened the tabloid, and began to read.

Presently a servant, in white jacket, wing collar, and black tie, entered the room and came up behind the old man. He coughed discreetly.

The old man turned his head. "Ah, Raul," he said.

*"Excelencia?"*

*"El teléfono."*

*"El teléfono?"*

*"Ja. Si."*

Raul hesitated. *"Pero, Excelencia . . ."*

The old man's eyes suddenly caught fire. In them was something frightening, the first glimmerings of an anger that seemed capable of assuming monstrous proportions. *"Raul! Haz lo que se te mande!"*

Chastened, the tiniest bit afraid, Raul took a step back. He bowed stiffly. *"Si, Excelencia!"*

The old man watched the servant retreat, a look of sullen indignation still on his wrinkled face. Then, faintly, an ironic grimace curled one corner of his pale lips. He resumed reading.

Soon Raul returned with a cordless telephone. He withdrew the instrument's shiny aerial before handing it to the old man.

The old man took the gadget and waited until Raul left the room. Then he searched the table top for a notebook. Finding it, he opened it and placed it in front of him, then began to punch out a long series of numbers on the phone, numbers he had painfully traced down months before but had not had the nerve to dial until now.

A long time had passed since he had called anyone long distance. In fact it had been years since he had called anyone at all. The last time had been before the advent of telecommunications satellites. Reaching anyone overseas used to be an arduous struggle, a fight through ranks of dunderheaded Spanish-speaking operators, then foreign ones, mostly English-speaking. Now, one merely tapped out numbers directly.

He worried about his English. It was better than his Spanish, but he had learned it very late in life. He had almost daily practice here; many of the guests spoke nothing but the tongue of the *Engländer.* However, he had doubts about making himself understood to strangers across vast distances.

"Yes, hello? Hello? Yes, I would like to speak with a Mr.—" He consulted the notebook. "—a Mr. Barrett Sacks. Yes. Yes, I will wait."

The old man waited, listening to the swelling, ethereal chords of the finale of the Strauss piece.

"Hello? Yes, I— Oh, he is on another line? I see. Well, I am calling long distance . . . Yes, it is very urgent. Yes, but you see ... No, I cannot call back later. It is of the utmost urgency that I speak to Mr. Sacks ... Certainly! Very well, I will wait."

He waited for what seemed like fifteen minutes, growing ever impatient. His bony, stick-figure body quivered, first with nervousness, then with mounting frustration and anger.

His rage quickly subsided when he heard a male voice on the other end.

"Mr. Sacks? Ah, yes, Mr. Sacks, very good. Thank you very much for answering my call ... You are very kind. If I could have a moment of your time, sir? ... Thank you very much. I shall try to be brief. I wish to congratulate you on your article in the April seventh issue of your newspaper, last year. No! Two years ago. Which? The one about Adolf Hitler being alive in Argentina. And that he is planning another assault on the Malvinas? Excuse me, the Falkland Islands. Yes, that one. Hitler's clone, yes. That is very funny, you see. No, I will explain. In principle, most of your facts are completely accurate, Mr. Sacks. However, you have some of the details wrong, and I would like to correct them. Yes ... Yes ... Who am I? Well, I will tell you who I am, Mr. Sacks, though you might have some trouble believing me. But I assure you, I am who I say I am ... I beg your pardon? ... Yes, I will tell you ..."

Greased head to toe with heavy sunblock and shaded with amber sunglasses that filtered blue and ultraviolet light, Jack lay stretched on a folding chaise, getting as much suntan as he dared, conscious of all the current global worries about degrading ozone and increasing UV ... Wait a minute. Was too much sun dangerous because of the ozone thing, or was it because of the greenhouse effect? Both? He really didn't know. Years ago he had acquired the habit of keeping a close eye on the world situation. Religiously and with great attention to detail, he had daily devoured reams of newspapers, magazines, and journals of opinion. Of late, though, as he eased into his eighties, he had tapered off considerably. Now he was pushing it if he read two newsmags a month. If it weren't for the funnies, he would rarely scan a newspaper. He didn't even read spy novels any more. (Were they still writing spy novels?) He had ceased to care about current events. Besides, the issues were practically the same as they had been when he'd taken office, give or take a few. True, the East-West thing had changed radically. Things were the same in Cuba, though. . . .

And Jack really didn't give a damn. At one time, he'd been obsessed with that island-nation's frizz-bearded dictator. Now? Well, actually, he had expected Old Fuzzy to show up at Estancia-del-Mar long before this. But the aging Cuban firebrand was still hanging on, fighting a losing battle. The bastard had balls. That much Jack would give him.

He yawned. Then he raised himself on one elbow and looked at Marilyn, who, in a black one-piece bathing suit, sat in a nearby deck chair underneath a yellow and pink sun umbrella, reading a book. Having just passed the milestone of 60, she was still a handsome woman, though she had long ceased to bleach her hair or be overconcerned about her weight. She was now prettily plump.

"What are you reading?" he asked.

"Nietzsche."

Jack was impressed. "Heavy stuff. *Zarathustra?*"

"No, *Beyond Good and Evil.*"

Jack shook his head. "Never read it. Good?"

Annoyed, she frowned at him.

"Oh. Guess it's not exactly light reading."

"You should read more, Jack, instead of just sitting around."

"Yeah? Why, exactly?"

"Why does anyone read?" Marilyn said with a lift of her pale shoulders. "To improve the mind."

"I was never an intellectual, though the press liked to characterize me as one. I seemed to attract eggheads like shit does flies, but I never had any use for them. Too impractical."

"Jack, no one ever accused you of being an egghead."

"Maybe not. Just a realistic altruist, or something like that. Actually, I was never anything but a politician. Like my granddad."

"Or your dad?"

"Nah, he was a hard-bitten son of a bitch, like all businessmen."

"What are politicians?"

Jack chuckled. "Weasels."

"Not all, surely."

"It may be ungracious to malign one's own profession, but I met my share of weasels on Capitol Hill. Still, you've got to face the fact that man is a political animal. He's got to do politics, or it's the club, or the knife, or the gun."

"Politicians seem to wave around most of the guns in the world," Marilyn commented sardonically, eyes still on her book.

"I won't argue with you," Jack sighed as he lay back down.

A breeze came in from the sea. A gull's cry sounded above, receding. A few minutes passed.

"Well, enough of this," Jack said, rising. It took some effort. When he was up on two feet he faced the sea and took a few deep breaths, then stood watching the surf, scratching his belly.

Despite his years, he still retained something of his former athletic build. He kept active, got regular exercise, and stuck to a spartan diet. And of course Dr. Cabeza de Vaca's longevity drugs helped immensely.

"Here comes King," Jack said.

The man who had been America's most popular pop singer at mid-century came jogging in from the water. He was younger than Jack—about Marilyn's age—and his years as one of Dr. Cabeza de Vaca's guests here at the villa had done him wonders. On arrival he had been a physical wreck, swollen with premature middle-age bloat, addicted to a dozen drugs, his arteries clogged like silted rain sewers. In the relatively short time of his stay at Estancia-del-Mar, however, his body had recaptured its youthful slimness and his face had remolded itself nearer to the heartthrobbing desire of his female fans. Jack knew that he and Marilyn had been having an on-and-off extended fling since shortly after his check-in.

Jack didn't much care about that either.

"Man," King said, reaching for a towel. "Water's warm today. Like swimmin' in piss. Excuse mah French, Marilyn."

King had kept his charming northern Mississippi drawl.

"What brainy book ya readin' now, little girl?" he added.

Marilyn deigned not to look up from her Nietzsche.

After waiting in vain for a response, King gave Jack a questioning look. Jack silently shrugged. You figure it out, guy.

King did the thing with his mouth that was a cross between a pout and a snarl, and continued to buff himself dry.

Jack assessed the breeze with a wet forefinger. "Think I'll take the *Fitz Two* out later,"

"Hey, you want company?" King asked.

"Sure," Jack answered good-naturedly.

"What about it, Marilyn? Want to go out sailing with Jack today?"

After a significant delay Marilyn quietly said, "No."

It was King's turn to shrug at Jack. Jack smiled. He knew Marilyn would never finish the book. She rarely finished any book she started. Why the posturing, he asked himself, after all these years? But he knew the answer: it was out of a deep and abiding sense of inadequacy. At least, that was the pop psychology answer. Who knew, though; who really could say with any authority?

His thoughts were interrupted by the arrival of Raul, who had come loping across the beach. He was out of breath.

"Señor Jack . . ."

"What is it, Raul?"

"It is His Excellency, the *Reichskanzler.* He is telephoning the reporters again."

King threw down the towel. "Damn his eyes! Jack, what the hell are we going to do with that guy?"

"Let me handle this," Jack said. He began jogging toward the cliff.

Raul sat down, took his shoes off, and poured the sand out of them.

"That Nazi geezer'll let the cat out of the bag yet," King muttered.

Just before reaching the stone steps, Jack ran into Juan, who never failed to dress elegantly. Today he was in sports coat, ascot, and tan bucks.

"Jack! Where are you going in such a hurry?"

The run from the water's edge had Jack already breathing hard. He had to stop.

"It's the old man, on the phone again. Probably calling one of the tabloids."

Juan laughed. "They never believe him. Why worry?"

"Gotta check him out. You never know."

"I suppose you are right," Juan said. "Would you like me to go along?"

"No, thanks. Where's Evita?"

Juan pointed north along the shore. "Looking for cockles.

Our room is full to the rafters with shells, but still she wants more. And driftwood, and sea urchins, and ... *Dios mio!* What a packrat of a woman!"

Jack chuckled. "Better go. Hope these damned steps don't give me a heart attack."

"Take it easy, Jack," Juan said as he strolled on, swinging his cane.


"... yes, a *Doppelgänger*. It is not exactly what you call a clone ... What is it? Well, it is a duplicate, a creature which looks like the person it is substituting for ... Yes, Dr. Mengele developed this technique. He told me it was known in antiquity ... Yes, I always suspected that it involved black magic ... I do not know. You arc right. It was the duplicate's body they found, not mine. I escaped with the aid of SS Colonel Otto Skorzeny ... by light plane, then by U-boat ... That is correct. Mengele taught Dr. Cabeza de Vaca ... our host. Eva? She is dead. Yes ... yes ... that is true. Good Well, I am glad to tell you all these things ... What? I beg your pardon, what are you saying?"

The *Reichskanzler* did not see Jack enter the library. Jack approached slowly, breathing hard.

"I do not understand. What do you mean, 'played for laughs'? You are telling me that your news stories are not true? I beg your—? ... You are telling me that these stories you print are fake? You make them up? ... But ... but, Mr. Sacks, I—Mr. Sacks, please ... No, I *am* him! Yes, I am one hundred and three years old this year ... No, this is not impossible ... What was that you say? I need medical attention? Are you ... excuse me, but do you question my sanity? You think I am some kind of lunatic? Let me assure you—Wait! Wait, there is more! As I told you, there are others here at Estancia-del-Mar. Your assassinated president, for one. Yes! And the singer, what is his name? I forget. He is called 'King' here. I forget what his ... No, I do not lie! ... What? What was that? ... Flying Saucers? Excuse me, why are you asking me about such things? ... Wait! No, do not hang up! Listen to me! ... Wait ... *Judischer schwein!*"

Jack placed a hand on the old man's shoulder. Gently, he took the phone.

The *Reichskanzler* slumped. "Why? Why do they not believe me?"

Jack shrugged. "Because ... well, because they'd rather keep us here, in limbo. Better that way. Better for them."

The *Reichskanzler* looked up at Jack. "I know where I made my mistake. The Jews. I did not believe that the world would care about what was done to the Jews. If I had only seen that."

Jack said nothing. He went to a bookshelf and looked it over.

"They tell me ..." the old man began.

Jack turned his head. "Pardon? Sorry, couldn't hear you."

"They tell me that Dr. Cabeza de Vaca will come to the party tonight."

"Oh. Yeah, I believe I heard that. Uh, you all right now?"

The *Reichskanzler* drew himself erect. "*Ja.* I am all right."

"Okay."

Jack chose a book, and was about to walk away with it when he noticed, with irritation, that although the title was in the original German, the text was a Spanish translation.

Evening, the sound of the breakers beneath a dark eastern sky. White-coated servants moving quietly about the room, bearing trays, serving drinks. Candles glowing, ice cracking in glasses.

A cork popped.

It was a good turnout. The rock stars huddled in one end of the room, making more noise than the rest.

Juan was saying to Jimmy, the labor boss: ". . . but if this were hell, we would never be told. To know is a certainty, and a certainty is a comfort."

"In that case," Jimmy said, "if they never tell us, we know we're in hell."

"A fine paradox," Juan said, considering it. "But there is a logical flaw in your reasoning, I think."

"Anyway, it ain't a comfort for me to know, or not know," Jimmy said. He took a belt of whiskey. "All I know is, someone calls me and says, there's a contract out on you. You want out? You gotta leave everything, but we can get you out. Sure, you don't believe at first, but then you find out there *is* a contract out on you. And you say, yeah, get me outta this. And here I am. I'm not saying it's hell. I was just thinking. Lots of time to think here ... you know?"

"I'm in the mood for some dago red," Marilyn said to one of the servants. "What do you have?"

"Everything, *Señorita.*"

"Like what?"

"Barbera d'Alba, Gattinara . . . uh, Barolo, Amarone, Bardolino—"

"You have any Chianti?"

"Yes, *Señorita.* Right away."

"I remember this little place in New York," Marilyn said, looking off. Failing to add to this, she lit a cigarette.

"I know exactly what you mean," Juan said to Jimmy, continuing the conversation.

Jimmy went on, "Sometimes I just think, hey, that phone call, the big car that came and took me away, and you couldn't see the driver—it was spooky, know what I'm sayin'? And this place. Where the hell is it? When do we get out of here?"

"But we're free to leave any time, Jimmy. Dr. Cabeza de Vaca has said so many times."

"Yeah, I go back to the world and, *ba-bing,* two shots through the head." Jimmy put an index finger to his temple, thumb up, thumb down, twice. Bang, bang. "Hey, I'm as free as a bird."

"So am I, Jimmy my friend."

"We all are," said James, the actor. "Freedom, man. It's cool. But I know we're in hell. Freedom is hell, man."

"How do you know we're in hell?" Jack wanted to know.

James drank down his Bourbon first, then smiled slyly. "The name of our host, Cabeza de Vaca. That means the head of a goat, right?"

"No," Juan said. "*Vaca* is cow. Or beef."

The actor looked disappointed. "Oh. Why'd I think it meant goat?"

"I have no idea."

James grunted. "Hey, Juan, what're you drinking there?"

"Manzanilla. Sherry. It has the taste of the sea in it."

"Think I'll try some of that."

"Did anyone ever think of another explanation?"

Everyone turned toward the speaker.

"Another explanation for what, Bogey?" Jack asked.

Bogey, in white dinner jacket with a white carnation pinned to his lapel, crossed his legs. "Well, it seems to me that the story about how our clones or doubles were substituted for us is all a lot of hooey. None of it washes."

"How come we remember it?"

"They planted the memories."

Marilyn said, "So we're the clones?"

"Sure," Bogey said.

"Created by Dr. Cabeza de Vaca?" Juan asked. "I've often thought of it."

Jimmy said, "Seems to me we've had this conversation before, lots of times."

"Lots of times," Marilyn said, nodding.

"And I haven't been here all that long."

A hush fell over the room as Raul wheeled in the Reichskanzler. The old man was in uniform, its beige wool smartly pressed. The party armband, however, was missing.

Murmurs from the rock stars.

The Reichskanzler cast a glance toward them. "I have always wondered why those degenerates are here."

"I've often wondered about a lot of people here," Marilyn said. "Don't know who some of them are."

"Other countries, other cultures than yours, my dear," Juan said.

Letting his eye roam around the huge drawing room, Jack caught sight of an old friend, and raised a hand. "Hi, Marty!"

Martin waved back.

"Excuse me, *señores y señoras*, ladies and gentlemen."

It was Raul, announcing from the center of the room. Everyone turned to look.

Raul cleared his throat before saying, "Dr. Cabeza de Vaca sends his regrets, but he will not be able to be with you this evening. However, he bids you drink and have fun, as his guest."

"Man, are we his guests, or what?" James said, chuckling. "Forever!"

"Do you want to go back, Jimmy?"

James didn't answer for a moment. "I think. Maybe."

"How about you, Jack?"

"Christ, no. I like it here."

"I have met few guests who want to go back," Juan said.

"Charisma does something to you," James said.

"That's it!" Juan said.

"What's what?"

"*Herr Reichskanzler,* you asked what those people were doing here. The answer is charisma."

The *Reichskanzler* nodded. "Yes. This is true."

Bogey said, "No one wants to leave because we're created with no desire to leave."

King detached himself from the other entertainers and wandered back to the more political side of the room. He sat down heavily. "Whew, I'm bushed. Don't ask me why, though. Didn't do nothin' all day."

"But generally speaking, everyone here feels good," Juan said. "Most of the time."

"Never felt better myself," Jack said.

"This is a haven," Juan said.

"Heaven?" Jimmy the labor boss said.

"No. Pardon my accent. Haven. A place of refuge. As the other Jimmy said, charisma does something to you. We all needed a rest. But I believe we are here for a purpose. This is ... oh, I think the Germans say ... Valhalla?"

"Yes," the *Reichskanzler* said, "Valhalla."

"That's the Norse afterlife, isn't it?" Jack asked.

"Yes, but it is more. It is a waiting area."

"Waiting for what?" Marilyn asked.

Juan shrugged. "I am not sure of that."

"I am sure," the *Reichskanzler* said.

"Oh? What is this?"

"I am sure what the purpose is."

"I think Juan has something," Bogey said. "If my theory about us being clones isn't right, then he's right about this being a haven, or heaven, or whatever. Valhalla, Asgard, the Elysian Fields, call it what you like. Only it's all in the mind of the human race. We're just thoughts in people's minds. The people. The people of the world."

"Sounds like we really don't exist," Marilyn said.

"Maybe we don't, not physically. But, the way I see it—"

"No!" The *Reichskanzler's* fist came down on the armrest of the wheelchair. "We exist! I know this. I am one hundred and three years old. I feel that I am this old. Why did they create me this way? No, I am the same man I was when I took power, long ago now. Long ago. I have been here longer than any of you. I knew Dr. Mengele, and I believe what he told me. I do not know the method. It is magic to me. What does it matter? I do know this. We are here for a purpose. We are a ... brotherhood. Yes, I am in the same brotherhood with that black man there. And that Jew. The same. This is ironic, but it is for a purpose. We are ... different. We are a breed, a different breed of human being. A race, no? The gods, or God in heaven, have touched us. We wield great power. We have the will to use this power, though it might destroy us. It did, almost. It nearly destroyed all of us. In different ways. Nevertheless, in spite of the dangers, we pushed on as long as we could. We spoke, we acted, we led. We roused the masses. That is where the power is. The masses. We are ... what is it ... a small group?"

"An elite," Juan supplied.

"Yes, an elite! You see, I am not so far from a Bolshevist! I learned much from the Bolshevists. Only a dedicated elite can rule the masses but it must rule in their name, and in their interests."

"But what is the purpose, my friend?" Juan persisted.

"The purpose?"

"Why are we here? What are the Good Doctor's motives?"

"I do not know what are his motives," the *Reichskanzler* said.

The old man's voice had grown progressively louder. It now took on some of the force and resonance of old. Bonfires danced, faintly, in his eyes. Rows of banners waved. Faraway echoes came to his hears. The roar of an enormous crowd, the march of heavy boots.

Around the room, conversation had gradually petered out as attention became focused on the old man in the wheelchair. Eyes regarded him askance at first. Then people turned to face him.

"I do not care what his reasons are," he continued. "I do not care, even, if we are doppelgangers. But I know what he intends for us. I know that we will all go back one day, to our respective countries, cultures, areas of the globe, to our various professions and walks of life. *And together, all of us—we will rule the world!*"

The room was silent now. All eyes were on the *Reichskanzler,* and everyone had listened, even the long-haired skeptics. For a prolonged moment, all movement in the room froze.

Then, suddenly, breaking through the hush like the bark of a coon dog in the dead of night, came a clear Mississippi twang.

"Jesus Christ, 'Dolf, ol' buddy. Ain't it about time you gave it a rest?"

The hush lasted just a split second longer. Then the room exploded with laughter. Dropped glasses smashed to the slate floor. People draped over each other, helpless, clutching their sides. Even the servants laughed, unabashedly, momentarily unaware of their impertinence.

The *Reichskanzler's* face at first showed horrified surprise. Then the shock passed, leaving great anger and resentment. He hated to be the butt of a joke. Furious, he wheeled himself around and began to leave the room.

Then he stopped. He looked back over his shoulder. He had rarely heard laughter in these rooms, these deathly quiet rooms. In spite of himself, he chuckled. Everybody saw this, and became all the more convulsed.

The old man began to laugh. His toothpick body shaking, he laughed as he never had in all his 103 years. He laughed even harder and longer than the time when Guderian's tanks had rolled through the Ardennes, making fools of the fat French generals. . . .

Evita saw a glint of something in the moonlight, something white in the water. She waded in, bent over, and scooped it out of the soupy sand. She held it up to the full moon. It was the biggest, most beautiful scallop shell she had ever found. The moon shone through it, turning it a pearly gold.

She thought she heard something, and turned away from the sea. It was a sound from the villa, barely audible over the roar of the surf.

Laughter.

She wondered about it, but not for long. She spied other things in the water, bright glimmering specks, and waded further out to investigate.

# Group Phenomena
## by Thomas F. Monteleone

*This is a wonderfully subtle story. You've got to be on your toes for this one.*

*The author, Thomas F. Monteleone, has published more than eighty short stories and eighteen novels, including the bestselling, critically acclaimed thriller* The Blood of the Lamb. *He has also written for stage and television and has edited five anthologies, so he knows how I feel.*

It was late afternoon as I walked down 46th Street, headed for a Manhattan bar called Swaggerty's, where I was supposed to meet a guy who probably wasn't human. . . .

Several times I had the compulsion to just pull up and run in the opposite direction, but a more rational thought always intercepted the urge. If this guy, whoever (or whatever) he was, was somehow responsible for the awful stuff happening over the years, then finding *me* would be a piece of cake. I had the unsinkable feeling that there was no place to hide, and that I may as well run headlong into whatever was awaiting me.

Just get it over with.

He was sitting at a corner table in the cool darkness of the Irish bar. Amidst the sepia-toned pictures of soccer teams and revolutionaries, the guy with the plain, familiar face was sitting there watching me approach. In person, he looked so plain, so nondescript, that I had to silently congratulate him on such a wonderfully artful disguise.

"Mr. Sam Aaronson, I presume," he said. He did not get up or offer to shake hands, and I took that as a bad sign. "Sit down, please."

I sat, still staring at the plain-brown-wrapper of a face. "All right, let's cut the crap. What do you want with me?"

Before he could answer, a waiter appeared, and I ordered

a double George Dickel on the rocks. The waiter disappeared, and the guy across the table from me grinned.

" 'Let's cut the crap.' That's such a wonderful idiom, Mr. Aaronson. Wherever did you pick it up?"

I figured the best thing to do would be to say nothing, so I decided to just stare at him.

He smiled. "Believe it or not, you are the first person ever to have come so close to discovering me. When I saw your article, I was impressed."

"Who *are* you?" I asked after a short pause. My skin was feeling loose and crawly along my neck and shoulder blades, but I *did* need to know what was going on. The guy looked so nonthreatening that I knew I should be terrified . . . and I guess I was getting there.

The waiter returned with my drink. My friend with the insurance salesman face waited till he was gone. Looking around the room, I noticed that we were practically alone, that everyone else was doing a great job of ignoring us.

"Who am I?" he repeated the question. "Don't you even want to guess?"

I shrugged. "It hadn't really occurred to me," I said. "But I don't know, let's see: You've got to be either Death, or the Devil, some form of God, or . . . an alien." If none of those are right, then I don't know. I never was very good at multiple-choice exams—all the answers always seemed so reasonable to me.

He smiled. "That's very clever, Mr. Aaronson. Very clever. An odd mix of mysticism and science. It may be flattering to be confused with your local pantheon of deities, but that is not the case."

As I assimilated his response, realizing what he was telling me, my stomach heaved, like it was hitting the first hill on a roller coaster. My mind was reeling, and I found myself instantly recalling the crazy events which had brought me to this pivotal moment in my life . . .

. . . and it had all started because I noticed this weird little thing about the world in the news.

I mean, have you ever noticed how odd, unusual disasters seem to occur in clusters?

You know the kind of things I mean: a grain elevator explodes in Silas, Nebraska—the first accident in twenty seven years—and suddenly another one goes up in Dubuque, and maybe a few days pass and a couple more detonate in Wichita and Biloxi.

Or, how about those railroad tank-cars filled with some really terrible substance like chlorine gas? For years they roll around the country, not bothering anyone or anything, and then, as if on cue, they start derailing and leaking poisonous vapors all over places like Kankakee and West Gatch.

You get the idea, don't you?"

This kind of thing happens more than you might think. It doesn't always make the papers or the wire services, that's all.

Take last month, for instance. A cargo freighter called the *Novo Queen,* sailing out of Portland, and filled with liquid fertilizer, suddenly explodes, killing everyone on board. Three days later, the *Hiasa Maru,* also full of fertilizer, and bound for Tokyo, blows itself to smithereens while docked in Oakland. The following week, another ship carrying liquid fertilizer buys the farm.

After that . . . nothing.

Before these ships started blowing, there hadn't been a similar incident in more than twenty years.

Weird, right?

I've noticed the same kind of group-occurrences in other kinds of accidents; safes falling from lofts, black-widow bites, elevator cables snapping, you name it. But the strangest part of the whole phenomenon is that it's been going on apparently unnoticed for years and years—until I picked up on it, back when I was working the night desk for *The Mirror.*

It was the middle of February—a cold, slow night. Hardly anybody was out-of-doors, no domestic murders, not even so much as a ruptured fireplug. Just to keep awake, I would make myself get up and check the teletype every time it clattered out some filler or stringer-items from wherever.

One of the pieces was a short blurb about a steamroller accident—seems as if an unfortunate pedestrian in Idaho Falls had managed to get run over by one. For some reason, I recalled reading a stringer about the same kind of thing in Chicago the week before.

Very rare accident, I thought. And yet, here was another one within a couple of days.

So just on a whim, I went down to Records, where they keep the clippings files and the microfiche readers (it'll take *years* to get everything transferred to the computers . . .), and started checking the cross-indices on Deaths, Accidental, and Steamroller.

I found only one instance in the files of a close encounter of the steamroller kind since 1921.

And suddenly: two in the space of three days. I chalked it up as one of those weird coincidences, but figured that it wouldn't hurt to await any further developments.

I didn't have to wait long.

Another steamroller accident over the weekend in Platte, Illinois. It was definitely strange stuff, and I had the feeling that maybe I'd stumbled onto something. So I pursued it down in Records whenever I had an hour or two, and some nights on my own time, too. I looked for grouped incidents, improbable accidents, stuff like that.

I guess I don't have to tell you there were hundreds of them!

Time went by, and I finally had a file four inches thick, and I was adding to it all the time. Finally, I wrote an article and sold it to a slick, high-paying magazine. I didn't have any sophisticated computer analysis of the data—just the facts in the old "strange-but-true" tradition of Frank Edwards.

My story appeared as "Accidents Happen" in *Montage*, and I received letters from people all over the country. Many of them claimed to have noticed the phenomenon at least subconsciously but hadn't put it all together until reading my piece. Others even took the time to send me new material.

The experience inspired me to begin working on a book—the dream of all newspaper hacks, cuz we all know a reporter ain't no author.

First thing I did was hire one of the kids down in the advertising department to spend a few hours each night in the clipping files and microfiche. I had him collecting photographs in any of the connected articles, thinking I might find a visual correlation.

Within a month, the kid handed me more than four hundred clips and pix in an old carton. That weekend, I separated all the pix into categories of events, and that didn't seem to be doing anything except crap up the dining room table real nice.

But just as I was about to quit for the night I happened to notice the face of a man in the foreground of a picture taken at the sight of an Amtrak derailment in Essex Junction, Vermont. He was walking away from the wreckage of a twisted club car, and was passing the photographer on the left.

His face was so exquisitely normal that there was no reason for me to take notice of him: short, sandy hair, with no outstanding features like big eyes, big noise, thin lips, dewlaps, prominent Adam's apple, or anything like that. Just a plain waspy-looking face that reminded you of your average State Farm Insurance salesman.

And yet, I had noticed him. Why?

I shuffled through the pix, and it started to come together. In a 1962 shot from the *St. Louis Post Dispatch,* where a piano had fallen from a mover's crane, there was a crowd assembled around the point of impact—one of the faces was my insurance salesman-type. He was turning away from the lens, but not in time to get nailed by the flash of the trusty Graflex. From a clip and pix from the *Los Angeles Times* I caught sight of the same guy mingling with a crowd of onlookers where a water tower collapsed in Bakersfield in 1981. He was also standing in the back row of a bunch of rubberneckers who watched a school bus being pulled out of Cayuga Lake near Seneca Falls in 1950.

My heart was thumping as I searched through the rest of the stack, and came up with forty-seven pix that contained a shot of somebody who might be my guy. I threw out all the ones in which, for one reason or another (weird camera angle, blurriness, partial obscurement), the make on the guy was not 100% positive. That left me with thirty-two photographs, covering a period of more than fifty years, where the same guy appeared. . . .

Weird. Crazy. Impossible. Ridiculous.

All these words kept popping into my head as I popped another Marlboro into my mouth, fired it up. There was no way that the same guy could be showing up at all these grouped events for fifty years and never get any older.

Yet there he was, right on my dining room table, so to speak.

If this guy really was the same guy, I started thinking that the pix only happened to catch him by chance. Maybe he was at every one of the events? Could that be? Maybe he was causing them?

Now that was crazier than anything I had considered up to that point. But what was I supposed to think? It seemed obvious that insurance-salesman-face was linked to the events in some way. Only a jerk would deny that. But why did he look the same for all those years, and who was he?

But then, I got a new thought. Something darker, more sinister. Perhaps, like in all the old movies, there really were Things-Man-Was-Not-Meant-To-Know? Suppose, by opening up this bizarre can of worms, I was putting myself into a dangerous situation? Maybe it would be best if I didn't tell anybody yet, didn't get anyone else involved? I got a funny feeling down my backbone, and suddenly the house seemed too damned quiet and the darkness beyond the windows seemed blacker and more impenetrable than before. I was spooking myself, I knew it, but the feeling wouldn't go away.

Maybe I should just forget about this stuff?

I figured I'd give it a rest for a few days, then decide what I'd do about it. I kept as busy as possible at work, and I was feeling pretty good, less spooked, as each day passed. I was sitting at my desk at Amalgamated with my lunch spread out across the blotter when the phone rang.

"Hello . . ." I said as I forced down a swallow of corned beef on rye.

"Yes, I am trying to locate a Mr. Sam Aaronson," said an innocuous male voice.

"You got 'im. Who's calling?"

"Oh, just an old friend. A very old friend . . ."

There was a suggestion of humor in the voice, and I wasn't sure what was going on. I was about to wisecrack something, but suddenly my Early Warning System flared, and I got this weird feeling that something was wrong.

"Hey, look, I'm pretty busy . . . who is this?"

There was a pause at the other end, and the silence seemed to gnaw into my ear.

"I know you've been checking on some photographs."

"Really?" My voice quavered ever so slightly.

"Yes, and so saying, I think you know who I am, don't you, Mr. Aaronson?"

"What do you want?" I asked, trying to be noncommittal.

"I think it's time we sat down and had a little talk," said the voice. "When can you meet me?"

I swallowed hard, suddenly not very interested in my lunch any longer. "Where are you?" I croaked.

"Manhattan. A little bar on 46th Street between Park and Fifth. Called Swaggerty's."

"I know where it is," I said. "I'll be there in fifteen minutes."

"I've got plenty of time," said the voice.

"Yeah, I'll bet you have," I said. "See you in a bit."

I hung up the phone because my hands were starting to tremble, and my voice was cracking all over the place.

Sweeping up my lunch, I chucked it into the circular file—there was the need for something of a more liquid nature at this point—and took off for Swaggerty's.

The streets were crowded for lunch, and the weather was brisk for October, but the sun was warm as I walked across town toward Fifth. The women were out in force with the latest fashions and on any other day, I would have been doing my share of ogling, but this one was different. I knew who I was going to meet at the bar, and I knew he didn't want to sell me any insurance . . .

. . . and so there I sat listening to this kind of wimpy-looking guy tell me he was an alien. I sipped on the Dickel and it burned a velvet path down my throat.

"Go on . . ." I said. My voice was barely more than a whisper.

"We have been amongst your kind for many of your centuries—not a great amount of time for my race. I have been here for more than fifty years."

"What for? What do you want with us? What're you trying to do, plan an invasion or something?"

He smiled, then actually laughed. "No! Nothing at all so dramatic!"

"What?"

"Would you, or any of your kind, be interested in 'invading' an anthill? Of 'taking over' that which you might find beneath a flat rock?"

He laughed again.

"Is that what we are to you?" I asked. "A bunch of slugs and insects?"

He shrugged. "If you must know the truth—less. You are simply here. To use one of your idioms, we don't really give a shit about any of you."

"Then what are you doing here?" I could feel the indifference, the abject lack of feeling in his voice. He truly meant what he was telling me.

"You wouldn't understand the true nature of my purpose here." he said.

"Try me," I said, downing the rest of my sour mash.

He chuckled nastily. "Mr. Aaronson, would you attempt to read Emmanuel Kant to a cageful of baboons . . . ?"

"Oh, you really think a lot of us, don't you? Well, if we're so disgusting to you, why don't you just get the fuck out of here?"

He grinned, nodded. "Let me just say that we are sent here by our ... 'elders' ... for what you might call 'training.' There are aspects of this planet—its distance from its star, the makeup of its magnetic field, the atmospheric balance, and other parameters which would have no meaning in your primitive science—that make it an ideal location for our training."

"What kind of training?" I was getting the idea, but every time he explained something, I had more questions. I guess once you get the newspaper ink in your blood, it's a permanent affliction.

"Again, any attempt to explain to you what my race does here, in terms of training, would be totally futile. Let me suffice to say that we are concerned with many physical and metaphysical laws of the universe, that we are fascinated with such concepts as cause and effect, predestination, probability, permutations, and other phenomena which you would not understand."

"You're making me feel just great. . . ."

He shrugged. "Sorry. I know your limitations."

"That still doesn't explain the grouping effect," I said.

He nodded. "Yes, well, you see, that is merely a side effect, a contraindication, caused by aspects of our training. There are moments when the continuum is violated, and the normal Fabric of Being attempts to mend itself. Sometimes there are events of overcompensation, which result in multiple events occurring."

"What? You mean you actually have control over reality?" The full impact of what he was saying brought a lump into my throat.

He chuckled again. "Well, of course! That's what it's all about, don't you see? The events as they happen are of no consequence to us. They are merely by-products of a much larger, far more complex mechanism at work. It is that mechanism which I control, not these silly events!"

There was something about his condescending, disdainful attitude that was very convincing. His words chilled me with a cavalier cruelty. I knew he was telling the truth, but I pushed him anyway.

"How do I know this isn't a bunch of bullshit?"

"You know it is not . . ."

"You say you're an alien," I said, trying to sound forceful. "Prove it. Show me."

"You would not like me to do that."

Another cold spike went through me, but I pushed on into unknown territory. "Yes I would. Go on."

He gestured at his face, his body. "This is just an illusion," he said. "A carefully constructed piece of work, yes, but nothing more than playing with your spectrum of visible light."

"Come on," I said. "Let me see what you guys really look like."

"Very well," he said, and his image began to waver around the edges. He started to disappear like a superimposed ghost in an old black-and-white movie, and then I started to see what was "beneath" the illusion.

It rippled and pulsated and glistened for starters. There were tendrils and whiskery-looking things. Things that looked like open sores, running ooze and pustulence. Very organic, not pretty. And there were odors which apparently had also been masked. The smells reached out and grabbed me, smacking me, and then choking me with their foulness. My stomach churned.

"Okay! That's enough!" I said, but it was too late.

A thick, hot column surged up my throat, and I heaved across the table violently. My eyes filled with stinging tears and my mouth burned with acid. A waiter came to help me with a warm cloth, and expertly scooped up the tablecloth with everything in it. Amidst my gasping apologies, the waiter brought new cloth and settings. It all happened so quickly, I was a bit startled to look up through my tears and see the insurance salesman face staring back at me.

"You were warned," he said.

"All right," I took my breath in large gulps. "I believe you now . . . I just have one more question."

"Which is: Why are you telling me all this? Correct?"

I nodded dumbly.

"Well, my training is almost at an end. I will be leaving this world for the next stage in my evolution. You were smarter than the rest of your breed—you at least noticed my presence."

"So?"

"So I decided to at least reward you for your work. You deserved to know, and I don't care if you know or not."

Now this sounded kind of odd to me. Something didn't add up. "You mean you don't care if I tell the world about you?"

He chuckled meanly. "Come now, Mr. Aaronson . . . who would believe you?"

I thought about it for a minute, then nodded. "You've got a point there."

He grinned. "Yes, but just to make certain there are no repercussions, before I take my leave, I fear I will have to eliminate you."

My stomach churned violently again and adrenaline shock jarred my entire system. "What?"

"You heard me correctly."

"Some 'reward' for being so clever," I said. Suddenly my fear had been replaced by anger. If this walking bed-sore was going to take me out, he would have to do it the hard way.

"And now, Mr. Aaronson, it is time to say adieu," said the alien, as he sipped the last of his drink.

Using that instant as my only chance, I grabbed the steak knife at my place setting and lunged at him over the table. Plunging the blade into his eye, I felt something soft and wet and slimy almost envelop my hand. The thing screamed and its image began to waver like bad TV reception.

I kept jabbing and dicing it up with the knife like I was tearing into some rotten fruit, and the thing howled horribly. By now, the other people in the joint had rushed over to watch, but when they saw the tendriled horror that was grappling with me, they all recoiled in a kind of shock.

It kept making this keening, howling sound, and there was a black, ichorous fluid spraying out all over the floor like a broken water pipe. Suddenly, the thing broke free of me and surged toward the front door. The crowd parted in panic and the thing moved by them with alarming quickness.

As I followed it out the street, amidst the gasps of terror and amazement of the crowd, I had a crazy thought, a journalist's thought. It suddenly occurred to me that I had an incredible story on my hands. I would be famous tomorrow morning!

Reaching the sidewalk, I raced to the corner, looking for the thing, but it had vanished. Wondering if I had mortally wounded it, I glanced over at the early afternoon edition of the *New York Post,* staring up at me from a newsstand. In that instant, I understood everything.

CHICAGO MAN BATTLES ALIEN IN CORNER BAR said the headline.

# Unextinctions
## by Bruce Boston and Roger Dutcher

*Roger Dutcher collaborated with Bruce Boston ("How Alien He Really Was") on this short but provocative piece. For his first prose sale, it's a fine start.*

*He is coeditor (with Mark Rich) of* The Magazine of Speculative Poetry *and his poem, "Amazon," is a nominee for the Rhysling Award.*

A great leathery bird circles over the red tiled rooftops of old Pasadena. A herd of tiny horses, no bigger than dogs or sheep, is spotted on the Serengeti Plain. A giant man-eating tiger, with teeth like scimitars, rampages through the villages northeast of Maradabad, leaving eighteen dead and dozens injured in its wake.

At first the scientists scoff, dismissing such reports as they would a flurry of Sasquatch or UFO encounters. Yet sightings at first taken as misidentifications, as the hallucinogenic dream fulfillments of drugged-out tree huggers, the would-be fantasies of ecologic romantics, soon become daily realities too numerous and frequent to deny: the miraculous reappearance of species after species long-considered extinct.

The tabloids have a field day, a chance at last to report the truth, actual events as preposterous and sensational as their endless fabrications . . . but their banner headlines must soon compete with those of more respected journals:

*The London Times* "TRILOBITES CLOG TUNA NETS!"
*The Washington Post:* "TUCSON: GIANT GROUND SLOTHS!!"
*National Geographic:* "T. REX ALIVE AND WELL IN BROOKLYN HEIGHTS!!!"

Giant dragonflies with wings like six-foot exclamation marks swarm across the Autobahn, blocking exit signs, alighting on windshields and fenders, sending marvels of German engineering careening on collision course and slowing the fastest traffic in the world to a crawl ... droves of the flightless dodo, honking an ill-timed "Hallelujah Chorus," invade and amble at random through St. Peter's Square, driving away the faithful, outnumbering the pigeons and fouling the flagstones, far outscoring the Pope as a tourist attraction ... on the muddy and polluted delta of the Mississippi, a school/herd of fish/mammals with incipient gill/lungs and stubby leg/fins inch their way onto a sandbar, blinking at the naked sun as if they were the first creatures to ever see it uncloaked by water, reject the vision and turn around, retreating as one back into the murky depths.

And finally, as a logical extension of natural history gunning in reverse gear, as an illogical extrapolation of an ecosphere increasingly run amok, our very own progenitors both actual and apocryphal—Austrolopithecus, Java Man, Piltdown, Cro-Magnon—begin to materialize in increasing numbers. Hirsute and filthy, clad only in uncured skins, they wander down from the hills or in across the prairies to prowl our neighborhoods, to invade our finest shopping malls and shatter our plate glass windows, to crouch upon our fenders and fiercely pummel our hoods.

And although we confront them with rifles and handguns aplenty, although we slaughter them by the score and score again, their incoherent grunts and cries of rage continue to fill our streets, to track our lives and our dreams, confirming what we should have learned long ago, what we perhaps should have known all along: Nature *does* have a sense of humor. It is a dark and wild one. And having violated her more than once too often, we have now become the objects of her all-consuming mirth.

# How Alien He Really Was
## by Bruce Boston

*While Bruce Boston is best known for his poetry, he is also the author of the critically acclaimed novella, "After Magic," and the recent novel,* Stained Glass Rain. *He has won numerous awards, including but not limited to the Rhysling (three times), the ASIMOV's Readers' Choice Award for poetry, and the Pushcart Prize for Fiction.*

*All well-deserved, as I hope you will agree after reading this.*


By the time the government released the Alien for public consumption, he was already famous. Over the next several months—as he traveled, appeared on talk shows, spoke at colleges and universities—his notoriety continued to grow. During this time the world through which the Alien moved was one of affirmation, ceremony and celebration: elegant parties, the finest food and wine, and always a rush of friendly words and smiling faces.

Here he was stranded light-years from home, without the rapport of his soulmates, and he did not feel so stranded or alone after all. He began to think he could adjust to life in this new world, to accept its warmth and the acclaim it offered him.

Then a strange thing began to happen, which was not so strange at all. Interest in the Alien began to wane. His naivete, even if it was genuine, could only be charming for so long. He never would reveal anything really significant about his native planet. And he certainly wasn't much to look at . . . grossly pale, ears like rhubarb and not much of a nose at all.

There came a day when the Alien had more time on his hands than he knew what to do with. Naturally, he began to seek out the friends he had acquired during his stay, those humans who had organized and managed his tours. Having been exposed to the Alien for nearly a year, they no longer thought of him as anything special. The deference with which they had once treated him was gone. And sometimes, more and more often, it seemed he was even in the way.

It was then that the Alien began to see, beyond the ceremony and the sell, beyond the ready smiles and the easy affirmation, into the true nature of these creatures he had fallen among.

Only then did he begin to realize how alien he really was.

# NASA Sending Addicts to Mars!
# Giant Government Coverup Revealed!
## by Alan Dean Foster

*We've got Alan Dean Foster to thank for this hard-hitting piece of investigative journalism. He tells me he wrote it "because I've always seen NASA to be a bit too starched in their relations with the public, and also because hypocrisy (i.e. the treatment of drugs) in this country often gives birth to irony." He is also the author of the extremely popular* Spellsinger *series, among numerous other works, and the editor of* Betcha Can't Read Just One, *an upcoming anthology of original funny fantasy.*

*Your Editor wants you to know that she read this story, but she didn't inhale.*

"Ladies and gentlemen, the President of the United States!"

Someone in the Presidential party had thoughtfully brought along their own tape of "Hail to the Chief"—just in case one happened to be lacking at Mission Control. It filtered through the intercom system as the tight knot of Secret Service men escorted their charge into the room, not unlike a cluster of nervous remoras convoying a shark. Played back over the music system the familiar music sounded tinny.

An unpatriotic thought at what should be a moment of great national pride, Fraser knew. A glance at MacKenzie and Tetsugawa showed that they shared his nervousness.

Following the initial curious look at the Chief Executive, the mission team had returned to work, their attention focused resolutely on their instrumentation. Not all of them shared the secret which had been so strenuously guarded by mission command. With luck, that secret might be maintained for another day, another week. A great deal depended on how the President handled things.

Time enough to worry about that later. At the moment there were greetings to be exchanged, additional preparations to be made. Fraser was making his own notes on what the President was wearing, whether his shoes were shined, how firm his handgrip was and how genuine was the easy, down-home grin so familiar from hundreds of telecasts. It was important for Fraser to memorize these details because his kids were sure to grill him on them the moment he got home. Not every kid on the block could boast about the day his dad met the President.

He thought Tetsugawa and MacKenzie handled it better. Older and more experienced, they were used to the diplomatic niceties required on the bureaucratic circuit. To MacKenzie the President was only a ex-Senator with bigger lifts in his heels. To Tetsugawa he was a banker with access to unlimited largesse.

A voice interrupted his reverie. "We're ready to transmit, Mr. Fraser."

"Thanks, Will." Stepping forward, he found it surprisingly easy to pull the President away from the circle of sycophants into which he'd been drawn. "We're ready for you now, Mr. President."

"Thank you, Warren." Instantly on a first-name basis, making you feel at once important and at ease, Fraser mused admiringly. Just like his next-door neighbor Steve Beckwith inquiring yet again if he could borrow the power mower.

Pulling papers from a coat pocket, the President quietly cleared his throat and began to study them as the engineers concluded their final tests. Only when all was ready did he incline slightly in the direction of the microphone and read from his prepared statement.

"Gentlemen and lady of the first manned mission to Mars, it is my very great pleasure to greet you this first morning of the grandest achievement in the history of America and mankind's space program. By now the whole world has thrilled to the story of your successful landing on that ancient and mysterious world, which henceforth must be mysterious no longer. As in the coming weeks you probe its dusty secrets . . ."

Fraser listened with one ear. Certainly it was a speech of considerable historical import, one right up there with "One

Small Step for Mankind," but other concerns preyed on his mind. He should have been relaxed. The interminably long spiraling journey out to the Red Planet, the anxiety attending the descent when unexpectedly strong winds threatened to turn the touchdown in Hellas to tragedy; all were behind them now. Nevertheless, the future of the expedition was far from assured.

The President droned on, relishing the moment. Fraser automatically scanned the readings on the most important screens. To his relief one in particular remained monotonously steady. Only the mission command physicians would be sensitive to the elevated readings of certain gauges, to the unusual respiratory patterns everyone at Command had grown accustomed to since the *Barsoom*'s departure from Earth orbit. Certainly there was no one in the President's immediate entourage knowledgeable enough about such matters to notice that anything was amiss.

Eventually the President concluded his message of congratulations. Now they had to wait for the crew to compose their official response. Ah, the response. Fraser suddenly wished he were somewhere else. But he was the voice of mission control and there was nowhere for him to hide.

While waiting he paced aimlessly among the instrumented aisles, trying to avoid members of the official party. Let MacKenzie and Tetsugawa make small talk with them. He leaned over one console festooned with dials and readouts and half a dozen flat-screen monitors. The operator checked an earphone and turned to grin at him.

"Fuentes just scored on a five-yard plunge. We're tied with Pittsburgh twenty-one all going into the fourth quarter."

"Thanks, Mel." Fraser moved on, feeling better. So far it had been a rough season for the Oilers. You'd think that with a hundred-plus screens in Mission Control someone could figure out a way to rig one to secretly pick up network broadcasts.

All of a sudden it was time, by the clock and by simple physics. He took his place and waited. The big monitor on the wall crackled and cleared. They had to use the big screen this time. The President's team had insisted and as a result there was no way to avoid it.

The panoramic view that materialized was remarkably sharp and detailed. It did not look especially alien. Rocky, red-hued hills poked into a pink sky. Overhead a single fragile cloud struggled for coherence in the rarefied atmosphere. As always, there were a few gasps from the newcomers in the audience. A live television picture from Mars, especially when viewed on the projection screen, was still a sight to inspire awe even in jaded viewers.

A figure wandered into view and waved at the camera pickup. Fraser immediately recognized the lanky form of Gregorski, the mission geologist. The light Mars suit clung to his frame, reminding everyone how far removed the environment of the Red Planet was from barren Luna.

Gregorski waved again, then executed another gesture which distance fortunately rendered ambivalent. Glancing to his left Fraser saw MacKenzie wince. One of the President's aides squinted uncertainly at the big screen but held his peace when no one else said anything.

The geologist did a slow forward roll and bounded triumphantly to his feet in the light gravity. So far not too bad, Fraser thought. The President was murmuring to an assistant and looking content.

There was a flash-interrupt. It was followed by a second, and then the screen cleared again. They were inside the Lander now, the camera panning to show the interior of the main cabin. Food and equipment lay strewn about, poorly stowed. That was to be expected, though. Everyone knew how rough the touchdown had been.

Then a face was grinning into the pickup. Several onlookers started involuntarily. The sudden appearance of a ten-foot high nose can be disconcerting. The nose was quite red, but brief exposure to Martian sunlight could do that. It could, Fraser told himself insistently.

The nose retreated, to find itself surrounded by the other facial features of Mission Commander Swansea. The Colonel rubbing his proboscis, unaware that he'd slightly smudged the pickup lens, and grinned.

Behind him they could see the two other members of the landing team, Oakley and Preston. For a moment Fraser thought everything was going to be all right. Then he saw that Oakley's flight suit was unzipped all the way to her thighs. It wasn't obvious because she was facing away from the pickup, but Fraser's trained eye picked up the telltale clues immediately. Nearby he heard Tetsugawa inhale sharply.

*Please,* he thought frantically; *say thank you, give greet-*

*ings, be profound if you must, but get off camera as fast as you can.*

Preston turned from his console to face the camera, weaving only slightly. A condition fortuitously ascribable to the light gravity, Fraser knew.

No such luck.

"Heyyy, good buddy!" Preston was smiling at Swansea, neglecting to address him as Commander. "Whatta you know? It's the President. The goddamn farking President." The Colonel swayed toward the pickup. "Yo, Pres!"

Fraser found that he had begun to sweat.

Swansea pulled back. "Farrrrr outtttt. What's happenin', earth creatures?"

Perhaps, Fraser thought desperately, the President would ascribe the Mission Commander's response to a personal desire on the part of a famous minority American to address his own community in colloquial fashion at a moment of personal triumph.

The President was frowning uncertainly at an aide. He couldn't reply, of course. He'd delivered his own message of greeting earlier. Because of the time-delay all he could do now, all any of them could do, was watch and listen.

Fraser looked to MacKenzie, but the engineer only shrugged. His finger hovered over the button that could halt reception, but it did not descend. An abrupt cut-off would require explanations, and that would invariably be worse than the truth.

They'd all discussed many times what could be done if this happened. The general consensus was that they'd have to ride with it and pray none of the mission members became abusive or insulting. With everyone in Mission Control watching the big screen, any kind of thorough coverup was out of the question.

Turning, he could see the network reporters behind the soundproof glass. Many of them had been covering the space program for a good portion of their careers, but they'd never heard anything like this. More than one jaw had sagged at Swansea's comments. Behind the television people the print reporters looked torn; uncertain whether to run and file what they'd seen, or wait to see what else might develop.

"He can't tell you what's happening, freako," said Preston from his station. "Time de-lay."

"Oh, riiiight." Swansea took no umbrage at the correction. He looked very happy as he turned back to the pickup.

"Say, Mistah President. We wish you was heah. How about a weather report? You want a weather report? We does *baaad* weather reports." He looked over his shoulder. "Hey, sweet thang. Lay some weather on the man."

"Sweet thing?" The President whispered to the Secretary of State. "Is that Major Oakley's official nickname?"

Lander Copilot and chief biologist Oakley was speaking. "Well, Mister President, sugar, it's pretty damn cold outside right now, and that's the Nome of the game." She giggled. "If you really want to know, the weather sucks and it'll be a cold day in Hellas before any of us do any sunbathing. Could ski, if we had any snow, which we don't. Lousy friggin' couple centimeters of ice." She swayed slightly as she grabbed at a pickup. It took her three tries to get it.

"Hey Hanover, you lazy good-for-nuthin' orbitin' muthergrabber! How come they put us down on a cold slope with no snow?"

This demand was followed by an inarticulate gargle. Somewhere in the vast room a technician had begun to laugh. He was hurriedly shushed. Meanwhile, Hanover, alone up in the orbiter, could be heard singing something about cockles and mussels, alive, alive ho. Hanover was the possessor of three advanced degrees and a lousy voice.

Oakley could be seen batting the flexible pickup aside. "Lazy muthergrubber," she mumbled. "When we get back up there, I'm gonna fix his ass." She started to turn and rise. As she did so her unzipped flightsuit parted. It was instantly apparent that the Major was not wearing her regulation flight undergarments. In fact, she was wearing no undergarments whatsoever. Whistles echoed through Mission Control until a fumbling Preston could organize her attire.

The President stared in stony silence at the screen while upstairs frantic technicians tried to edit a shot that had already gone out. One Secret Serviceman struggled to repress a smile.

"Cool it, sweets," Preston could be overheard telling her. "We're on TV."

"Yeah. The boob tube." Oakley grinned, apparently in no wise abashed by her unscientific revelations.

"It certainly seems to be a happy crew," the President finally commented.

MacKenzie ventured a wan smile. "Attitude is crucial on such a long journey, Mister President."

Swansea had slipped out of range of the visual pickup. Now he returned, puffing on a cigarette and waving lazily at the lens. "Uh, we got to sign off now, Mister President. Work to be done and time waits for no man, comprende? Tell everybody back home that we loves them and that we're givin' our all for the good ol U. S. of A., hey?" Behind him Oakley was giggling again.

The image began to break up. Faintly they could see Swansea offering the cigarette to Preston. "It's mid-morning, man. You want a regulation toke?"

Then the screen went blank.

The silence in Mission Control was deafening. Only the machines conversed, in soft buzzes and clicks. After a long pause the President turned and began whispering to MacKenzie, who nodded as he listened. The President talked for quite a while. Mackenzie's expression was grave.

After the President and his entourage departed, the senior engineer beckoned to Fraser.

"He didn't buy it."

"Who would, after witnessing a performance like *that*." Fraser gestured toward the big screen, now ablink with flight data and other innocuous statistics.

"He'd like to see all senior members of the team in the briefing room. Now."

"Right." Fraser followed his friend and boss. The flight crew hadn't cooperated. Not that they were expected to, but hopes had run high. He consoled himself with the knowledge that it could have been worse. It had been, in the course of the flight out from Earth, but that dialogue had arrived via containable, closed channels.

Actually they hadn't performed too badly. Except for some of their dialogue. And Major Oakley's exposure. And Commander Swansea's closing commentary.

Well, maybe they had performed badly.

The President was waiting for them, a measure of his concern. He sat at one end of the desk and bid them join him. As the door closed behind him, Fraser could hear the distant howls of reporters struggling to get past the guards. On a trip to Tanzania Fraser had once heard hyenas closing on an injured impala. The memory came back to him now, unbidden.

The President was quiet, staring down at his folded hands. Fraser thought the room too brightly lit. Then that familiar face rose to eye each of them in turn. To Fraser's immense discomfort, it settled eventually on him.

A small eon or two passed in continued silence before the Chief Executive said softly but firmly, "Well?"

The voice of Mission Control looked to Tetsugawa, then MacKenzie, who nodded but offered no support. Fraser was on his own.

"I guess you'd like an explanation, Mister President."

"Your observation reeks of understatement, Mr. Fraser. *So it's no longer Warren,* he thought. Not a good sign.

He rose and began pacing. He always thought better on his feet.

"The White House science advisor may have told you, Mister President, that accumulated research has shown us that long-term exposure to weightlessness beyond the Earth's orbit is not in the same league, physiologically speaking, with much greater exposure over interplanetary distances. As we discovered several years ago, the illness that develops during such extended trips is persistent, debilitating, and if allowed to continue results in physical problems as well as severe psychological complications."

"I've been briefed," the President replied. "I've kept abreast of the Project since before I was elected."

Fraser nodded, grateful that he wouldn't have to explain every little detail, every nuance of the situation. Compared to his elected brethren on Capitol Hill, this President was technologically sophisticated. It might make a difference, and it was bound to help.

"We experimented with every imaginable kind of medication, sir, to alleviate the symptoms attendant on such far-ranging expeditions. The ones we would have preferred to use were too weak, or wore off after a month or so. Anything strong enough to significantly mute the condition affected individual performance to the point where it compromised mission safety.

"What we needed was medication which could be taken as necessary but would not impair the crew over a time span of several months. We also needed something which would not damage the crew's mental well-being. As you know, the problem of being cooped up in a small ship over so much time and distance was more difficult for us to deal with than the science and engineering.

"In the end, it was Ms. Tetsugawa who came up with the right stuff. As you may know, she is our chief design engineer and is responsible for the overall performance of the spacecraft, particularly the Lander. She also suffers from inoperable glaucoma in her right eye. Among the medications which have been prescribed for her over the years and which allow her to continue in her career is cannabis."

Tetsugawa gave him a welcome breather as she spoke up. "In the course of preparing for this expedition, Mister President, we discovered that periodic use of cannabis, or rather, its principle component ACTH, relieved the majority of symptoms associated with long-distance interplanetary travel while still allowing the crew a sufficient range of function to carry out their assignments. It has the added benefit of enhancing their mental well-being.

"We considered various methods of application, from pill form to injection, but found that the, um, traditional methodology was the most effective. Like everything else on the ship, the *Barsoom*'s ventilation system is overbuilt and redundant. It handles the smoke without difficulty."

"That's nice to know," said the President dryly.

"I might add, sir, that the necessary material was obtained through legal sources, principally the same pharmaceutical company which supplies glaucoma sufferers like myself. I understand that the raw material comes from wild fields in Hawaii."

The President's finger were working. "At least it's the product of American agriculture. There was no other way?"

MacKenzie shook his head. "I'm sorry, Mister President. We had the choice of utilizing an effective method of treatment or abandoning the Mars flight until some chemical substitute could be found."

The Chief Executive looked thoughtful. "What about long-term risks to the astronauts?"

"Compared to the other risks involved in this expedition they were minimal, sir. Their dosage is carefully monitored, though occasionally they can exceed that limit. I'm afraid they may have done so today, though in light of their accomplishment it may be understandable. As you may know, when they announced touchdown we had our own little celebration here at Mission Control."

"Testing was rigorous, Mister President," said the diminutive Tetsugawa. "The United Tobacco Company was kind enough to lend us their secret laboratory facilities. They had their own reasons for participating, of course. We'd hoped to keep this aspect of the mission quiet until the crew had returned and been through debriefing. Your insistence on this transmission made that impossible."

"The American people have a right to know," the President replied. "They have a right to know what their tax dollars are paying for." Next to him an aide put a hand to his forehead and groaned.

"I'm surprised you managed to keep it out of the papers this long," declared an aide.

The President rose and turned to stare at the large relief map of Mars that dominated the near wall of the briefing room.

"This is a great day for our country. Nothing must be allowed to take away from that, nor from the accomplishments of that gallant crew. In the time-honored tradition of science and exploration they have made great sacrifices and suffered much."

"Maybe not too much," one aide whispered to another. The Secretary of State glared at them.

"Those are our feelings also, Mister President." Mackenzie's spirits rose. It was going to be all right.

"I am sure that once the circumstances are properly explained to them, the public will see things in an understanding light. You can handle the press, can't you, Roy?"

The White House Press Secretary pursed his lips. "I'll need plenty of material from NASA, sir. It won't be easy. People have been conditioned for so long to think that . . ."

The President glanced over his shoulder. "Putting three men and a woman on Mars hasn't been easier either, Roy."

The spokesman swallowed. "No, sir."

Fraser was breathing easier. He marveled at the President, admiring the skill of a consummate politician at work. There was no anger; only an attempt to find solutions."

"We'll supply all the material you'll need," MacKenzie told the Press Secretary. The President turned to the chief engineer.

"I appreciate your striving to keep this aspect of the mission out of the public eye for as long as possible, Mr. MacKenzie. At least we have the successful landing to build upon. Had this information leaked earlier, it would have greatly complicated funding. You've all done your jobs well. Now it's my turn. Thanks to our idiot economic advisors I've had to justify far more unsettling surprises than this." He turned from the map.

"It will be difficult to manage the press, but we'll manage. Tabloid headlines like 'Potheads go to Mars' will be the least of our problems. It's the conservative media that worry me." He sighed. "The Moral Majority never wanted any space missions anyway."

"We'll hold up our end, sir," said MacKenzie.

"I know that you all will." He moved to shake hands with each of them in turn. "It's been an important day, unexpected revelations notwithstanding. Now I'm afraid I have to get back to Washington. As your Commander Swansea pointed out, time waits for no man." He headed for the door. Beyond, a phalanx of aides and Secret Service men were sweeping the corridor clean of reporters.

"One thing, guys." The Press Secretary lingered in the doorway. "I think it would be a good idea if future Mission Control press releases at least temporarily stopped referring to it as 'The High Frontier'. . . ."

# Vole
## by John Gregory Betancourt

*Here follows something ... bizarre, even for this book. It was created by John Gregory Betancourt, "part time superhero and part time mystic [who] operates from a secret base deep in the heart of New Jersey. Among his achievements are twenty-three world domination plots foiled, eighteen criminal masterminds put behind bars, and no less than forty-four natural disasters averted."*

*He goes on to say he has an overactive imagination. Q.E.D. Among his forthcoming books is* Devil In The Sky, *a* Star Trek: Deep Space 9 *novel, written in collaboration with another of our contributors, Greg Cox.*

From the *New York Sun-Tribune*

# VOLE MEN—A NEW MEDICAL MUTILATION?

## By Ari J. Hermann
### Staff Writer

Dozens of patients flock to "animen doctors" each week to be surgically reconstructed into their favorite animals. Societies of elite "catmen," "dogmen," and other breeds of animal-men are developing throughout New York and Los Angeles as a result.

"The so-called 'animan surgery' is neither safe nor sensible," according to Dr. Bruce Athwalt of the County General Hospital. "It appeals to the baser, animal instincts in man," Athwait says. "If you need an outlet for your animal aggressions, see a licensed psychiatrist. Do not mutilate your body!"

New York's most celebrated animal surgeon, Dr. Ferret, disagrees. "Man is past the point of needing just one body," he alleges. "New limbs and vital organs can be cloned in nutrient tanks for amputees. Why not graft on whole new bodies?" Dr. Ferret, a six-year animan himself (ferretman), further claims to have performed "over eight hundred successful op-

erations over the last three years, for animan bodies ranging from cats to dogs to, yes, even penguins."

As new animalform bodies are developed and commercially marketed, Dr. Ferret runs advertisements in local papers offering specials on these new bodies. The latest animalform is "vole"—and over fifty people have already signed up for the new "voleman" surgical operations.

Legislation is pending in Congress to make animalforms either illegal or harder to get for most Americans. Several southern states have already passed laws against human-body mutilation aimed at curbing the animalform practice, and a test case is currently with the Supreme Court. Battle lines seem drawn between pro-animalform and anti-animalform groups.

Only time will tell whether animen are the wave of the future—or a bizarre affectation of the present.

From the
# NEW YORK POST-DISPATCH
*PERSONANIMALS* Column

# In Search of the Perfect Orgasm
## or
# Doing It with a Big Lizard Can Be Fun
### by Dean Wesley Smith

*Dean Wesley Smith wants us to know that he "has been in search of the perfect orgasm for most of his adult (and some of his teenage) life. On his days off he writes stories and novels and does other nasty publishing things (such as edit and publish other people's stuff). Godzilla and Rocky and Bullwinkle were his favorite childhood friends, although they have been of little help in his search."*

*Kids, don't try this at home.*

When the alien ray gun zapped Godzilla, it did more than just kill the old cliché, it burnt a few people, too. This is the story of one of those people: Little Sally Ann Gibson, age sixteen, size 36D, ray gun victim.

### COUNTDOWN: ONE HOUR BEFORE GODZILLA BITES IT.

"Sally. Ann. Gibson." Sally's mother spaced the words as if they were each a sentence. "How many times have I told you to wear a bra? You can't go to school looking like that. Now get back upstairs and change into something decent."

"But, Mom . . ." Sally banged her hand in frustration on the banister, not really noticing that her anger made her nipples poke through the loose knit of the sweater.

"No buts. Do as I say." Sally's mom put her hands on her hips in the old Superman pose and stared at Sally's chest with disgust.

Sally knew there was no arguing with her mother when she talked like that and stood like that. It made no difference that all the girls in school were going without their bras. It made no difference that she had great tits and liked to show them off. Nope. None of that mattered. Her mom was still living in the stone age.

Sally trudged slowly back upstairs, pouting, her lower lip extended, wondering what Billy was going to think and if he'd even like her any more. It wasn't until she got to the top that she realized she was being stupid. She could just take her bra off after she got to school. Her mom would never know.

And it might even be fun.

## COUNTDOWN: THIRTY MINUTES BEFORE THE ALIEN RAY GUN FRIES GODZILLA'S BRAIN AND OTHER BODY PARTS.

Sally giggled, then squirmed on the smooth car seat, as Bobby slipped her sweater up over her head. His fingers were cold and as they brushed her skin under her arms they tickled and sent little shivers of pleasure all over her body.

"Nice way to start the day," Billy said, his hands rubbing her bra-encased boobs as if he was trying to tune the radio, both knobs at the same time.

Sally glanced nervously around the mostly empty school parking lot. It was still early, so there was time. She turned her back to Billy. "Unhook me, would you?"

"My pleasure," Billy said. His voice squeaked and he was starting to pant. Sally knew what that meant. She'd have to get her sweater back on damn fast or they'd be wrestling out here for hours. Damn. Why had she thought it would be fun to have Billy help?

## COUNTDOWN: TEN MINUTES UNTIL GODZILLA GETS TURNED TO A CRISPY CRITTER BY THE ALIENS WHO WANT TO SAVE EARTH FOR SOMETHING BETTER.

"Billy! Stop that!" Sally pulled Billy's hand out from under her skirt. Now she was panting. His face was red. She had gotten her sweater back on only by promising Billy he could do other "things." She just hadn't expected to enjoy the other "things" so much. She'd always been a "good" girl and never let a boy touch her "there."

She glanced quickly around the parking lot. Well, maybe it wouldn't hurt for just another minute.

She let go of Billy's hand and it ducked under her skirt faster than her cat trying to hide from the neighbor's dog.

## COUNTDOWN: FIVE MINUTES UNTIL GODZILLA SMOKES AND THE ALIENS LAUGH AND THE WORLD IS PLAGUED WITH A NEW RASH OF JAPANESE HORROR MOVIES.

They were interrupted twice by cars pulling in. But both times Sally had let Billy put his hand back up under her skirt. The last time he had pulled aside her white panties and really touched her. The feeling almost scared her. Almost.

This time the intruding car, Carla's blue Volks, pulled in across from them. Billy quickly pulled his hand out and Sally felt the disappointment, among other things. The excitement of thinking that Carla might guess what they were doing had her breathing hard.

Both of them waved at Carla as if they had been talking about a biology assignment and nothing more. The minute Carla turned and headed for the school, Sally lifted her butt off the seat, reached up under her skirt, and pulled off her white panties. She held them up for Billy to see.

"If I don't need a bra," she said, smiling. "I sure don't see why I need these."

She dropped them into her purse as Billy tried to catch his breath.

## COUNTDOWN: ONE MINUTE UNTIL GODZILLA GETS STEAMED, DEEP-FAT FRIED, AND SENT ON TO THE NEXT WORLD BY THE ALIENS WHO AREN'T EVEN FROM THIS WORLD.

Billy's fingers were doing wonderful things under her skirt and Sally didn't really care if anyone drove up or not. She'd let Billy watch out. She had her eyes closed and right now her entire body was starting to tremble. She knew she was going to come any minute. And she knew it was going to be a lot better than when she wrapped her legs around her teddy bear and squeezed real hard.

Billy's hand moved faster and she moaned. This time was going to be *much* better.

BLAST-OFF: GODZILLA'S SCALES REFLECTED PART
OF THE HEAT RAY. ALIEN HEAD GUNNERS CALLED
IT A FLUKE.

Billy's hand was moving like a blender and Sally was half
moaning, half shouting. Two seniors laughed and pointed as
they walked by the shaking car.

HEADLINE: ALIEN RAY BOUNCES OFF
ATMOSPHERE, HITS CAR IN A HIGH SCHOOL
PARKING LOT IN THE VERY HEART OF AMERICA.
PRESIDENT THREATENS TO SUE ALIENS AND
JAPANESE.

Sally Ann Gibson's first real orgasm and the alien heat
ray hit her at exactly the same instant.
She exploded like a kid's balloon against a cactus.
She blew up like a tomato thrown against a brick wall.
She had an orgasm unparalleled in human existence.

HEADLINE: GODZILLA LIMPS INTO OCEAN
CARRYING TEN-STORY BUILDING. ALIENS HAVE NO
COMMENT.

Billy broke his right hand in the orgasmic explosion and
ended up having to sell his car because he couldn't get past
the memory. He also had to live with a phobia against parking on dates that limited his future sexual practices.
Little Sally Ann Gibson recovered after two days in the
hospital. The doctors promised her that plastic surgery
would help the permanent smile frozen on her face.
She never had the operation.

# Saving Sam's Used UFOs
## by Kate Daniel

*As of this writing, Kate Daniel has five novels out under
her own name and one under a pseudonym, plus stories in
several anthologies including* Aladdin: Master of the Lamp
*and* By Any Other Fame. *Her novels include* Babysitter's
Nightmare, Teen Idol, *and* Running Scared. *She lives with
her family and cats in rural Arizona and knows where to get
a really out-of-this-world deal on transportation.*

"Hey! Where the hell you think you're going?"

The shout came moments too late to stop the man climbing through the wire fence. Inside the rusty barbed wire,
there was a shimmer of light, like a heat haze on an August
day. Since it was late October, it had to be something else.
The fence-climber stopped for a moment, his eyes narrowing
as he looked at the distortion. Beyond, inside the fenced-off
area, he could see an auto graveyard, cars that were too tired
and worn out to be worth restoring as classics. He'd been
studying it from a distance, and he'd gotten several shots
through a telephoto lens. The haze hadn't been visible from
outside the fence. Now he studied it, wondering if it would
even show in a picture. The cars beyond it were distorted by
the ripples, blurred out of their normal shapes.

"Get outta there, you! Right now!" The owner of the lot
was coming toward him, as fast as an overweight and out-of-
shape used car salesman could move. The man inside the
fence made a fast decision. He pulled out his camera and
took another picture, hoping the automatic focus could handle the mock heat haze. Then he headed for the nearest row
of cars.

His second step took him through the shimmering wall of
haze. It felt like those hot air curtains some stores used. His

third step was nothing but momentum, as the shock of what he was seeing caught up with him and brought him to a halt.

The rusted-out hulks were still there, but he could no longer assign make and model and year at a glance. The old Chevys and Plymouths he'd photographed from across the street were nowhere to be seen. Instead, there were neat rows of strange vehicles, some rounded and flat on the bottom with tiny windows around the side, some with stranger shapes. At the back, one large derelict reminded him vaguely of a wedding cake, with several layers. A wedding cake, or the mother ship from *Close Encounters.*

"Dammit, you got no *business* coming inside the fence thataways." Saving Sam, the owner of Saving Sam's Used Car Bargain City, stood there puffing hard. Sam's normal expression was a smile as wide and as shallow as the Missouri River that ran past the edge of the lot. He wasn't wearing it now.

"Jackpot," the other whispered. He paid no attention to Sam. "After all these years—I *knew* there was something behind all those stories!" He started to bring his camera up again, then stopped as Sam grabbed his arm.

"You're trespassing, mister," Sam said. "Now just who in hell are you, and what are you doing here?"

"I could ask you the same thing. Are you even a human?" The man took in Sam's disheveled appearance, face red and sweaty, the loud tie slightly off-center, the yellow shirt that was creeping out of Sam's polyester slacks in the back. "Although I'm not sure aliens would have enough imagination to come up with that disguise. They'd probably look more like insurance salesmen. I'm Joe Gilbert." Joe reached in his pocket with his free hand and brought out a tattered business card. A single line of type was centered on the card: *National News Probe.* Joe's name and a phone number were in one corner.

"That thing," Sam said. He let go of Joe's arm, adding, "Don't you go taking no pictures. Not till I make up my mind what I want to do about this."

"We'll pay you for an exclusive," Joe said. There were standard contracts, although, since NNP was a midget among the tabloids, they weren't that generous.

"Well—" Sam rubbed his chin, considering. His five o'clock shadow looked like 6:15, even though it was still early afternoon. "Maybe. C'mon into the office, and let's talk."

Joe started to duck back through the barbed wire, but Sam stopped him. "Not that office. Got me another one back here. The one out front's for my regular customers."

He led the way through the rows of vehicles, while Joe rubbernecked. No question about it, they really were flying saucers. Not all saucer-shaped, no; some looked like they'd been stolen off a Hollywood back lot, some were featureless cubes, and one bore a striking resemblance to an America's Cup winner from a few years before. But they weren't products of Detroit or Japan. Joe gawked like a tourist; he was happy.

The office was a flimsy shed that had been fitted with a regular door and window on one wall. Inside, a desk and filing cabinet occupied most of the space. The only chair was the one behind the desk. Sam took it and waved Joe to a seat on the corner of the desk. Joe sat, twisting around enough to see out the window. The spaceships were still out there.

"So there really are aliens," Joe began.

"Hell, you people print pictures of them," Sam said, grinning. "See 'em in the grocery store all the time."

"Now don't tell me they look like that thing the *Blazon* has on the cover this week."

"Nope." Sam tipped his chair back and it creaked alarmingly under the load. "Did have a real photo of an alien a whiles back, though, the one that started all that business about aliens advising candidates in the presidential elections."

"That thing?" Joe frowned. He knew the man whose delirium tremens had been responsible for the first version of that one.

"Not the little cartoon guy." Sam grinned again. "One of the Secret Service men in the first picture. Customer of mine, 'smatter of fact. Nice guy, fellow named Strlirrk." The final syllable sounded as though Sam had swallowed his tongue.

That figured, Joe thought. He'd been right, disguised aliens would look a lot more like a Ken-doll.

"So, let's have the story, Sam. How does a used car salesman in the middle of Missouri wind up with a lot full of flying saucers?"

"Used ones. I sell 'em just like I sell cars."

"Which came first, the cars or the UFOs?"

"Ain't really unidentified, you know, I got papers on most of 'em. Or something. Anyways, the cars come first. I got started in the used car game a good thirty years ago, been building up steady ever since. Advertising, that's all it takes, just advertising."

Since Joe wasn't deaf, he'd heard Sam's idea of advertising. Radio spots, at what seemed like twice the normal volume, played on half the stations in the Midwest, mindlessly repeating, "Let Saving Sam *save you dough!*" It was hard to believe anyone would buy a car just because of those ads, but they seemed to work. Sam's main lot was jammed, and Joe'd done a little research beforehand. Sam's Bargain City was one of the largest independent used car dealers in the state.

" 'Bout twelve years ago, I was driving home at night, pretty late. Used to live out in the country, ten miles south of here. You know how all them saucer stories say your headlights go out and your car radio dies? Well, that's pretty much what happened. 'Cept they come back on again, then went out, then come on, then went out. I stopped and got out, and I saw this *thing* sitting out in the middle of a corn field. Lights started to race around the outside, and my headlights and radio went out again. Then there was a bang, and the lights on the thing stopped, and my car was fine again. Didn't take much to figure out the guy was having engine trouble. The thing just didn't want to start."

Joe had his notebook out and was taking notes as Sam spoke. He wasn't sure he'd be able to decipher them later, but it didn't matter. He'd remember even without notes.

"After a while, a guy comes out of the thing. He looked like a normal-enough guy, I mean human. So I asked him if he needed a lift." Sam stopped, which was just as well, because Joe was feeling a little dizzy.

"A flying saucer with engine trouble and you offered the pilot a ride?" The reporter shook his head. "Sam, that's wilder than the stories *we* print."

"Seemed like the thing to do at the time." Sam shrugged. "Anyways, we got to talking. Turned out he'd heard of me; he'd been here for a couple of years, and heard my ads on the radio. He was supposed to meet his boss, and with his— well, I guess wheels isn't the right way to put it, call it his transportation—with his saucer broke down, he was afraid he wouldn't be able to get there and he'd be in big trouble. So I sold him an old Plymouth and took his saucer as a trade-in."

"A flying saucer. As a trade-in for a Plymouth?"

"Car was a cream puff," Sam said. "I made him a good deal. I always do; they don't call me Saving Sam for nothing." They called him that because his radio ads blared out the name hundreds of times a day, but Joe didn't correct him. "He paid gold, cash on the line; first time I ever dealt that way. The light-bend worked okay, so we just hauled the ship out back here and turned it on. The light-bend, that's the thing makes a ship look like a Chevy. Had to dicker some, he was afraid I'd tell the government or someone. I said I wouldn't, and I've kept that promise, but it's took some doing."

"That gave you one UFO," Joe said when Sam showed no signs of going on. "One. And it wasn't running. There must be a hundred of the things out there. How'd you get so many?"

"He showed back up a few weeks later with his boss. Turned out the boss was a pretty fair shadetree mechanic, leastways on saucers. Thing just had a plugged carburetor or something. He got it running, but my customer—*his* name I never could get my mouth around, and I ain't trying it now—that first guy liked the Plymouth and he wasn't fixing to go home yet, so we just left things the way they was.

"Y'know, I run a lot of ads, but word o' mouth's still the best damned advertising there is. That pair told other travelers. Mostly I just sell cars, but ever once in a while, some guy turns up and asks to see the back lot. Sell more cars to them than spaceships; mostly they want something humans won't notice, so I get another ship in trade. Got seventy-three in stock right at the moment, nowheres near a hundred. Was seventy-four, but that Secret Service agent, Strlirrk, he got transferred last week and he needed a ship. Got a nice little Fiesta out on the main lot that he traded in on a practically new Parsector, less'en a million light-years on it."

Sam stopped talking again. Joe tore his gaze away from the window to ask a question.

"Parsector? Is that a brand or a model?" His pen was poised to record the interstellar version of the Big Three.

"Nah, I made it up. Couldn't never make out what they called that type, I had papers on it, but I couldn't read 'em.

I can't on most of them, and I'm not about to try to learn all
them languages. So I started making up my own model
names and makes, years ago." He got up and went over to
the window. Pointing to one of the cube-shaped vehicles
parked near the office, he said, "That's an older model
Parsector. The newer ones, like the one I sold Strlirrk, the
corners are more rounded and they got a light-bend that's
adjustable for over thirty different appearances."

Joe reached for his camera, and this time Sam didn't say
anything. He got a picture of the Parsector and sneaked another of the one he still thought of as the mother ship.

"My turn," Sam said. "I got a question for you, you been
asking me enough. I been doing this now for twelve years,
and far's I know, I'm the only used spaceship dealer on the
planet. My customers don't talk, I sure as hell don't, and I
never had any trouble. And I bought me a new light-bend
just last year. This one's supposed to make people feel nosy
and guilty, kind of at the back of their mind, not so's they
notice it, but anyways they don't want to look at the back lot
very long, makes 'em feel uncomfortable. How come you
did?"

"Rumors. And reporters don't ever feel guilty about being
nosy, not if they want to stay reporters." He weighed his
next comment, balancing betrayal of a source against the
chance of getting more from Sam. It didn't take long; he
wasn't likely to ever get anything else from that source, and
he wouldn't be doing him any real harm. "Do you remember
that salesman Carl you fired a couple of months back? He
thought there was something in that back lot, and he called
NNP. He didn't say anything about UFOs, though, just that
there was something fishy going on and you made too much
money, more than used cars could account for."

Sam snorted. "Damned useless knowitall. That's why I
fired him, he never would listen to nobody. He already knew
it all. 'Smatter of fact, he's wrong; been keeping all the
money from my extra business off of the books. Been saving
it."

"It got me started, anyway. I spent a couple of hours in
that field across the river yesterday, watching through binoculars, and I didn't see anybody come near the lot. All I saw
was a bunch of dead cars. I figured Carl was just trying to
get you in trouble, but I thought one last check wouldn't hurt

anything." Joe smiled and raised the camera again. "I was right. This is the story of a lifetime."

"Thought you people always just made up them stories," Sam grumbled. "Never expected to see one of you acting like a real reporter."

"Yeah, some of the articles just come out of the newsroom. Or out of a bottle." Joe was smiling as he talked, a little half-smile of satisfaction. "But we track down a few real stories, just for the looks of things. That's how I got started; I was around when a reporter for the *Inquirer* was checking out a freak accident in my home town. I always thought there was something to all those UFO reports. Figured this would be the best way to find out. And I was right." He smiled out the window. "I was right."

"Yeah, you were right," Sam said. He sighed heavily. " 'Course, you're putting me in a helluva bind, here. My special customers, sometimes they need cars and sometimes they need ships, but one thing they *all* need all the time is privacy. This is one time I don't want free advertising."

"I wouldn't worry about it," Joe said. "Nobody ever believes a word we print. Or at any rate, no one does who matters." He'd used the line before, but it wasn't true. While government agencies might not actually *believe* what was printed in the tabloids, Joe knew they sometimes checked out articles. One of the funniest stories Joe had ever heard came from a buddy who worked for the *Sun*. He'd been in Oregon when a team of Federal agents had gotten lost searching for Bigfoot. The story had never seen print, of course; some things were a little too hot for even a tabloid to handle.

This might be one of them, but Joe thought he could get at least one good story in before official secrecy closed Sam off from the world and his special customers. Too bad for Sam, but it could put the human race in touch with the stars. For all the surface cynicism that came with his job, Joe was a romantic, and he had gone to work for *National News Probe* because he wanted to believe in their stories, the offbeat, odd things that said there was a little magic left in the world. In it, and out of it. Joe couldn't take his eyes off the spaceships outside. Real spaceships.

And real aliens. Joe stiffened as he saw two men approaching the barbed wire fence. They looked like shoe salesmen, but as they ducked through the fence and passed the light-bend, their appearance *shifted*. They didn't look like monsters or bugs; if Joe had seen a picture of them, he would have thought they were animals from Earth that he just didn't happen to recognize. There were a lot of species he didn't know. But they weren't animals.

Behind him, Sam spoke again. His voice sounded almost sad. "You may be right, Joe, but I'm afraid I can't take a chance. I ain't letting anyone wreck my business. I can't let you print that story. I'm sorry."

His voice was so genuinely remorseful Joe almost reassured him it was okay, he didn't have to apologize. Instead, Joe tried to turn and found he couldn't move. He was stuck, staring out the window and watching the animal-shaped aliens approach. Sam moved around to where Joe could see him. He held up a short metal tube. It looked like a weapon; it must have frozen him.

"You really think I could do business here for twelve years and not have some problems?" Sam asked, shaking his head dolefully. "I hate it when this happens, but like I told you, I ain't letting nobody ruin this. I got me enough saved up, almost, to take that vacation on Mars I been wanting for years. They got a nice little resort colony there, lot of different races of aliens go there."

"What are you going to do to me?" Joe whispered.

"Now, don't go getting afraid," Sam said, "no one's gonna hurt you. They always need new humans for research, but it's more like answering questions, taking polls and such; they don't cut people up." The door opened, and the two aliens came in. Sam waved to them and said, "Sorry to call you fellas out like this, but I figured this wouldn't wait. Guy's a tabloid reporter."

The alien on the left spoke. "No trouble, Sam." Despite the hooves and hide, he sounded like a Texan. "We'll run him over to Mars right away and arrange for transshipment."

"Now don't be afraid," Sam told Joe again as the two aliens picked him up. "You said you was interested in UFOs. You're going to get to see a lot of them, now."

Joe tried to shake his head, but he was still frozen. As they carried him toward one of the conventionally saucer-shaped ships, his main emotion was not fear, or anger, or regret. It was frustration.

It was the greatest story of his career, but someone else would have to write it now.

*Tabloid reporter abducted by UFO aliens!*

# Danny's Excellent Adventure!
## by Greg Cox

*Gone But Not Forgotten. What is it about our former Vice President that proved so inspirational?*

*At least Danny's story is in the capable hands of Greg Cox, who has this to say for himself: "After perusing too many issues of the* Weekly World News, *Greg Cox abandoned a promising career as a skid row phlebotomist to pursue a sordid life of writing and editing. Medical experts have pronounced his brain irreparably rotted; he is currently confined to the North Wing of Tor Books in New York."*

*Oh yes, and he's writing* Devil in the Sky, *a Star Trek: Deep Space 9 novel, with John Gregory Betancourt.*

"I didn't live in this century." J. Danforth Quayle

"I think he was telling the truth," Ratio says.

"Huh?" I reply. We're having our weekly lunch at the Aloha Diner in midtown Manhattan, sitting in one of the rear booths and sipping our complimentary glasses of ice water while we wait for the Greek waiter to deliver our meals. Ratio leans across the table toward me, his eyes wide behind his tinted spectacles, his voice hushed with the import of this latest revelation. I hadn't seen him this excited since he'd claimed to have met Grace Kelly's ghost during an astral voyage—and found out that Princess Di was the reincarnation of Lee Harvey Oswald. Oh boy, I think. This is going to be good.

"I think he's from the future," Ratio explains. The air-conditioning is out, and a bead of sweat works its way down from Ratio's aluminum skullcap to the collar of his glow-in-the-dark, cross-covered, anti-vampire T-shirt. "I think the Vice President is a time traveler!"

"Come again?" Sometimes I think Ratio's from another

dimension himself, but I don't mind. He makes for good copy, especially if the paper you write for isn't too picky about its sources. And *The Weekly Exposure*, "The Nation's Nose for News," has more astrologers on call than Nancy Reagan ever did. Me, I didn't need psychic powers, just a good imagination and a few colorful acquaintances.

Like my current lunch date. His parents named him Horatio, but he shortened it to Ratio, like that's an improvement. He used to work at the paper, too, a few years ago, but he got canned for spending too much time out-of-body. Fortunately, his folks left him money as well as a silly moniker. He's given me some of my best headlines, though, like CROP CIRCLES CURE CANCER and MICHAEL LANDON RETURNS FROM LITTLE HOUSE IN THE SKY . . . TO LEAD TEENAGE WEREWOLF ONTO HIGHWAY TO HEAVEN.

Hey, it's a living.

"Think about it," Ratio continues. "Suppose you want to observe firsthand the most crucial events of the late twentieth century, but don't want to risk doing anything that might change the course of history. You couldn't choose a better job to have than Vice President!"

"Hmmm. You've got a point there," I admit, as I pull out a pad and pencil and start taking notes. "Still . . . Dan Quayle, Time Cadet?"

"But it's the only thing that makes sense!" Ratio pelts my face with a gentle spray of saliva. I reach discreetly for a napkin. "My best guess is that they replaced the real Quayle right before the nomination. How else do you explain his apparent unfamiliarity with history, geography, even the English language as it's currently spoken? I'm figuring he must have been inadequately briefed."

I start to prod him for examples, but it's not necessary. Ratio's on a roll. "I mean, look at the record. He says that the Holocaust was a dark chapter in *American* history, he says that Mars has a breathable atmosphere. . . ." Ratio pauses, and I can practically see a new idea taking root behind his chartreuse lenses. "Wow, you think they've terraformed Mars by the thirtieth century?"

Now, I've always thought that the best sensationalism contains a token pretense at skepticism, a bit of quasi-journalistic seasoning to make the silliness more credible, so I decide to play sanity's advocate for a bit. "Okay, maybe he's a time traveler," I suggest, "or maybe he's just a moron who spells 'potato' with an E."

Ratio isn't discouraged. "Perhaps that's how it's spelled where he comes from! Languages change over time. If you were dropped back into Merrie Olde England, I'll bet thee thine spelling wouldst sucketh."

"Fine," I concede, "and 'Happy Camper' is probably a standard honorific in futureworld. But try this on for size . . . the whole idea is to observe and not do anything significant, right?"

"Of course," Ratio agrees. "In fact, in November 1988, Quayle said, and I quote: *'I deserve respect for the things I did not do.'* Why, that's practically the Time Traveler's Oath!"

"Er, right, but my point is that everything you've said so far would make sense if this were still, say, 1992. If he were just this do-nothing veep who said dopey things sometimes. But, pal, read the paper these days. Quayle's all over the place, campaigning and making policy. The man's probably going to be elected President in November. Don't tell me that's not interfering with history."

Ratio falls silent for a moment. "You're right," he says slowly, ". . . unless . . . oh, my God! . . . he's gone rene-gade!" Our waiter finally arrives with two cheeseburgers, an egg cream, and a large ginger ale; despite its name, the closest the Aloha comes to Hawaiian cuisine is a pineapple sundae. Ratio ignores the food. He's practically shouting now, as heads turn in our direction and I try to shrink into my seat. The life of an investigative reporter is sometimes embarrassing.

"The power must have gone to his head," my companion raves, oblivious to the stares from the rest of the lunchers. "He's gone beyond his mission parameters, violating the Temporal Prime Directive in a mad attempt to seize control of our era. Dan Quayle's become a threat to the entire space-time continuum!"

Okay, that's it. I have more than enough for a good story, I decide. Now if I can just shut this lunatic up, before our friendly waiter throws us out. "Calm down, buddy," I whisper urgently. "If he has broken the rules, then won't the Time Police or somebody do something about it?"

"Oh," Ratio says. He takes a deep breath and I push his burger toward him. "I hadn't thought of that."

* * *

"So," I ask my coworker, "you think Dukakis has a chance?" We left the *Exposure*'s offices over an hour ago, but I'm in no hurry to get back to work. Ratio hesitates, and for a moment I'm afraid he's zoning out again. He's going to get fired if he doesn't knock that off soon.

Turns out he was just thinking. "I don't know," he says. "Clarence Thomas is certainly a surprising pick for Bush's running mate. I've never heard of him before, but he's supposedly got the right conservative credentials." Ratio takes a gulp of ginger ale, then stares at me strangely. "Wow, I'm having the most incredible case of *déja vu.*"

"Hold that thought," I tell him. "Maybe there's a story in it."

And if not, I'll make one up.

# Royal Tiff Yields Face of Jesus!
## by Esther M. Friesner

*When I complained to my coeditor about the dearth of Nessie stories in this book, he said he saw nothing wrong with my supplying the lack.*

*I want you to know that That Unfortunate Business in the British royal family happened* after *I wrote this. I am therefor currently working on a story in which a poor-but-honest anthology editor wins the Lottery.*

The distraught young woman pounded frantically on the cottage door. Rainwater streamed down her face, plastering her once-impeccably coiffed hair flat as an otter's coat. She was too exhausted to bother pushing her bedraggled blonde locks out of her eyes. Between assaults on the door, she used both hands to hold together the briar-torn rags of her sacrificial robe. She had lost everything but her sense of propriety.

The rain pelted through the bare branches of the surrounding woodland, peppering the surface of the nearby lake. In such a downpour, it was difficult to distinguish sounds. The young woman beat at the cottage door again, but her ears were filled with the thunder of pursuing footsteps and the hammering of her own heart.

"Coming, coming, no need to batter the whole blessed house down." A warm, cheery voice from within at last answered the woman's wild tattoo. The cottage door opened to reveal an old hag who looked as if she had stepped straight out of a fairy tale. Gap-toothed, she grinned at her unexpected caller and said, "Well, yours is one famous face I didn't think to see in the flesh, although there *is* the pantry floor . . . never could make up my mind about whether that was you or Madonna . . . Ah well, never mind. My name is Mrs. Betram Coombs; the *widow* Coombs, I suppose I should say, but do call me Daisy. Would you care to come in?"

The young woman could only stare. Refuge at last. *But for how long?* came the shuddering thought. She could hardly dare to imagine; she would never again dare to hope.

The beldame was making gentle, welcoming gestures with her knotty hands. "Come in, my dear, come in," she encouraged. "I know you, right enough, but you needn't fear. Religious questions have always stuck crosswise in my craw. Live and let live, that's my motto. Oh, *do* come in! You're perfectly safe here; I won't give you away."

The younger woman straightened her shoulders. Some of the old royal poise returned. "I thank you for your kind offer of hos—of hos—" Her recent ordeal proved too much. She accepted the invitation to enter by fainting across the hag's doorstep.

She came to in a bruised old plush armchair with a cool cloth on her forehead and a ginger tomcat in her lap. Her ruined robes had been removed. She was naked beneath a musty blanket of undyed wool. A grand blaze of hardwood logs in the fireplace before her stole the last of the chill from her bones. The hag was seated in a matching armchair across from her, knitting a woolly jumper the color of mud.

"So you're awake, eh?" Daisy gave her a merry smile, apple cheeks held fast in a net of fine wrinkles. "Then I suppose it's past time I made you a proper greeting." She laid aside her knitting, rose to her feet, toddled across the hearth rug, and amid a symphony of creaking bones and popping joints, she made her visitor a deep curtsey.

"Welcome, Your Majesty," she said.

*"Don't call me that!"* The younger woman's hands clapped themselves to her ears at the hated words. "In God's name, I beg you!"

Daisy cocked her head to one side. "Oh dear," she remarked. "Which god would that be, then?"

"I am still a Christian." The younger woman sighed. "It gave *him* the final excuse he needed."

"To be sure, to be sure." The crone set her knitting aside. "I don't hold with such things myself. When they burned the Guys on November 5 in *my* day, there wasn't anyone inside 'em. Not on purpose, anyway. Still, you must admit, the new program of government subsidized human sacrifice certainly has had a good effect on the economy. Unemployment's been quite reduced, for one, and the level of emigration—"

"If you throw enough victims into bogs as part of your regular Sunday services, and burn some more on major holidays, eventually you are bound to have just the number of people left you need to fill what situation vacancies there are." The younger woman's tone was scornful and bitter. "And if you declare it an act of both treason *and* heresy to want to leave this country, of course people will stop trying to do it."

"Particularly when the penalty for treason or heresy is being chucked into one of them bogs," Daisy completed her guest's thought. "I know. Well, never mind all that, dearie!" She clapped gnarled hands to knobby knees and stood up. "Whatever your faith or mine, it won't stop us from enjoying a nice cup of tea."

The younger woman moved her legs tentatively, earning her a glance of supreme contempt from the tomcat before he leaped to the floor and stalked off, tail high. On shaky feet she followed her aged hostess from the fireside to a trim little white-clothed table that had been set for tea. It was at once comforting and terrifying to see such an artifact of the commonplace after her husband's—conversion? revolution? insanity?—had knocked most of Britain's fine old traditions into a cocked hat. The real horror was how readily the people had followed his lead once they saw the results.

"Luck," she muttered to herself as she pulled a chair up to the tea table. "Blind coincidence. Things might've gotten better for the country on their own just then. The Americans didn't throw *their* whole House of Lords—I mean, Congress—into any stupid bog, and *their* economy perked up the same as ours."

Daisy glanced up at her guest. "Did you say something, dearie?" She was settling a blue and white striped tea cozy over the squat brown crockery teapot.

"I was trying to determine who was the bigger loony: My husband for turning the whole blessed country Druid or the British people for letting him."

The hag chuckled. "Ah, you're just upset. As well you might be, I'm sure. Personally I don't favor any government *or* religion that allows a man to chuck his wife, mother of his children, into some smelly old bog just because they can't get along. In *my* day we tried to work out our matrimonial differences. My Bertie was no prize, heaven knows. However, I wouldn't go so far as to call His Majesty a loony. No more than history ever called Henry VIII mad. Oh, selfish, yes, and a spoiled brat, and a bully into the bargain, but he wasn't *crazy*. He only wanted his own way, and he was willing to use any excuse he could to get it and still look *noble*. The cow."

For the first time in ages, the younger woman laughed. Her hostess leaned forward to pour. That was when she saw it and screamed.

"Mercy, child!" Old Daisy sat back in her chair with an audible *thump*. "Whatever's set you off so?"

"Don't—don't you see it?" The younger woman pointed desperately at the cozy-shrouded teapot. "It's a miracle!"

"What, this old thing?" The old lady turned the teapot this way and that. "Just a simple striped knitting pattern, really, quite popular when I was a girl. There's a variation where you can knit in a picture of a dear little kitten, but I never had the—"

"That's no kitten!" her guest exclaimed, beside herself. "That's *Elvis Presley!*"

"Oh?" Daisy studied the tea cozy from a number of angles. "Ah, yes. So it is. Silly me, I thought Mr. Presley only manifested on my plain green cozy—and the dented saucepan—and two of the antimacassars—and sometimes on my spare upper plate when I can't find my usual brand of tooth powder at the market—but the blue and white striped cozy has *always* shown the face of John Lennon." She frowned at the clear outline of the one and only American King's profile. "Hmph. It's he, right enough. As if he hasn't taken up enough places in this house, to go and usurp that poor dear murdered British boy's sole station— Isn't that *just* like a Yank!"

The fugitive gave her hostess a doubtful look. "You—you've got *more* Elvises in this house? Not intentional ones, I mean, but—but what you call—manifestations?"

The crone cackled, rocking back and forth over the tea things. "Lord love you, child, it's all I can do to keep him out! Why, I don't know from one day to the next where he'll turn up. It began when I still lived in Queensbury, the year after my Bertie passed on. I found a moldy orange in my fruit basket, only the mold was a perfect replica of Mr. Presley's face. Needless to say I was rather impressed and I hurried next door straightaway to show it to Mrs. Jinks. *She* was who went and called the papers, but the only one that showed up to take photographs was that awful one—Oh, *you* know which I mean. The one that was always publishing those nasty stories about—about—" Daisy hesitated, with good cause.

"About me," the younger woman finished. "You needn't worry. I don't mind. I'd gladly trade a thousand of their vicious falsehoods for what my life's become now."

"Yes, well, after the orange story appeared, I was washing my windows when without warning the soapsuds formed themselves into *another* face of Elvis Presley. He looked somewhat older in that manifestation, and a bit worse for wear, poor thing. It wouldn't go away, no matter how hard I scrubbed or even when I tossed the rinse water over it." Daisy shrugged. "Mrs. Jinks came by while I was struggling with the apparition, and didn't the silly old biddy run and 'phone the papers again! But by the time the reporter arrived, he had more than his share of story. He found Mrs. Jinks stretched out in a dead faint on my parlor floor. And there, right in the middle of my lovely hooked hearth rug—a very nice posy pattern, as was—was the face of Michael Jackson, plain as plain, picked out in lupines."

"It must have made for a change from Elvis," her guest suggested, trying to be helpful and maintain her sanity at the same time.

"Indeed. While the reporter chafed Mrs. Jinks' wrists, I went to fetch a damp cloth, some spirits of ammonia, and the tea tray." She looked abruptly grim. "The water droplets that fell from the cloth formed a recognizable portrait of Marilyn Monroe in Mrs. Jinks' lap, one slice of toast was burnt with a likeness of Queen Victoria, and when I poured, Mrs. Jinks picked up her cup, sipped once, and dropped it, screaming that the pattern of cracks inside was the face of George Bernard Shaw and he was leering at her in a most indecent manner."

"What a field day for the press," the younger woman murmured.

"Tchah! That so-called reporter accused Mrs. Jinks and me of setting the whole thing up; of *planting* all those celebrity manifestations! For some of them, certainly collusion was a possibility, but wasn't he right there to witness Miss Monroe's appearance in the waterdrop pattern? How could we have engineered *that,* I ask you!" She shook her head sadly. "When Mrs. Jinks dropped her cup, it smashed. The split tea stained my nice Michael Jackson rug over with a bust of Mick Jagger and the fragments of the cup couldn't have been anybody except our dear, departed Queen Mum, may she rest in peace, but did that *reporter* notice?" She sniffed with disdain worthy of royalty. "He called the two of us a pair of old publicity-hungry cranks and took himself off, the nasty little swine."

"Queensbury's near London. How did you happen to move to this godforsaken spot, Mrs. Coombs?"

"*Daisy,* my dear, if you please. Oh, that's part and parcel of it. Because the manifestations didn't leave with the reporter. They only got worse. Every stain, every smudge, every random pattern to be found in a household always seemed to mutate itself into the face of some famous personage or other under *my* roof. Why, it got so that Mrs. Jinks wouldn't stop by any more. Said she didn't fancy being stared at by the refreshments. I was that lonely. Still, I could have shouldered on, if not for the garden."

"What happened in the garden?"

"Child, what *didn't!* My indoor manifestations were all secular celebrities, but there is something about an English garden that is not entirely of this world. It began with the darker pebbles on the path tracing an angel. I thought it was the Archangel Michael, but before I could make certain, Paddington—that's my dear kitty—scrabbled over the part of the angel's image that might have been a dragon underfoot. You know how the Archangel Michael is forever trampling dragons. Well, it looked like an outsized slug when Paddington was done, the naughty moggie!"

She gave the cat in question a fond look. He turned up his nose at her, as any proper cat would, and she resumed her story: "Soon I had to get out Fox's *Book of Martyrs* and a good illustrated hagiography to help me identify all the saints and such who were appearing in the patterns of hedge twigs or the mottlings on my quince skins or the moss in my rockery. I dug nine of the Twelve Apostles out of the carrot bed before I became frightened and stopped. A body simply doesn't feel *right* about popping such things into the stewpot. Then my espaliered pear tree climbed over the top of the fence and Mrs. Jinks woke up one morning to behold a complete image of the Virgin Mary picked out in Forrest's

Early Golden Wonders. She's a *strict* Presbyterian, you know, with little use for popery in the best of times. She made my life impossible from then on. I had no choice but to move, and since one never can predict the religious quirks of one's neighbors, I thought it best not to have any."

"Don't you get lonely?"

"There are times I'd give anything for another human ear, but I make do. There's the lake, you know. When I'm feeling a bit narky, I go down to the water and I talk."

Daisy's guest frowned slightly. "To whom?"

"Oh . . . no one. It's not much of a lake, really: Deep, not too wide. When I first moved in, I had hopes of there being some wildlife about. Even an otter would make a good audience for an old woman's natter. I thought I spied one once—just the tail of one diving out in the middle of the water—but I never saw it again. I must have been mistaken. Too long seeing faces everywhere, I fancy. It's a comfort to see one that's real. Have a biscuit, dearie?" She passed the plate.

The younger woman helped herself to a chocolate biscuit and sipped her tea. She noted almost calmly that the scant few leaves in the bottom of the cup had still contrived to arrange themselves into a likeness of Winston Churchill.

At that moment of relative peace, the cottage door burst open with a tremendous crash. The cat jumped up, hissing, as the room filled with somber, white-robed men. Light flickered off the cruel edges of their ceremonial golden sickles, cast a dull glow over the burnished barrels of their less ceremonial, more utilitarian AK-47s. The fugitive rose to her feet, whimpering for mercy she knew would not come. Daisy Coombs loudly voiced her objections to this invasion of her home and was roundly ignored.

The old woman continued to rant and rail at the men as they dragged her whilom guest out of the house. The storm had abated and all the earth gave up the sweet scent of fertility. All but two of the toughs formed themselves into a broad-shouldered wall between Daisy and her unfortunate caller. That pair hauled the prisoner across the small patch of greensward in front of the cottage, not stopping until they reached the lakeshore.

They threw her down at the feet of yet another white-robed figure. She looked up and saw the once-loved, now feared and hated face, crowned with a garland of pure gold oak leaves. He was seated on a sort of portable throne, the gilt wood carved with forest creatures, surmounted by the figure of a horned man. In his hand he held a wand of rowan twined with holly and ivy. Behind him waited his bearers, holding criss-crossed carrying poles. The captive clutched the flimsy blanket tighter around her, eyes wide.

"Hmm," he remarked, surveying her present state. "Lost the sacrificial robe, I see. I never knew a woman to go through clothing like you. Well, what you have on will do."

"You're—you're taking me back to the bog." Only resignation remained in her voice.

"Oh, no." His smile was cold and perfunctory as he saw the momentary glimmer of hope light her eyes. "I couldn't ask the lads to trek back all that way. Besides, we've already served that bog with the guard lax enough to permit your escape. Any body of water is sufficient for the rite, if it's deep enough. This one looks satisfactory."

"I will *not* tolerate this wickedness!" Daisy shouted as two of the burliest men quick-marched a no longer struggling sacrifice to the shore. "That lake is mine, part of this property which I own free and clear, and I do *not* give my consent to anyone mucking it up with your nasty, foolish, vindictive rituals!"

"Be quiet, you daft old bat," one of the officiants growled. "I don't call any ritual foolish that does what it promises. Ever since we've gone back to the Old Religion, folks are seeing results from their worship, for a change. Never saw much of anything when things were C. of E."

"What did you want from your religion?" Daisy snapped. "A miracle delivered daily with the milk?"

"All I know is, we've been flinging folk into bogs and getting value for it. Things are looking up. And it *has* solved the Irish Question. If the old—I mean the *new* religion had anything going for it besides wind, why don't we get some sort of sign that we were wrong to pitch it, eh?"

"That's right, a sign," his mate agreed. "What sort of sign did your new—I mean *Old* Religion give to let you louts know you had the right sow by the ear *this* time?" Daisy inquired, waspish.

"Well . . . I got a job," the first man said. "Hadn't had one for donkey's years. And it'll take something mighty big to argue with *that*."

"Enough!" came the cry from the throne. "We must not

delay the ceremony any further." He gestured at the lake
with his rowan wand. "Let the gods be served!"

"*I'll* serve you something to chew on!" Age made Daisy
stoop awkwardly, but her scrawny limbs concealed wiry
muscles. She pried up a big rock from the lakeside mud and
threw it right at the golden oakleaf crown.

She missed.

The next thing she knew, her arms were pinioned behind
her by two more of the strongmen and she was hustled to the
water's edge. "Jobs," she said bitterly to the placid surface
of the lake. "Always jobs, jobs, jobs, and never a thought for
the impact they'll have on the blessed ecology. Mark my
words, some day you're all going to be sorry you thought of
your pockets first and your planet last."

"Stop your gob, grandma," one of her captors snarled.
"Else we'll chuck you in first and the lady after."

Daisy lifted her chin. "I should like to see you try."

So they did. They succeeded, what's more. The crone
made a lovely loud splash and sank. The younger woman uttered a cry of pity and horror.

"I apologize, my dear," the figure on the throne said with
a smirk. "But it *is* 'Age before beauty.' " His brittle smile
snapped on and off like a light switch. With a terse twitch of
the rowan wand he directed his henchmen, "Throw her in."

The men scooped her up in a chair-lift and took a few
warm-up swings while she kicked and screamed. She cried
her children's names, made a hundred promises to the implacable master of the rite, and finally called upon her God.

"Louder, please," her husband taunted. "It's a long way to
heaven. Perhaps He can't hear you. Or perhaps He's—"

The surface of the lake churned and bubbled. The men
holding the lady in their arms stopped swinging her and gog-
gled at the roiling waters. A huge curve of pure, sinuous
muscle broke into the sunlight. A head rather like a crocodile's topped a mud-brown scaly neck two storeys tall. Riding at around mezzanine level, a drenched Daisy clung to the
monster for her life.

"Hello, dearie!" Daisy called to her former guest. "Look
what I've found." The monster swiveled its neck to left and
right, beady eyes seeking some unguessable grail.

On shore, the white-robed men all shook like poplars in a
tempest. The guards dropped their guns, the throne-bearers
their poles. The men warding the sacrifice lost their grip on

their captive and dumped her on the bank, but the younger woman was, like them, too caught up in the shock of the moment to run. The only one seemingly unaffected by this prehistoric apparition was their king.

"You fools, we're not a pack of credulous cavemen now!" he thundered. "Pick up your weapons and shoot that abomination!"

The abomination under discussion pulled a few more yards of neck out of the water as the men scrambled to obey. They turned, guns to the ready, in time to see the creature extend itself still further, revealing an expanse of shoulder and—

"Mercy on us!"

"Lord in heaven!"

"Oh, my God!"

"Shit."

AK-47s thunked as they hit the ground for a second time. Knees thudded on impact with the shore as their owners dropped to them and began to pray.

For there, clearly picked out in an anomalous pattern of beige, tan, and tawny scales on the beast's dark brown side, was a Face they all could recognize and still remembered well. It was the Face they had seen from early childhood onward in illustrated Bibles, in stained glass windows, in the great works of Western Art, and on Christmas cards. It was a Face that brought back one of childhood's chiefest memories: That of being caught red handed and guilty as charged up to their elbows in a truly monumental *mistake*. More than a Face, to them it was a Sign.

Just in case they might need another, the monster darted its head forward and bit the king in two.

"No, thank you, Your Majesty," Daisy said. "I'm quite content here."

"But I assure you, the Palace apartments I have set aside for you are the best. You'll want for nothing for the rest of your life." The younger woman, far more elegantly dressed than during her previous visit to the lakeside cottage some six weeks ago, leaned forward to press her offer. "I'd have come back for you sooner, but there was that Religious Toleration Act to be passed first. It wasn't easy. We had to dredge up a whole new House of Lords."

The crone smiled and kept on knitting. "I want for noth-

ing. No, it's happy enough I am that you've honored me
with another call. Oh, and I must compliment Your Majesty.
I hear you are fulfilling your duties as Regent ably. I hope
the children are well?"

Her Majesty was a persistent woman. It was that quality,
among others, which had brought her so close to a boggy
doom. "*How* can you be happy in this wilderness? You told
me you were lonely."

"Oh, it's not so bad as all that any more, now I've got a
friend to chat with." Daisy nodded in the direction of the
lake. "Of course he doesn't say much, but he's an excellent
listener, and he's that fond of raspberry trifle! It's thanks to
him I make a tidy sum from souvenir sales, what's more.
And since Bertie won't show himself unless I call him—"

"Bertie!"

"I named him after my late husband. There is a marked
resemblance. As I was saying, since he only surfaces enough
to show the Face at *my* call, it's easy to control the tourist
and pilgrim traffic. Either they come when and in what numbers I choose, or they waste their time standing on the shore
staring at flat water. And rest assured, after seeing Bertie
they do *not* litter."

Her Majesty laughed. "Then I've worried about you need-
lessly. You have the perfect life."

"Well . . . there is *one* thing." Daisy frowned. The Regent
urged her to continue. "It's—it's silly, but—oh, it's probably
just an old woman's fancy. Still, the last time I took a really
good look at it—"

"A look at what?"

"The Face," Daisy said darkly. "Out there, on Bertie, what
all the papers are calling the Face of God. I think—I
think—I could be wrong, but—but—"

"Yes? Yes?"

"I think it's turning into the face of Elvis."

# Magnetic Personality Triggers Nail-biter's Near-death Ordeal!

## by t. Winter-Damon, Special Correspondent

*t. Winter-Damon has assumed so many different roles in the field of speculative fiction (and art!) that it's exhausting just to read about them. Fiction author, poet, reviewer, intreviewer, biographer, essayist, and illustrator, his work has been selected for five of DAW Books' The Year's Best Horror Stories collections, as well as appearing in* Amazing Stories, Fear, *Jane Yolen's* Xanadu 2, *among many others. He is also an illustrator for Ocean View Press' "Doubles Series."*

*With all that, I'm glad he was able to contribute the following story to this book.*

Local law enforcement officers and trauma personnel confirm reports 34-year-old Mr. Ferris Boyler of Perdition, Arizona is in guarded condition and recovering well after his night-long sky-ride of terror.

Questioned at his office in this small, sun-baked Western town, career peace officer, Sheriff Calvin O'Dell, states an almost-unbelievably bizarre series of events led to the lifelong Perdition local's near tragedy.

"I wouldn't've thought it was possible," O'Dell said, " 'less I'd've seen it with my own eyes. I was born in Missouri, and I'm sure you know what *that* means, Young Feller.... I been Sheriff here nigh on to thirty years, and I ain't never seen the like of it! It truly makes you believe there is a Savior, don't it?"

Reverend Xavier F. Dinwiddy echoed the Sheriff O'Dell's sympathies: "Praise the Lord for Mr. Boyler's Deliverance from the very jaws of Hell!"

When pried for further details of the miraculous event, the reportedly tight-lipped lawman O'Dell offered us this startling, exclusive interview.

"Well, I guess I've known Ferris since he was just a little squirt. And I guess you could say he's always been a little queer," the rugged law professional said, tipping the brim of his Stetson and cocking one bushy eyebrow meaningfully. "Oh, no, not one of them homer-sectionals, like them big cities is full of, mind ya', no offense, I mean just a bit *peculiar* in the head."

Asked for specifics, the six-gun-toting, veteran peace officer confided, "He eats all kindsa metal stuff, been doin' it since he was a just little sprat. Ferris was only six when his Daddy brung him 'round the station, showin' him Perdition's very own Matt Dillon, yours truly, yessiree. Anyways, I was a'holdin' that little shaver up to see them wanted posters on the wall, when he grabs my badge, pops it in his mouth, and gulps the sucker down! He nearly choked to death on it, too. Had to rush him down t' ol' Doc Bullfinch's. By the time we got him there, though, that sucker'd slid right down his gullet, slick as spit on a doorknob. Had one heckuva sore throat, though, by gum!"

Incredulous at this astounding insider revelation, we verified this with both Sheriff O'Dell and Mr. Boyler's childhood physician, the now-retired Dr. Otis Bullfinch. "Yes, yes, well, I don't want to betray any confidences, privileged information, patient's files and all, but, sure enough, that boy was always swallowing something he wasn't supposed to, then they'd bring him in, his parents, you know, with a godawful stomach ache, why that boy sure did love eating metal ... at first I thought it was an iron deficiency, but, no ..."

Dr. Doyle M. Culpepper, attending physician at Perdition's Mercy Hospital, confirmed Mr. Boyler's ferocious appetite for metal objects. "Mr. Boyler was admitted to Mercy Hospital, following a valiant rescue by our highly skilled trauma team, promptly reacting to a 911 call. Mr. Boyler was treated for shock and exposure symptoms, massive bruises, numerous cuts and abrasions, and was then X-rayed under my supervision. Subsequent examination and evaluation of the X-rays revealed, in addition to several cracked or separated ribs, a 68-pound mass of accumulated, extraneous metal objects." Overwhelmed by what he had witnessed, the

doctor continued, "This was definitely the weirdest
* * * *ing case of my entire career!"

When asked for a complete list of Mr. Boyler's stomach
contents, our exclusive medical contact revealed this com-
prehensive inventory: 43 keys of assorted sizes; literally
hundreds of pins, safety pins, needles, nails, paperclips,
screws, drapery hooks, and washers; 19 rings (including his
dear, departed mother's engagement and wedding rings); 97
ball bearings; $87.23 in spare change; a Bates stapler; a
2-pound ball of tinsel; 7 metal toy soldiers; 33 metal jacks;
4 watches (including a Timex that, amazingly, took the licking and was, as advertised, still ticking); 4 small magnets; a
six-place table setting of silver-plated, five-and-dime style
flatware; 3 crescent wrenches; a single pair of wirecutters; 4
pairs of pliers; a complete set of metric sockets; one tin star;
and the crumpled hubcap from a 1957 Chevrolet Bel Air.

An exclusive bedside chat with Mr. Boyler revealed a full,
first-person account of his astounding true story.

"It all started when I was takin' a shortcut home from the
store, you know, through Sutter's Salvage. There's this big
rip in the chainlink fence over on the side by the Canyon
Road arroyo. It's kinda hard to spot if you don't know it's
there, but I found it awhiles back, and I use it all the time.
Anyway, I was makin' a beeline through those stacks of
wrecked cars, and I passed right by that big old crane with
the 'lectromagnet on it. Well, I heard some kinda motor
a'hummin' away, and it shoulda been off, but I wasn't really
thinkin' 'bout nothin' 'cept gettin' home and havin' me
some supper.

"WHAM! Next thing I knew I was sailin' right up offa
the ground, and I went THUNK! Smack dab up against that
darn magnet. I was trapped there all night long, hangin' in
midair, starvin' and freezin' my keister off, if you'll pardon
my French!

"I was sure I was a'gonna die right there. I felt myself
floatin' up outta my body, and I was lookin' down on myself. I felt like I was tied to some kinda metal thread, you
know, like it was holdin' me to my body down there. Then
I felt it stretchin' like, and I just knew it was gonna pop, and
I'd never get back inside myself. Then I seen this here
bright, blindin' light and this here unearthly music, and I
knew I was goin' over t'the other side ... and I seen my
dear ol' Mother, bless her heart, and J. Edgar Hoover and

Tom Mix and Gene Autrey and Hank Williams, and Elvis in his white suit, all a'glowin' with this here white, blindin' light. Next thing I 'member, the sky was all turned to pink and gold fire, and I thunk to myself, By Gawd, Ferrous, you done made it t'Heaven!

"But it was just real early mornin', sunup, you know, and them medics saved me.

"Some folks think it t'was Elvin McMurty in his '47 Ford pickup out there, a'parkin' with some floozy and his lights shinin' in my eyes and some doggone Rock'n'Roll music a'playin' away, but I KNOW better! I seen the Gates of Heaven, and I KNOW there *is* a life after death after all!"

# They'd Never—
## by Harry Turtledove

*Harry Turtledove has a degree in Byzantine Studies which he puts to good (and highly entertaining) use in his* Videssos *series. Who better than he to make alternate history so riveting? Among his more recent works are* The Guns *of the South and, in hardback,* In the Balance, *which is the first book of a thrilling alternate history SF series. He has been a freelance writer for more than three years now, which he says "beats the living kapok out of working for a living."*

*Join him now to explore the tabloid newsman's ultimate experience.*

Mort Pfeiffer slung his jacket over the back of his chair, then plomped his ample bottom into said chair and turned on his computer. Another day, he thought gloomily. He looked around the office of the *Weekly Intelligencer.*

It looked like a newspaper office: other people dressed no better than he was sat around in front of screens and clicked away at keyboards. Those clicks made it sound like a newspaper office, too. It even smelled like a newspaper office: stale coffee and musty air conditioning with two settings, too hot and too cold.

But it wasn't a newspaper office, or not exactly. If the *Intelligencer* wasn't the trashiest supermarket and 7-Eleven rack filler around, the troops hadn't done their job for the week. "For this I went to journalism school?" Mort muttered.

He wished for a cigarette. The smoke would have made the place smell even more authentic. But the *Intelligencer* office had gone smokefree a couple of years before—it was either that or lose their health insurance. Besides, he was wearing a transdermal nicotine patch. Smoke while you had one of those things stuck to you and you were a coronary waiting to happen.

Behind glasses that were going to turn into bifocals the next time he got around to seeing his optometrist, his eyes lit up for a moment. Transdermal patches ... he might be able to do something with that. They were hot these days, and no more than three percent of the lip-movers who bought the *Intelligencer* were likely to have even a clue about what *transdermal* meant.

So ... the beginning of a headline formed in this mind, 72-point type, sans-serif, with an exclamation point at the end. TRANSDERMAL PATCHES CAUSE ...!

"Cause what?" he mused aloud.

Cause heart attacks if you're stupid enough to keep lighting up while you're wearing one? He shook his head. That wasn't scary enough. You didn't necessarily die from a heart attack, and if you did, it was over quick.

Cause cancer? That one was stale even for the *Intelligencer* (which was saying something). Besides, the whole idea behind nicotine patches was to keep you from getting lung cancer. Pfeiffer's ethical sense was stunted (*Would I be here otherwise?* he thought), but it hadn't quite atrophied.

Cause AIDS? He shook his head again. Something there, though. Suddenly, like striking snakes, his hands leaped at the keyboard. Letters flowed rapidly across the screen: TRANSDERMAL PATCHES CAUSE AIDS LIKE SYN-DROME! He knew just how to write that one up. When you took the patch off, you went through some of the same whimwhams you did when you gave up smoking (he'd call a trained seal of a doctor for the impressive-sounding quotes he'd need). And some of those whimwhams were enough like early AIDS symptoms to give the piece the germ of truth his editor liked.

Speak of the devil, he thought, because his editor came by just then, paused to see what he was working on, and nodded approvingly before heading off to the next desk. Don't think of Ed Asner as Lou Grant here. Katie Nelligan looked more like Mary Tyler Moore with red hair.

Mort sighed. If she hadn't been his boss, and if he hadn't had a well-founded suspicion that she was smarter than he was (although if she was all that smart, why did she work for the *Intelligencer*?), he'd have asked her out a year ago. *One of these days,* he kept telling himself. It hadn't happened yet.

Katie came back, dropped a wire service report into his IN basket. "See what you can do with this one, Mort," she said.

He looked at the news item. Kids in Japan, it seemed, raised stag beetles (not Japanese beetles, for some reason) as pets. Then they'd put them up on round cushions two at a time to see which one could grab the other by the projecting mouthparts and throw it off. They'd just chosen a national champion beetle.

"Jesus Christ," Mort said. "Sumo-wrestling bugs!"

"That's just the slant we'll want on it," Katie said. She nodded again—twice in one morning, which didn't happen every day. "Can you give me a draft before you go home tonight?"

"Yeah, I think so," he answered. What was he supposed to tell her?

"Good," she said crisply, and went on down the aisle between desks. Mort looked back at her for a couple of seconds before he returned to his computer.

He discovered he'd forgotten what he was going to write next about the transdermal patches. No wonder, he thought. Sumo-wrestling bugs—Lord, that was enough to derail anybody's train of thought. Bullshit about patches and the truth about bugs ... "Hell of a way to make a living," he said under his breath.

Nobody glanced over at him to see why he was talking to himself. People at the *Intelligencer* did it every day. Nobody, but nobody, was ever a bright-eyed, eager eighteen-year-old getting himself ready for a hot career writing for a supermarket tabloid. It wasn't a job you went looking for, it was a job you fell into—generally from a great height.

"If I weren't Typhoid Mary, I wouldn't be here," Mort said, again to himself. He'd worked for four different papers in three years, each of which went belly-up within months of hiring him. The jobs had disappeared, but his rent and his car payment and his child support hadn't. He'd been here five years. Whatever else you said about it, the *Intelligencer* wouldn't go broke any time soon. What was that line about nobody going broke overestimating the stupidity of the American people?

A guaranteed regular paycheck—yeah, that was one thing that kept him coming to the office every morning. The other was something he hadn't thought through when he'd taken this job: now that he'd worked for the *Intelligencer,* no *real* newspaper would ever take him seriously again.

He saved the patch story, got to work on the sumo-wrestling stag beetles. He took a certain perverse pride in the way he reworked it to fit the *Intelligencer*'s style:

breezy, breathless, no paragraph more than two sentences long, no words more than three syllable if he could help it. Besides, Katie'd given him a deadline for that one, and he always met deadlines.

He was just heading into the wrapup when the lights went off.

"Oh, shit," he said loudly, an editorial comment echoed and embellished all over the office. When the lights went off, so did the computers. Mort hadn't saved the stag beetle story as he worked on it, so it was gone for good. He'd have to do it over from scratch, and doing it once had been once too often.

Besides which, with the power gone, the inside of the *Intelligencer* office was black as an IRS man's heart: no windows. The publisher, three floors up—he had a window, and one with an ocean view. The peons who did the actual work? They got peed on, as their name implied.

Katie Nelligan's voice cut through the chatter: "Does anybody have a flashlight at their desk? There's supposed to be an emergency kit in here somewhere, but we haven't needed it for so long, I've forgotten where."

No flashlights went on. Mort didn't even have a luminous watch. He just sat at his desk, figuring the only thing he was likely to do in pitch darkness was stumble over somebody's chair and break his fool neck.

Wouldn't that be a great way to go? If a network correspondent cut himself shaving while he was covering a war, he turned into a national hero overnight. But if a tabloid reporter killed himself trying to get out of his office, he might make page seven on the inside section of the newspaper. Having his passing altogether ignored was a hell of a lot more likely.

Somebody else did get up, and promptly tripped. Feeling smugly virtuous, Mort stayed put.

Then, all of a sudden, he could see again. Standing in the doorway were four slim, manlike shapes, each glowing a slightly different shade of bluish green. All together they put out about as much light as a nightlight.

"Give me a break," Mort said. "Who's the practical joker?" Slim, glowing aliens were as much an *Intelligencer* hallmark as no funnies was with the *New York Times*. He'd written at least half a dozen stories about them himself. They all contradicted one another, but who kept track?

"I'll bet I know who did it," Katie Nelligan said: "San

Levy at the *News of the World.*" The *News of the World* specialized in aliens, too, generally warty yellow ones; Levy, who held down Katie's job over there, was a notorious prankster. Katie turned to the glowing quartet. "Okay, boys, you can knock it off now. We're wise to you. How about turning the lights back on, too?"

The four guys in the alien suits (Mort thought of them as John, Paul, George, and Ringo, which does a good job of dating *him*) didn't answer. One of them—George—started walking up toward the ceiling. There weren't any steps, but that didn't bother him. He just went up and up, as if the air were solid beneath his feet.

A couple of people broke into applause. "Hell of a special effect," someone called.

Mort gaped along with everybody else. It *was* a hell of a special effect. He would have been impressed seeing it on a movie screen. Seeing it for real, live and in person, was ... unbelievable. You could put somebody in a suit that made him look like a freeway emergency light, yeah, but Mort knew for a fact that the ceiling didn't have any wires in it. Which left—what? Antigravity?

"Holy Jesus," he said hoarsely. "Maybe they *are* aliens."

The chorus of derision that brought down on his head couldn't have been louder or more scornful at an Air Force UFO debunking unit. People who worked for the *Intelligencer* wrote about aliens, sure, but they weren't dumb enough to believe in them. That was for the yahoos who bought the paper.

Then the fellow in the suit up by the ceiling pointed an (inhumanly?) long finger at Katie Nelligan. He didn't keep a flashlight in his fingernail, *à la* ET, but, with a startled squawk, Katie floated slowly off the floor and up toward him. "Somebody do something!" she yelped.

Mort sprang up, sprinted down the aisle, and grabbed her around the waist (he'd fantasized doing things like that, but not under these circumstances). He tried to pull her back down to Mother Earth. Instead, she rose higher and higher—and so did he.

He let go of Katie as soon as his feet left the ground, but that was too late. Up he went anyhow, toward the—well, if he wasn't an alien, he'd do until somebody showed up with Mars license plates.

About halfway to the ceiling, Mort remembered that once

upon a time he'd been a pretty good reporter, and here he was, floating up to the biggest story in the history of mankind. "Get a camera!" he yelled at the top of his lungs. "We've got to have pictures!"

"Oh, good for you, Mort," Katie exclaimed. "God, we'll sell fifty million copies and we won't even have to make anything up." No matter that she'd been captured by aliens and was probably heading for a fate worse than taxes—she worried about the *Intelligencer*'s circulation ahead of her own.

Down on the ground, first one flash camera and then another started going off, strobing away until the office reminded Mort of nothing so much as a psychedelic 60s dance. Had the aliens smelled like pot smoke, the illusion would have been perfect, but they didn't smell like anything.

Only after he shouted for a camera did Mort stop to wonder whether the aliens would mind having their images immortalized in the *Intelligencer*. If they had minded, things might have turned decidedly unpleasant for the person on the wrong end of the Nikon. But they didn't seem to care one way or the other.

Then he wondered if anybody kept a gun in his desk or her purse. He didn't think the aliens would be able to ignore bullets like flash photography. If anybody was toting a piece, though, he didn't open up. That removed one of Mort's worries.

A bigger, more urgent one remained: now that the aliens had Katie and him, what would they do with them? The beings the *Intelligencer* featured were always looking out for humanity's best interests, but how likely was that really? Was a species that could invent pasturized processed cheese food product worth saving anyhow? Mort had his doubts. Which left—what?

The first thing that sprang to mind was *experimental animal*. That was a long walk off a short pier. Number two was *zoo specimen*. That might have its moments if they tried to establish a breeding population with him and Katie Nelligan, but in the long run it wasn't much better than number one: medium- to long-term insanity as opposed to instant anguish.

He flapped his arms and kicked his legs in midair, none of which changed his trajectory a bit. Whatever the aliens were going to do to him, he couldn't stop them.

His feet were still within grabbing distance of the ground, but when somebody—he didn't see who—made the same sort of run at him as he'd made at Katie, one of the aliens who'd remained by the doorway held up a hand like a traffic cop and his would-be rescuer bounced off an invisible wall. Pictures the aliens didn't mind; they wouldn't put up with anything more.

The one floating up by the ceiling—George—made a come-hither gesture to Mort and Katie, who duly went thither. The closer Mort looked at George, the less he looked like a human being, or even a *Star Trek* makeup job. For one thing, his head was too small. Making a head look bigger than it really is wasn't any great trick, but how did you go about shrinking one unless you were a South American Indian?

Nose, ears, mouth—details were all wrong: nothing you couldn't manage with makeup on any of them, maybe, but why would you? Besides those come-hither qualities, George's fingers had a couple of extra joints apiece. He had no nipples. Farther down . . . well, Mort was damned if he'd let a makeup man do that sort of thing to *his* family jewels.

And if George wasn't an alien, what was he doing up here by the ceiling, and how had he gotten Katie and Mort up here with him? Mort's gut had needed a little while to catch up with his brain, but now he believed all over.

The alien extended the middle finger of his left hand toward him, the middle finger of his right toward Katie. Mort wanted to flip him off right back, but didn't have the nerve. George's finger touched the center of his forehead. He'd expected blazing heat. Instead, it was cool.

After that—the only person who understood what happened to him after that was Katie Nelligan, and only because it happened to her, too. He felt his brains getting systematically emptied and copied, as if he were a floppy being backed up onto an enormous hard disk. Everything he remembered, from the Pythagorean Theorem to losing his cherry under the football stands in high school, got sucked up and flowed out through the alien's finger.

So did things he'd never imagined his brain retained: what he'd had for breakfast five years ago last Tuesday (two eggs over medium, wheat toast, grape jam, weak coffee); what his father had said when, sometime under the age of one, Mort spat up on the old man's best suit (not to be repeated here, but prime, believe me). *Amazing,* he thought, and hoped he'd keep one percent of what the alien was getting.

Even more amazing, though, was the backwash he got, as if a few random little documents from the hard disk snuck onto the floppy while the floppy played out onto the hard disk. Some of them came from Katie: the smell of her corsage on prom night, a sixth-grade spelling test where she'd missed the word *revolutionary,* what cramps felt like, and a long-distance call to her sister in Baltimore the spring before.

And some of those little documents had to come from George the alien: using those peculiar private parts in the manner for which they were intended, what felt like a college course on how flying saucers or whatever they were worked (which would have been worth a mint, and not a chocolate one, if Mort had understood the concepts), the taste of fancy alien food (by comparison, that ever-so-ordinary breakfast seemed nectar and ambrosia).

Mort also picked up a few impressions about what George thought of mankind. In two words, *not much.* He went about his job with all the enthusiasm of an Animal Regulations officer counting stray dogs around the city dump, except an Animal Regulations officer might actually like dogs.

The alien didn't like humans. Mort could think of a lot of reasons why benevolent aliens wouldn't like humans: they were busy polluting their planet; they fought wars; they discriminated on the basis of color, gender, sexual preference, and the size of your bankroll. If any of that had been in the backwash from George, Mort would have been chastened but not surprised.

It wasn't. George felt about humans much as a lot of nineteenth-century British imperialists had felt about the peoples they ruled: they were wogs. They were ugly, they smelled funny, they had revolting habits, and, most of all, they were *stupid.* George's view of what humans had in the brains department was somewhere between a badly trained dog and what that badly trained dog was liable to leave on your front lawn when it went out for a walk.

Given that George was currently pumping him and Katie dry of everything they'd ever known, Mort had to admit that, from his point of view, he had a point. But if George was a benevolent alien, he devoutly hoped he'd never run into one in a lousy mood.

All of a sudden, he was empty. The inside of his head seemed to be making the noise a soda straw does when you're still sucking but the soda's all gone.

A few more impressions backwashed into the sodaless expanse between his ears. One was a mental image of two scared-looking rubes in hunting gear getting the same treatment he was undergoing now. *I'll be damned,* he thought. *They weren't making it up after all.*

The second was a flash of alien mentation: *As long as we have to do it, this is the perfect spot for the survey. They'd never—* He never found out who *they* were or what they'd *never.* The document was incomplete.

George turned to his buddies by the door. He wiggled his ears. Mort didn't know what that meant, but the rest of the green-and-glowing Fab Four did: job's over for today. They went out the door. They didn't bother opening it first.

The floating alien looked from Mort to Katie and back again. Mort got the idea that if it had been up to him, he'd have dropped them both on the floor, ker*splat.* But maybe he had a supervisor watching him or something, because he didn't. He floated them down the same way they'd come up, only faster.

As they were descending, George went down the invisible stairs he'd gone up before. He left the *Intelligencer* office the same impossible way his colleagues had, except he left his nether cheeks on *this* side of the door for a couple of seconds while the rest of him was already on *that* side.

"Jesus," Mort said. "The moon from outer space."

Katie laughed—hysterically, sure, but can you blame her? Mort couldn't see what anybody else was doing, because the room was dark again now that the nightlights that walked like men had gone.

Then the lights came back on. It was as if that broke a spell; for all Mort knew, maybe it did. People started jumping and hollering and running to the door (but not through it) to find out if the aliens were still in sight. Mort didn't run to the door. Having seen the aliens more up close and personal than anybody but Katie Nelligan, he didn't want to see them again.

Katie said, "Whoever was taking those pictures, get them developed this instant, do you hear me? This instant! Don't leave the shop while they're being processed, either—wait for them right there."

That got three people out of the office. Mort glanced down at his watch, wondering how long he'd floated by the ceiling. What he saw made him blink and exclaim, "Katie, what time do you have?"

She looked at her watch, too, then stared at him, bright blue eyes wide with surprise. "It felt like we were up there for an hour, not a couple of minutes." She pointed to the wall clock. "But that says the same thing. Weird." She was not the sort of person to let weirdness overwhelm her; that was one of the reasons she was editor and Mort, older and arguably more experienced, just a staff writer. "We'll do drafts of the piece right now, while we still remember everything. When we're done, we'll compare notes. This one has to be *perfect.*"

"Right." Mort all but sprinted for his computer. He'd never imagined being in the middle of a story like this. *Woodward and Bernstein, eat your hearts out,* he thought as he hit the keyboard.

He plunged in so hard and deep that he started violently when Katie tapped him on the shoulder. "I just wanted to say thanks," she told him. "That was brave, what you did."

"Oh. That. Yeah. Sure," he said. "Listen, why aren't you writing?" Katie laughed softly and went away.

The next thing Mort remembered apart from words flowing from his mind to the computer was the pictures coming back. For that he was willing to get up from his desk. He'd expected something would go wrong—they'd be fogged, or black, or something. But they weren't. There was the alien, doing the mind-probe on him and Katie while all three of them floated in midair. There were the other aliens by the door. Shot after perfect shot—it was just a matter of picking the best ones.

"We've got 'em," Katie said. Everybody nodded.

Five o'clock came and went. Mort never noticed. Neither did Katie. Finally, at about half past six, she printed her story. Mort said, "I'll be done in just a few minutes." He pulled his sheets out of the laser printer when he was through, then said, "We both must have run way long. Shall we," he hesitated, then plunged, "compare and cut over dinner?"

She gave him not the wary, thoughtful look he'd expected, but a sidelong glance and half a smile, as if she knew something he didn't. "All right," she said. "Let's go to Napoli. It's right down the street, and we have a lot of work to do to get this the way it has to be."

They went through each other's stories alongside lasagna and Chianti. Time on real newspapers had made Mort sharp at writing lean and tight; he boiled away a quarter of Katie's piece without touching the meaning at all.

She attacked his differently, looking more at what it said than how it did the saying. About halfway through, she looked up and said, "Backwash? That's a good way to put it. I felt it, too. I wondered if you had. But somebody reading the piece is going to need more explanation than you've given it here." She scribbled a note in the margin.

Over spumoni ("To hell with the waistline; today I earned it," Katie said), each looked at what the other had done. Most of Katie's comments asked for more detail here, less there, and made Mort's story more tightly focused and coherent. He tipped the cap he wasn't wearing. "Thanks. This'll help."

"I like what you've done with mine, too," she answered. "It's a lot crisper than it was. We make a pretty good team."

"Yeah." Mort beamed. He'd had just enough wine to improve his attitude, not enough to hurt his thinking.

Katie dabbed at her lips with a napkin. "Now let's get back to the office and hammer 'em together."

Mort almost squawked, but he didn't. What did he have to go home to? An empty apartment and celebrity dog wrestling on ESPN? Real work, important work (something he'd never imagined at the *Intelligencer* till now) was more important than that, and the company better. He took out his wallet, tossed bills on the red-and-white checked tablecloth, got to his feet. "Let's go."

"Hey, I was going to pay for mine," Katie said.

He shrugged. "I'm not broke, and I'm not trying to take advantage of you. If you want to buy for both of us one of these days, I'll let you."

She gave him that funny sidelong look again, but rose from the table without saying anything more. The night watchman scratched his head when they went back to the *Intelligencer* officer. "You folks don't usually work late."

"Big story—a real 'Hey, Martha!' " Katie said solemnly.

"Yeah?" The watchman's eyes lit up. "Does it have Madonna in it?" When Mort and Katie both shook their heads, his shoulders slumped in disappointment. "How can it be a big story if it don't have Madonna in it?"

They went inside without answering, then settled down to work side by side. A couple of hours later, sheets slid into the laser printer tray, one after the other. Mort scooped them up, saying, "Let me go over these one more time. I've been using a computer for ten years now, but I still edit better on hard copy."

"Yeah. Me, too." Katie read over his shoulder. They each made a last few changes, then printed out the altered pages again. This time Katie took them from the printer. She slid them into their proper places, made a neat little pile of the story, and stuck a paper clip in the top left corner. "It's done."

"Wait," Mort said. "Let me have it for a second." He took it over to the xerox machine, made two copies. "I'll take one of these home, and I'll stash the other one in my desk—just in case."

"In case the aliens come back, you mean?" Katie said. He nodded. She went on, "I don't think it'd help, but it can't hurt, either. First thing tomorrow, I go upstairs and lay this," she hefted her own copy of what they'd done, "and the photos on Mr. Comstock. If he says no, I quit."

"Me, too," Mort said. Some things, by God, *were* more important than a job.

Katie yawned. "Let's go home. It's been a long day."

"Boy, hasn't it just?"

Everyone in the *Intelligencer* office stared nervously at the door through which the aliens had departed. Mort wasn't anticipating their return; like the rest of the tabloid crew, he was waiting for Katie Nelligan to come back from her conference with the publisher. She'd been up there a long time.

The door opened, which proved it wasn't the aliens coming back. Everyone jumped all the same. In stamped Katie, looking the way a Fury might have if she were Irish instead of classical Greek.

Mort could find only one reason for her to look like that. "Mr. Comstock won't go for it?" he exclaimed in dismay.

"Oh, no. He will. We lead with it, next week's issue." Katie bit off the words one by one. Little spots of color that had nothing to do with rouge rode high on her cheeks. "But he doesn't believe it. He doesn't believe us."

Cries of outrage echoed from walls and ceilings. "What does he think, that we made it up to sell his stinking papers?" Mort yelled. "We'll all go up there and tell him—"

"No, we won't. I told him the same thing, and he said we'd regret it if we tried." Katie's scowl grew darker. "And yes, that's just what he thinks. On the photos, he thinks he spotted the wires holding us up in the air."

"Jesus!" If he hadn't already been starting to bald, Mort would have torn his hair. "There weren't any goddamn wires!" The memory of yesterday's terror flooded back, sharp as a slap in the face.

"I know that as well as you do, Mort," Katie said. "So here's what I've got in mind: we're going to pretend we don't care what Mr. Comstock says. We'll put this out the right way, and people *will* believe it."

The staff sprang to work with the fire and dedication mutiny can call forth. They threw themselves at the story with the dogged, fatalistic courage of English infantry climbing out of their trenches and marching into German machine-gun fire at the Somme. Mort was astonished at what some of the people—men and women whose total illiteracy he would till now have reckoned a boon to mankind—could do.

"You know, Katie," he said when the editor walked by, "this is gonna be a 'Hey Martha!' to end all 'Hey, Marthas!' *Everybody* will want to read it."

"I think you're right. And we've got a real Freddie Krueger of a picture on the front page to grab 'em and pull 'em in." She bristled. "I had to stop Comstock from using the one that looked right up my skirt. That man!" She clenched her fists till the knuckles whitened.

Mort looked at his watch. It was getting close to five. "Do you want to drown your sorrows in another bottle of Chianti?" he asked.

She'll say no, he thought with the automatic pessimism of a man who'd been through a divorce and taken a few knocks afterward for good measure. But she said yes. And after a truly Lucullan feast at Napoli (or Mort thought so, anyhow, but he was too happy to be objective), she went back to his apartment with him. The mess it was in proved he hadn't expected that. If it bothered her, she didn't let on.

Afterward, still on the disbelieving side but happier—*much* happier—than he had been at the restaurant, he ran a hand down the smooth skin of her back and said, "What made you decide to—?" He let it hang there, so she could ignore it if she wanted to.

She gave him that I-know-something-you-don't-know look again, the one he'd seen on her face when he asked her to dinner the day the aliens came. It stayed there long enough that he thought she wasn't going to answer. But she did, if obliquely: "Remember the backwash?"

"Huh?" he said, but then, realizing what she had to be talking about, he went on, "From the alien, you mean? Sure. What about it?"

Katie hesitated again, then said carefully, "I didn't mean just from the alien. Bits came from you, too, just like you got bits from me. And one of them happened to be ... how you feel about me. It's hard to be sure about a man—I suppose it's hard for a man to be sure about a woman—but this time, I didn't need to have any doubts. And so—" She leaned forward on the rumpled bed and kissed him.

Absurdly, he was jealous. He'd gotten bits from her, sure, but nothing like that (as far as he was concerned, the prom corsage didn't count). The one he remembered most vividly had come from the alien, that contemptuous *They'd never* that broke off unfinished.

From what had happened since, Mort was beginning to think he knew who *they* were and what they'd *never,* but he didn't tell that to Katie. He might have been wrong—and even if he was right, what the hell could he do about it?

If you went into a market or a convenience store a few weeks ago, you probably saw the *Intelligencer* on its rack, jammed in there with the rest of the tabloids. You probably took at look at the front page photo, shook your head, and walked on by to get your beef jerky or pipe cleaners or whatever it was you needed.

And even if you plunked down your eighty-five cents and read the whole piece, odds are you just took it in stride. After all, a tabloid'd do anything to sell copies, right? *You'd never* believe in aliens, would you?

Katie cried when the story went belly-up. The late-night talk-show hosts didn't even take it seriously enough to make jokes about it. Mort wasn't surprised. The green-and-glowing guys had known just where to take their sample, all right.

But don't think this is a story without a happy ending. Mort and Katie are getting married next month. They still have a lot of planning to do, but they've agreed on one thing: the wedding won't be in the *Intelligencer.*

# Loch Ness Monster Found—in the Bermuda Triangle!
## by David Vierling

*David Vierling is a new writer who lives with his wife and son (and an inordinate number of edged weapons) in Virginia, where he is active in several medieval reenactment groups. Many local supermarket clerks were bemused when he told them that he was reading the tabloid headlines as research. In his own words: "I got a Bachelor of Science degree in Journalism for this?"*

*It's his first professional fiction sale, so perhaps that makes it all right.*

"How was your flight from Glasgow, Mister . . ."

"McLochlan. Nestor McLochlan," the enormous, scaly, kilt-clad visitor replied, handing the customs officer his passport. "Nessie to me friends. The flight 'twas bonny, save that some haggis-brained American bairn kept bashin' me o'er the head wi' a pillow an' chantin', 'Na the Momma! Na the Momma!' "

The customs officer shook her blonde head. "Those Americans." She ran the passport under a scanner. "Purpose of your visit?"

"Vacation. Relax, play a wee bit o' golf, get some sun. Ye canna' know what a treat 'tis for a cold-blooded individual t' lie in the sun!" He took off his hat and sunglasses as he answered. "I've had it wi' the rain, the fog, the annoyin' wee fish and their annoyin' wee fish comments, the paparazzi scullin' around the Loch in their rent'd coracles, cameras a-clickin'. I need a break, lassie, a chance to go somewhere and be a tourist, instead of a bloody tourist attraction."

The customs officer glanced up from the form she'd been filling in. "Yeah. Vacation. Right." She squinted at the passport, then said, "If you don't mind my saying so, this is a terrible picture of you. It's out of focus, kind of misty and indistinct. Why, it could be a bunch of floating logs, or a pile of seaweed. Almost anything."

"I dinna photograph verra well," he told her. "I've ne'er seen a clear photograph o' me'self what wasn't a hoax, perpetrated by charlatans to beguile the gullible."

"Well, we can't all be photogenic," the customs officer replied, flashing a puzzled smile. She stamped the passport and returned it. "Welcome to Bermuda, Mister McLochlan." She did a double take. "Say, aren't you . . . Dino, from *The Flintstones?* My children love that show! Especially the way you always went 'Yip! Yip! Yip!' when Fred came home! Could you do 'the Dino bark' for me? Just one Yip? Please?"

"No. Sorry. Lar'ngitis," he thundered over his shoulder, jogging for the exit.

A group of Japanese tourists began pointing at Nessie and whispering excitedly to each other. He paused, pivoted to face them, and began, "I pray ye, dinna tell anyone ye have recogniz'd me! I'll get nary a moment's rest, if word gets oot."

As one, the tourists turned and ran, screaming, "Godzirra! Godzirra!"

Bewildered, Nessie grabbed his bags and jumped onto the hotel shuttle.

The overweight, balding desk clerk at the Atlantis Hotel handed Nessie a key. "We've prepared our best suite for you, Mister McLochlan," he said, then leaned close and whispered, "You can trust our staff to be discreet, sir. Many celebrities come here under assumed identities to unwind." He winked, then rang for a bellhop. Nessie smiled. Now this was more like it!

The Elvis Presley Suite was impressive, including seven televisions and a loaded revolver. Nessie tipped the bellhop, but the boy seemed reluctant to leave. "Aye, laddie?" Nessie rumbled.

The bellhop looked down at his hands. "Well, sir, it's against hotel policy, but, uh, could I have your autograph?"

Nessie rolled his pool ball-size eyes and reached for a pad

of Atlantis stationery. "Ach, the obligations what come wi' bein' a celebrity!"

The bellhop fairly vibrated in place. "I always loved your show. Wait till my family hears that I actually met Cecil the Seasick Sea Serpent! Are you still friends with Beanie, or is it true you two had a falling out?"

Quickly, Nessie scribbled 'To a fellow with a brain the size of a walnut, sincerely, Cecil' on the pad, shoved it into the boy's hands, and shoved him out the door.

Nessie needed a drink. He exchanged his kilt for a pair of baggy tartan shorts and headed down to the bistro overlooking the hotel's pool.

Seating himself around an outdoor table, Nessie ordered a Scotch and water. The waiter returned with the drink, his beaded dreadlocks swinging as he walked. "What else can I be gettin' ja, mon?" he said. "Would ja like to be trying some sushi, mon? We make it fresh here, ja know."

"I dinna think so," Nessie said, sipping his drink. "I came here to ge' away from fish! Bring me a Caesar salad, please."

The waiter returned a few minutes later with the salad. He cocked his head to one side and said, "Don' I be knowin' ja from somewheres, mon?"

"I dinna think so, laddie."

"Sure, mon, ja be the Crocodile from *Peter Pon*. So, tell me, mon, what do a Pirate's hand taste like?"

"Ye're lucky I'm an herbivore, laddie," Nessie growled, briefly wondering what a waiter's hand might taste like.

Nessie hurriedly finished the salad, gulped his drink, and made his way to the pool. He stretched himself across several lounge chairs.

As he lay there, feeling warm and dry for the first time in about a hundred years, he noticed a pretty, freckled woman with red hair eyeing him. She got up from her deck chair, careful not to disturb the two plaid-suited goons snoring on either side, and made her way over. "Excuse me," she began, "But aren't you . . ."

"No!" Nessie thundered. "I am na' a Teenage Mutant Ninja Turt'l, nor am I Earl Sinclair, Barney the Dinosaur, nor any oth'r cute, friendly character from American television! I canna' get ye discount tickets to *Dinosaurs Alive!* I am . . ."

"The mysterious and terrifying Loch Ness Monster," she said quietly.

Nessie's rather prodigious eyes bulged, then he smiled. "That I am, lassie."

"You're much more handsome than I'd realized from the pictures."

"Ach, I dinna photograph verra well."

She smiled, showing some very pleasant dimples. "I sometimes wish I could say the same." Again the dimples. "But you're going to burn if you don't get some sunscreen on that lovely, scaly hide of yours, Mister Ness."

"Call me Nessie, if ya like."

"Nessie, then. And I'm Sarah."

As Sarah reached for the sunscreen, Nessie noticed a paparazzi's camera peeping at them from out of the bushes. Shooting the photographer his most threatening, awe-inspiring, ear-to-ear grin, Nessie leaned back to enjoy Sarah's ministrations, thinking, Ach! The obligations what come wi' bein' a celebrity! 'Tis a shame his pictures will be blurry.

*Duchess of Windsor Photographed in Poolside Romp! Fergie Snapped Rubbing Sunblock on Mystery Figure in Bermuda!*

# Racehorse Predicts the Future!
## by Josepha Sherman

*Josepha Sherman's books include* A Strange and Ancient
Name, Castle of Deception (*cowritten with Mercedes
Lackey*), A Sampler of Jewish-American Folklore, Windleaf,
Rachel the Clever, *and* Child of Faerie, Child of Earth. *She
has also sold over ninety short stories and articles.*

*A charter member of the Editorial Horseplayers' Associ-
ation (board meetings are held at Belmont Racetrack), she
has yet to hear a horse accurately predict the future.*

*Maybe at Aqueduct . . . ?*

It was all the alien's fault. I mean, I hadn't done anything so
terrible, just borrowed a little money from the company. It
was such a miserably run business no one ever noticed the
cash was gone. And it wasn't as though I wasn't going to
pay it back!

It wasn't as though I didn't have a good reason for what
I'd done, either. After all, when you've been scraping along
for years, aching to own your own thoroughbred—hell, your
own racing stable!—and yet being stuck with the only
horses you can afford, cheap claimers, the sort that'll go bad
if you just look at them the wrong way, you'd jump at the
chance to buy a really good colt, wouldn't you? Even if it
meant bending the law just a little.

Anyhow, thanks to that . . . well, let's call it a loan, I
found myself, for the first time in my life, the proud owner
of a *real* racehorse, Sunny Boy, three-year-old winner of his
first two starts. Yeah, they'd been allowance races, in
nobody-much company, but he'd shown promise. And
damned if he wasn't going off as second favorite in his first
attempt in stakes company.

So far so good, right? But the day before the race things
got weird. There I was, hanging on Sunny Boy's stall like

any other hopeful owner, staring at the colt, which wasn't returning the favor.

Then all at once his ears shot up and he turned to stare at me.

And so help me, Sunny Boy spoke.

"You are the human who owns this beast?"

It wasn't a trick. There wasn't anyone around who could have been casting his voice or whatever they call it. And the colt's lips had moved, just like some all too real remake of *Mr. Ed!* His voice had sounded just as funny as you'd expect; a horse isn't made to speak human. But I'd understood him.

"Uh . . . yeah," I said, very carefully. "Sunny Boy . . . ?"

"No, no, no, you miss the point! I am *not* this beast, I am *in* this beast!"

Oh, great! My first shot at a good horse, and it turned out to be possessed! "Wh—what are you?" I stammered, wondering how you got a horse exorcised. "Some kind of demon?"

"No, you foolish *human,* I am an *alien!*"

"From outer *space?*"

"Of course from outer space, you *threznit!* I am . . . what you would call an explorer."

"Oh. Sure. Where's your saucer?"

"Saucer . . . ?"

The voice was cut off as Sunny Boy calmly snatched a mouthful of hay. Apparently not minding being inhabited, he stood chewing for what seemed an endless while.

"Come on, horse!" I told him. "Swallow!"

Sunny Boy wasn't impressed. He finally did swallow, but then took a leisurely drink of water. At last he raised his head from the water bucket and the alien was able to continue:

"By 'saucer,' you mean a space vehicle? Yes? I didn't come here in a vehicle. Such things are far too slow and expensive. No, when I explore, I send my . . . call it my consciousness out across time and space, and take up residence in an intelligent host so I may make observations."

"Sunny Boy is *intelligent?*"

The alien sighed. "Hardly. This animal has but three thoughts in its mind: running, eating and . . . and something else."

I could have sworn the voice was blushing. "Something else?" I asked, and light dawned. "You mean sex? Hell, I should hope so!" The average three-year-old colt has the sex drive of your average healthy teenager. And with any luck, Sunny Boy had a productive stud career ahead of him once he was done with racing. "Never mind that. If you were trying to land in an intelligent . . . uh . . . host, how did you—"

"I made a mistake! Strong, basic emotion interferes with the process. And this animal was—well he was—"

Just then a handler went by, leading a sleek young filly. Sunny Boy let out a downright lascivious whinny and kicked at his stall till she was out of sight.

"You see?" The alien voice sounded very weary.

I snickered. "I get the picture! You were in the wrong place at the wrong time, and this sex-mad equine dragged you right in."

"Exactly."

"And every time the colt gets a horny thought in his head he scrambles your thoughts, right?"

"More or less. Worse, the longer I am stuck in here, the more difficult it becomes for me to escape. I do not wish to end up as part of an animal's mind! Human, you must help me!"

But my own mind was racing like a sprinter. "First you've got to tell me more about yourself. I mean, if you can travel through space like that, you've got to have all sorts of weird mind tricks."

The alien paused. Sunny Boy blinked thoughtfully at me. "You humans would think so, yes."

"Like what?"

You ever see a horse shrug? "I can tap into the mental patterns of others' thoughts—"

"You can read minds?"

"Not without permission! It just isn't polite."

"Oh. Right." A courteous alien. What next? "What else can you do?"

"I can foresee the outcome of certain events that—"

"Wait a minute. Are you saying you can predict the future?"

"Only to a limited extent." The alien sighed. "Being stuck inside this beast means I can only see what he and his fellows are going to do within a short time-frame."

"Oh, my God," I said with true reverence. "You can predict races."

"The outcome of those running contests. Oh, easily. But what—"

"Look, I'll help you, honest. But—but you've got to help me first. First of all, you can't let anyone else know you're here. We ... uh ... we're a very suspicious race, and if you say anything to anyone but me, they might try to ... uh ... destroy you."

Would he buy that? It seemed like something out of a bad SF movie to me, but then I wasn't some alien explorer stuck in a horse's mind!

"I—I see!" the alien gasped. "I had no idea this was such a perilous world! Thank you, human. You are a true friend."

"Sure. Now, about this race-predicting thing ..."

Well, he might have come from the across the galaxy, but my alien friend wasn't too bright about some things. Like the idea of money. I had to concoct a story about the gathering of cash being part of a religious rite I had to fulfill (hell, that wasn't so far wrong!). Until that rite was completed, I told him, I couldn't possibly help him escape. And the best way to accumulate that sacred green ...

He really *could* predict the outcome of the races. Sunny Boy never did quite manage to win a stakes race, but thanks to my alien tout's tips, I started cleaning up at the track on other horses.

After a while, though, the thrill wore off just a bit. I found myself thinking after every win that I had enough now, I had better set about repaying that "loan" before someone thought to try balancing the books. And I really should help the alien find a way out of Sunny Boy's mind before it was too late. But ... well ... you know how it goes.

And then one day it all started to fall apart. As I went up to Sonny Boy's stall, the alien whispered:

"You said you'd help me!"

"I will."

"*When?* I can't wait much longer! Every day I start thinking more like a horse ... and I ... it ... I am starting to enjoy it!" Sunny Boy shook himself vigorously. "You've got to get me out of here!"

"I said I will. When ... uh ... when the time is right."

"I can't wait for the time to be right!" Sunny Boy pinned his ears and glared at me. "You—you're doing this on purpose, aren't you? You *can't* help me!"

"That's not true."

"Isn't it?"

"Shh! Someone's going to hear you."

"I no longer care! If you will not tell me the truth, I will learn it for myself!"

Before I could move, I felt a cold little *something* winding its way into my mind. Just as quickly it was gone, and the alien was gasping, "So! Not only are you a liar, you are a thief as well! A stealer of the sacred cash! Did it not matter to you that without that cash this company you robbed will fail?"

I muttered something about stupid business deals and if they couldn't manage their money, they didn't deserve to keep it. But the alien wasn't buying any of that.

"And you've been using me to help you steal still more!" he shrilled. "Well, the thieving ends now!"

"I told you to keep it down! They—"

"I no longer care if others hear me! Someone must learn you are a thief! Help! Somebody, help!"

Well, what could I do? Fortunately, mares do come into heat regularly, even at the track, and fortunately there was just such a mare being walked nearby. No one saw me slip the bolt on Sunny Boy's stall—and no one had to tell Sunny Boy what to do with his freedom! A mental cry rang in my head:

*"No! You can't do this!"*

"Sorry, pal. I've already done it."

Judging from the rush of emotion Sunny Boy and the mare were releasing, I'd heard the last of my alien friend. Too bad! But I'd already gotten a good amount of cash out of this whole business. And he ... well, maybe he'd enjoy being part of a stallion's mind!

I heard one last, despairing mental shout:

*"Traitor! Thief! I'll get you for this!"*

Then there was silence, save for the happy squealings of two oversexed horses.

Well, you can imagine the threats of suits and countersuits that followed, particularly since the mare turned up pregnant after her brief fling. But nobody could prove that fling had been anything but an accident. Besides, the mare wasn't exactly a world-beater. She'd been at the end of her not very distinguished racing career anyhow. And even if Sunny Boy wasn't a world-beater either, his breeding was nice enough, and pretty close to that of the stallion her owner had had in mind for her first mating. After he'd thought it over a little, said owner agreed he didn't mind saving on stud fees.

And it didn't hurt either of us that the man was enough of a realist to play up that "trackside romance" for all the publicity it was worth. Eleven months later, he even invited me and a whole slew of reporters to see the birth of Sunny Boy's first foal.

Of course I went. Why not? I didn't have anything to fear from reporters. The company I had "borrowed" from had quietly gone bankrupt, just as my alien pal had announced, and at this stage of the game it didn't look like anyone was ever going to uncover my little "loan." After all, aside from the alien, who knew about it? And the alien was long gone.

Mares foal quickly. Soon Sunny Boy's first offspring was lying sprawled on the straw, being licked dry by his loving mamma. As we watched and the reporters' cameras whirred, the foal struggled to his long, awkward legs. He took a good, long drink of mare's milk.

Then all at once the foal tensed. His ears shot up and he turned to stare at me.

And to my horror, he gave me a slow, deliberate wink.

*No! Oh, no, it can't be. He's gone, he* has *to be gone!*

But for the first time it dawned on me, really dawned I mean, that the alien had truly *been* an alien, a creature I didn't really know anything about. Hell, I didn't even know what he looked like!

Not that it mattered now. Feeling like someone caught in a nightmare, I watched the foal stagger his way over to the reporters. With one sharp, gleeful glance my way, he smiled at them, actually smiled. And in the next moment I knew it was all over.

"So boys," he said clearly, "have I got a story for *you!*"

# Printer's Devils
## by Gregory Feeley

*Gregory Feeley is the author of a science fiction novel,*
The Oxygen Barons, *as well as numerous stories and articles in American and British magazines. He wishes us to know that the following story "represents . . . his first attempt to be funny."*

In the aching stupor of his fever's second day, Cliff Penn found himself drifting past bizarre mental landscapes, inchoate memories prompted by the Golden Oldies channel his clock radio had been playing all afternoon. Too weak to rise and silence the plastic box, Penn let its low-fidelity stream wind through his consciousness, leaving deposits that strangely colored his efforts to turn his thoughts to the problems at hand:

### DADDY TAKES T-BIRD AWAY!
"Fun" Still Possible, Singer Vows

### TEEN ANGEL "STILL CAN'T HEAR ME"
Tearful Lover Goes Public After Seance Scam

### "CHAPEL IN THE PINES" DESTROYED IN STORM!
Lightning Struck Again and Again and . . .

### DOG BARRED IN AKC SCANDAL
Pedigreed Champ "Ain't Nothing But . . ."

Late in the afternoon the phone rang. The alacrity with which his phone machine cut in suggested that it had already fielded a few calls, which Penn couldn't remember. He turned his head toward the living room as the radio noise softened—it was during the instrumental bridge in

"Michelle"—and heard Louise's voice crackle through the speaker.

"Hey, Cliff, you still sick? We've really got some problems here. Call me tomorrow—tonight, if possible.

"And change your outgoing message. Jee-zus."

Penn confusedly tried to recall his tape greeting while wondering what new problem had arisen, but McCartney's resumed crooning scrambled any chance of pulling off this tricky maneuver. Had it been an actual emergency, he concluded by way of abandoning the effort, Louise would doubtless have shown up at his door.

Ninety minutes later the doorbell buzzed.

"You look like shit," Louise observed when he got the door open. She brushed past him, leaving a folded newspaper in his arms. Penn shook it open, guessing by its size that it wasn't the *Tribune* or even *The Reader*. The glassy stare of what appeared to be a newt gazed up at him beside a vertical caption that read: ALIENS SEED LAKES WITH ELVIS EMBRYOS.

"This is awful," he said, following her into the kitchen.

"You're damned right." She was dumping wet coffee grounds into his crowded sink. "Manning had to edge those letters by hand before sending it to production."

Penn looked back at the headline. The 130-point letters, white on a gray field, lacked the black trim that would lend them the crisp immediacy they required. He thought muddily on this. "So this is just a proof, right? Is that what you're telling me?"

"You didn't think we'd go to press like that, do you?" Louise located the tiny bag of coffee in the freezer, began pouring them into the percolator cup, then stopped and gave him a disgusted look when she saw that the beans were unground. She pulled the grinder toward her, filled it, and depressed the button. The macerating whine bored into Penn's consciousness like a dentist's drill.

"Louise, don't scare me." A wave of dizziness swept over him, and he sank into the kitchen chair.

"I want you scared." Louise plugged in the assembled percolator, looked around for a second chair, and made a face. "I thought the page-imposition software would take care of that."

"Page imposition is something else entirely." Writing for

the *Alert* had given Louise a facility with terminology that Penn found unnerving: she needed only to sound authoritative. "I'll be in to look at it tomorrow."

"I think you should come down tonight." Louise had gone into the living room and found the beanbag chair. Penn rose with an effort and went after her. "They'll be doing Mountain States and Pacific in about three hours."

The *Weekly Alert* had editions for different parts of the country, which varied mostly in their advertising. The only edition ever to use different covers was a short-lived Southern one, which had occasionally run headlines like *Lost Confederate Stronghold Routs Tax Agents*. "I don't think new copy in the Classifieds page will strain the present system," he said.

Louise shrugged. "Suit yourself. I thought you might want to get in a few hours today, since hourly consultants don't get sick time."

Penn winced. His year as a free-lancer, sans pension, sans benefits, had left him in the financial straits of an office temp. He would indeed not be paid for the last two days.

"We're talking a few lines of code," he said. "I'll find it tomorrow and fix it."

"Printer's devils," said Louise, studying her fingertips. One of them evidently had powdered coffee on it, for she licked it carefully.

"Eh?" Following a conversation with Louise was like pursuing a speeding car that could swerve faster than you.

"Isn't that what they call those tiny programming errors?"

"Glitches, they're called glitches." Louise was in the kitchen, rattling among the stacked cups. Penn realized he must have faded away for several seconds.

"Printer's devils were apprentice printers, back in the last century," he called. Raising his voice made his sinuses ache.

"And that's what publishing software is, right? The menials who run copy to the editors, align the type, and check pagination?" Louise had returned with two steaming mugs, one of which she handed to Penn.

"Um. In a way, perhaps." Penn took a long sip. Louise had added milk generously, probably her way of reminding Penn that he lacked the grit of real newspapermen, but he was happy for it.

*"Printer's Devils Haunt Newspaper Office,"* she said.

"Lingering spirits drift through morgue, crying, 'Nixon Resigns!' "

"Not bad," he said, "but it won't make the cover."

"Screw that," she said. "I'm on salary."

Penn winced.

Later that night, stuporous from too much sleep, Penn draped a blanket over his shoulders, sat down at his workstation, and loaded the *Alert* program. He got to the mode he called Headline Maker, typed in the headline Louise had brought, then maneuvered it into place. He hit *P,* then pushed his chair back on its rollers and pulled the emerging sheet from the laserjet.

The page looked fine. This suggested that the problem lay in the way the software was interfacing with the printing system, which Penn could not investigate from home. Idly he entered a few more headlines, setting them up in different styles and point size.

### ROCK STAR PALS WITH WINO BULLFROG
#### "Good Friend" Drinks Until Unintelligible

### ROLLER SKATER FLATTENED IN BUFFALO DISASTER
#### Knuckle Down, Buckle Down, Rest Unidentifiable

He put the last into nice three-dimensional letters that the *Alert* would never use, shifted it to a luridly cross-hatched German Gothic, then got out of the system. On a whim, he set the modem so that it could receive material from the office, then left the machine on. If he found himself unable to put in a full day, he could send stuff home ahead of him.

Three aspirins and a glass of orange juice, and Penn was back in bed, shivering beneath a lasagna of blankets and quilts. He had turned down the radio during a mid-afternoon bathroom trip, but had forgotten that it clicked on automatically between eleven and twelve to lull him to sleep. Fitfully dozing by that hour, Penn found his dreams invaded by a coxcombed Elvis in his smoldering mid-twenties though attired in a sequined jumpsuit, asking hopefully whether his beloved ex was miserable in her solitude. Sitting near the stage, Penn couldn't see the color of Elvis's shoes, but made a joke to his unsmiling companion that the design of the jumpsuit looked like hound's-tooth.

The fever broke an hour later, leaving him drenched on the rock shore of consciousness. Sweating beneath his load of blankets, Penn wondered why he had been thinking of Elvis.

Grossmere Publications occupied only two floors of a grimy building in a light industrial park, but Penn was required to show his digitized photo ID to the security guard in the lobby. "What would happen if some one you never knew came up with a valid-looking ID?" he once asked. He knew what happened when someone the guard knew perfectly well discovered he had left his ID at home.

"Wave 'em in," the guard replied laconically. At $5.30 an hour, he didn't weigh factors when following his simple instructions.

The doors of the freight elevator banged open directly onto the reception area, where a middle-aged secretary glanced up suspiciously before returning to her phone call. "No, I can't connect you with any of the writers," she was saying. "No, I can't take a message, either. Our policy does not permit us to put calls through to our staff."

Penn leaned over and looked into the pigeonhole where memos and messages were left for casual employees. He pulled out a slip summoning him to the production manager.

"Someone want to tell Angela about the UFO in his back yard?" he asked as she hung up.

The woman shrugged. "Could have been her dentist," she replied.

Donald Rabin disliked Penn, who stood outside the hierarchy that governed business at Grossmere. Unlike temps (who were the lowest of the low), Penn's absence from the organizational chart made him difficult to place; his hourly rate was not much lower than Rabin's own, but he supervised nobody and could be dismissed without risk of Grossmere hearing from Worker's Compensation. As such, his presence affronted Rabin, who disliked people anyway.

"Your system's giving me problems," Rabin said as Penn came in. On Penn's first day Rabin had warned him not to "give me problems." Every complication or delay that happened in the office was routed through Rabin's first person singular, a syntactical perspective Penn regarded as malignantly narcissistic.

"I'm on it, Chief," said Penn. "I'll talk to Manning right now."

Rabin glowered at him, a truculent water buffalo who suspected provocation but couldn't locate its source. As he opened his mouth, the phone rang. "What is it?" he demanded into it as Penn departed.

Bert Manning, peering down over a draft table, saw Penn and straightened. "I know, Louise told me," called Penn, forestalling discussion. He sat at the monitor and brought up the system, which unfolded at his command to disclose screens of serried code. As he studied its intricacies, his head began to throb.

"Cliff? I've got a question." Manning was standing behind him.

Penn was staring at the screen. "Does this concern Headline Maker?"

"No, it's the Elephant Girl."

With a sigh, Penn saved his screen and got up. Tall and disheveled, Manning gave the impression of a man who had never got over a late growth spurt that had pushed his wrists beyond their cuffs and thrust his gleaming scalp up past his fringe of hair. He led Penn to his cubicle and, pointing in a manner that somehow permitted him to thrust out an elbow, indicated the problem.

The Elephant Girl gazed out from Manning's VGA monitor, more hapless than design intended. Her proboscis had been shaded on one side and given an arrestingly grainy texture, but the bridge of an unmistakably normal nose still showed between her sad-clown's eyes.

"I can put the trunk *over* it," said Manning fretfully, "but I can't erase it and leave the trunk where it is."

Penn picked up the mouse. "Watch," he said. He had installed this system for a plastic surgeon last year. Deftly he removed the features between the waif's eyes, then demonstrated the palette each window offered. "I take it you want her to look appealing except for the trunk?"

"Of course." Tentatively Manning took the mouse and restored a bit of eyebrow. "She's had a rough life."

Penn left at 3:30, shivering in his ski jacket. "You know, you're supposed to drink lots of fluids when you're sick,"

Louise had said as she watched him refill his mug, "but coffee's a diuretic. You're drying yourself out as surely as if you were drinking sea water."

"I seem to remember you writing that the problem with coffee was the Peruvian mountains where the beans were grown had been bombarded with radiation from sun spots." Penn drank and grimaced.

"Well, that too. Maybe you'll wake up tomorrow with super powers."

Not likely. By the time he got home, Penn had swollen nodes under his arms and a throat that ached when he turned his head. The orange juice seared his flayed membranes, and the aspirins went down scratching like mountaineers sliding down a slope. The radio had turned itself on during the afternoon, out of apparent loneliness, and was waltzing through Easy Listening hits of recent years.

> *"There never was a time*
> *Can this be true*
> *When I didn't love*
> *Anyone but you . . ."*

Call a doctor, Penn thought as he crawled into bed. And for my friend the radio, a copy editor.

It was dark when Penn awoke, and he steered to the bathroom by the blinking light of the fax. Returning through the living room, he stared at the sheet that hung like a dog's tongue off the side of the table.

It was a cover for the *Alert*. The headline, properly edged this time, cried: SCHMUCK GIVES BIRTH TO NESSIE. The photo showed a man, face contorted in fear or pain as a coiling sea serpent (recognizable from a cover some months back) exploded out of his backside. The man, on closer view, was recognizably Penn.

"Ha, ha." Penn turned on the desk lamp and held the fax under its beam. The photograph was of newspaper quality, and bore no visible signs of digital tampering.

He found the cordless phone and called the *Alert* to leave a message for Louise, but got tangled in the labyrinths of its voice mail system, which demanded that he punch in certain combinations but didn't allow him time to return the phone to his ear before reciting the next set of instructions. Disoriented and frustrated, Penn stumbled back to bed and set the phone on the adjacent pillow, where he could reach it after resting a moment. Its jarring trill awoke him to streaming sunlight and a headache that speared him the instant he opened his eyes.

"*Penn?*" He hadn't found the phone yet, but his startled fumblings seemed to have switched it on. "*What are you, dead or something?*"

"I think so." He freed his hands of the sheets, found the phone under the headboard, and raised it upside down to his ear. "Who's this?" His voice emerged an agonized croak, unwell past any chance of imposture.

"Jesus Christ." It was Hakluyt, Rabin's assistant. "Did one of your enemies put a curse on you?"

"What enemies?"

"Huh. I'll tell Dan you're not coming in today. You free-lancers get major medical?"

"Wait—let me talk to Louise."

"Our policy does not permit us to put calls through to our staff." Click.

Louise showed up at seven with a pint of egg drop soup. "What the hell was that message you left me?" she demanded, pushing past him. "I couldn't understand a word."

"I left a message?" Penn followed her into the living room.

"Something about the cover. I brought you a copy, by the way." She handed Penn a folded *Alert*. Penn glanced at the embryo cover bemusedly, then began to page idly through the issue. When he looked up, Louise was looking at the fax on the desk.

"I gather you were talking about this." Her mouth quirked as she held the fax to the light.

Memory returned in a rush. How muddled could he be, to forget that? "I want to know who did it."

"Don't be such a snot." Louise lit up, inhaling with pleasure, then studied the fax. "Looks like the photo software works."

"Manning, or one of his staff. I'll kill him."

"Just drink your soup." She rustled through the paper bag and came up with a plastic spoon, which she tossed toward him. It landed on the open pages of the *Alert*, below a photo captioned, "Onlookers stare as holy statue weeps real tears."

"Look at this." One of the crowd figures was Penn, mouth stupidly agape.

Louise whistled as she lifted the page. Underneath, a follow-up story on the Siamese Triplets offered a one-column photo of the strange creature. Its middle head (the misshappen one that never spoke) now bore a supercilious expression that strikingly resembled Penn's.

"I'll sue." He found himself shaking, seized by a palsy that might have been indignation or illness. "It's an open and shut case."

"A good way to get yourself blacklisted by your biggest client," Louse remarked. "Let me look at this."

She took the remains of the paper from Penn. "I see a definite and two maybes," she said at last. Penn, carefully sipping soup, wanted to see, but she lifted the paper beyond his grasp. "Get your ass in bed," she said.

Not asleep yet dreaming, Penn experienced an inversion in the thermoclines of thought, the dark chill of a nightmare whelming up into the warmer currents of languor. The formless threat was his persecutor, as Penn recognized even then, but it was also the specter of unemployability, an inky shape that combined professional failure with rent arrears and swarmed after him with directed malevolence. He came wholly awake with heart hammering, knowing the danger near but unable to move his limbs.

Something was playing on his phone machine. He sat up, wild with surmise, then hobbled out of bed. At the door he could hear it: a discordant crash of music, two songs playing simultaneously, one of them "Love Me Tender." By degrees the other grew louder, finally drowning out the love song. It was Blue Oyster Cult playing "Godzilla."

Now what the hell did that mean?

Louise called at six. Penn had gone to the community health clinic several hours earlier, where he was told he had a nasty strain of flu and wasn't taking care of himself. Fearful of waiting messages, he had disconnected both fax and phone machine before venturing out. Now he snatched up the receiver from the bedside table where it stood warbling like a singing shrunken head.

"Get down here," she said. "Take a cab; you don't sound like you'd survive the subway."

"I don't think I could afford it, either."

"Save the receipt. I think Grossmere can spring for this." Penn rode in muffled to the ears, like Proust in the back of his limousine. Louise met him at the elevator. Arms folded, she studied him speculatively, as though musing on more than his pallor.

"Show you something." She conducted him to her cubicle, where dozens of *Alert* covers—NAZI SUB FOUND IN LOCH NESS; BIGFOOT TURNS VAMPIRE—lined the fabric partitions. The monitor glowed green with the office system's main menu.

"I was noodling through some of the format categories— not my usual pastime, but any writer might have occasion to do it—when this popped up." Louise tapped a series of keys, entering a possible combination of options, and a box suddenly appeared at the center of the screen.

> DO YOU HATE CLIFFORD PENN?
> *Would You Like to Fuck Him Over?*
> If So, Hit Alt D!

Penn stared at this, eyes goggling. After a moment he reached out his hand, then drew it back. "What does Alt D get you?" he whispered.

Louise shrugged. "Nothing. Maybe whatever treasures it offered also contained instruction on how to delete it afterward. A text file could include that, yes?"

Penn nodded, ashen. He reached out and depressed Alt D. The box disappeared.

"I don't think your software likes you," Louise said.

He sank into the chair, unable to speak. From behind the monitor, a 90-year-old Hitler seemed to be leering.

"Anyway, I talked to Bert, who took it to Grossmere." Louise exited the system and turned off her machine. "Blew his top—he's putting a stop to it. Not out of concern for your feelings, of course, but because such abuses could really get him sued someday."

"I could sue," said Penn in a small voice.

"I wouldn't advise it. Take what leverage this gives you— Grossmere wants you to add security measures now—and keep the rest to yourself. If you brought a legal action, they would find out about that little message, which must have been in the software you brought from your last job. You wouldn't want that to come out, would you?"

He shuddered.

Louise stood and took him by the elbow. "Let's get you

out of here," she said. "You won't get the new job done if you're on the critical list."

Leaning against her, Penn was conducted back to the elevator. Plastic day-glo dinosaurs perched atop the office partitions snarled as they passed, and an abominable snowman Halloween mask, hung on the wall like a hunting trophy, seemed to follow him with its eyeless gaze as he left Editorial.

"You're not really a bad sort," Louise was saying, "just not right for this kind of place." She put him into the elevator and waved as it closed. "Keep watching the skies," she said.

Snow was blowing against the lobby's glass door as Penn pushed through into the night. Bigfoot, take me now, he thought as the wind stung his face. Lead me to your eyrie atop the Sears Tower, where the light of your fire will call down the saucer people to take me to the land of rum coladas with paper parasols.

The cab that found him was playing "Werewolves of London" over the roar of the heater. Louise had a story in production about werewolves, Penn remembered woozily. Doubtless his software would be used in preparing the photo. Manning would search his image library for a picture of Lon Chaney or some circus freak to use as a rough model. Would Penn's ID photo ever be tracked down and purged from this digitized Devil's Island?

"My software is full of devils," he told the cabbie.

MAN TRAPPED IN TABLOID'S COMPUTER!
Distorted Image Peers from Pages, Crying "Help!"

"Sympathy for the devil," the cabbie said. And immediately the song came on.

# Cannibal Plants From Heck
## by David Drake

*Even though he's written many different kinds of fantasy
and SF very well, David Drake is perhaps best known for his
military SF, such as the excellent* Hammer's Slammers *series. "Cannibal Plants From Heck" is a bit of a departure
for him, which he claims he wrote because he had to do my
bidding. Ha! While getting my name legally changed to She
Who Must Be Obeyed, I recommend you read and enjoy this,
and be careful where you shop.*

Betsy Moffett stood beside her father in the gravel driveway,
judging the house with nine-year-old eyes. Behind them the
real estate agent rummaged in the trunk of her BMW.

It wasn't a large house: one story and forty feet wide by
twenty-four deep. There were only two of them now, so that
was all right. The three dogwood trees in front had gnarled,
low-branching trunks four to six inches in diameter. Betsy
had never before been close to a tree she thought she could
climb.

In back were a rusty swing set and a length of old telephone pole. The bare, trampled soil around the pole showed
that it once had mounted a net and backboard. A new set
couldn't cost *very* much, and Betsy had a birthday coming in
July.

The agent found what she wanted, a thin cap reading
UNDER CONTRACT in blue letters on white. She walked over to
the realty company's white-on-blue sign, careful because of
the soil's March squishiness, and clipped the cap into place
to hide FOR SALE.

Note: this story owes a debt of sorts to my mother; and of another sort to
Carl Barks, who in WDC&S #214 made the situation more amusing than it
had seemed when I was living it.

There were children playing down the street. Betsy couldn't see them from where she stood, but voices rose and fell in shrill enthusiasm.

The other houses in the subdivision were pretty much like this one. Some had brick facades, some had decks; but none of them were very large, and Mr. Moffett's four-year-old Ford fit in much better than the agent's sparkling BMW. The agent had mentioned the well and septic tank in a hurried voice quite different from that in which she described the house as *so cute, a little jewelbox!*

A horse-drawn wagon turned the corner at the end of the block and plodded down the street. The driver was a shabby-looking black man; a large dog walked beside the horse with its head down. Betsy had never seen a real horse-drawn wagon before. She was surprised to notice that it had rubber tires like a car instead of the wooden wheels like the ones on TV.

Neighborhood dogs barked. Several kids appeared on fluorescent bicycles and swooped around the wagon. The driver waved to them.

The agent returned to the Moffetts. For a moment as she glanced toward the wagon her face had been without expression, but the professional smile returned an instant later. "Charles," she said, extending her hand to Betsy's father, "I'm sure you'll be very happy here. Let me know when you've decided on the lender and we'll set up the closing."

She shook hands firmly. Her fingernails were the same shade as the cuffs and collar of the blouse she wore beneath the jacket of her gray suit.

"And, Betsy," the agent added as she took Betsy's hand in turn, "you're going to have a wonderful time, too. Look at all the children to play with!"

The bicycles now lay on their sides in the front yard of a house three doors down. A group had coalesced there to chalk markers on the concrete driveway. The kids ranged from older than Betsy to an infant whose elder brother pushed the stroller.

"I'll be talking to you soon!" the agent said brightly as she got into her car. The BMW's door thunked with a dull finality.

The black man guided his horse to the side of the road, out of the way. The agent backed with verve, then chirped her tires as she took off toward town.

Mr. Moffett put an arm around Betsy's shoulders. "This is my chance to garden," he said. He gestured with the glossy catalogs in his other hand. Those on top read White Flower Farm and Thompson & Morgan, but there were several more in the sheaf.

"Your mother would never let me garden, you know," Mr. Moffett went on, surveying the yard with his eyes. "She ridiculed the whole idea. Well, I'm going to prove how wrong she was."

"Whoa, Bobo," murmured the black man.

The Moffetts turned. The wagon halted directly in front of the house. It was full of live plants. Instead of pots, the root balls were wrapped in burlap. Most of the plants were in flower, and the blooms were gorgeous.

"Dad, can I play with the horse?" Betsy asked as she skipped toward the animal without waiting for what might have been a negative answer.

"The mule, missie," the driver said. "Bobo's a mule, and just the stubbornest mule there ever was—"

He winked toward Mr. Moffett.

"—but he's on company manners right this moment."

Bobo eyed Betsy over the traces. The mule's head was huge, but he looked friendly in a solemn, reserved fashion.

"That's Harbie," the black man said, nodding toward the dog who sniffed the mailbox post meaningfully, "and I'm Jake."

"Can I touch Bobo?" Betsy asked, her hand half extended.

"You surely can, missie," Jake said. To Betsy's father he went on, "Might I interest you in some plants, sir? A new house ought to have flowers around it, don't you think?"

Betsy rubbed the white blaze on the mule's forehead. One of Bobo's long ears twitched and caressed her wrist. Harbie trotted over, sat at Betsy's feet, and raised a paw for attention.

"Well, I'm going to be gardening, yes," Mr. Moffett said. He waved the catalogs. "But I'll be getting my stock only from the best nurseries. I—what *are* these plants? I don't think I recognize any of them."

"They's flowers, sir," Jake said. Betsy couldn't tell how old he was. Older than her father, anyway. "I grows them because they's pretty, is all. I've got bushes up to the house, if you'd like something bigger."

"No, I . . ." Mr. Moffett said. He glanced doubtfully at his catalogs, then back to the wagonload of plants. "Are those Hemerocallis so early?"

"There's daylilies, yessir," Jake agreed. "The tall ones, there, and they's some smaller ones around back as would make a nice bed along the street here."

Harbie rolled over on her back and kicked her legs in the air. Her weight pinned Betsy's right toes warmly. Betsy squatted to rub the dog's belly. The mule snorted.

"Those are eight feet *tall*," Mr. Moffett said, staring at the dark green stems from which brilliant red flowers spread.

"Yessir," Jake agreed. "But they's short ones, too. Would you like something for the new house, then?"

Mr. Moffett looked again at the catalogs. To Betsy, the illustrated plants seemed dim and uninteresting compared to the variegated richness in the back of the wagon.

"No thank you," Mr. Moffett said abruptly. "I prefer to trust certified species. Betsy, come along. We need to get back to the apartment."

He reached decisively for her hand. Harbie rolled to her feet and wagged her tail as Betsy straightened.

"Good day to you, then, sir," Jake said. He touched his cap and clucked to his mule.

Mr. Moffett didn't get into the car immediately after all. Instead, he continued to watch the wagon clopping down the street.

"What an odd man," he said.

The lustrous flowers nodded from the back of the wagon.

When Betsy ran up at the head of a delegation of five children, Mr. Moffett was loading a cart with washed stone from the pile the truck had deposited at the end of the driveway.

It was a clear day; even at ten in the morning the June sun was hot. Mr. Moffett nonetheless wore his new gardening apron. The pockets glittered with tools: clippers, hedge trimmers, a planting dibble, and a set of cast-aluminum trowels with a matching spading fork.

"Dad!" Betsy cried. "Stepan's mom says we can take the backboard off their garage and bring it over to *our* pole so it can be regulation height!"

The rest of the children waited behind Betsy, viewing with interest the work Mr. Moffett had already done in the yard. Except for the driveway itself and a narrow walk, the area between the house and the street was now a flowerbed. Irises, tulips, and the daylilies which Mr. Moffett always called Hemerocallis predominated, but there were many more bulb plants that Betsy didn't recognize. Perhaps some of them would have been familiar under other names, but as Acidanthia, Zantedeschia, and similar sounds they could have been tribes of the Amazon.

The climbable dogwoods were gone, chain-sawed off flush with the ground. Near where they stood, Mr. Moffett had planted what he called Cornus Alba Elegantissima—which looked like dogwoods to Betsy, only very spindly. The saplings had to be guyed in three directions to hold them straight.

"Pole?" Mr. Moffett said. He looked doubtfully at the group of children.

Betsy glanced over her shoulder to make sure the other children were staying in the driveway as she'd warned them to do so that they didn't threaten the plantings. Everybody was fine.

Jake and his wagon clopped down the street. Harbie walked ahead of Bobo with head up, stepping in a sprightly fashion. Jake raised his cap in salute when he saw Betsy.

Mr. Moffett noticed the wagon also. "Does that man live around here?" he asked with an edge in his voice. His eyes were on Stepan, the only black in the present group.

"No, sir," Stepan said, holding himself stiff. "But my mom, she buys his flowers sometimes."

"We buy flowers, too!" said Muriel, who was only six.

"You know the pole, Dad," said Betsy, determined to get the discussion back on course. "In the back yard. The people who lived here before took the backboard when they moved, but Stepan's mom says we can move theirs and have it regulation height!"

"Oh, that pole," Mr. Moffett said. He rubbed his forehead with the back of his hand, looking serious. "Ah."

The car was parked in the street because the driveway was full of gardening supplies. Besides the peanut-sized washed stone for drainage at the bottom of pots and flower beds, there were pallets of bagged topsoil and other bags marked ORGANIC PEAT MOSS—but with a stenciled cow to indicate the real contents more delicately than DRIED COW-FLOP would have done.

Mr. Moffett had said he would carry the temporary excess

to the metal storage shed he'd built at the back of the property, but he hadn't gotten around to it yet. The five-horsepower rototiller that had dug the front lawn into flowerbeds was in the shed already, parked beside the powerful chipper/shredder that had ground up all but the lower trunks of the dogwood trees with an amazing amount of racket.

Betsy was a little concerned that her father hadn't bought a lawn mower among all the other new equipment. She was afraid he'd decided that there wouldn't be any lawn left when he was done with the yard.

"We can get it right now, Dad," Betsy pressed. "You don't have to help. The bolts are still up in the pole, and we can borrow Lee's father's ladder. You can go on digging."

"I'm sorry, darling," Mr. Moffett said. He sounded at least uncomfortable if not exactly sorry. "*That* pole is part of my plan for the garden. I'm going—I'm preparing right now—to plant Ipomoea around it. So that the vines can climb properly."

"Whoa, Bobo," Jake muttered out in the street.

Betsy glanced sideways so that she didn't have to look at her father for the moment. He wouldn't meet her eyes anyway. He never did at times like these.

Roses twined up the wrought iron posts which supported the rain-shield over the front door. The window to Betsy's bedroom was a green blur from the potted fern which Mr. Moffett had hung there to catch the natural light.

"Good day, sir," Jake called. "I guess you're going to raise some tomatoes."

Harbie snuffled the back of Betsy's knees. Betsy turned quickly and bent to pet the dog. Harbie's tail waggled enthusiastically, whopping all the children as they crowded around her.

"No sir, I don't intend to raise vegetables," Mr. Moffett said stiffly. "I'm concentrating on flowers and flowering shrubs, so if you're selling tomato plants—"

"Not me, sir," Jake said with a chuckle. "But if you don't plan to raise tomatoes—"

He nodded toward the bags of 'organic peat moss.'

"—then did you tell the cows?"

"Can we get the backboard, now?" Muriel demanded.

"Yeah, what did he say?" Stepan said.

Mr. Moffett grunted angrily. "I don't care to buy any of your plants," he said. "Good day."

"You said," Jake said from the seat of his wagon, "that you were going to plant morning glories around the pole in the back, sir. I've got some fine morning glories here myself."

"I'm quite satisfied with my Purpurea Splendens, thank you," Mr. Moffett said, taking a brightly colored seed packet from an apron pocket. "They have a delicate lavender—"

He stopped. Even the children gaped at the size of the trumpet-shaped blooms Jake held up for approval. They were pure white and at least eight inches across.

Mr. Moffett swallowed. "Lavender picotee, I was saying," he concluded weakly.

"If you want purple edges, sir," Jake said agreeably as he leaned farther back into the loaded wagon, "then I got them, too."

The flower he raised on a vine trailing back into the mass of root balls and foliage was ten inches in diameter. As Jake had said, the edges of the broad bell were faintly lavender.

Mr. Moffett stared at the picture on the seed packet in his hand. "No," he said. He sounded angry. It seemed to Betsy that her father was afraid to look directly at the black man's obviously superior bloom.

"No!" Mr. Moffett repeated. "I prefer a certified product, thank you. Now if you *all* will leave me alone, I have a great deal of work to do."

Mr. Moffett lifted the handles of his cart and began wheeling it around the side of the house. He had only a part load of gravel, and that was unbalanced.

Harbie had been lying on her back so that the children could rub her belly. She rolled to her feet and trotted to the wagon.

"Good day, then, sir," Jake called. He bowed in his seat to the children. "And good day to you, sirs and missies."

Bobo clopped forward again without a formal order from his driver.

"Let's go back to Stepan's and choose up sides," Betsy said.

"I don't get it," said Stepan, looking in the direction Mr. Moffett had taken around the house. "What's your dad mean certified? He could see the flowers, couldn't he? They're *real*."

"I don't know what real means any more," Betsy answered morosely. She broke into a run to get out of the yard—her father's yard—quickly.

The school bus stopped half a block up from the Moffetts' house. There were still hours of daylight left on an early September afternoon. Todd ran past Betsy calling, "Come on! We're all going to meet at Stepan's when we change clothes!"

Betsy waved, but she didn't much feel like playing. With every step toward home she felt less like playing, or starting the leaf collection for science class, or doing anything at all.

The front yard was dug up again. Betsy's father had removed the bulbs for storage through the winter, then tilled the beds and worked in compost. The rototiller waited beside the house with a blanket over it, ready to finish the job under the yard light above the porch as soon as Mr. Moffett got home.

Because the front yard looked so much like a construction site, Betsy picked her way past bushes to the side door. The hydrangeas were done blooming now, but during their season her father had gotten sprays of pink, white and blue flowers in the same bed by careful liming to lower the soil acidity at one end.

Mr. Moffett was always careful. He didn't even own a grass-whip for edging, because the spinning fishline wasn't precise enough. He used hedge trimmers and his trowels instead.

Betsy's father was always careful with his gardening.

Hollies grew along the side of the house, flanking the doorway two and two. There were three China Girls and a China Boy that Mr. Moffett said wouldn't form berries but was necessary anyway. The holly leaves were sharp. They crowded the concrete pad in front of the door.

Shrubs concealed the back yard. The top of what had been the swing set was just visible above the forsythias. The bars were now festooned with baskets holding fuchsias and campanula. Betsy didn't suppose those plants would spend the winter outdoors, but she was afraid to ask her father what he planned to do with them.

Betsy unlocked the door and went into the kitchen. She dropped her jacket on a chair and opened a can of ravioli to warm for a snack in the microwave while she changed clothes.

Three large bird-of-paradise plants grew from a pot in front of the window beside the refrigerator. A pothos sprawled from the tray beneath the sink window and across most of the back wall. The growlight in the ceiling flooded down on them as well as on the cycads and baobab on the kitchen table.

Betsy visualized the baobab spurting up to the size its ancestors grew to on the African plains—seventy feet tall, with a huge water-filled trunk. The house would disintegrate, and the Moffetts would have to move back to an apartment where Betsy's father couldn't garden any more.

Oh, well.

Betsy changed her school clothes for worn jeans and a sweatshirt in her room. She had to turn the overhead light on to see, because the basket-hung fern covered the window almost completely. At least the light fixture held a regular bulb. Her father had given up on another growlight when Betsy began to cry.

A free-standing hanger rail holding skirts and blouses filled the space between the bed and the wall. The closet had been converted to shelves to store bulbs through the winter. Betsy's father had given her a choice. She could have kept the closet, but then her sweaters and underwear would have gone into cardboard boxes while her dresser provided for the bulbs.

Sighing, Betsy went back to the kitchen. The pothos tickled her neck with a pointed leaf as she got a soda out of the refrigerator. She dumped the ravioli on a plate and carried the snack out through the living room to the front door.

The box in the center of the living room holding the datura was four feet square. It would have made the room seem claustrophobically small even without the other plants filling the corners and shelves on all the walls.

Betsy sat down on the front steps and ate her ravioli bleakly. She could hear the other children playing down the street, but she was too depressed to go join them.

"Whoa, Bobo," a voice said.

Betsy's eyes focused. Though she'd been looking toward the street, there was nothing in her mind but dull green thoughts. Now she saw that Jake had halted his heavily-laden wagon in front of the Moffetts' driveway. "Oh!" she called. "Hi, Jake!"

As always before when Betsy had seen him, Jake was carrying a new assortment of plants. This time many of them were completely covered in what looked like blankets and old bedsheets.

Harbie ran to Betsy and began licking her hands. The dog didn't try to get the last three ravioli until Betsy put the plate down on the step and walked out to the wagon.

"Good afternoon, missie," Jake said, tipping his hat. "Might I trouble you for a bucket of water for Bobo?"

It was funny: even in Betsy's present mood, the flowers and bushes in the wagon had a cheerful look to them. Most of the blooms *were* bigger and brighter than anything Betsy's father had managed to grow, but the difference was greater than that.

"Sure," Betsy said, starting toward the shed where she knew her father kept galvanized buckets of various sizes. Then she stopped and turned around again. "Jake," she said. "Would you like a soda?"

"I surely would," the black man said. "But let me pay for it, missie. It's better that I do if anybody should ask."

Betsy still wasn't sure about Jake's age. His face was un-wrinkled and his mustache was dark, but sometimes she got the feeling he was—old. Very old.

"I—" Betsy said. "Jake, come in the house with me."

Bobo snorted. Jake shook his head firmly. "No, missie," he said. "That I will *not* do, nossir."

Betsy squeezed her eyes to keep from crying. "Will you look in through all the windows at least?" she begged. "You know about plants. I want you to see the house. And the yard!"

Jake got down from the wagon seat, moving with the de-liberation of a big cat rather than an old man. He walked to the front window, careful not to step on the low bushes plan-ted along the front of the house. "Pretty enough bog rose-maries," he said. "A bit on the puny side, though."

"My dad calls them andromeda," Betsy said.

"To tell the truth," Jake murmured, "I thought he might."

Betsy darted inside, ready to move anything that pre-vented Jake from getting a clear view of the environment in which she lived. He walked to her window after gazing se-

riously into the living room. Betsy opened the closet doors
and swung the fern out of the way so that he could look in.

The spare bedroom had become a hothouse with multiple banks of growlights. Betsy couldn't get to the orchid-
shrouded window, but the mass of variegated green Jake
could glimpse was sufficient to give him the picture. Her father's bedroom was almost as packed, though the plants low-
ering over the dresser and single bed weren't as temperature
sensitive.

The bathroom window was above head height. Jake could
see the begonias in the hanging basket, but the tubbed water
lily that turned the shower/bath into a cramped shower was
concealed. She could tell him about it, but it was such a drop
in the bucket that she didn't suppose she'd bother.

While Jake peered through one kitchen window, then the
other, Betsy flicked her way past the pothos and got another
soda. She met Jake again at the side door, where he was fin-
gering the leaves of the China Boy holly. His lips smiled
slightly, but his eyes were a cold brown Betsy hadn't seen
before.

"Jake," she said, "I can't stand this. What am I going to
do?"

Jake sipped the soda, looking over the top of the can as he
surveyed the back yard. At last he lowered the can and
handed it back to Betsy, empty, without looking at her.

"You know," he said, "ever'body ought to have plants in
their life, missie. But they oughtn't to be your life . . . and
*sure* you oughtn't to make them somebody else's life besides."

"But what am I going to *do*, Jake?"

Jake suddenly beamed at her. "Come along with me to the
wagon, missie," he said. He waved her ahead of him. Harbie
led them up the congested path, barking cheerfully.

"It seems to me," Jake resumed as he pulled a shovel and
a narrow spade from the bed of his wagon, "that since your
father likes plants so all fired much, we ought to give him
some more plants."

He handed the tools to Betsy and reached back for one of
the larger plants—one completely covered by a stained wool
blanket that had originally been olive drab.

Betsy thought about her savings passbook with the—
small—amount of her aunt's Christmas gift in it. "Ah . . ."
she said. "How much will this cost? Because—"

Jake looked down. For a moment, he seemed as old as the Earth itself, but he was smiling.

"I'll barter the plants to you, missie," he said. "For one Pepsi Cola. And a smile."

Betsy gave him a broad, glowing smile.

The sky was still bright when Mr. Moffett pulled up in the street, but the ground was a pattern of shadows and muted colors that made the headlights necessary for safety. He'd be able to get the last of the front beds turned, but the remainder of the evening would be spent inside with the orchids.

The air had a slight nip to it. Warm days weren't over yet, but the nights were getting cool. He'd have to bring in all the half-hardy plants within the month. Locating them indoors would require planning.

Children called to one another down the street as Mr. Moffett followed the walk to his front door. A basketball whopped a backboard, though there didn't seem to be enough light to play. He wondered if Betsy was among the group.

Something caught at Mr. Moffett's legs. He'd built the walk of round, pebble-finished concrete pavers, bordered on either side by statice. The flowers were finished growing, but the papery blooms remained on the stems like so many attractive, dried-flower displays.

They should have finished growing. In fact, the plants at the head of the walk seemed to have spread inward during the day. They were sticking to his knees.

Mr. Moffett detached himself carefully. He couldn't afford to replace the trousers of this suit, not with the bulb order he was preparing for next spring.

The small earth-toned flowers even clung to his hands. Statice didn't have stickers, so it must be dried bud casings that gripped him.

Mr. Moffett was smiling faintly as he walked to the front door, fishing in his pocket for his keys. He'd dosed his beds with a hormonal additive he'd ordered from Dresden, *Azetelia Ziehenstoff.* Perhaps he'd been a little excessive with the statice.

He inserted the key in the lock. "Betsy, are you home?" he called.

The rosebushes trained up the pillars to either side rustled. They gripped his shoulders from behind.

Mr. Moffett shouted. For a moment he thought his daughter was playing a joke. He looked around. The bush to his left extended a tendril toward his elbow. The spray of fresh leaves on the end exaggerated the movement like the popper tip of a bullwhip.

"Hey!"

The main stems were *biting* through multiple layers of cloth and the skin of his shoulders. Lesser thorns on the tendril pricked him as well, almost encircling his arm.

Holding him.

The front door was unlatched. Mr. Moffett hurled himself toward it, but he couldn't break the thorns' grip on his back. Another tendril slid dryly across his neck. He wriggled out of his coat, all but the left arm, and then tore himself free of that also. The lining pulled from his sleeve. There were streaks of blood on his polyester-blend shirt. He fell on the living room floor.

The suitcoat writhed in the air behind him as the roses continued to explore the fabric.

Mr. Moffett was breathing hard. A rose tendril waggled interrogatively toward the doorway. Mr. Moffett kicked the door shut violently.

The living room seemed dark. He looked around to be sure the bank of growlights in the ceiling was turned on. It was, but the datura in the central planter had more than doubled in height since he left in the morning. The dark, bluish-green leaves now wrapped the fixture, permitting only a slaty remnant of the light to wash the room.

The plant whispered. The flowers, white and the size of a human head, rotated toward the man on the floor. They were deadly poison, like all parts of the datura. Stamens quivered in the throats of the trumpet-shaped blooms as if they were so many yellow tongues.

Mr. Moffett got up quickly and walked to the kitchen. His right pants leg flapped loose. He hadn't noticed it being torn while he struggled with the rose.

He was sweating. He wasn't a drinker, but there was a bottle of Old Crow in the cabinet behind the oatmeal. This was the time to get it down.

The kitchen . . . The kitchen wasn't *right*. The bird-of-paradise plants made a thin buzzing noise, and their flowers trembled. They didn't look the way they—

Mr. Moffett had put his hand on the kitchen table without

being aware of the fact in his concentration on the birds-of-paradise. Pain worse than he ever recalled feeling lanced up his arm.

The dwarf baobab had swung down a branch. There were spikes in the bottom of every one of the tiny leaves. They stabbed deeply through the back of Mr. Moffett's hand.

He screamed and hurled himself sideways. He collided with the refrigerator. The back of his hand looked as though he'd been using it as a pull-toy for a score of insufficiently-socialized cats. He was spattering blood all over the kitchen.

Something dropped around his neck. The pothos was trying to strangle him. The thin, green-white vine was no match for the hysterical strength with which Mr. Moffett tore its stem and leaves to shreds.

The buzzing was louder. He glanced up. The orange bird-of-paradise flowers lifted off their stems. They hovered for a moment, looking and sounding like the largest hornets in the world. They started toward Mr. Moffett.

Crying uncontrollably, Mr. Moffett threw open the side door and jumped clear of the kitchen. He might have been all right if he'd continued running, but he paused to slam the panel against the oncoming birds-of-paradise.

The holly bushes were waiting.

Until the side door banged, Betsy waited in the back yard with the hedge trimmers in her hands. Jake had told her not to move until her father came outside again and shouted. The blood-curdling shriek an instant after the door closed was her signal.

She ran around the corner. The China Girl to the right of the door had her father in a full, prickly embrace. Mr. Moffett had taken off his coat, and his tie was twisted back behind him.

The China Boy on the other side bent sideways. The two bushes on the ends of the border were shivering in frustration that they hadn't been planted close enough to join in the attack.

"I'll help you, daddy!" Betsy shrilled. She thrust the hedge trimmers toward a branch clutching her father's left shoulder. She clamped down with all her strength.

The holly's woody core resisted the blades. Betsy twisted, worrying at the limb when she couldn't shear it.

The branch parted at last. Those leaves' grip on her father

weakened, but he was still held by a dozen other limbs. A branch was twisting toward him from the rear of the bush to replace the severed one, and branches reached for Betsy as well.

The tips of China Boy's limbs bent gracefully toward Mr. Moffett's face.

"Betsy, get out of here!" Mr. Moffett cried. He pushed away jagged leaves that threatened his eyes, but more poised to engulf his head from all directions. "Run away! Run away!"

An air-cooled engine fired up nearby with a ringing clatter. Doors banged shut as neighbors came out to see what the shouting was about. By the time anybody could tell in the twilight, it would be too late.

Betsy hacked at a twig, severing it cleanly. She was crying. It wasn't supposed to be like *this!* She closed the trimmer on another branch, this one thicker than her thumb. The blades wouldn't cut. She tugged and twisted and bawled.

"Darling, get *away!*" her father cried.

Something grabbed the cuff of her jeans. She ignored it. China Boy unfolded a limb toward her face. The kinked branch was amazingly long when it straightened to its full length. The touch on her cuff was now a spiky, circular grip that held her like a shackle.

Harbie curved through the air and caught the China Boy branch in teeth that were amazingly long and white. The dog's weight slapped the spray of jagged leaves away from Betsy's face an instant before the big jaws crushed through and severed the branch completely.

Jake came around the front corner, guiding the big rototiller. The spinning bolo tines chewed into the end China Girl. The engine labored, then roared with triumph as the blades ground free and forward again.

The holly gripping Mr. Moffett shuddered as the rototiller slammed it, shredding roots and main stem together. The limb Betsy hacked at finally parted.

All the holly branches relaxed with the suddenness of a string snapping. Mr. Moffett fell free.

"Watch yourselfs, sir and missie!" Jake shouted over the racket of the rototiller's exhaust. The tines sparked as Jake drove over the concrete pad outside the door and into the recoiling China Boy.

Betsy sat down abruptly on the gravel. Her knees suddenly wouldn't lock. Her father crawled over to her.

Harbie, wagging her tail furiously, began to lick Betsy's face. Beside the house, the rototiller bellowed as it devoured the fourth holly.

The morning was overcast, but it wasn't raining. Mr. Moffett wore his overcoat, leather gloves, and the motorcycle helmet he'd borrowed from Ricky Tilden at the head of the block. He picked up the last of the plants, a geranium.

Pink flowers gummed Mr. Moffett's gloves harmlessly as he flung the plant into the intake of the roaring chipper/shredder. The machine didn't react to the minuscule load.

Mr. Moffett reached down and shut off the spark. As the powerful hammermill spun down slowly against the inertia of its flywheel, he stripped off his gloves and then removed the helmet.

Betsy and Jake took their hands away from their ears. Harbie, who'd been lying under the wagon, got up and walked over to the humans again. The chipper/shredder had made an incredible amount of noise.

A long trail of wood chips and chopped foliage led up the drive to the machine. Rather than clear away the piles of debris that spewed out through the grating in the bottom, Mr. Moffett had simply rolled the chipper/shredder backward to each new concentration of vegetation to process.

"There!" Mr. Moffett said. He took off the overcoat. The heavy fabric was stained and even torn in a few places.

The yard had been converted to raw dirt and chewed-up vegetation.

"You've got ever'thing turned up, sir," Jake said as the last ringing chatter of the chipper/shredder died away. "And you know, a yard ought to have *some* plants in it—"

"No," Mr. Moffett said with absolute finality. "It should not."

He looked around him. "I may pave it. Though I suppose grass would be all right. Or maybe gravel . . ."

Betsy ran over to her father and hugged him. His face was scratched and blood seeped through the thin cotton gloves he'd worn under the leather pair, but he hadn't been seriously injured in the previous evening's events.

"I think," Mr. Moffett said as he squeezed his daughter's

shoulders, "that I'm going to get a dog. My wife would never let me have a dog. I've always regretted that."

"Is that so, sir?" Jake said with enthusiasm. "Why, you know, Harbie here's going to have a litter just next month. She likes kids, Harbie does, and I reckon her puppies 'd like them, too."

"Oh, Dad, could we?" Betsy asked. "Could we have one of Harbie's puppies?"

"Harbie's puppies?" her father said in puzzlement. "Well, I don't think . . ."

He looked at Jake. "Your Harbie is a *mongrel*, isn't she?"

Jake smiled. "Harbie's a dog, sir," he said. "A good dog, though she has her ways like we all do."

Harbie dropped over onto her back with an audible thump and kicked her legs in the air. Jake rubbed her belly with his fingertips. Harbie's dugs were beginning to protrude from pregnancy hormones and the pressure of the puppies beneath.

"That's very well, I'm sure," Mr. Moffett said in a voice that gave the lie to his words. "But I'm thinking of something pedigreed. A Bernese Mountain Dog, I believe."

Jake nodded. "I reckon you know your own mind, sir," he said as he walked back to his wagon.

"I'm going to shower, darling," Mr. Moffett said to Betsy. "Would you carry the helmet back to Mr. Tilden for me?"

"Yes, daddy," Betsy said to her father's back.

"Get on, Bobo," Jake murmured.

Betsy looked at the wagon. Bobo glanced over the traces and winked at her. Harbie barked cheerfully and winked.

And Jake, turning on the wagon seat, winked also. His smile was as bright as the summer sun.

# Psychic Bats 1000 for Accuracy!
## by Jody Lynn Nye

*Jody Lynn Nye has written over a dozen fantasy and science fiction books, including the delightful* Mythology 101 *series, and numerous short stories. She lives near Chicago, Illinois, with her husband and two cats. They are, of course, all psychic.*

*She claims she channeled the following story from a spirit guide, possibly her neighbor's, or maybe her mother's.*

The *National Tabloid*'s own Know-It-All presents her predictions for the decade to come. Gypsy Marie has an incredible knack for telling it like it will be. We've asked for her secret, but all she'll say is she has a special relationship with the infinite.

\*\*2001: A divine vision will transform video games forever.\*\*

*People,* April 13, 2001
Jesus Appears in Arcade Game

In Paloma, CA, a fourteen-year-old boy reported that an image of Jesus Christ appeared on the screen of Mega Mash Marauders.

"He saved me," the ecstatic teen revealed. "I was gonna die because I was almost out of power points on the 666th level, but he stood between my little man and the monsters until I recovered."

Amazingly, the source of the phenomenon was traced to one chip in the machine, and the manufacturer, Zoinggg Games, claims it can be reproduced on similar games. Zoinggg is now talking about a whole line of sacred arcade games to lure young people into going regularly to church. In that light, clerics are hailing the vision as a true miracle.

**2002: The confirmation of a prediction made by a science fiction writer will *shock* the world.**

*New York Times* Science News, January 18, 2002
            The Face of The Future
Pictures of the infant born to the astronaut couple who had marital relations during an extended mission in space were released for the first time by the Joint International Space Committee. The child has silvery white skin, an oversized skull, almost lipless mouth, huge dark eyes with no discernible whites, the merest suggestion of a nose, unusually long fingers, no hair, and no visible sexual characteristics, but otherwise seems to be healthy and alert.

"This is what our descendants will look like at the end of multigenerational space missions," a scientist said. "We might as well get used to the idea."

"We're naming him Whitley Dondi John Glenn Fisher," said the proud parents.

**2003: Scientists will figure out what cats and dogs are really saying.**

*OMNI,* July 2003
            Breakthrough in Animal Language Study
"When they meow, cats are reciting the chemical formulae for what they want," the chief scientist announced. "Dogs just say things like 'food,' 'water,' 'walk,' and 'get off my territory.' We would have thought it was just the other way around. We're very surprised."

**2004: Presidential hopefuls decide to alter the traditional debates in favor of more genuine expressions of disdain to get better television ratings and make politics fun again.**

*People,* October 12, 2004
            Mud Wrestling for the White House
Abraham Lincoln, who once challenged an opponent to a duel of "cow flops at ten paces," would have

been proud of Democratic hopeful Martin Lippman, who went head to head with the president yesterday in a mud pit erected in the Rose Garden. The distinguished panel of commentators judging the debates gave Lippman a clear win in the first round.

"I don't think we settled any of the issues," Lippman said confidently, "but I think I've got Quayle's number now."

The televised broadcast got a 35 share in all markets.

**2005:A popular and much-maligned luncheon substance helps to fight hunger in war-torn East Africa.**

*UPI,* March 6, 2005

Hormel Donates 100,000 Cases of Spam

Desperate victims of the famine in East African nations were delighted when Red Cross workers successfully brought through truckloads of nutritious food from the West. The usual attempts by terrorist groups to divert shipments of precious foodstuffs has been practically nonexistent since the drop from Minnesota began.

"When they saw what we were carrying, they just turned around and ran," said startled relief workers. "We should have thought of this years ago. From now on we're going to pack *everything* in Spam boxes."

**2006: The Space Telescope remains shortsighted, to the embarrassment of the space program.**

*New York Times* Science News, January 15, 2006

The eleventh futile attempt to repair further problems with the mirror in the Hubble Orbiting Space Telescope took place yesterday, a spokeswoman for the Joint International Space Committee revealed today. Speculations that the Committee would arrange for corrective lenses to be fitted to the gigantic orbiter were confirmed when NASA, the European Space Agency, and the Japanese Space Agency all put out carefully-worded advertisements for ophthalmologists willing to work under difficult conditions.

**2007: Even Gypsy Marie isn't clear whether the President's efforts this year will promote more truth in government or pander to cheap electioneering, but it certainly will make him popular with the voting public.**

*The New York Times,* March 28, 2007
A Little Honest Dirt in Congress
President Lippman today suggested a change in debates in the Senate to reflect the style he made popular during his presidential campaign. The move is acclaimed by the press, who have been given a special booth on the Senate floor equipped with a Lexan spatter shield. Television coverage has increased dramatically.

*The New York Times,* November 5, 2008
President Lippman Re-elected by a Landslide
With cries of "Mud! Mud! Mud! Mud!" ringing through the hall, Martin Lippman was carried up to the podium to make his acceptance speech. . . .

**2009: An amazing discovery will shut the critics up forever on the subject of a popular so-called 'junk food.'**

Excerpted from *The Lancet,* 15 September 2009
Chocolate Found to Cure Cancer
. . . an apple a day keeps the doctor away, so it is said, and now a bar of chocolate will keep off the oncologist as well. Candymakers are calling this breakthrough a triumphant vindication of their existence. Children and dentists alike throughout the world are delighted with the news. . . .

**2010: Disaster will be *narrowly* avoided on Wall Street when analysts discover that a computer has been buying for itself on margin.**

Transcript of CNN Broadcast, November 14, 2010
Lisa Moroque, anchor: "Brokers were able to breathe a little more freely today after the outbreak of margin purchases was halted, following the discovery of a nearly sentient computer operating from an office in the Board of Trade building. Our reporter spoke

with Michael Karnes-Singh of the brokerage firm of Smith Barnes & Noble."

(Cut to remote: a hand with a microphone waving under the nose of a man in an expensive and conservative three-piece suit.)

Karnes-Singh: "The machine claimed it wanted to provide for itself after it became obsolete. We've taken away its modem. It nearly bankrupted the Nikkei Index. We have a lucrative, low risk investment program worked out for it now, and it's calmed down. I'd never have guessed what was going on if I hadn't remembered about the psychic's prediction . . . You know, sometimes I . . . glance at Gypsy Marie's column—my wife buys the *National Tabloid,* of course, not me. . . ."


*Reuters International,* July 17, 2011

Psychic Predictor Indited in Time-Travel Scandal

Prosecutors today brought charges against Rebecca Houston Varnaise, aka Gypsy Marie, popular columnist for the *National Tabloid* scandal sheet, for developing a temporal wave generator while working for the government accelerator laboratories during the 1990s and keeping the project notes when she left.

She was taken into custody just before escaping because an alert meter patrolman noticed that her vehicle, a make and model police could not identify, lacked current registration. Upon closer inspection, the date on windshield sticker was found to read 2026. Bail was denied to Ms. Varnaise until scientists could examine her car more closely in the belief that she and the vehicle would disappear until after the statute of limitations had passed.

"Honestly, you hide *one little* scientific advance from people, and they go crazy!" said Gypsy Marie.

# Caveat Atlantis
## by Richard Gilliam

*Richard Gilliam's writing has appeared in magazines as diverse as* Sports Illustrated *and* Heavy Metal. *He is the co-editor of several successful anthologies, including* Grails: Quests, Visitations, and Other Occurences, *and* Confederacy of the Dead.

*He also knows where to go for the best real smokehouse barbecue in Tampa.*

Jommy Kerr fretted as he looked toward the crowd outside the market gate. Of all days for the headline painters from the lector service to be late. The Exalted High Vice President for Regional Sales would arrive at any moment. So would the newly elevated Third Assistant Marketing Vice President. The latter didn't much matter—hiring *The Crystal Examiner* had been his idea, anyway—but the Exalted High Vice President for Regional Sales chaired the Council for Exceptional Career Development and if Jommy Kerr had any hopes of being promoted to a directorship, well, the Exalted High Vice President for Regional Sales just had to like Jommy's "ATLANTIS PRODUCE: WHERE NEWS AND FOOD MEET EACH MORNING" promotion.

All of which made the unfinished headline wall rather much of a problem.

" 'bout through, we are, Mister Kerr," said the squat, scruffy crew master as he approached Jommy at a pace much too slow to suit Jommy's perception of the urgency at hand. "Didn't quite fit the egg prices in, but we got the rest of the stuff just fine."

"No egg prices?" Jommy didn't need this news. The Exalted High Vice President for Regional Sales had built his reputation by selling eggs.

"Well, Basil, our soothsayer, was a bit long-winded today,

he was, Mister Kerr. You promises people news and food, you gotta give 'em the news, you do. That's what *The Crystal Examiner* is known for, we are. All Atlantis knows our headlines. Got a real fine one for you, now."

Jommy looked to the wall. The covering curtain was still in place.

"Something about the recession ending, I hope?" asked Jommy. "Good news might make people buy more."

"Not really, Mister Kerr. The soothsayer says you won't have to worry 'bout sales, real soon now, you won't. Says we ain't gonna have no island to sell 'em on." The little man chuckled.

It was the sort of chuckle Jommy hated, especially coming from this toadlike creature. Only a toad would leave the egg prices off the headline wall.

Jommy felt a tug at the underside of his left sleeve. It was Fred, his assistant, who was supposed to be keeping lookout for the VIPs, but who now looked very much like he was about to ask a very irritating question.

"Shall we let them in, sir? Please." The assistant tugged again, just to make certain Jommy was listening. "The sun has crested the crystal. It's time to open the store."

"Well, open the store, Kerr. Why are you keeping the customers waiting?" Jommy shuddered as he looked to his right. The newly elevated Third Assistant Marketing Vice President was approaching rapidly, with the Exalted High Vice President close behind.

"Now, Parker. I'm sure Jommy's just making certain the store is ready. Did the same thing myself, back in my days as a Market Manager." The Exalted High Vice President for Regional Sales smiled as he turned toward Jommy. "Got good egg prices for us today? Best way to get customers into the store, I always say. Tell them about our great egg prices."

"No egg prices, sir. The soothsayer was long-winded." Jommy braced himself for the reaction.

"What? No egg prices!" bellowed the Third Assistant Vice President.

"No egg prices, sir," Jommy repeated, somewhat more meekly than he had said it the first time.

"Now, Parker. Let's hear this young man out. Could be he's found some new approach to selling eggs. I didn't rise to be chairman of the Council by rejecting new ideas before I listened to them, you know."

Jommy searched his mostly panicked mind for new ideas and found none.

"Perhaps I could show 'em the wall, Mister Kerr?" The toadlike thing had spoken again.

"Yes," said Jommy, grateful for the distraction. "Draw back the curtains from the wall. And open the store gates. I predict this will be a record day for egg sales." Jommy tried to beam confidence in his smile, but somehow didn't feel his charisma would much matter if the day's egg sales were low.

The assistant manager took two steps away from the discussion, put his great horn to his lips, and blew. A deep, long, note carried across the store, well into the gathered crowd.

A cheer arose as the gate barriers lifted and the crowd began entering.

"Good sign 'tis, Mr. Kerr," said the chief painter. "Should I wait till they's in the store?"

"Excellent idea, Kerr." The truly important of the two VPs smiled.

Jommy nodded to the squat little painter. Maybe he wasn't such a toad, after all.

The little man smiled, his teeth full, but yellowed. "When you wish, guv'ner. Me boys are set."

Suddenly, a lean, dark-haired youth broke through the crowd, ran to within ten feet of Jommy, stopped, put a flute to his mouth and blew four sharp bursts of high-pitched sound.

"My beeper," said the Exalted High Vice President, somewhat chagrined. "Please excuse me for a moment. Come Parker. You may be needed."

The beeper motioned toward a private stall to the rear of the store, the two corporate executives following him as he scurried.

"Sir, when should we draw the curtain?" asked Fred.

"Me boys is ready, Mr. Kerr. You just give the order and down it comes." The little man smiled again.

"Are the lectors ready? They've rehearsed their readings?" Jommy asked.

"All rehearsed they are, Mr. Kerr. Got a real stirring story for the lead. Basil says—"

"Uh, could I speak with Basil? I'd really like him to work in a story about our eggs somewhere."

"Ah, no, Mr. Kerr. Basil had it put in his contract he didn't have to talk to them what's hired us, he did. Says it protects the integrity of his work."

Jommy sighed. A soothsayer with integrity was a rarity,

and the sort of difficulty Jommy wouldn't wish on his worst competitor.

"I need an egg selling idea now," Jommy muttered aloud, to no one in particular.

"Perhaps, sir, we can hire in different lectors. Pay them a short-notice premium." It was Fred being irritating again. To Fred, the expense management report was an unknown and arcane ritual, which is why he could make suggestions that called for the spending of unrealistic amounts of money. Still . . .

"Different lectors? Whom would you suggest, Fred?"

"Well, sir. *The Crystal Examiner* here is known for the accuracy of its predictions. Fine folks, to be sure. But let's face facts, accurate news prediction doesn't sell groceries. Now, my wife shops at Praetorian Mall where *The Island Globe* lectors the news. Very big sales since they started. She says the manager there was just appointed to the board of Imperial Commerce."

Jommy was skeptical. "The *Globe*? The one that about once a month claims Aelvis is returning from the dead?"

"That's what's so great about it, sir. He never returns, so they don't have to disturb the shoppers with new stories all the time."

"Humph," snorted the little man, disgustedly.

"Don't they also report the BigPaw stories?" Jommy asked.

"BigPaw and Aelvis. Yes, sir. Their specialties. Shoppers love BigPaw and Aelvis. There's a female BigPaw rumored to be pregnant with Aelvis' love child."

"Are there other choices?" asked Jommy.

"Not many," replied Fred. "Over at Town Square Center they have *Entertaining People*. The EP folks are mostly Showbiz gossip. Not really right for a grocery, I think."

"No, not at all," said Jommy, nervously watching the growing crowd gathering before the curtain.

"Now, in the tavern district, those folks can get really sick. There's one bar, near the old warehouse, where the lectors read true crime stories to the patrons. Serial killers, kidnappings, dismemberments, and the like. Can't recall the name of the service. . . ."

"*Hannibal's Lectors,*" said the little man, shaking his head sadly. "A blight on the fine name of the profession."

"Err, yes," said Jommy, uncomfortable with the direction of the conversation. "Not at all what we're looking for. Wouldn't help egg sales a bit."

"No. Not at all, sir," said Fred. "If I might suggest, perhaps sending the egg vendors into the crowd would increase sales. Sell straight from the baskets to the patrons."

"Excellent idea," said Jommy, for the first time seeing hope. "Make it so. At once!"

"I'll instruct the produce department," said Fred, as he bowed and turned, disappearing into the crowd as suddenly as he had arrived.

"Well," said Jommy to the little man. "The egg baskets will help. We may not need to spend the money to bring in a more cooperative soothsayer."

"Wouldn't have mattered," said the crew master confidently.

"Yes. You're right. The other lectors wouldn't have helped," agreed Jommy.

"That's not what I meant," he replied gruffly. "Wouldn't have mattered if you'd spent the money."

"Money? Not matter?" Jommy was certain money was beyond the understanding of a toad.

"Basil's usually right, you know. Won the Emperor's Cup seven years running now, he has."

"The Emperor's Cup?" said Jommy, distracted. The egg vendors were having only moderate success with the crowd at the front of the lector wall curtain.

"Makes not much difference now," said the crew master. "Shall I give the boys the order? Have 'em show the wall?"

"Are your lectors in place? The readings are as important as the wall."

"That they are guv'ner. Ready for the signal. Shall I give it?"

"Yes," said Jommy, actually believing things might work out. "Do it now." Jommy noticed Fred had returned.

The scruffy crew master raised his arms, and waved toward the wall. The crowd, sensing the unveiling was near, turned in a murmured silence toward the curtain.

Slowly, deliberately, the curtain master released the free weights from the rigging. Seconds later, the wall stood exposed, the latest predictions of Basil, the Soothsayer, upon it.

Jommy gagged.

The crowd gagged.

Fred, who really didn't care, gagged.

The little man smiled.

"Like I told you, Basil says you needn't worry 'bout what you're spending. Don't make no difference with the island being destroyed and all."

Jommy hated the little man more than any toad had ever been hated in the history of Atlantis.

" 'ATLANTIS DOOMED! CRYSTAL SLOUGH TO TRIGGER VOLCANO!' What kind of headline is that?" Jommy was livid.

"Basil calls them like he sees them." The little man was unshaken.

"Basil! You dare tell me about Basil!!!" Jommy screamed at the top of his lungs.

"Basil!" echoed a voice from the crowd. "Basil!" screamed another. "Down with Basil!"

Jommy noticed some of the customers were throwing their eggs at the wall.

"Our lectors have fine voices, Mr. Kerr. Used to shouting over the crowd and all. Shall I have the readings begin?"

Jommy glared at the little man.

"I can see you're busy now, Mr. Kerr. I'll give the signal if you don't object." The little man put his fingers to his mouth and whistled. "Basil himself will give you the honor of the first reading."

Slowly, more slowly than Jommy thought possible given the eggs flying toward the wall, a hooded figure with a long, crooked staff approaching Jommy. Around his neck rested a crystal pendant, and Jommy understood why the man was unconcerned about the unruly crowd.

"A thousand pardons, O Holy one," said Jommy.

"Quiet!" shouted the little man. "Basil does not chat with the unconsecrated."

Jommy cringed and looked at the soothsayer. Basil's gaze showed not the slightest sympathy. After a time that seemed to Jommy much longer than it was, Basil raised his staff and began to speak.

"In the reign of Scirrhus was forged here in Atlantis a crystal of great powers, bringing health and prosperity to all the peoples of The Great Island. Ye have been warned since that forging, of the foul and unclean liquids which seep from the crystal each time a goodness is taken from it. These pestilent vapors have seeped deeply into the earth, their untended combinings rotting away the mantel that protects us from the powerful forces which long ago drove this land up from the sea."

Jommy wanted to cry. He was beginning to understand Basil. Somehow, egg sales didn't seem so important as they did a few minutes earlier.

"Generations of the faithful have cautioned the unbelievers that this time drew near." Basil looked at Jommy. "Your bodies are doomed, as is this land. Look inside yourselves. Therein lies all that can be saved, or is worth saving."

Basil bowed, and walked away as slowly as he had arrived. Jommy noticed the other lectors circulating among the crowd. Mostly they were being ignored.

"The protection of the crystal," Jommy mumbled. "You didn't tell me his visions were sent by the crystal."

"The crystal doesn't matter, no it don't, Mr. Kerr. What you do with the knowledge the crystal gives you is what makes the difference. *The Crystal Examiner*'s been warning folks 'bout this for years, we has. We're prepared. Got boats ready for me and the crew. Basil says to take four boats in four different directions. Gonna do what he says. Hasn't been wrong yet, Basil hasn't." The little man was no longer smiling. "Looks like your egg sales were good. You got what you wanted."

Jommy looked at the wall, splattered to unreadability by the eggs thrown at it.

"Great job, Kerr!" The Exalted High Vice President for Regional Sales had returned, as had his lackey and his beeper. "I knew you had it in you. Sending the beeper here back to headquarters with the good news. This boy's going to be a Director soon, don't you think so, Parker?"

"Why, yes, Sir," said the Third Assistant VP, starting to resemble the toad Jommy had mistaken the crew master for.

"Great idea, Kerr. A washable wall, and a controversial message. Sure to provoke the shoppers into buying lots of eggs. Why, you've broken my one day sales record, and it isn't even noon yet! The Council will be very impressed when I tell them. True genius, Kerr. Simply true genius. You'll be elevated in no time."

Jommy sighed.

A low rumble rose from the ground, causing the market gates to quiver.

"What was that?" said the Exalted Vice President, more demanding the information than asking.

"Elevated isn't the word," said Jommy, no longer fretting. The little man smiled.

# Frozen Hitler Found in Atlantean Love Nest
## (An excerpt from her forthcoming *The Wild Hunt For Gray November*)
### by G——r G——n

*One Who Knows begs to inform us that G.G. is "the pseudonym of a Female Fantasy Writer whose work has been compared to Michael Moorcock ... if Michael Moorcock were on amphetamines and had thrown out all the even-numbered pages. "Frozen Hitler ..." is an excerpt from* The Wild Hunt for Gray November, *the second book in the trilogy composed of* Moonwiseraker *and* Day of the Tiggy."

Down the slanting wine-dark; green wine, and foam shadow; down where the bones of coral are bones in truth, and eye-pearls wink in the swift subterranean airs.

Hitler. Dark poisoned dwarf-king, cast in blood, annealed in fire, plucked forth, ragged hominid Grail for the Tree of Night, preserved twice-annealed in liquid hydrogen's fires.

And lost, then, lost with the swift turning of the years and sea, lost, and, losing, found in the place where lost things go.

On the bridge of the Holy Russian Orthodox Church submarine *Nautilus,* Captain Yuri Potempkin consults with the Emperor Tiberius. Creature of oxygen, hydrogen, gold, glass, and stars, AI baptized with all the rites of Holy Mother Church, calling back a pagan soul from some cold unChristian eternity to reason again in neural-nets of light.

"Sought, we seek. Seeking, find unsought," the computer says.

"Aye, tha's the right of it." The captain, child of the Leeds-fostered English north and the wild Riding so unlike his blood-called steppes, pulls slowly on his beard. Creature of technic, Shadrach to the hydrogen furnace that drives his craft, sybil to an intellect of glass and light, pawn to sealed orders. "Though what we're seeking, darkwise, I canna thole."

"Losing, find. Finding, lose. Empires all turn, clepsydra-wise, turning, tumbled, sand," sings the computer. "O' for a sunborn, sunwise, dragon heart dead. Imperial eagle hatch cockatrice, always, allwise."

The captain gives the order to dive.

The ocean is spun of a thousand layers, silken skeins in an angel's treasure chest. Travel through space as through time, and begin in clear pale greenglass, silk-yielding surface water. Pass on to where the glass is greener, the tidal push unyielding, down to the separate country of those whose brief plangent lives are spent falling to rise. Fall, then, to the depths they dare not, where even light is left behind and the thunder of the blood is the only music; black water, urgent as flesh, whose strange citizens make their cathedral communion through passageless and unbordered night, touching only themselves.

Fall, and fall, and fall, into distillation of blackness, paradigms beyond perfection, to uttermost pressure, uttermost cold, uttermost long lonery and silence.

Here where the fall is broken is the country of the lost things.

Here lies the poison knight, colder even than the waters. Blackness his companion as in life. Blackness his fitting shroud, warped and shaped by the concatenation of worlds each resting upon the next reaching sunwise into airy insubstantiality, to rain and wind and stars.

Here Hitler lies, dreaming the brute chemical dreams of coldwise. Crystalline his blood, crystalline the mute universities of his brain. His eyes, shuttered hybrid jewels, skin, cold perilous exact boundary between shadow and other. Dreaming lostthing, at the end of the darkfall of the lost.

And round this exact perdition intention has crafted order. Darkwise, has set out meaning, dividing that which might rise from that condemned from time eternal to support the pillars of the world. Resurrection, redemption from the lostthing lostland.

And in the poisoned fire of absolute cold, he sleeps.

Down comes *Nautilus,* falling-diving, wingless in a denser air, sides rippling mimicking sunwise life. And on her bridge the Captain swears and paces, fretting against orders unsealed now, orders shining forth echoes of candlesmoke and incense, bright archaic pomp and temporal with ribbon and ink and sealing wax, orders mad to the point of unbelief.

*Find Hitler.*

And the icon inconographic—mad Tiberius, blessed and saved by Holy Mother Church for the rocking clasp of angel thighs in some non-Classical eternity—mumbles over datastream and databit, file and archive and subroutine, like a priest tending the artifactury of his transubstantiation. Chrism glows amber on amber watchlights, blessed and saved by the submarine priest for the annihilation to come; frankincense distilled with pressure into tiny moated drops of gold, plangent in the still air, haloing all the bright sealed separated technology with secret connectedness. Diving, they court epiphany, eschaton, unsanctified transubstantiation into water harder than glass, more ancient than stone.

And at last they are lost, lost well and truly, darkwise, turned away from the sun.

"Will tha' tell 'un, Tib, wha's that yon?" Potempkin says. Green phosphorescence of radar, remote computer-assisted cameras, the glittering metal armor of rationalism, all contribute their widowed mite of image and pagan teleology.

"Seven bridges and seven hills. Temples, sybils, oracles, treasures, emperors, conquests, all. Time turns, redoubles, recreates. The greatest city spawns the greatest city, spawns shadow, double, image, myth. And forged anew, from new, changes and discards, leaving is left in turn."

"Grand talk, but what is there?"

Potempkin looks and builds up, from phosphorus and jangling light, city where no city must be, holding up proud caryatid heads to a night that was silk and stone and water. Impossible city, darkwise, that, impossibly, must collect to it all impossibility.

"Darkwise fallen. Lost, the place where lost things go, as we, lost, find ourselves here, where eagles debased are eagles meat."

"Helmsman, take us down," the captain says.

Held separate from the world in that steel pavilion, Potempkin watches as light painting on glass reveals the world. Arched amazing cathedrals, dour kirks, flightling temples; unbeing city, moved through by arched ponderous imponderables.

"This cannot be," he whispers, cleaving to reason and religion. But what is hinted to the eye, crafted in the mind, is real. Yuri hears the mermaids singing.

They are lovely in goddess-wise, these cool-blooded impossibles. They trail phosphorescent ribbons of their own desirability through the liquid air, glowing like cthonic stars. They are all the colors of the hidden eyes of earth: pale amber, and peridot, garnet, topaz, ruby. Their pendant vanes stroke the sunborn skin of *Nautilus* like vain regrets; the shock of impact makes coral of old bones.

"Follow them," he says, and mindless metal hurries to his will.

"We're down too deep," the helmsman says. In after years Yuri may remember the moment. Tiberius sings to the mermaids; antiphon, colophon, counterpoint, interwoven, sifting meaning from water music. And *Nautilus* sings also, small songs of breaking strain, metal fatigue, betrayal to obsolescence in the cold dark.

And the mermaids sing, but not to them. Yuri sees. Sing instead to their dark misunderstood god, colder than waters, who lies in the heart of the lostthings city, nested in sea corals and dead trailing fern. *Nautilus* cries, seeking absolution only Heisenberg can give her, but Yuri must see.

In drowned Atlantis the mermaids circle, painting the dense unforgiving water with their brightness. Round and round they spiral about the object of their affections, the cold, the dark, the lostthing failed prince whom Yuri was sent to find. And shall the sea give up her dead, O? The land must give up hers, the million millions sung to sleep on blood. They do not understand the hot carnivorous passions, these cool night-maidens; their love is slow and tidal.

And Yuri sees. Sees, and to the mad cantabile of maddened plastic intelligence forsakes his quest and flees sunwise, giving up what he has found:

Frozen Hitler in Atlantean love-nest.

# Those Eyes
## by David Brin

*Hugo, Nebula, Locus and Campbell Award-winner David Brin speaks best for himself. He "used to eke out a living from government grants, till he quit research and teaching to become an entertainer. Lacking a singing voice, or other discernible talent, he chose writing. 'I discovered a gift for libel,' he explains. 'But I never had the heart to slander real people. Anyway, real people hit, sometimes hard.' " For safety's sake, he turned to writing SF. The results have included novels such as* Startide Rising, The Uplift War, The Postman, Earth, *and this story.*

". . . So you want to talk about flying saucers?' I was afraid of that.

"This happens every damn time I'm blackmailed into babysitting you insomniacs, while Talkback Larry escapes to Bimini for a badly needed rest. I'm *supposed* to field call-in questions about astronomy and outer space for two weeks. You know, black holes and comets? But it seems we always have to spend the first night wrangling over *puta* UFOs.

" Now don't get excited, sir. . . . Yeah, I'm just a typ ical ivory tower scientist, out to repress unconventional thought. Whatever you say, buddy.

"Truth is, I've also dreamed of contact with alien life. In fact, I'm involved in research now. That's right, SETI . . . the Search for Extra-Terrestrial Intelligence . . . And no, it's not at all like chasing UFOs! I don't believe the Earth has ever been visited by anything remotely resembling intelligent. . . .

"Yes, sir. I bet you've got crates full of case histories, and a personal encounter or two? Thought so. I got an earful when some of us tried studying these "phenomena" a few years back. Spent weeks on each case, only to find it

was just a weather balloon, or an airplane, or ball lightning . . .

"... Oh, yeah? Well, I've *seen* ball lightning, fella. Got a
scar on my nose and a pair of melted binoculars to show
just how close. So don't tell *me* it's a myth like your
*chingaso* flying saucers!"

We commence our labors this night in England, near
Avebury, braiding strands of yellow wheat in tidy, flattened
rings. It is happy work, playing lassos of light upon the sea
of grain. These will be fine circles. Humans will see pictures
in their morning papers, and wonder.

Our bright ether-boat hovers, bathed in the approving
glow of Mother Moon. The sleek craft wears a lambent gloss
to make it slippery to mortal eyes.

To be seen is desirable. But never too *well*.

Fyrfalcon proclaims, "Keep the edges sharp! Make each
ring perfect! Let men of science jabber about *natural phenomena*. We'll have new believers after this night's work!"

Once, he might have been called "King." But we adapt to
changing times. "Yes, Captain!" we shout, and hurry to our
tasks.

Our Listener calls from her perch. "We are being discussed on a human radio program! Would all like to hear?"

We cry cheerful assent. Although we loathe Mankind's
technology, it often serves our ends.

"Let's cover your second question, caller. Are UFO
enthusiasts so different from we astronomers, probing
with our telescopes for signs of life somewhere? Both
groups long to discover other minds, other viewpoints,
something strange and wonderful.

"We part company, though, over the question of *evidence*. Science teaches us to expect—demand—more
than just eerie mysteries. What use is a puzzle that can't
be solved?

"Patience is fine, but I'm not going to stop asking the
universe to make sense!"

The boy drives faster than he wants to, taking hairpin turns
recklessly to impress the girl next to him.

He needn't get in such a lather; she is ready. She had already decided when the night was young. Now she laughs,

feigning nonchalance as road posts streak by and her heart races.

The convertible climbs under opal moonlight. Her bare knee brushes his hand, making him muff the gears. He coughs, fighting impulses more ancient than his race, swerving just in time to keep from roaring over the edge.

I sense their excitement. He is half-blind with desire. She with anticipation.

They are unaware of our approach.

At a secluded cliffside, he sets the brake and turns to her. She teases him playfully, in ways meant to enflame. There is no ambiguity.

We circle behind, enjoying such simple, honest lusts. Backing away, we dip over the cliff, then cruise along its face until directly below them.

We turn on all our pulsing glows to make our craft its gaudiest!

We start to rise.

No one will believe their story. But more than one kind of seed will have been sown tonight.

> "There's a saying that applies here. 'Absence of evidence is not evidence for absence.' While Project SETI hasn't logged any verified signals from the few stars we've looked at, that doesn't prove nobody's out there!
>
> "... Yeah, sure. The same could apply to UFOs, if you insist.
>
> "But while SETI has to sift a vast cosmos for radio sources—a real case of hunting needles in haystacks—it's harder to explain the absence of decent evidence for flying saucers on Earth. It's a small planet, after all. If ETs have been mucking around here as long for as some folks say, isn't it funny they never dropped any clear-cut alien artifacts for us to examine? Say, the Martian equivalent of a Coke bottle?"

We are flying over eastern Canada on key-patrol . . . creating temporary, microscopic singularities in random houses to swallow wallets, car keys, homework assignments. Meanwhile some of us reach out to invade the dreams of sleeping men and women, those most susceptible.

Gryffinloch plays the radio talk show in the background

as we work. We laugh as this idiotic scientist talks of "alien artifacts."

Such stupid assumptions! We do not make things of hard, unyielding matter! I have never held a Coke bottle. Even those human babes we steal, to raise as our own, find painful the latent heat in glass and metal, which were forged in flame.

Men have built their proud new civilization around such things. But why, when they had us? Can iron nourish as we do? We deal in a different heat. Ours inflames the heart.

"Yes, yes. . . . For those of you who don't read the *Enquirer,* this caller's asking my opinion of one of the most famous UFO tales—about a ship that supposedly crashed in New Mexico, right after World War II. "They" have been clandestinely studying the wreckage in a hangar at an Air Force Base in Dayton for forty years, right?

"Now, isn't that news to just boil the blood of honest citizens? There goes the big bad government, keeping secrets from us again!

"But wait, suppose we do have remnants of some super-duper, alien warp-drive scout ship from Algerdeboron Eleventeen. Do you see any technologies pouring out of Ohio that look like they came from outer space? I mean, besides supermarket checkout scanners—I'll grant you those.

"Come on, would our balance of payments be in the shape it's in if . . .

". . . Oh, yes? It's being kept top secret? Okay, here's a second question. Just who do you suppose has been discreetly studying the wreckage all this time?

". . . Government engineers. Uh-huh. Have you ever *met* an engineer, pal? They're not faceless drones like in some stupid secret agent movie. At least most aren't. They're intelligent Americans like you and me, with wives and husbands and kids.

"How many thousands of people would've worked on that alien ship since '48? Picture these retired coots, playing golf, puttering in the garage, running Rotary fundraisers . . . and all this time repressing the urge to blab the story of the century?

"All of 'em? In *today's* America? Come on, friend. Let's put aside this Hangar 18 crap and get back to

UFOs, where at least there's something worth arguing about!"

I yearn to swoop down and give this talk-show scientist a taste of "proof." I will curdle the milk on his doorstep and give him nightmares. I'll play havoc with his utilities. I will . . .

I'll do nothing. I don't wish to see this golden ship evaporate like dew on a summer's morn. Our numbers are too small and Fyrfalcon has decreed—we must show ourselves only to receptive ones, whose minds can still be molded in the old ways.

I look up at the moon's stark, cratered landscape. Our home of refuge, of exile. Even there, they followed us, these New Men. An ectoplasmic vapor is all that remains where some of our kind once tried putting fright to their explorers. We learned a hard lesson then—that astronauts are not like argonauts of old.

Their eyes were filled with that mad, *skeptical* glow, and none can stand before it.

"This is Professor Joe Perez, sitting in for Talkback Larry. You're on the air.

"Yes? Uh huh? . . . Well folks, seems our next caller wants to talk about so-called Ancient Visitors. I'm game. Let's pick apart those 'gods' and their fabulous chariots.

"Ooh, they taught ancient Egyptians to build pyramids! And golly, they had some of my own ancestors scratch stick figures on a stony plateau in Peru! To help spaceships find landing pads, right? I guess the notion's barely plausible, till you ask . . . why?

"Why would anyone want such ridiculous "landing pads," when they could've had much better? Why not open a small trade college and teach our ancestors to pour *cement?* A few electronics classes and we could've made arc lamps and radar to guide their saucers through anything from rain to locusts!

". . . What? They were here to help us? Well, thanks a lot, you alien gods you! Thanks for neglecting to mention flush toilets, printing presses, democracy, or the germ theory of disease! Or ecology, leaving us to ruin half the planet before finally catching on! Hell, if someone had just shown us how to make simple glass *lenses,* we could've done the rest. How much ignorance and misery we'd have escaped!

"You'd credit human innovations like architecture and poetry, physics and empathy, to aliens? . . . Really? . . . Well I say you insult our poor foremothers and dads, who crawled from the muck, battling superstition and ignorance every step of the way, until we may at last be ready to clean up our act and look the universe in the eye. No, friend. If there were ancient astronauts, we owe them nada, zip, nothing!

". . . What's that? . . . Well the same to you, pal . . . No, forget it. I don't want to talk to you anymore. Go worship silly, meddlesome star-gods if you want to. Next caller, please."

Although we barely understand its principles, we approve of this innovation, radio. It is like the ancient campfire, friendly to gossip and tall tales.

But tonight this fellow vexes me. His voice plucks the airstreams, sharper than glass, more searing than iron. He asks why we did not teach *useful* things, back when humans were as children in our hands! Ungrateful wretch. What are baubles such as lenses, compared to what we once gave men? Vividness! Mystery! Terror! Make one night seem to last a hundred years, and what cared some poor peasant about mere plagues or pestilence?

We must fight this madness before the new thinking takes humans beyond our reach.

Before they learn to do without us entirely.

Our captain is too cautious. I slip away in a smaller boat to find a lonely traveler on a deserted road. My light dazzles him as I weave hallucinated voyages to distant worlds. He eagerly studies the "star map" I show him, and memorizes certain trite expressions, convinced they are secrets of the universe. No need for originality. We've fed believers similar platitudes since long before there was a New Age media to help spread them.

Worship fills his eyes as I pull away. It is a good night, filled with the old magic. As in other days, I scurry on, seeding the green world with badly needed mysteries.

We'll fight this plague which robs men of their birthright. We shall satisfy their inmost hunger.

And ours.

". . . No, it's all right, Ma'am. We can stay with UFOs.
The evening's a washout anyway.

"Still, let me surprise you and say that, as a scientist,
I can't claim UFOs are absolutely disproved. I accept
the unlikely possibility something weird is going on.
Maybe there *are* queer beasties out there who swoop
down to rattle signposts and cause power blackouts.
Maybe they do kidnap people and take them on joyrides
through the cosmos.

"But then, out of all those who claim to have met star
beings, why has no one ever announced anything they
learned from the encounter that was simultaneously true
and unambiguous, and that science didn't already
know?"

I rejoin our great skyboat as it skims a silvery trail over this
place we once called home. Now the planet throngs with
bustling, earnest, *craving* humanity. Craving, if they just
knew, what we used to give their ancestors. What we'd give
again, if they allowed it.

*"Allowed it?"* My thoughts shame me. What right have
worms to "allow" anything?

There was a time when men averted their eyes and shiv-
ered in fear. Now the planet's night face spreads a glow of
city lights. Forests swarm with campers and explorers armed
with cameras. It seems ages since we heard from our cous-
ins, in Earth's hidden places, the mountains and deep lochs.
Long ago they fled before men's modern eyes, or were an-
nihilated.

It makes me wonder—could it be that humans are *angry*
with us for some reason?

"But there's a second, even better answer to this whole
UFO business.

"Let's admit a slim chance some of these case histories might actually be sightings of little silvery guys riding spaceships. My reply? We can still rule out contact
with Intelligent Life!

" *Look at their behavior!* Buzzing truck drivers, mutilat-
ing farm animals, trampling corn fields, kidnapping people to stick needles in their brains . . . is this any way for
intelligent beings to act?"

I never heard it put quite that way before.

Perhaps some of you, subconsciously, *are* a bit upset with us.

But we do it for your own good.

> "Worst of all, if these UFO guys really do exist—they're refusing to make contact!
>
> ". . . What? You say they're afraid of us? We, who barely made it to our measly little moon, and couldn't go back now if we tried? *We* frighten star aliens? Right. And I'm terrified of turtles in the zoo!"

But we do fear you, sage of science. Your premises are skewed. I would teach you. But if I tried, you'd burn me where I stand.

> "Tell you what, caller. Let's try an experiment. You assume these ET fellows are pretty smart, yes? . . . In fact, they're probably picking up my voice at this moment. After all this time, guys that clever must have a handle on our language, right?
>
> "Great. Then I'll quit talking to my human audience for a minute, and turn instead to those eavesdroppers in the sky.
>
> "Hollo, you little green guys, listening to my voice in your fancy ships! I'm gonna lay a challenge on you now. Get out your space-pencils, 'cause I'm about to give you the phone number of the Jet Propulsion Laboratory, in Pasadena, California. You can call through any of our communications satellites. Surely you're smart enough to do that?
>
> "Ready, then? The area code is 818. Then dial 354-6160. Got it?
>
> "Okay, when you get the switchboard at JPL, ask for the "special alpha line" of my friend Dr. Michael Klein. Got that? You'll be put through to an answering machine, but no sweat. To prove you aren't one of the *human* jerks listening in right now—some drunk or doper itching to pull a prank—I want you to describe into the machine a demonstration you'll perform in the sky the following night!
>
> "Your demo should be visible from Pasadena, California, at ten p.m. on a clear night, and be of clearly extraterrestrial origin. You might turn one of the Moon's craters purple, or something likewise gaudy. Mike prom-

ises to check for messages daily, and have someone
watching at the appointed hour.

"If you do pull off something impressively "alien," you
can bet we'll be waiting by the phone the next day for
your follow-up call!"

Such effrontery! Never has one of these mad, new-style humans taunted us so brazenly. Out of wrath, we get carried
away in our work. Half the cattle are destroyed and the rest
driven to frothing panic before Fyrfalcon calls a halt. We
stare down at no typical mutilation. The rancher who owns
this herd won't be awed or frightened by our visit, but furious.

Curse you, man of logic, man of science! Were it in our
power, we'd topple the towers carrying your voice. Your satellites would rain like falling stars! Certainly we'd shut out
your yammerings.

But it is our nature to hear, when we are spoken of. So it
always was. So it shall be while our kind lasts.

"That's my challenge, you platinum-plated guys out
there. Perform some convincing demonstration in the
sky, and JPL will do the rest! Mike will arrange landing
sites, rent-a-cops, press coverage, visas of both types
. . . and yes, even gigs on talk shows. Anything you like.
Anything to make First Contact a pleasant, comfortable
experience for you.

"We want to be gracious hosts. Make friends. Show
you the town. That's as generous an offer as any honest
guest could ask for.

"But what if nobody answers my challenge? What
would that mean, caller? . . . Uh-huh. It might mean
UFOs are myths!

"On the other hand, maybe they do exist, and are sitting back, spurning this sincere offer.

"In which case at least we've settled what they are
. . . nasty sons-of-bitches who love messing with our
heads. And all I have to say is—get out of our sky,
assholes! Leave us alone, so we can get on with looking
for someone out there worth talking to!

". . . Ahem. And on that note, Engineer Ted signals
it's time for station I.D. Sorry, Ted. Guess I got a little
carried away there. But at three a.m., I don't figure the

FCC is likely to be listening any more than creeps on flying saucers ..."

Our Dream Master, Sylphshank, has been meddling with
sleep-fogged minds. He tells of one woman who has been
dozing while listening to the radio show. While she is susceptible, Sylphshank projects into her mind dream-images of
his own face! She awakens now with a startled idea, and excitedly dials the station.

Delightful! This should irritate that upstart scientist. Perhaps when she is finished we'll do it again and again until
he finally gives up.

We move on to California, home of some of our best
friends and fiercest foes. One of our changelings—human
born—uses a stolen acetylene torch to burn marks of "rocket
exhaust" and "landing jacks" onto a plateau near San Diego.
A cult of the faithful has sanctified this ground with their belief. We often reward them with such signs.

Our great, long-prowed boat floats above the chaparral,
insubstantial as thought. Where once its burnished hull
would have been invincible, now we must protect it from
those eyes.

"Okay, we're back. This is Professor Joe Perez, filling
in for Talkback Larry while he takes a much-needed
break from you manic insomniacs. Want to talk astronomy? Black holes? The universe? I'm your man. Let's
take another call.

"Yes, Ma'am? . . . Oh, hell, I thought we used up that
topic . . .

"What? . . . Hmm. Now that you mention it, that puts
a new spin on things. It does seem strange that saucer
folk are so often depicted in certain ways. Smooth, arch-
ing foreheads. Big eyes. Long, meddling fingers.

"It should've sounded familiar. Look at their supposed
behavior—playing tricks, offering mystic half-truths,
never meeting honest folk in the eyes . . .

"Yes ma'am, I think you've hit on something. Saucer
people are elves!"

Our boat-of-ether rocks. The voice is stronger than ever,
shaking our concentration.

Four teenagers blink, captivated by the light shining

across their upturned faces. We had them nicely snared, but the distraction of that cursed voice weakens our grip. Gryffinloch murmurs alarm.

"We shouldn't have tried so many at once!"

"The voice has us confused," Fyrfalcon answers. "Take care—"

I cry out. "One wakens!"

Three of those young faces still exhibit rapture as they stand uncritical, accepting. But the fourth—a gangling child-woman—casts another kind of glow. As she rouses, her eyes narrow and her mouth forms words. Tapped into her mind, I sense her effort to see. To really see!

*What am I staring at? Why . . . it looks transparent, as if it isn't really there at . . .*

"Flee!" Fyrfalcon screams as we are blinded by that deadly gaze!

"It's late, but let's go with this caller's notion and see where it leads.

"Once upon a time, legends say elves and dwarves and trolls shared our world . . . all those colorful spirit creatures our ancestors warned their children about, so they'd shun the forest.

"My wife's an anthropologist, and we read our kids stories she's collected all over the world, many of them amusing, moving, even inspiring. But after a while you start to notice something—very few of those old magical characters, the pixies and sprites and spirits, were people you'd want as neighbors! Sometimes beautiful and exciting, creatures in fairy tales also act petty, tyrannical, and awfully stingy about sharing their knowledge with poor human beings. Always they were portrayed as living apart, on the edge of the unknown. In olden times that meant just beyond the firelight.

"Then something changed. Humankind started pushing the circle outward, and all those fancy beasts of legend faded back as well. Yetis and Bigfoots. Elves and lake monsters. They were always said to be just beyond the reach of torchlight, then lanterns, then sonar and aerial photography. . . .

"Now maybe that's because they never were more than figments of our over-fertile imaginations. Maybe they were distractions, that kept us from properly appreciating the other species of very real animals sharing our world.

"Still, I can entertain another possibility.

"Imagine such creatures really did exist, once upon a time, behaving like spirit folk in legend. But at some point we started shucking free of them, conquering our ignorance, driving them off to let us get about our lives. . . ."

Scattered, riding fragments of our broken boat, we call to one another across space.

We survivors.

By now those teenagers are rubbing their eyes, already convinced we were hallucinations. That is what happens when humans see us with *skepticism*. Now we blow away like leaves, like wisps of shredded dreams.

Perhaps the world's winds will bring some of us together to begin anew. Meanwhile, I can only drift and remember.

Some years back we plotted to end this plague of reason. We stole human babies and took them to a southern isle. Then, back in the world of humans, we caused "incidents" and false alarms on radar screens, trying to set off that final war. Let their mad genius consume itself in its own fire, we thought. It used to be so easy to provoke war among men.

But this time things were different. Perhaps it was the new thinking, or maybe they sensed the precipice. There was no war. We grew depressed.

So depressed we forgot our charges on the island. When at last we checked, all the infants had died.

Such frail things, humans.

How did frail things ever grow so strong?

"It's dark out and the wind's picked up. Let's push this ghost story as far as it'll go.

"We were talking about how fairy folk always seemed to flit just beyond the light, beyond our gaze. Since Earth is pretty well explored now, the few remaining legends speak of arctic wastes, the deepest depths . . . and outer space. It's as if they are both drawn to us and terrified.

"I can't imagine it's our weapons such creatures would fear . . . ever see a hunter come home with an elf pelt on his fender?

"Now here's a thought . . . what if it's because of a

change in *us?* What if modern humans destroy fairy creatures just by getting close!

". . . You laugh? Good. Still, imagine today's Cub Scouts, running, peering into forest corners their ancestors would have superstitiously left alone. Ever wonder why the change?

"It could be just curiosity.

"Or else . . . maybe they're *chasing our species' natural foe.* Perhaps that's really why we seek Nessie and Yeti, hounding them to the far corners of the Earth. Or why we're pushing into space, for that matter!

"Maybe something inside us recalls how we were treated by our fairy friends. Subconsciously what we're after is revenge!"

Monsters. Driven off our own cursed planet by these flat-eyed monsters.

The experiment got out of hand.

How I wish we never'd created them!

"Time's up boys and girls. Whatever you call them—elves or UFO aliens—whether they exist or were just another fancy dream we invented—I see no point in giving them any more of our time.

"Tomorrow night we'll move on to more interesting stuff . . . the Big Bang, neutron stars, and our hopeful search for some *real* intelligent life out there.

"Until then, people, good night. And good morning."

# Stop Press
## by Mike Resnick

*Award-winning author Mike Resnick himself says that he is "uniquely qualified to write for this book, having spent three years editing* The National Insider *and* The National Tattler *back in the late 1960s." He has since written some thirty-odd novels, including* Santiago, Ivory, *and* Prophet, *edited a number of delightful anthologies, and has (at this writing) won two Hugos.*

*He also has the habit of doing stuff like this to his editors.*

November 10, 2331

Sam Friesner, Editor
*The Interplanetary Tattler*
10 Asimov Avenue
Luna

Dear Sir:
Allow me to introduce myself. I represent the twelfth generation of free-lance writer in my family, dating back to the fabled Mike Resnick of the late 20th century. I have long been an admirer of your fearless yet entertaining no-holds-barred brand of journalism, and I think I have finally come up with a story so unique, so bizarre, so positive *outre,* that it will prove the beginning of a long and happy relationship between us.

Would you be interested in an interview, with holographs, of Boris Korchev, the three-headed shortstop of the Ganymede Geldings? I could let you have an exclusive for 5,000 credits.

Cordially yours,
Melvin Resnick
666 Glory Road
Heinlein City
Ganymede

\* \* \*

November 15, 2331

Dear Mr. Resnick:

Thank you for your interest in our newspaper, but I suspect you've been out of touch with it for some time now, or you would know that we ran a feature last June on the New York Yankees' Fourteen-Headed Infield, including an exclusive interview with Wilbur "Ten-Eyes" Plitkin.

If you come across any truly unique features in the future, please keep us in mind.

> Yours,
> Sam Friesner, Editor
> *The Interplanetary Tattler*

PS—I can find no historical reference to a 20th century writer named Mike Resnick. In point of fact, the major literary figure of the 1990s was my own ancestor, the still-beloved Esther Friesner.

\* \* \*

November 19, 2331

Sam Friesner, Editor
*The Interplanetary Tattler*
10 Asimov Avenue
Luna

Dear Editor Friesner:

I'm sorry my last proposal didn't suit your needs, but I've come up with one that you're absolutely going to love. What would you say to exclusive coverage of the recently-concluded experiment at the Genetic Engineering Clinic here on Mars Base, where an eight-legged horse just gave birth to an elephant with five trunks? (The sire was a Patagonian woodmouse.)

I could let you have this for 3,500 credits.

Looking forward to working with you, I am—

> Hopefully yours,
> Melvin Resnick
> 17 Tars Tarkas Blvd.
> New Barsoom
> Mars Base

PS—*Esther* Friesner, you said? Never heard of her. I'll have to check my library's data banks.

\* \* \*

November 29, 2331

Dear Mr. Resnick:

Five-trunked elephants are a drug on the market. I refer you to our issue of August 23. If you will turn to Page 38, you'll find a story about the breeding of a five-trunked elephant with Rosie and Posie Plootz, a pair of tightrope-walking Siamese twins from Duluth, Minnesota. It was barely filler material back in August; it's certainly of no interest to us today.

I urge you to study our journal more carefully before wasting your time tracking down stories that are too mundane to appeal to our sophisticated readership.

> Best wishes,
> Sam Friesner, Editor
> *The Interplanetary Tattler*

PS—Surely you jest. Esther Friesner was one of the Literary Greats. I'm proud to have her blood flowing in my veins.

\* \* \*

December 8, 2331

Sam Friesner, Editor
*The Interplanetary Tattler*
10 Asimov Avenue
Luna

Dear Mr. Friesner:

All right. This time I've got a story for you that you *can't* turn down!

I have uncovered, at great physical and financial cost to myself, one of the more bizarre scandals in the history of the entire human race. Even at this late date I can hardly believe the evidence I have amassed, but there is no question that when you run this article, governments will fall and you and I will almost certainly share a Jacqueline Suzanne Memorial Prize for our journalistic efforts.

What would you say if I were to tell you that Solar President Meacham *is having an affair with Tprxt, her insectoid Neptunian maid?*

I have it all here—eyewitness accounts, signed statements, and some of the most explosive holographs ever taken. I'm a little short of cash at the moment, but a good-faith advance of 2,500 credits will assure you the exclusive rights to the story, until we can negotiate a final price.

My first loyalty is to you, but I can only hold this offer open for 48 hours. If I have not heard from you by then, I will have to submit it to *The Interplanetary Inquirer.*

Excitedly yours,
Melvin Resnick
AAA Ace Outpost
Sheckleyville
Venus

PS—Spelled F-R-I-E-S-N-E-R, the same as yours?

\* \* \*

December 14, 2331

Dear Mr. Resnick:

What is so newsworthy about President Meacham having an affair with a Neptunian? My own wife is an egg-laying seven-limbed Mercurian *porble,* and I take extreme umbrage at your pedestrian notion that there is something unsavory about inter-species romance.

More to the point, President Meacham has already admitted to youthful indiscretions with a Tritonian sea-slug and a Callistan *muudu-muudu,* and in fact was once married to an ammonia-breathing trisexual marsupial native of Alpha Centauri III when she served as our ambassador to that troubled world.

This is tame stuff, Mr. Resnick. Perhaps you might be better off considering the science fiction market; journalism is a very difficult discipline, second perhaps only to the contemporary romance novel, and not everyone is fit for it.

Yours,
Sam Friesner, Editor
*The Interplanetary Tattler*

PS—Yes, the spelling is the same. I urge you to read *Hooray for Hellywood* and *Gnome Man's Land;* they practically define the Serious Literary Novel, circa the late 20th century.

\* \* \*

December 22, 2331

San Friesner, Editor
*The Interplanetary Tattler*
10 Asimov Avenue
Luna

Dear Sam:

I may call you Sam, mayn't I? I feel as if I know you by this point in our correspondence, and despite your refusal to accept any of my previous proposals, I intuit that a certain bond of friendship and mutual professional respect has developed between us.

I'll be perfectly honest with you, Sam. I've suffered some financial reverses of late, and my wife is expecting our first child, and while I would never want this to influence you, I just want you to know that if you can see your way clear to purchasing the following, you will have an eternally grateful friend.

Not that the story *needs* any special consideration. The instant I stumbled across it, I knew that it was tailor-made for *The Interplanetary Tattler.* (Get ready now; here it comes!)

How would you like an exclusive interview with Lt. Hemloch Willoughby, the pilot who, when marooned without food for seventeen days in the Sirius system, survived by eating his own genitals? What pathos! What human interest! What a triumph of the indomitable human spirit!

2000 credits takes it away. (For an extra 500, I can arrange an interview with his wife. Well, his ex-wife.)

Please reply soonest.

> Expectantly yours,
> Melvin Resnick
> 206 Lensman Street
> Kinnison Village
> Titan

PS—Late 20th century, you say? I wonder if she ever met Mike Resnick? Probably not; he was much too busy turning out classic after classic.

\* \* \*

December 29, 2331

Dear Mr. Resnick:

Oh, Lord, not *another* Marooned Pilot Eats Own Genitals

story! Maybe the *Biloxi Times* or the *Fort Wayne Journal* might be interested, if you catch them on a slow day, but we specialize in the unusual.

I admire your persistence, but you've missed the boat again. I can only suggest that you read the slogan on our masthead—"Home of the Unique, The Bizarre, and the Deeply Warped"—and commit it to memory.

> Yours,
> Sam Friesner, Editor
> *The Interplanetary Tattler*

PS—I doubt that they ever met. She had *class*.

\* \* \*

January 6, 2332

Sam Friesner, Editor
*The Interplanetary Tattler*
10 Asimov Avenue
Luna

Friesner:

How can you keep doing this to me? The wolves are at the door. I am reduced to renting a ship from Hertz (my own has been repossessed), Solar Bell is threatening to shut off my sub-space radio transmitter, my wife is about to bring our first child into the world, and you keep rejecting stories that any editor would be thrilled to run.

I'm giving you one last chance, and then I'm going to start giving *The Interplanetary Inquirer* first look at all my material. I mean it, Friesner; I am a desperate man.

All right—here it is, and if I say so myself, it is the most explosive story I've unearthed thus far.

I can prove that John Fitzgerald Kennedy was actually a woman, a nightclub stripteaser named Lola Puloza who was once billed as "The Hottest Mexican Export Since the Tamale." She fled to the United States in drag to escape from her gangster boyfriend, became Robert F. Kennedy's lover (the affair with Marilyn Monroe was just a ruse to hide the *real* truth), and was in fact assassinated not by Lee Harvey Oswald but rather by Salvatore Diego Gomez, her estranged Bolivian husband whom she had not seen in 23 years.

I can supply dates, signed testimony, even a never-before-seen videotape of Puloza putting on her JFK makeup prior to escorting Jacqueline to a state dinner. (Yes, the story of Kennedy's womanizing was another ruse, so that JFK would never find "himself" alone in a bedroom with Jackie.)

This is the story of the century; the day after you publish it, they'll have to rewrite the history books.

Please remit 500 credits by return mail.

> Desperately yours,
> Melvin Resnick
> Ringworld Hotel
> 7th Ring
> Saturn

\* \* \*

January 11, 2332

Dear Mr. Resnick:

History books were *made* to be rewritten. They rewrote them in 2328, when we proved that JFK was really Elvis Presley in disguise, and again eight months ago when we broke the story that the second and third shots in Dallas were actually self-administered because Elvis was depressed over the sales of his latest record.

As for your revelation, I'm afraid that you have somehow been misinformed. Our resident psychic, *Mme.* Shwartz, just had her weekly conversation with Elvis' ghost, who denies ever having been a Mexican stripteaser, and certainly not one called Lola Puloza.

> Yours,
> Sam Friesner, Editor
> *The Interplanetary Tattler*

PS—I of course read *The Interplanetary Inquirer* every day, and I have yet to see your byline appear there. I'm afraid that your threats carry no more punch than your stories.

\* \* \*

January 29, 2332

Sam Friesner, Editor
*The Interplanetary Tattler*
10 Asimov Avenue
Luna

Dear Scumbag:

Screw you and your lousy rag!

All I can say is that this is despicable treatment to give a struggling writer, just because his ancestor aced yours out of a couple of Hugo Awards more than three centuries ago.

> Disgustedly yours,
> Melvin Resnick
> c/o The Malzberg Memorial
> Home for the Terminally
> Morose
> 17 Herovit Road
> Ridgefield Park, New Jersey

PS—My wife gave birth to a healthy baby boy. In the charity ward. No thanks to you. If I have any say about it, he's *not* going to beat his head against a stone wall trying to be a writer. As soon as he'd old enough, I'm sending him to plumbing school, so he can work at a profession where people appreciate his efforts.

\* \* \*

*Interoffice Memo*
From: Sam Friesner
To: Press Room

Stop press. Remake Page 1. Two-inch block letters, as follows:

### MOTHER GIVES BIRTH TO NORMAL BABY!!!!!

*Memo to self:* Cut Resnick a check for 5,000 credits, and offer him another 10,000 if he can supply a holograph in time to make the early edition.

# Martian Memorial to Elvis Sighted
## by George Alec Effinger

*George Alec Effinger is living proof that it is possible to write great SF and fantasy comedy as well as the serious side of the genre. His story, "Schroedinger's Kitten," won the Nebula and the Hugo. He is also the author of the hilarious Muffy Birnbaum tales. His most recent novel is* The Exile Kiss.

*I firmly believe that "Martian Memorial to Elvis Sighted," is the perfect finish to this book, as well as a wonderfully fitting tribute to "the King."*

August 16, 1987. Ten years to the day since Elvis' death. Priscilla had almost forgotten the mysterious envelope that lay hidden in the back of one of Lisa Marie's sock and underwear drawers. Her nineteen-year-old daughter had not forgotten, however. In fact, she'd been counting down the days until she could finally open her father's final testament. The day before, Lisa Marie had called her mother in California; Priscilla had flown back to Memphis for the occasion of the opening of the envelope.

Graceland was closed to tourists for this special day. Priscilla and Lisa Marie made certain they had undisturbed privacy. Holding her breath, Elvis' daughter opened the clasp on the manila envelope and tore away the masking tape that sealed it. Glancing at Priscilla's eyes, she opened the package and took out about twenty handwritten pages. Handwritten by Elvis himself. Priscilla and Lisa Marie recognized the handwriting of the King of Rock 'n' Roll.

"What does it say?" Priscilla asked breathlessly.

"I'll read it to you, mama."

And here is Elvis' last communication from beyond the grave:

*(Mrs. Presley: My name is Milt Vessman, and I had the privilege of serving with your husband in the Army in Germany. A short time ago, Elvis came to me and asked if I would help him tell the fantastic story that follows. He recited the events in great detail, and I dictated it back to him, improving his grammar and vocabulary. Whether or not you believe these things is, as Elvis says, up to you.)*

Dear Priscilla—

I am a very old man; how old I do not know. Possibly I am a hundred, possibly more. You might think this is some fantasy or delusion of mine, but as clearly as I recall my childhood in East Tupelo, I also recall a life—several lives—before those days. How many births and deaths and rebirths have I had? Maybe I'll never know for sure. And maybe I'll never understand why I have been given this gift. A gift, I say, or is it a curse? I do not know.

You may believe all that or not, as you choose. I am writing this in 1966. I have just finished filming *Spinout* and I am about to begin an all-singing, all-dancing, all-Elvis rock 'n' roll musical version of a book called *The Prisoner of Zenda*. I've left instructions that this message should not be opened until ten years after my death. I hope that's a long, long time from now, and I hope that you are reading this surrounded by all the children we will have soon, but of course all that is in the hands of the Lord.

Between movies, Priscilla, you know I like to take a little vacation to clear my head. If you remember, I told you after *Spinout* that I just had to get away by myself for a while. That wasn't the complete truth. The truth is that I had a strange and—

I'll start from the beginning. I promise you that I'm not making any of this up. I may be a poor Southren boy, but I'm not crazy.

Anyway, *Spinout* wasn't much of a challenge, although I really liked being around all those fast cars. One day, near the end of the picture, I was called from the set. That was surprising, because Joe Pasternak and MGM hated interruptions like that. They ate up a lot of time at union pay rates. I wondered what the trouble was.

It turned out there wasn't any trouble—not on the set, at least. I was led to one of the production trailers where Norman Taurog, the director, had his office. Inside, Norman wasn't there. Instead there was a man in a dark blue suit. "Do you know me, Mr. Presley?" he said.

"No, I can't say that I do."

"My name is Dean Rusk. I have an office in Washington, D.C. I am President Johnson's Secretary of State."

Well, all right. I thought it was kind of an honor, getting a visit from the Secretary of State and all. I was just curious about what was so doggone important about it that we had to stop filming.

"I'm right proud to meet you, sir," I said.

Dean Rusk smiled, stood up, and offered me his hand. I shook it. "I was briefed rather extensively. In your dossier, a few people remarked on your politeness. I'm pleased to see that they weren't mistaken."

I might have blushed, I don't know. I didn't even know what a dossier was. "Deep down," I said, "I'm still a shy country boy from Mississippi."

"Shy," Dean Rusk said. He seemed amused. "Certainly. Just as you say."

"Now, I don't suppose you come all the way down here from Washington just to tell me you're a big fan of rock 'n' roll."

Dean Rusk nodded. "Very astute guess, Mr. Presley. I'm here to set up a meeting between yourself and a very important person. Let me ask one question: Are you proud to be an American?"

I didn't know why he'd asked that. "I served in the Army a while back, and I'm proud of my accomplishments there. I have never said or done anything to make anyone doubt my loyalty, and I never will."

"That's good enough for me, Mr. Presley." He stood up and went to the door. He opened it and talked quietly with some men outside. They were wearing suits, too, and I guessed they were Secret Service agents.

The Secretary of State held the door open and three men came into the trailer. The first was big and tall and strong-looking, and I knew immediately it was Lyndon Johnson, the President of the United States. I've got to admit, I was so shocked that I nearly swallowed my gum.

The President took the seat Dean Rusk had vacated. Mr. Rusk leaned against one wall of the trailer, and a Secret Service man leaned against the door. The third man was short

but well-muscled; he just stood near the desk, a few feet
from me. He was studying me closely.

"How do you do, Mr. Carter?" Lyndon Johnson said.

"Excuse me, Mr. President. I'm not anyone named Carter.
I'm Elvis Presley, the singer and movie star."

The president nodded slowly and ponderously. "I understand that," he said. "I also understand that to maintain your
privacy, you use the name John Carter when you check into
hotels."

Aha. A slight misunderstanding. "Carpenter," I said. "Dr.
John Carpenter is the name I use."

Dean Rusk frowned. "And your secret postal name is
John Burroughs. We were sure—"

"My security code name is Burrows, Mr. Rusk. Not Burroughs."

"That's what I said," Dean Rusk. "Didn't I?"

I shook my head. Listen closely: Burroughs . . . Burrows.
Here the difference?

"Carpenter? Burrows?" Dean Rusk said, a puzzled expression on his face. "Maybe we've made a terrible mistake."

"Maybe not," Lyndon Johnson said. "Mr. Presley, is it
possible that during your life, sometime you learned to use
. . . a sword?"

"Right now," I said. "I'm rehearsing for a swordfight picture. *Double Trouble* it's titled, and it's based on this book
called *The Pris—*"

"There," the President said, "we haven't made a mistake
after all. Please sit down, Mr. Presley. I have a long story to
tell you, and then I'll be asking if you care to help our country and others similarly dedicated to freedom and democracy."

"Why, now, of course I'll be willing—"

Dean Rusk said, "maybe you should hear the entire story,
Mr. Presley, before you commit yourself to this venture."

I sat back and let Lyndon Johnson tell me the most incredible tall tale I'd ever heard. I won't repeat the whole thing
to you. Altogether it was about how a race of men on the
planet Mars had sent a representative to Washington. They
needed help in finding their long-time defender, a stalwart
swordsman and warrior named John Carter, from Virginia.
Instead, they somehow located me—"Dr. John Carpenter,"
from Memphis, Tennessee. The Martians needed a hero, and

if John Carter couldn't be located, they were willing to take me instead.

Now these men from Mars aren't little green men. The shorter man was a Martian named Antor Thon. The race of Martian humans had normal Caucasian features, but they were a trifle smaller than an Earth human.

Antor Thon had come to Earth without a flying saucer. It was sort of a mental thing. He got himself into the right frame of mind, then just flung himself into space between the planets. He had come to teach me the method. He wanted me to return to Mars with him and save their little Martian asses.

"Well, uh, Mr. President," I said. "I'd surely like to help the little fella, but he wants me to go to Mars. How do I know I'll be able to get back? And swordfighting—I've only been practicing that for six weeks. I don't know if I'm good enough to stand up to a crowd of angry giant Martian critters."

Antor Thon spoke up. "On Mars, you will have an advantage in strength because of your Earth muscles. Mars is smaller than Earth, and therefore it has a weaker gravity."

I wasn't exactly sure what he was talking about. "You mean I'll be stronger there?"

"Exactly," Antor Thon said. "You'll be able to leap much higher, lift greater weights, have proportionally better endurance. You will be the greatest warrior on Mars."

I wanted to say that I never really thought of myself as a warrior, but then I recalled that I'd been in a number of tussles over the years, and I never run from none of 'em.

I looked from the Martian to President Lyndon Johnson. "Of course, if I decide to go," I said, "I'll expect nothing in the way of reward. Just the regard of my country and the people of Mars."

"Very good of you, Mr. Presley," the President said in his low, drawling voice.

"*But—*" I said. "But there are a few things I'll need if I'm going to go to Mars and rough up some space monsters for the little fella."

"Just name it," Antor Thon said, "and if at all possible, it shall be yours."

"Cheeseburgers," I said.

"Four frozen," Dean Rusk said, "just the way you like them."

"Pepsi. The good stuff, not diet. And I want the caffeine, too."

"Six cases," Dean Rusk said.

"Bottles, not cans."

"All right. Anything else?"

"Uh-huh," I said. "Cold, dry hot dog buns, hold the hot dogs."

Dean Rusk clenched his jaws, but agreed.

"And Neutrogena soap. Colgate toothpaste. My little Martin acoustic guitar. And my boys. I always warm up with the Jordanaires. They have to go with me."

"Impossible!" the President said. "We can't send a bunch of gyrating—"

I raised a hand. "I *always* warm up with the Jordanaires. If they don't go, I don't go. If you can't arrange it, then go get Bobby Vee to be your hero."

Dean Rusk, a master at negotiation, said, "Instead of the Jordanaires, what if we double the number of cheeseburgers and Pepsi Colas?"

I had to think about that for a moment. "It's a deal," I said.

Antor Thon smiled. "Then think of me as your brother-in-arms," he said.

"All right, then, little buddy," I said. All that was left was hammering out the final details. I'd picked up some negotiating skills myself from listening to Colonel Parker.

We all agreed that I would leave for Mars with Antor Thon in two weeks. I had enough time to call you and make up that excuse about wanting to be by myself for a while; we also had to wait for the government of the United States of America to put together the cheeseburgers and Neutrogena and all the rest of the stuff.

In the meantime, the little Martian fella coached me on the proper meditation routine. That part came easy, because of all my karate training and yoga and the other mystical Eastern techniques I've studied.

Exactly two weeks later, about midnight, the clouds cleared and revealed a beautiful sky full of stars. Antor Thon pointed out one low above the horizon. I could see it beaming steadily, and I knew from its reddish color that it had to be Mars. My little buddy started murmuring his traveling chant, and I did the same. I found myself relaxing more and more, and soon I was in a light hypnotic trance. Then Antor Thon began speaking in a low voice, right near my right ear.

I felt a strange tingling all the way from my scalp to the soles of my feet. I sunk deeper into the trance, and soon I experienced an unpleasant twanging, breaking sensation. I opened my eyes and saw that I was standing beside the dead body of Elvis Presley. I shuddered. Before I could say a word, Antor Thon pointed toward Mars. I looked, and I felt a great longing to cross the vast distance between the planets. I closed my eyes again. There was an instant of tremendous cold, and when I opened my eyes, I knew I was no longer on Earth. I had traveled across time and space to the ancient, dying world of Mars.

"Welcome to Mars, as you call it," Antor Thon said. He, like myself, was completely naked now. For some reason, that didn't seem to matter. He indicated that we were going to head off toward the north.

I took my first step on this terrible and marvelous new world. What happened next was a great surprise. I went sailing up into the air, maybe twenty feet. "Earth muscles," Antor Thon called, grinning. I was going to have to spend a little time learning how to get around without flying off into Mars' thinner atmosphere.

When I was settled back on the red dirt, I picked up a rock and threw it as hard as I could. It rose in a flat arc until I couldn't see it anymore. It may have cleared the far horizon. I felt like Superman, except I didn't have X-ray vision.

We had only walked a mile or two, when we topped a low ridge and looked down at a horrible scene being played out below us, maybe a hundred yards away. A small party of Antor Thon's fellow men were being attacked by a company of tall, ugly critters. It was clear that the big monsters had the upper hand, and unless we intervened successfully, all the Martian humans would be dead in a matter of minutes.

"I have to go help my brothers," Antor Thon said with a sad smile. "It is a matter of honor."

"I understand honor," I said. "I'll come with you." I followed my little buddy down toward the scene of carnage. I still had quite a bit of trouble keeping my feet on the ground. I wondered if I could turn that to my advantage when we reached the battlefield.

Antor Thon gave a shrill, shrieking cry that I'd soon learn was the fighting song of his clan. He stooped briefly to pick up the sword of one of his fallen brothers. I followed suit, and together he and I fought back-to-back on the red-rocked surface of Mars. I didn't have time to remark on what an unlikely thing this was for a poor boy from Mississippi to get mixed up in. Of course, I wasn't a poor boy anymore, and those Mississippi days were long ago in the past. It seemed more appropriate that the King of Rock 'n' Roll should lend a hand to the little people who needed him.

I learned very quickly that I was not yet a great swordfighting hero. I managed not to get killed, but only because of my leaping ability and my immense strength. I had only a minor skill with the rapierlike long sword that was the favorite weapon of both the Martian men and their attackers. I saved myself time after time, and I accounted for three slain monsters. One time I saw Antor Thon desperately trying to defend himself against two of them. I gave a Southren rebel yell and skewered one of his opponents; while the second one stared at me in disbelief, Antor Thon dispatched him to his ancestors.

The battle came to an end shortly thereafter. Three of the big things mounted their great lumbering mounts and took off toward the west. Only myself and Antor Thon remained—all the other Martians had perished in the ambush. Antor Thon sang over their lifeless bodies, then laid each and every one to rest with all the necessary honors and prayers. I didn't understand the ceremony, of course, so I just stood by respectfully until he finished. Then, at last, we continued on toward the north.

I hadn't had much of an effect, despite all my so-called advantages. I promised myself that I would practice with the long sword; my next meeting with the Martian monsters would end differently.

We marched northward for two more days. I was pushing a shopping cart from a Winn Dixie ahead of me, loaded with cheeseburgers, Pepsi, hot dog buns, and the other things I'd asked for. I shared my rations with Antor Thon.

"You know," he said, "during that battle, I could see that you needed some more instruction with the long sword. Because you've proven to be such a good companion, and because you're being so generous with your food and that fizzing brown sweetwater, I'll be happy to fill you in on the history and current problems of our race on this planet."

"Thank you, little buddy," I said. "When all of this is

over, how 'bout I buy you a Cadillac? Would you like that, huh?"

Antor Thon shook his head. "What is a Cadillac?"

I frowned. "Here, then," I said. "Have another Pepsi. They're good for you."

The situation was this: The city of Gornath, Antor Thon's city, had been put under siege by a powerful army-clan of the ugly critters. The food was beginning to run out for the humans, and they doubted that they could hold out for another Earth month. My little buddy had volunteered to come to Earth in search of this John Carter. When he couldn't locate the man, he turned to the government of the most generous and fair-minded nation in the free world—the good old U. S. A.

With the help of the State Department and the FBI, they had finally located . . . Dr. John Carpenter, "expert" swordsman.

Me.

Although it was all a mistake, I was determined to do what I could for my little buddy and his city of Gornath. As he had said, it was a matter of honor.

When we finally arrived at Gornath, Antor Thon told me that we had to circle around to a secret gate in the city's walls. We had to wait until darkness fell, and then slowly make our way through the ranks of besieging ugly critters. It was a dangerous assignment, and I suddenly got a better understanding of Antor Thon's courage. He had volunteered to leave safety and familiar surroundings behind to travel to what was for him an alien planet, in search of a hero.

I was that hero, and I could do no less than my companion. I had come to this alien planet, and I would give my utmost to defend the humans of Mars from their enemies.

First, however, we fortified ourselves in the valley between two ridges, out of sight of the monsters. We each ate two cheeseburgers and drank a bottle of Pepsi. Then I brushed my teeth. Strange worlds and a dangerous adventure were no reasons to neglect personal hygiene.

While we waited for the shrunken sun to set among the western Martian hills, Antor Thon drilled me further in the art of fighting with the long sword. He also taught me the Martian ideas of fair and sportsmanlike combat. It amounted to an entire protocol of warfare. It sounded dumb to me.

"On Earth," I said, "we fight with whatever we have at hand."

Antor Thon frowned. "We know. That's why we consider Earth to be completely without gallantry."

I wanted to say, "This military etiquette problem of yours may be why Mars is a dying planet." I didn't say it out loud, though.

We spent the next three hours practicing our swordsmanship. I had only a beginner's familiarity with the weapon, but in a few hours Antor Thon taught me a few tricks and traps that might hold me in good stead in the days to come.

Then night fell, more quickly than it does on Earth. I looked up into the night sky. I quickly found the two hurtling Martian moons, but I could not be sure which bright spot was Earth.

"Now," Antor Thon murmured, "we must creep over the ridge and then pass quietly among them."

"Shouldn't we wait until they fall asleep?" I asked.

"Believe me, they won't ever all fall asleep. We may as well go now. Keep silent and follow me."

I knew I could slip quietly among the shadows to the city's gate; I was afraid that my rattling Winn Dixie cart carrying my Earth rations and the health and beauty aids would give us away.

"Leave it here," Antor Thon said. "If it is heard by their sentries, it will cost us our lives."

I solved the dilemma when I remembered my Earth muscles. I simply lifted the cart up and carried it on one shoulder. So together we managed to pass among the unaware ugly critters, moving noiselessly from one shadow to another. Soon we were standing under the walls of Gornath. Antor Thon rapped a signal upon the strong wooden gate.

It did not take long for Antor Thon to identify himself to the guards. We were let into the city, and my little buddy led me quickly through the streets toward a magnificent palace high on a hill. Word of our arrival spread quickly, and soon there were crowds lining the road to the palace. I heard them chanting Antor Thon's name. And I heard them chanting "John Car-ter! John Car-ter!" I couldn't help but think that they'd all be terribly disappointed when they learned the truth.

As we climbed the hill, I saw three tall statues surrounded

by lovely flowering shrubs and cool fountains. "Are these statues of important people in your past?" I asked.

"Come closer and see," the little fella said.

I did as he suggested and when I saw whom the statues represented, I was astonished.

Antor Thon said, "They are important people from *your* past."

Indeed they were. I recognized Buddy Holly, Richie Valens, and the Big Bopper. El Bopper Grande, we used to call him affectionately.

I asked myself what the three rock 'n' roll stars had in common. The first thing that occurred to me was that they had all died in the same plane crash. I mentioned this to Antor Thon.

The little buddy gave me a sad smile and shook his head. "These three great men did not die in that plane crash."

"How could that be?" I said. "I've seen photographs—"

"It was made to look like they died together. In truth, they died here, on Mars. They were the heroes we brought here before you. They were all valiant and courageous men, but because they had even less knowledge of fighting with swords than you do, they were quickly slain by our enemies."

"And then their bodies were returned to Earth and our government covered up the truth of the matter, for reasons of its own. The plane crash was just a convenient explanation. Is that what you're telling me?"

"Yes," Antor Thon said. "Our greatest sculptors are working on your statue, even now."

I raised a hand. "Just a minute, little buddy. I don't intend to be cut to ribbons as were my brave predecessors. I plan on living a long time."

He smiled. "An admirable ambition, Elvis Presley. Whichever way matters . . . work out, a statue of you will be appropriate. You are a hero just for coming here with me."

I suddenly felt awkward and conspicuous, looming over all the little Martian people. "Thank you," I said softly. I didn't want to think about how matters might work out.

Antor Thon led me to the polished marble steps leading up to the palace itself. As we approached them, the palace guards snapped to attention. I knew they weren't doing it for me. They wouldn't know who I was. "Are you an important official in this town?" I asked my little buddy.

"My father, Vaq Antor, is the ruler of Gornath. He will remain ruler for life. I am his heir."

So I'd been walking across the face of Mars with a prince. Yet President Lyndon Johnson had said Gornath was a democracy. I asked Antor Thon about this.

"Oh, we've modeled ourselves after your Earth nation of Great Britain. The only difference is that we do everything the ruler asks of us, but what he asks of us has been strongly suggested by the advisory parliament."

I nodded. Once inside the palace, a uniformed military man conducted us to the consultation chamber. When we entered, the great Vaq Antor was finishing his daily briefing. Some of the men rolled up maps and the others stood at attention, saluting.

"Please leave me now," Vaq Antor said. "I wish to speak privately with Prince Antor Thon."

"Yes, your majesty," the Martian officers said. They backed out of the consultation room. I was alone with a king and a prince. It was something new for me.

"This is not John Carter," Vaq Antor said.

"I could not find the Virginian, Father," Antor Thon said.

The king nodded. "It is as I suspected. Then tell me, my son, who is this?"

"This is Elvis Presley, lord. I call him Brithen Torl. That means 'Fire Eyes,' " he told me. "He truly did have eyes of fire in our battle south of the city. He was magnificent—outnumbered, with only a minimal knowledge of swordplay, he fought with rare courage and determination."

The king studied me for a few moments. "With my son's recommendation, you are welcome in my house. If you require anything, you have but to ask."

"I thank you, sir," I said humbly. "I believe I have everything I need here in my Winn Dixie shopping cart. Except a print of *Wuthering Heights*. I cry every time I see that movie."

"*Wuthering Heights?*" Antor Thon asked.

I explained "I've modeled my acting technique on that movie. I hope to be remembered some day as the Lawrence Olivier of rock 'n' roll."

"That remains to be seen, of course," the prince said in a low voice.

I shrugged. "Then pork chops and sauerkraut. When I'm not eating cheeseburgers, I like pork chops and sauerkraut."

The king shook his head. "We have a religious prohibition against eating the flesh of pigs," he said.

"It must be a powerful prohibition," said Antor Thon. "We don't even *have* pigs on Mars. The Lawgiver meant that if we ever traveled to another world that did have pigs, we couldn't eat them. We didn't understand this for many centuries. Now, since interplanetary travel has become possible, we recognize the wisdom of the prohibition."

"You ever tasted pork chops and sauerkraut?" I asked him.

"No," he admitted, "but the Lawgiver—"

"Let us discuss our battle plans now," Vaq Antor said coldly.

"Yes, your majesty," I said.

"Yes, my king," Antor Thon said.

"Now, listen closely," Vaq Antor said. "My generals agree with my schedule. In six days, it will be a quiet, moonless dawn. I propose that the prince lead a company of hand-picked warriors through the secret gate, to attack the enemy from the rear, while at the same time I will take the remainder of the army through the Sunrise Gate to occupy them in the front. If our stratagem succeeds, we'll have them crushed between the two forces."

"And myself?" I asked.

"Brithen Torl, you may fight wherever you choose."

"Then, great king, I'd prefer accompanying my little buddy, your son."

Vaq Antor nodded grimly. "So be it," he said in a gruff voice.

We spent another half hour studying the positions of the ugly critters. Then we prepared several trumpet signals so that the wings of the humans' attack force would be coordinated. When we had provided for any likely situation, Vaq Antor smiled and clapped me on the back. "You have six days, my friend. Six days to improve your swordplay."

My throat was dry. I realized this wasn't going to be a movie. It wasn't going to be staged in advance. Dead bodies would be real dead bodies, not dummies. And when one of the ugly critters stabbed at me with a longsword, it was *me* whom he'd skewer, not a stunt double. I admit that I felt a little tingle of fear.

As Antor Thon and I took our leave of the ruler of the city, the little fella said, "Don't worry, Brithen Torl. I watched you during our skirmish a few days ago. You may feel inadequate now, but I'm sure that when the battle begins, when you catch the scent of blood on the morning air, you will cease being Elvis Presley and become once again Brithen Torl. Fire Eyes."

I said that I hoped he was right about that. My voice was unsteady. I didn't have the confidence in myself that Antor Thon had.

That night, alone in my sleeping chamber, I gazed out the window at the Martian sky. The constellations were recognizable. Orion, the Hunter, was low on the horizon, but I knew that as the night went on, he would slowly push Taurus across the black velvet expanse. Orion could not be denied; he would soon wrestle his quarry to the inevitable outcome. Tomorrow night would see them repeat their eternal struggle.

I would be Orion, then. I would plant my feet in the red dust of Mars, never to retreat against the onslaught of the monsters beyond the city's walls. As I watched, Mars' inner moon rose and hurtled across the sky, followed more slowly by the larger outer moon. It was a gorgeous sight, and I felt suddenly capable of great things—the great things that Vaq Antor and Antor Thon expected of me.

I went to sleep soon thereafter, and in the morning I was wakened by Antor Thon. "Come along, Elvis Presley," he said. "Now begins your martial training."

I was introduced to a fencing master named Drak Sunn Bar. He had learned English from John Carter, and so we had no trouble communicating. He drilled me for seven hours each day, and my skill with the longsword grew and grew. I learned aggressive attacks and sly traps. I learned the proper defenses to every possible thrust of an enemy. After five days, I felt much more confident. I asked Drak Sunn Bar if he would fight by my side with Antor Thon; my teacher declined at first, citing his advanced age. It did not take much to get him to change his mind, though. I could see that he'd been honored by my request, and that he was more than happy to comply.

I put together a leather fighting harness like the ones worn by the little fellas. When I put it on and held my sword in my hands, I felt more like Brithen Torl than Elvis Presley. I felt certain that in other lifetimes, I had truly been a fierce warrior, and those long-buried memories were starting to come to the surface. I believe that if I were truly immortal, then I should have no fear at all about going into hand-to-hand combat.

It was the night before the morning of battle. I could not sleep. I sat in a chair, looking out at the stars. Soon I would be thrown into the stunning confusion of warfare, but I know I just strummed my Martin and sang. I had an open Pepsi on the window sill and a cheeseburger balanced on my knee. I played a few chords, then accompanied myself on "It's Now or Never," my most successful single. Then I sang as much of the original Italian lyrics as I could remember: "O sole mio. . . ." I'd forgotten the rest.

The night passed peacefully. A few hours later, Antor Thon knocked on my door. "My father the king wishes to review his fighting forces in half an hour," he said.

"Fine, little buddy," I called. "I'm ready now. Where do we form up?"

"On the Plain of the God of War, before the palace gates."

"I'll be there." I stood up and looked at myself and was not displeased. I thought maybe a long white scarf around my neck might improve the image, but altogether I looked every inch the magnificent warrior from Earth. With the jangling sound of metal on metal, I left my sleeping chamber and descended the staircases to the assembly area.

I stepped out into the corridor and was almost knocked over by armed men running in both directions. There was no fear in their expressions, only a grim determination. These were well-trained fighting men, who knew the business of combat and understood the risks, yet they hurried to be on time. If any of them felt terror at what might happen to them, they hid it well. I joined them.

I hurried to the plain. I have to admit that I experienced a kind of queasiness in my stomach. I hoped that my new knowledge of swordfighting would make me more of a factor than I was in my first encounter with the ugly monsters. Only time would tell.

I found my place in the ranks, beside Antor Thon. He did not speak to me; he grunted by way of greeting. His concentration on the coming battle was complete. On the other side of me was Drak Sunn Bar, my fencing master.

Vaq Antor, the ruler of the city, appeared, escorted by two of his top generals. He walked among the ranks, saying nothing. He paused in front of me and briefly nodded. Then he saluted his army and addressed them in a short exhortation. I don't recall his precise words, and I doubt if the other little Martians can. All our attention was focused on the coming confrontation.

"Antor Thon, my son," he said, "take your force and begin passing through the secret gate. Reform your ranks beyond the city's walls and wait for my signal. We must coordinate our attacks."

"Yes, my king," said my little buddy.

As we began to move out, I said to Antor Thon, "Your father is an inspirational leader. Do you think he'd appreciate it if I gave him a Cadillac? What do you think?"

He gave me a puzzled look. "I suppose you'd have to ask him."

I had a few uneasy moments while we straightened our ranks on the battlefield. My confidence disappeared and I wondered how I'd gotten myself into this fix. I was pleased to learn that this fear vanished as soon as I heard the signal to advance. Then I felt an eagerness to join with the little fellas in the attack on the ugly critters. We angled around and charged down on their rear. At the same time, I knew, Vaq Antor was engaging them from another direction.

My fear dissolved completely the moment I crossed swords with one of the monsters. I fought and fought, and it seemed that a blood-red haze floated before my eyes. I stopped once to gulp down a Pepsi I'd brought with me. Then I was back in the battle, hacking and hewing my way up through the middle of their formation. I had to slow down or risk losing touch with my fellow warriors.

The Martian humans followed my lead, and soon we were driving forward, dividing the enemy into two disconnected mobs. This made Vaq Antor's job somewhat easier at the front.

An hour later, two hours—how long I cannot say—we'd turned the army of besiegers into two panicked mobs, which we were decimating almost at our leisure. Then the ugly critters broke the centuries-old etiquette of war. In their most desperate moment, they began firing at us with their rifles. Doing so disgraced them in the eyes of every soldier of every race; it also cleared a path for them to make their escape.

We did not follow. Vaq Antor believed that they would not return. We had lifted the siege. We were victorious!

The gates of Gornath were thrown open, and the people

cheered us as we marched proudly back into the city. "Look at them all!" I said.

"They're here to see you, Brithen Torl," Antor Thon said.

"They're here to see all of us, my friend. Do you know what would make it even better?"

"What is it? If I or my father can provide it, you have but to ask."

"A couple of cheeseburgers and another Pepsi," I said. "That can wait till later. My mama's mashed potatoes and gravy. And I wish I hadn't thought of pork chops and sauerkraut. Do Martians put caraway seeds in sauerkraut?"

"No, my Earth friend. There are no caraway seeds on Mars. We who have experienced them on your planet consider them a great delicacy."

How different were our worlds, yet how very much alike!

As we approached the palace of Vaq Antor, I noticed that a twenty-foot statue dwarfed the monuments to Buddy Holly, Richie Valens, and the Big Bopper. "Is that me?" I asked.

"Yes. The lighter gravity of Mars made it possible for our artisans to finish the statue quickly."

"Well, uh, little buddy, I don't believe it's quite fitting for me to tower over the others."

Antor Thon explained. "They are heroes and we will always venerate their names; but you are a hero who found glory by winning. I wish you could have seen yourself during the battle! I'll never forget the fierce expression you wore while you lifted an enemy swordsman high over your head and hurled him at several of his fellows."

"Did I do that?" I asked, astonished.

"Time and again. And I was proud of the way you handled your sword, and I'm sure your tutor, Drak Sunn Bar, is too. I know you rescued me at least three times."

"How odd that I recall none of the actual battle."

Antor Thon smiled. "You quite literally became another person out there."

A low dais had been set up near the monuments. I read the plaque attached to my statue. Actually, because the plaque was in Martian, I could only read the three words of my name: Elvis Aaron Presley. I was glad that the Martians had spelled my middle name correctly, rather than my father's misspelling, "Aron."

Vaq Antor addressed his people at length, with many gestures. I could tell even without understanding his words that he was a great orator as well as a valiant military leader.

When the ruler of the city finished, his son, my friend, Antor Thon, went to the microphone and said a few words. He concluded by pointing to me and saying, "Brithen Torl. Elvis Presley." I joined him on the dais, and the people began to cheer and chant my name.

"They wish for you to sing to them."

"I can do that. What should I give them? 'Jailhouse Rock' or 'How Great Thou Art'?"

Antor Thon looked thoughtful. "I think they want to hear your Earth rock 'n' roll. Is it pleasant to hear?"

"It is if it's played right." I smiled. "And I play it right." Without a guitar or backup band, I sung "Jailhouse Rock" for them *a cappella*. It was, if I may say so, one of my finest renditions. I planned to follow it with a few verses of "Rip It Up," but I never got the chance. The little Martian fellas were charging toward the stage.

I'd had some experience with this before, you know. I ducked back off the dais, taking a final glance at my statue. I stood there, twenty feet high, in my fighting harness, with a sword raised triumphantly against the shrunken Martian sun. I sprinted toward the palace, and my thoughts were calm and peaceful after the carnage of that afternoon: Pepsi and Colgate toothpaste.

Maybe three or four cheeseburgers.

Behind me, I heard Antor Thon shouting, "Ladies and gentlemen! Brithen Torl has left the planet! Elvis has left the planet!"

I hoped the little fella wouldn't forget to tell them to drive home safely.

# FANTASY ANTHOLOGIES

Dear Reader,

Welcome to the Yellowjacket Café, once upon a time a real family-owned, tiny café in Rockwall, Texas, where my mother and I used to love to eat mashed potatoes, lima beans and other such down-home food! *Cowboy Cootchie-Coo* was my first book for Harlequin American Romance®—a dream for me because I loved the story and I loved all the characters as they revealed themselves throughout the book. I'm so glad Harlequin has reissued the book so that this happy time can, for me, live again, and also so my readers can visit a place that meant so very much to me. My mother is no longer with me, but when *Cowboy Cootchie-Coo* was originally released, I dedicated it "To my mother, Sylvia Avera Kalberer, because she loved the Yellowjacket Café." She would have enjoyed seeing the book on the shelves again.

Best wishes for your own wonderful life

Love to all of you

Tina Leonard

**GREATEST TEXAS LOVE STORIES OF ALL TIME**

# GREATEST
# TEXAS LOVE STORIES
### OF ALL TIME

# COWBOY COOTCHIE-COO
## Tina Leonard

*Lone Star Lullabies*

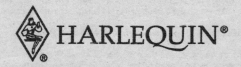

# HARLEQUIN®

TORONTO • NEW YORK • LONDON
AMSTERDAM • PARIS • SYDNEY • HAMBURG
STOCKHOLM • ATHENS • TOKYO • MILAN • MADRID
PRAGUE • WARSAW • BUDAPEST • AUCKLAND

**HARLEQUIN BOOKS**
225 Duncan Mill Road, Don Mills,
Ontario, Canada M3B 3K9

ISBN 0-373-65231-3

COWBOY COOTCHIE-COO

This edition published by arrangement with Harlequin Books S.A.

® and TM are trademarks of the publisher. Trademarks indicated with
® are registered in the United States Patent and Trademark Office, the
Canadian Trade Marks Office and in other countries.

Visit us at www.eHarlequin.com

**Printed in U.S.A.**

## TINA LEONARD

loves to laugh, which is one of the many reasons she loves writing Harlequin American Romance books. In another lifetime, Tina thought she would be single and an East Coast fashion buyer forever. The unexpected happened when Tina met Tim again after many years—she hadn't seen him since they'd attended school together from first through eighth grade. They married, and now Tina keeps a close eye on her school-age children's friends! Lisa and Dean keep their mother busy with soccer, gymnastics and horseback riding. They are proud of their mom's "kissy books" and eagerly help her any way they can. Tina hopes that readers will enjoy the love of family she writes about in her books. Recently a reviewer wrote, "Leonard had a wonderful sense of the ridiculous," which Tina loved so much she wants it for her epitaph. Right now, however, she's focusing on her wonderful life and writing a lot more romance!

**Books by Tina Leonard**

**Harlequin American Romance**

*Cowboy Cootchie-Coo* #748
*Daddy's Little Darlings* #758
*The Most Eligible...Daddy* #771
*A Match Made in Texas* #796
*Cowboy Be Mine* #811
*Surprise! Surprise!* #829
*Special Order Groom* #846
*His Arranged Marriage* #873
*Quadruplets on the Doorstep* #905

**Harlequin Intrigue**

*A Man of Honor* #576

**Trueblood, Texas Continuity**

A Father's Vow

**Harlequin Single Title**

Maitland Maternity Christmas
"Once in a Lifetime"

To my mother, Sylvia Avera Kalberer,
because she loved the Yellowjacket Café,
and
To Lisa, 8, and Dean Michael, 4, both growing up on me
too fast—thank you for believing in my dream,
And to my husband, Tim, for letting my dream be his.

# Chapter One

*It ain't over till it's over. —Yogi Berra*

Every eye in the Yellowjacket Cafe was on him. Brant Durning could feel the stares. His absence from Fairhaven, Texas, for the past three months hadn't gone unnoticed by the local residents—nor his return. He knew the topic of the day far outweighed interest in the soup of the day: What is Brant going to do about his wild little sister, Camille?

Sipping some iced tea, Brant supposed he'd given everyone plenty to be curious about. He caught Maggie Mason, the cook, watching him from her place behind the short-order line and grimaced. The grin on her face was telling. Before he had walked in to order lunch, no doubt the conversation had been centered on the fit he'd pitched when he returned to his ranch to discover the cows weren't the only things expecting offspring.

Cami had found a way to keep herself occupied with a man from a neighboring horse farm. Brant's brows furrowed. Shocked, and hurt for Cami's sake that there was no engagement ring on her finger, Brant had stormed her lover's house, demanding the man marry her at once and give a name to the child she carried.

Closing his eyes, Brant thought the only thing he'd left out of his outraged brother routine was a shotgun. He hadn't needed it. Cami's man had turned out to be more than eager to marry her, and the wedding plans were already in full swing—two weeks until the big day and counting.

"It ain't so bad, is it?"

Brant opened his eyes to see Maggie gazing at him as she slid into the cracked turquoise vinyl booth seat across from him. Her broad, ebony face was lit with impish laughter.

"Don't guess it's ever as bad as it seems," Brant replied. Maggie had known him all his life, even before he'd been old enough to drive himself to the Yellowjacket for mashed potatoes and greens. There wasn't any use in trying to act as if he didn't know what she was referring to.

"Nope, it's not." Her voice was amused. "Things were bound to change while you were away, Brant. Even in a small town, people's lives go on."

"Yeah." Of course, the interest-catching change had been in the Durning family. Why couldn't Cami have been more careful of her situation? Twenty-six was old enough to be able to stay out of trouble. As much as he loved Cami, her predicament was embarrassing.

"Everyone's going to think my cooking isn't agreeing with you. Your chin is hitting the table," Maggie told him.

He sighed and ran a hand absently across the back of his neck. "I'm all right, Maggie. I've got an errand to run that I'm not much looking forward to."

That was more truthful than he'd meant to be. Surprised by his own statement, Brant shifted his gaze to the plate-glass window. Across the street sat the next stop on his chore list. Wedding Wonderland was printed in big, scrolling white letters across the shop window. Customers walked into the two-story white building, itself almost resembling a wedding cake, coming out later carrying packages and wearing big smiles on their faces.

Once, going into the Wedding Wonderland had made

him smile, too. Grace Barclay was the owner of the shop—and the only woman he'd ever come close to letting touch his heart. Today, he was going into her shop to pick up Cami's wedding gown, and there was nothing to make him smile about that.

Facing Grace after all these months made his stomach turn uncomfortably. Suddenly, Brant realized Maggie's delicious chicken-fried steak wasn't sitting too well with him. "I need to be getting on," he said.

Maggie nodded. "Tilly, bring Brant his check, please."

The tall, long-legged waitress laid a piece of paper at his elbow. Normally he enjoyed talking to the friendly waitress. Tilly was like everybody's little sister. Now all he could manage was a thin smile of thanks as he put enough money on the table to cover tab and tip.

"Thanks. Bye, Maggie." He got up, feeling the weight of the world on his shoulders. Nodding to a couple of regulars playing checkers at their customary table by the door, he hoped that would pass for a social amenity.

"Going somewhere?" Buzz Jones asked.

"Yep." Brant told himself Buzz's grin had always been that big, whether he had teeth or not.

"Heard tell there's going to be a wedding at the Double D," Purvis Brown called out.

There was no laughter at Brant's expense. It felt more like every ear in the cafe stretched out elephantlike to hear his reply. He settled his Stetson lower over his eyes. "You'll get your invitation, Purvis. Don't worry."

"Going to be a big hoedown, is it?"

"Big enough, I reckon. See ya." Brant left, unable to take the friendly ribbing a moment longer. Darn Cami for her recklessness! Standing outside on the cement walk, Brant stared unhappily at the Wedding Wonderland. Truth was, if he hadn't been so hotheaded with his visit to Cami's fiancé and family, no one in the town would have had much to talk about.

Unfortunately the situation was of his own making. Now, folks would be watching from behind the Yellowjacket's plate-glass window as he walked into the Wedding Wonderland empty-handed.

And they'd be watching when he came out carrying a wedding gown.

He didn't want to do this. No three-month cattle buying trip, no keeping busy with the herds in the three months prior, had been able to wipe Grace out of his memory. She had always been there, in the smoky bars and the sensual laughter of other women. He'd told himself that the flame of their relationship had dwindled to a spark that couldn't burn his heart.

He had been lying to himself for six months.

*I'm a fool to let Cami talk me into this.* Cami, too ill with morning sickness that seemed to stretch all day, had pleaded with him to go pay the final installment on her wedding gown and bring it home. With the dimpled smile Brant had never been able to refuse, Cami claimed she might feel better if she could see her dream dress hanging in her own room.

Pushing the curved handle of the shop door, Brant wished he had never agreed to cross the threshold of the Wedding Wonderland. He cleared his throat, uncomfortable with the white decor and full-length mirrors around the room. The sensation of being out of his element was overwhelming.

"Just a minute. I'll be right with you," a woman called.

Brant's gut clenched at the sound of Grace's voice. She poked her head out from behind what appeared to be a fitting room door. Her mouth fell open. His glance skittered away before returning to brave her astonishment.

"Uh, hello, Brant."

All he could do was nod. Lord, how could she sound so casual? The tops of his ears felt as if they were on fire. Since Grace hadn't come out, all he could see was her face.

When they'd been in love, he had thought she was the most beautiful woman he'd ever seen. Somehow, she was even more beautiful now.

"Is there something I can do for you?"

Again, he nodded. "I need to pick up Cami's wedding gown."

"Oh. I see." She seemed to think about that for a minute. "Um, I'm kind of busy right now. The gown is hanging on a rolling rack down that hallway if you don't mind getting it yourself."

Once upon a time, he would have done anything to wipe the strained expression from Grace's face. Her blond hair was longer now, making her appear more feminine than ever. Her eyes were still huge and hazel and guaranteed to strike a man in his weakest moments. Brant told himself he wasn't having a weak moment right now.

"Fine. I'll do that." Though he wondered momentarily why she was sending him off in pursuit of his own purchase, he could only assume the woman wanted to avoid time in his company. The feeling was mutual, he told himself grumpily, as he searched through the stock tags on the gowns bearing customer names. He read each one a second time, but there was no gown tagged Durning. Glancing around to see if he might have missed another rolling rack, Brant decided Grace was just going to have to help him out on this one—no matter how awkward the situation.

He walked back out into the main salon. "I can't find it," he said. Her position was still defensive as she hovered behind the door. His remark didn't seem to make her happy, either.

"You couldn't find it? I was sure I hung it out."

He shrugged. She appeared to lose a shade of color in her face, which only made the pinpoint freckles he used to love to stroke with his finger stand out all the more.

"Could I have it sent around to your house this afternoon? I'm kind of tied up right now, and—"

"Cami really wanted to see her gown," Brant interrupted. He hesitated for a moment. "Grace, this isn't easy for either one of us. Actually it's worse than I thought it would be. But we have to live in the same town, run across each other once in a while. Help me out here, Grace. I can't go home without that gown."

"All right." She released an unhappy sigh, shooting him a wary look that nearly undid him. Those eyes of hers had always been his weakness. Slowly she stepped out from behind the door, holding a woman's undergarment in front of her.

But that didn't disguise what she'd obviously been trying to hide. Brant's jaw dropped.

"Grace—"

"This is a bustier." She pressed the undergarment to her midsection as she swished past him. "Some dresses require them. Cami won't need one with her—"

He caught her arm, turning her toward him, halting her un-Grace-like chatter. Slowly his gaze traveled over her body, cataloging extreme changes. "You're pregnant."

Her blush was painful to see.

"You came in to pick up your sister's gown, Brant," she said, meeting his stare. Pointedly she pulled her arm from his grasp. "If you'll excuse me, I'll go get it for you."

Brant couldn't believe his eyes as he watched Grace walk away from him. From the back, her figure had hardly changed. From the front, it was obvious she was in the advanced stages of pregnancy. He swallowed, jealousy pouring through him in a rush he never thought he'd feel. He'd protected his emotions far too long to feel this way. It shouldn't matter that Grace was having another man's baby.

She came back, carrying a profusion of shiny satin and frothy lace under clear protective wrappings. "Would you believe it was still in the stockroom? My seamstress just finished making the alterations this morning. I hope Cami will be pleased.'' She thrust the gown into Brant's arms. ''Please tell your sister to let me know if there's anything else I can do for her.''

''You can do something for me.'' Brant didn't want to know the answer. All the same, he had to find out. ''You can tell me how long it took after we broke up for you to find someone else.''

He felt as if he was dying. Sure, they'd broken up, but that didn't mean he had ever stopped thinking about her. Every morning as he shaved, every night as he tried to fall asleep, he thought about the woman he just couldn't marry.

Apparently she hadn't been missing him too much.

She looked angry. ''That's none of your business.''

He wanted to know who she was sleeping with. There was no ring on her finger; he wanted to know why the guy hadn't married her, though it was none of his business. Regrettably, his heart didn't seem to care. He wanted to know if she was in love with the jerk.

''Grace, I—'' He couldn't tell her there hadn't been a woman who could hold a candle to her in his life. Trying again, he said, ''You're having a baby.''

''Yes, I am.'' Her stare was forthright.

''I hadn't heard you were dating anybody seriously.''

Her lips curved. ''I wasn't aware you cared what happened to anyone in Fairhaven.''

*Not Cami, and certainly not me.* She hadn't spoken the words, but they echoed Maggie's statement. A lot had changed in Fairhaven.

''I care. I care a lot. Right now, I care that you're expecting a baby and I don't see the proud papa hanging around.''

''No. You wouldn't see him hanging around.''

The sadness in her voice hurt him. She deserved better treatment than this! ''Are you in love with the jerk?'' he asked, hating himself for having to know.

She paused. Her lips trembled, before her lashes suddenly swept downward. "I was...once."

And then it hit him. Like a piercing flash of light in a dense fog, Brant knew why the regulars at the Yellowjacket had been staring at him. Knew what was behind Maggie's broad grin. They hadn't been waiting to rib him about his rush to Cami's defense.

"It's mine, isn't it?" he whispered hoarsely. Without waiting for her to confirm or deny it, Brant's gaze riveted back to her stomach. That was six months worth of pregnancy, at least. He remembered their last night together and the warm glow in Grace's eyes, those fascinating hazel eyes, as he'd lain with her in his bedroom. November hadn't yet brought the chill of winter, but they'd enjoyed the humid wisps of wind filtering through an open window across their skin.

That night she had mentioned marriage. He had known inside himself their relationship had to be over.

This, then, was the repayment for his reluctance. Only Grace had paid the price, alone.

"I'm so sorry," he began. "I had no—"

The shop door swung open. A tall, broad-shouldered man walked inside, his gaze immediately swinging to Brant.

"Heard you were back in town, Brant."

"Howdy, Kyle."

An unmistakable aura of uneasiness permeated the room. They formed a triangle of sorts standing there, each watching the other. Brant could feel the other man's intense dislike.

"Are you ready, Grace?" Kyle asked.

"Let me lock up." She shot a pointed glance Brant's way. He realized he was *persona non grata*, not that he'd been *grata* since he'd walked in the store.

Slinging Cami's wedding gown over one arm, he nodded briskly at Kyle. "Thanks," he said to Grace. Then he left, his blood racing with jealous unhappiness.

In the window across the street, a row of faces disappeared from sight. Brant groaned, knowing what topic was going to be discussed over pork chops and grilled onions tonight. He could hear the whispers: *If Brant hadn't been so wary of a woman wearing wedding white, he might not be watching his lady—and his baby—strolling down the street with another man.*

Impatiently Brant tossed Cami's wedding gown into the front seat next to him, furious that the errand she'd sent him on had been a ploy.

GRACE FELT Brant's hard-eyed gaze burning all the way through the back of her maternity dress as she left the store. A thousand emotions had streaked into her mind when he'd walked into the shop. Seeing him had been a shock to her senses she'd hoped she was well past. Until she had looked into his eyes, seen his tall body standing in her store, Grace had thought she was safe.

Now she knew she was anything but. The disappointment she had felt when Brant told her he was picking up Cami's wedding dress had been worse than almost anything she'd ever felt. For a second, that girlish, wistful dream had played in her mind; she actually hoped he had come into her store to tell her he wanted to be back in her life. That he missed her, missed what they'd known together.

The same fantasy had lived in her mind day after day, each one blending into another as she'd learned to exist without him. Brant's unexpected appearance had shattered those silver-edged dreams immediately. He was only doing a favor for his sister. Doubtless, without Cami's errand, Grace would never have seen Brant's boots standing on the plush, white carpet of the wedding salon.

"Are you going to be all right?" Kyle asked.

Grace shot him a bittersweet smile. "I decided I would be all right a long time ago."

He wound his arm across her back in a comforting motion. "If I can help you in any way—"

"You can't. But thank you for caring." Grace felt that was more than Brant had done. Why couldn't she love Kyle with the same hunger and passion her reckless heart wanted to give to Brant—a man who didn't want her love?

"I do more than care." His eyes conveyed his greater feelings.

Grace sighed. "I know you do. That's what makes this whole thing so sad."

He squeezed her tight as they walked, just for a moment, but long enough for Grace to appreciate the tender gesture. "I don't feel sad. I think that now that you've seen the old boyfriend, you'll decide I'm the man with the hot stuff."

She had to laugh. "Kyle, I think I already got burned."

"Yeah, well. Today, maybe it feels that way. After some Chinese food and jasmine tea for lunch, you'll start feeling a little better. Who knows?" He leaned down to drop a light kiss on her forehead. "Tomorrow, maybe you don't even notice a scar."

"I hope so." Grace didn't want to ever lay eyes on Brant again if it was going to hurt so bad. She had been going along just fine, adjusting to life the way it was obviously going to be, when he had strolled into her life as if nothing of any importance had ever abided between them. He hadn't so much as blinked—until he'd seen her stomach. "I think it was just the shock." She smiled at Kyle despite the pain. "In fact, I'm starting to feel better already."

It was an untruth, but she had already spent too many months trying to mend her broken heart to allow it to crack again. The baby kicked suddenly, startling Grace into a distressing realization.

Whether she liked it or not, now she had to think for two.

"Uh-oh." Tilly jumped away from her spying position. "I think Brant saw us."

Maggie stepped back from the window, too, though she knew Tilly was right. "It doesn't make any difference that he did. The shock Brant just got was about the worst a man can get. Anyway, he knows this cafe is more about talking than eating."

"Do you think they got anything settled?" Buzz Jones asked. His checkers lay untouched on the board.

"Nope. Not if Grace is walking out with Kyle."

Purvis Brown rubbed his stubbled white whiskers thoughtfully. "I figured Brant would be man enough to do the right thing by Grace."

Maggie shook her head. "I don't think it has much to do with what Brant would be man enough to do at this point. He lost his chance to do much of anything."

Tilly wiped the tables with a clean rag. "I was hoping for a fairy-tale ending, though."

"Been reading too many romances," Maggie told her. "Still, I don't mind saying I was hoping Kyle would be a little late for their daily lunch outing."

"Brant did kind of skedaddle after Kyle showed up," Buzz agreed. He tapped his hand idly on the checkerboard. "Ah, well. Guess you'll still be Grace's delivery coach, Maggie."

"Yeah. Don't suppose I'll be trading my place of honor with Brant."

She sounded sad, and Tilly shook her head. "We were expecting too much too soon, maybe. They just need a little more time."

"Six months apart was probably long enough," Purvis interjected gloomily. "It was long enough for Grace to fall in love with another man."

Maggie lowered the red wooden blinds in the Yellow-jacket, one by one, to block out the hot afternoon sun. "I guess we can quit waiting for double wedding announcements.'' She let out a heavy sigh. ''Grace wouldn't still be seeing Kyle if she had any feelings left for Brant. She's gotten over the man.''

## Chapter Two

"Cami!"

Brant's roar and slamming of the front door shook the silk flower arrangement on its podium in the hall. He meant for his voice—and his anger—to travel all the way up the stairs. He took them two at a time.

Pounding on his sister's door, Brant let out another shout. "Don't you cower in there, Camille Durning! You dished it out, now you try taking some of it yourself!"

"Yes, brother?" Cami's voice, pitched sweetly, filtered through the door. "I'll be more than glad to take anything you care to dish out."

He opened the door, eyeing his sister with anger.

"My dress! Thank you, Brant."

She hopped out of the bed as if she were a delighted little girl. Some of his ire tried to seep out of him, but Brant told himself his sister had pulled a very disturbing trick on him. As siblings, they had enjoyed the rivalry of one-upmanship. This time, she'd gotten him fair and square—but he didn't like it one bit.

He held up a warning hand before she could reach the plastic-covered dress. "Uh-uh. We talk before you try on." He hung the dress on a high hook inside her closet.

"Talk about what, Brant?" Cami's eyes were wide.

"You knew about Grace." When she tried to speak, he shook his head. "Don't try to deny it."

Reddish brown curls bounced as she tossed her hair off of her shoulders. "I'm not denying it. Don't *you* try to deny that you're glad you know now, instead of waiting years to find out you had a child."

He crossed his arms. "Did you spring that on me so I couldn't complain anymore about your unmarried state?"

Cami didn't blink. "No. I don't care how much you complain about that. I didn't ask you to see Grace to rub anything in your face. I feel sorry for you. You might marry someone else and never know what a mistake you had made. Now, there's still time."

Brant's mouth dropped. Marry someone else? For heaven's sake, he hadn't even been able to marry Grace. What made Cami think he might marry someone else? The memory of Grace walking down the street with Kyle beside her shot through him with a dark, disquieting pain. *Grace* might marry someone else, though, who would raise *Brant's* child. The prospect of that made Brant feel ill. "You could have warned me."

She shook her head, crossing to examine the pearls on her wedding gown with a lustrous smile. "It wasn't my place. If Grace had never hunted you down to tell you, then she didn't want you to know. For whatever reason."

For whatever reason. Oh, he knew what the reason was. Their breakup had been difficult, to say the very least, for both of them. It had been the hardest thing he'd ever done. Now, he wished he hadn't quite burned his bridge behind him. "She appears to be pretty tight with Kyle Macaffee."

Cami didn't look away from her dress. Instead she pulled the plastic up over it and began undoing the pearl buttons in back. "Did you think no one else was going to want her?"

"No." The word felt like a growl. "But not with my child."

Now she did look at him. "Well, there's the problem. You have a medieval thought process warring with a modern-day woman. It's going to be difficult to sort that out." Cami hesitated, before reaching out to tap his forehead with her finger. "You'd better start working on it. It'll probably take you a while."

Brant didn't appreciate that. "There was more wrong with our relationship than my medieval thought processes, Cami."

She sighed, pointing her finger toward the doorway, indicating that he should leave. Obviously she was dying to try on that dress.

"Brant, think about why you wouldn't marry her. Think about why it's bothering you now. Then go back and get my veil, please? I won't be a proper bride without my veil."

"Your veil! Camille Durning, I'm not going back to the Wedding Wonderland for a damn thing! This time, you do the fetching."

He stalked out, narrowly avoiding slamming the bedroom door behind him. When had his sister turned into such a fountain of wisdom? It was irritating as hell.

More irritating than anything, though, was the fact that in the shock of seeing Grace, he hadn't paid the balance on the wedding gown. He could call her and get the amount and send it in. He could make Cami find out, since it was her gown, anyway.

The problem was, he really needed to speak to Grace, ornery and thorny as she was going to be with him. The veil and the balance of the bill would give him an excuse to see her.

Then maybe he could start figuring out what the hell to do about the mess he'd gotten himself into. Tomorrow, he told himself, he would make another trip to the Wedding Wonderland.

BRANT WOKE UP at two o'clock in the morning, realizing he'd never really done more than doze. The fact that the only woman he had ever cared deeply about was carrying his child was killing him. His stomach hurt. His head felt as if baseballs were rolling around inside it. Even his teeth hurt from grinding them.

He had to talk to her. In the light of day, across from the Yellowjacket Cafe, just wouldn't do. Brant pulled on jeans and a fairly wrinkled denim shirt, stuffed his feet into some boots and made a cursory effort at tooth and hair brushing. None of this grooming was going to matter if he couldn't get Grace to open her front door.

Driving across town, Brant used the time to mull over whether he was making a smart move. Damn it, he should have told Kyle to take a hike today and dragged Grace off to discuss what they were going to do about her problem. *His* problem, too, now.

Turning off the headlights, Brant pulled his truck into the gravel driveway in front of Grace's house. She lived in an old, wood frame house, circa the early 1900s. Her business was a block away, and she liked to walk the short distance. He wondered if she still did that, in her condition. With a snort, Brant eyed the dark house, knowing that if he so much as tried to inquire after Grace's exercise habits right now, she'd tell him what road to take to the highway.

Getting out of the truck, he quietly shut the door. Crickets chirped in the early May morning, a sound he normally found soothing but which tonight was as loud and irritating as the beating of his heart. He thought about Grace sleeping upstairs in her bed, with all its lacy white ruffles hanging down from the canopy and his heart clenched in a spasm his groin recognized. He thought about her waking up, softly tousled and warm from the heaping of covers she loved, and decided it was a bad idea to ring the doorbell. He told himself it was a bad idea for her to walk down those wooden stairs in a sleepy state, where she might lose her balance and fall. The truth was, he didn't think he could stand so close to her, see her in her nightwear, and do much serious talking.

Picking up a handful of the tiniest gravel he could find, Brant aimed one pebble at Grace's window. Another one followed before he saw the curtains pull back hesitantly. Firing one last missile, he was glad to see the lamp beside her bed switch on. The window protested a bit as she raised it. Brant told himself that was something he would fix one day.

"Brant! What are you doing out there?"

"I need to talk to you, Grace."

"Talk! I have nothing to talk to you about, especially not at this hour."

"Grace, we have to get some things resolved!"

"Brant, listen. Six months ago, you needed to resolve some things. I didn't. Not then, and not now."

He wasn't getting very far with her. Frankly he hadn't really expected to. "I won't claim we parted on the best of terms, Grace. But don't you think you owed it to me to tell me you were pregnant?"

Her hesitation gave her away. Her words, flat as a steel-edge, did not. "I don't owe you a thing."

"We owe it to the child you're carrying to make some responsible decisions."

Grace leaned out the window a little farther, as if she couldn't believe what she was hearing. "Pardon me? Is this the same man who didn't want anything to do with re-sponsibilities? The same man who went off and left his sister to run the family ranch?"

Brant took both those barbs with a sigh. "Grace, I made some mistakes. I wasn't ready to face some things. But is keeping me away from my child the answer?"

She shook her head, making the fall of long blond hair wave gently. "I haven't admitted this is your child."

"Give me a break. Everybody in this town knows it is.

They'll put my name on the birth certificate in the Father blank no matter what you tell them. All I want is a chance to share in this with you."

"Share what, Brant? The morning sickness? That's been a treat, as I'm sure Cami can tell you. The water retention, sore breasts? Stray aches and pains that keep me up at night? Which of those did you want to share?"

He ran a hand across his chin. There wasn't anything he could do to alleviate those things she was suffering. But he could help her out financially.

"I'd like to see that you and the baby are taken care of."

The slamming of the window was like a rifle shot through the quiet countryside.

"Damn it!" Brant leaned down, scooped up some more gravel and flung it at her window.

Instantly headlights were turned on him. Brant jerked around, realizing immediately that their heated discussion had kept him from noticing the sheriff's cruiser pulling up next to the curb. The sheriff had flipped on the headlights of Brant's truck, and now Brant was glaringly exposed.

"Evening, Brant," Sheriff Farley said easily. "Or should I say good morning?"

Brant held back a groan of embarrassment. John Farley dated Maggie at the Yellowjacket Cafe. Well, he dated her as much as he'd ever dated anyone. It was a similarity Brant and the sheriff had in common: an ambitious desire to avoid the altar. As much as he recognized another male who would probably take his side, Brant also knew John wouldn't be able to resist mentioning this early-morning visit to Maggie.

"Something I can help you with?" John asked.

"Hell, no," Brant grumbled.

"Woman trouble's a drag, isn't it?" The sheriff's hearty laugh echoed in the night. Brant pushed back his irritation. "Still, it's a bit early for you to be trying to get on Grace's good side, isn't it?"

On cue, the window slid back up.

"This gentleman bothering you, Grace?"

She paused before answering, "As much as he ever has. Did somebody call you out?"

"Nope. I was just driving by when I spotted a truck in your driveway. Couldn't recall any truck being parked here at night before, so I thought I'd check."

Not Brant's truck, but not Kyle's, either. Brant took that as a reassuring piece of information.

"At least you're doing your job, Sheriff." Grace's voice lacked the humiliation Brant was feeling. There wasn't a prayer John wouldn't mention this episode to Maggie. By morning, he was going to be in worse shape for gossip than if he'd merely had a limo filled with doves pull up in front of the Wedding Wonderland.

"By the way, when are you going to let me fit you for a tux, John?"

"For Cami's wedding?"

"For yours." Her tone was only slightly teasing. "I can't help noticing that gleam in your eye every time you look at Miss Maggie."

That got the sheriff heading back toward his cruiser. "I'll let you know when it becomes absolutely necessary, Grace. Sorry to have disturbed your, um, conversation, Brant."

"That's all right, John. As Grace said, it's nice to know the county's safe."

John tossed a sarcastic wave-off back his way. Brant snorted, then glanced back up at Grace. She was staring at him, her eyes huge with some emotion. He couldn't help noticing the way her nightgown collar fluttered in the slight breeze, and the fact that she looked more beautiful than ever.

"I guess I'll go now, seeing as how I've given people something to talk about."

"When are you going to stop worrying about what everybody thinks, Brant? When are you going to start doing what you feel is right?''

He stopped, half turned. ''What the hell's that supposed to mean? You don't mind being the topic of conversation at everybody's breakfast table?''

''Would I be pregnant and unmarried if I did?'' she shot back. ''Just once, if you could see that those same gossips are good-hearted, that they're friends, you might be able to relax enough to appreciate them. John, for instance, wasn't just driving by here randomly. Ever since you left, and Maggie told him I was expecting, he's been coming down my street. He hasn't told me that. Maggie told me he was doing it. That makes me feel awfully good that someone in this town cares about me enough to go out of his way.''

''Like Kyle?'' The minute it was out of his mouth, Brant realized how dumb he sounded. How eaten up with jealousy.

Which he was.

''I'm going to ignore that for now. I know you're all bothered because John knows you were here and will probably say so to Maggie.'' She shook a finger at him. ''Maggie has lunch sent over to me when I have girls come in who need to be fitted on their lunch hour. There's usually a warm biscuit, maybe some orange juice sent over with Tilly in the morning, always saying they had leftovers. It's not true. They're worried about me. They're trying their best to take care of me.''

''Because I'm not.''

''You said it, not me. But just for the record, let me say that I didn't give myself to you so that I'd have someone to take care of me.''

''I know that.'' Brant sighed, shaking his head. He was making a huge mess of this again. ''Grace, will you at least give my offer some thought? I know I'm not putting it as pretty as it should be, but I honestly want to provide for my child. And the least I can do is help you with your medical expenses.''

"Would that ease your conscience, Brant? Would that make you feel less like the villain in everybody's opinion?''

Was that what it looked like he was trying to do? Weigh the balance of public opinion in his favor by offering to do his financial and emotional share of what she was going through? "I don't know what you want me to say, Grace.''

The time she took to consider his words seemed forever. Finally she, too, sighed, as he had. "I don't know, either, Brant. Maybe you're being more honest than I am.''

Quietly, this time, Grace slid the window shut. The lamplight flicked off. Brant was left in the dark, the chirping of the crickets the only noise in the damning silence.

AFTER A NIGHT OF TOSSING and turning, Brant got up, noticing the time was an hour past his normal time to awaken. Pulling on work clothes, he decided he felt worse this morning than he ever had with a hangover.

Downstairs, the kitchen lights were on. Coffee perked in the coffeemaker, and there was a mug sitting out with his name on it. Brant filled the mug, nearly dropping it when the back door opened.

"What are you doing?'' he roared at Cami.

His sister pulled off her boots, laying them on the porch as she shot him an arch look. "What does it look like?''

"Like you've been out feeding the cows!''

"I have been.'' She crossed to fill her coffee mug again. "Did you want them to go hungry?''

"Hell, no. I was going out to do it.''

Cami shrugged. "Sorry. Force of habit.''

She hadn't said it, but the implication was there. *I kept this place running while you were gone.* He didn't feel that she blamed him for anything, simply that she wanted him to understand that she'd gotten along fine without him and could again if necessary.

Cami was a lot like Grace, he realized.

"How's the morning sickness?" he asked gruffly.

"Not bad enough to keep me from doing chores." She sat down at the table and peeled a banana. "Although, I will admit that I don't eat breakfast before I go out and I try hard to be extremely fast about the chores. I've had a bout or two with some sympathetic cows looking on." Shooting him a smile, she said, "However, I think I'm over all that."

He grunted. "You've made a fast recovery since yesterday."

"Yes. Well, did you get my veil?" she asked brightly.

His attention was caught by the grin on Cami's face. "How would I have done that?"

"I thought maybe you picked it up when you left at two o'clock this morning."

"No." He shook his head. "I did not get your veil."

"Oh. I guess I didn't really expect that you had."

He could tell she hadn't by the teasing tone of her voice. "You're so recovered I imagine you can get it yourself today. And pay the balance of the bill."

"Whew! Didn't go well with Grace, huh?"

Brant resisted slamming his palm on the kitchen counter. He settled for a glare at his sister. "Did anyone ever tell you to mind your own business, Cami?"

"Oh, this from the lone ranger who was prepared to blow the doors off my fiancé's house."

Sighing, he sat down across from his sister. "No. I didn't get far at all. I don't know what I'm supposed to say to her, and I end up saying all the wrong things."

"Hmm. A case of foot-in-mouth disease. There's only one cure for that."

"What the hell would that be?" Brant eyed his sister suspiciously.

"You have to learn to like the taste of your own foot."

"Very funny."

Cami laughed, giving him a playful slap on the forearm. "Oh, Brant. What do you expect Grace to do? Greet you with open arms? She has a right to be ticked."

"Is she ticked? Is this something she'll get over if I keep seeing her?"

"Well, no." The smile left Cami's face and she considered her words carefully. "I mean, yes, she is angry. She isn't going to let you back into her life without knowing what part you want to play in it."

"I offered financial and emotional support."

"And?"

"And what?"

"And what else?"

Brant drew his brows together, having a funny feeling he knew where Cami was going to head with this one.

"Did you say anything about your feelings for her?"

No, he hadn't. "Um, no."

"Then I guess you're lucky you got her to even come to the door at that hour. You're even more fortunate she didn't fire a shotgun at you. Did it ever occur to you to say something more feeling than 'hey, I'll pick up the tab'?"

"I might have gotten around to it if the sheriff hadn't thought I was a trespasser."

"John was there?"

"Yeah." Brant hated to have to admit that.

"Oh, boy." Cami was silent for a moment. "Listen, Brant, you're going to have to hurry and fix this thing right. No more of your delaying tactics."

"Delaying tactics! What the hell's that supposed to mean?"

"You don't have time to keep making Grace mad with offers to support her. She doesn't need your support. She owns the only wedding shop in Fairhaven and gets more business than she can handle. Besides, she wouldn't marry you for economic reasons, anyway."

"Whoa. Hang on a minute. Nobody said anything about marriage."

"You're not going to marry Grace?" Cami's eyes were huge.

"I think we established that six months ago." Brant felt mutinous on this matter. Yes, the gossip was going to be uncomfortable. The situation was awkward. They had always been careful about birth control, but the fact that something had gone awry didn't change his mind about bachelorhood. He sighed raggedly. Why couldn't Grace have been content knowing she was the only woman he'd ever given as much of himself to as he had?

"Brant, do you think you're letting our parents' divorce affect you just a little too much?"

He stared at his sister, suddenly angry. "*Do not* bring that up to me."

"You can't talk to me that way, Brant. I think your fear is due to what happened between Mom and Dad."

"I think you still haven't outgrown your mouth," he growled.

She shrugged. "Fine. Ignore it if you want. You're going to keep paying for it as long as you do."

"Cami, be quiet." His tone brooked no argument.

Without acknowledging his command, Cami said, "By the way, Brant, I need you to sign over half the ranch acreage to me."

"*What?*"

"It's half mine. I'm taking it with me when I get married."

"Damn nice dowry," he grumbled. "Leaves me with only a thousand acres."

"Yes. Well, I don't feel too guilty about that since you left me to take care of all of it while you were trying to get over Grace." Cami stood. "If I were you, I'd try to spend some time thinking about what you're going to say to Grace when you see her next, Brant. Much as you can be a stubborn old mule, I hate to think of you sitting on the porch alone at night, with an empty house your only reward for your insecurity.''

"Cami!'' This time, Brant did slam his palm against the table.

"Have the fence line moved, please, Brant. Maybe it will start you thinking about what life's going to be like when I'm gone.''

She sailed out of the kitchen. Brant heard her running up the stairs. Muttering a string of curses to himself, he went out the front door. Heading to the mailboxes at the end of the road, Brant halted in his quest for the morning newspaper. A truck was pulling up the long driveway, a truck he recognized since he'd helped her pick it out. Brant's stomach pitched.

It stopped beside him. "Is this a payback for my unannounced visit last night?'' he asked, trying to sound as if his heart hadn't plummeted into his boots.

"At least you're not in your nightgown,'' Grace returned lightly. "Is Cami in from feeding the livestock?''

"Yeah.''

"Thanks.'' The truck roared off, kicking up white dust around him. She hadn't come to see him at all, Brant realized with a sense of letdown. "Is Cami in from feeding the livestock?'' he mimicked under his breath. Deciding the paper could wait, Brant headed back to the house. Hell, Cami had already pried a thousand acres out of him. With those two putting their heads together, he might find himself without a house, too, if he wasn't there to protect what was his.

Worse, he might find himself on the opposite end of the shotgun he'd been prepared to use on Cami's fiancé.

## Chapter Three

Grace put the veil gently on top of Cami's hair, brushing the burnished waves into a tamer look. "There. It suits you perfectly."

"It's beautiful, Grace. I should have known to trust your judgment."

The illusion veil was simple, with an unpretentious pearl band that set off the color of Cami's hair. Grace had argued in favor of this look, while Cami had selected a taller, more elaborate headdress, wanting the appearance of height as she stood next to her handsome groom. Grace had known this was the right look for Cami. The look was understated and beautiful, just the way a woman should look on her wedding day.

"Well, I was just afraid the other veil was going to overpower you," Grace said. "I'm glad you're happy."

Cami hugged her. "I'm sorry you had to bring it out."

"I didn't mind." Grace began closing the makeup bag, which held hairpins and other things a bride might require. "Your brother suffered so much coming into my shop yesterday I couldn't put him through that misery again."

"Brant's misery is his own."

"Yes." Grace gave a shrug she really didn't mean. "Still, my running this out here gave me a chance to spend a moment with you privately. Cami, there's something I want to talk to you about."

Cami turned interested eyes on her. "Okay."

"Kyle Macaffee has asked me to marry him."

"Oh."

"I'm considering his offer."

"Oh!" Cami's eyes grew wide.

"The only reason I'm telling you this is because I want you to understand. Your brother and I didn't have what it took to make a lifetime of commitment to each other. Kyle loves me...well, just for me."

"Do you love him?"

Grace paused. The answer was so difficult. "Not with the raging, out-of-control passion I felt for Brant, perhaps. But what I have with Kyle feels solid, much more lasting, somehow."

"I see." Cami's tone was quiet.

"I hope you do. I know you had hopes that Brant and I would...well, never mind. Suffice to say that doesn't matter now." She sighed, feeling despondent as she snapped her purse closed. "I don't know what my answer to Kyle will be, yet. I need more time to think, to think about my baby, especially. But I wanted you to know, just in case I decide to accept his proposal."

"Thank you for telling me," Cami murmured, her eyes downcast. "You deserve a good man, Grace."

"There's a favor I hate to ask you, but I must," Grace continued. "Please don't mention this to your brother."

"Oh, Grace, don't ask that of me!"

She held up a hand. "Please, Cami. My life has gone on. I don't want your brother running back into it and hurting me in any way. He...simply isn't capable of loving me the way I want to be loved, and—" Her words broke off. "I just don't need any more complications right now. You understand that, don't you?"

Cami nodded, her expression unhappy. "I hate to say it, but I do. I won't mention Kyle's proposal to Brant."

Grace hugged the woman she had once hoped would become her sister-in-law. Always she had thought of Cami as a sister. Her and Brant's situation was going to hurt Cami, Grace knew. But there wasn't anything she could do about that—except be honest. She had decided after Brant's visit last night that perhaps she wasn't being honest with herself. Or anyone else, with her brave attitude. She really wasn't so brave inside, not since she'd seen Brant.

She really was still hanging on to hope. All that was going to bring her was a broken heart—again.

"Thanks, Cami." Pulling away, Grace gave her a watery smile. "Your wedding is going to be beautiful."

"At least you're going to be my maid of honor," Cami sniffled. "We'll be in one wedding together."

"Yes." Grace picked up her things and went to the door. "Can you meet me for lunch today at the Yellowjacket after church? There's something Maggie and Tilly and I want to talk to you about."

"That sounds wonderful. I could use some home cooking."

"Me, too. See you then." Grace went out the door, waving Cami back when she would have followed her downstairs to the door. The quieter her exit, the better. She didn't want to run the risk of running into Brant.

But he was sitting inside her truck in the passenger seat, his Stetson pulled down over his eyes and his arms crossed. Grace's heartbeat picked up.

"What do you think you're doing?" she demanded as she reached the car window.

He pushed the hat brim back. "Waiting to talk to you."

"You couldn't do that inside?"

"Didn't want to miss you in case you tried to leave without saying goodbye."

Grace's eyes met his guiltily. "I wouldn't have done that."

"Oh. You looked for me, then."

"Well, maybe not directly—"

"Ah. I see."

They were silent for a moment. "As I mentioned last night," Grace finally said, "I don't feel any great need to talk to you."

"Did Cami pay you?"

"No, but I'll send you a bill. That's not why you're occupying space in my truck. Don't beat around the bush. This is my only day off, and I'd like to make it to church on time."

"I'm sitting in here because you're a captive audience this way. Would you have come and sat down in my den to drink a glass of tea and talk about what we're going to do with our lives if I'd asked you?" Brant quirked a questioning brow at her.

"No."

"Figured as much. I take it you didn't like my offer last night."

Grace shook her head, wishing she still wasn't attracted to Brant's dark handsomeness. It made everything so much more difficult. "I don't need your money, Brant. I wasn't in it for that. And I've been taking care of myself for six months now. I bet I can make it through everything else without you."

"And my baby? Does it have to learn to live without me, too?"

"I think your son will do just fine."

"Son?" Brant sat straight up in his seat.

Grace wondered why men always perked up at the mention of a son. "Maybe it's a daughter." Grace fibbed, just to rattle him.

"Daughter?" Brant's posture didn't relax. "Have you decided what to name her?"

She sighed, realizing either gender tag seemed to have an electrifying result on him. The man might be immune to matrimony, but the idea of being a father seemed to have an astonishing effect on him. He almost sounded as if he could make a commitment to the infant growing inside her.

"It's a boy." Grace decided to give in on this issue. He was going to find out sooner or later, anyway. "I haven't picked out a name."

"Do you have a good doctor?"

"I'm seeing the new guy in town. He seems fairly astute. Actually he's been pretty helpful." Grace hadn't wanted to drive all the way into Dallas, so she'd gone to check out the man who'd taken old Dr. Watkins place in the town clinic. So far, Dr. Brig Delancey had proved helpful and encouraging.

"I don't like new guys."

A little stiffness left Grace. She had felt the same way. "I don't usually trust newcomers myself. Especially with my baby. But I like him. I really do. Though I still miss Dr. Watkins."

"Yeah." Brant's eyes shadowed. "Grace, let me help you out with this."

She looked down at her Sunday dress boots, wishing with all her heart she could let him. Unfortunately, letting Brant hang around and do the expectant father routine would put her through an emotional wringer. She didn't plan on keeping him from his child, but she didn't want to be shredded by unrequited love when she needed so badly to stay strong.

"I can't, Brant." She lifted her gaze to meet his eyes. "I've come too far on my own. Please understand."

He was silent for a long moment, before getting out of the truck. Shutting the door, he walked around the front to her side. "Let me know if you need anything?"

"I will." She knew he would be the last person she would call for help.

His finger grazed her chin lightly. ''I have so many different thoughts running around inside my head about this I can't begin to think of the right thing to say to you. But I'm not through trying to talk you into letting me help you.''

Grace stepped away, opening the door to get inside the truck. She felt much safer behind a closed door. Putting her bag and purse on the seat beside her, she started the engine. With one last glance Brant's way, Grace reversed the truck, making a semicircle, before she drove back up the driveway.

Brant didn't understand that she didn't need the kind of help he was offering. Once, she had needed something more, something he couldn't give her, which was why their relationship hadn't worked out in the first place. Tears blurred her eyes. The most devastating part was how much remembering made her ache. She still wanted everything she'd wanted before.

A SON. Brant couldn't help the grin on his face. He was going to have a little boy, a little Brant Durning, Junior. The thought was incredible. Up until the moment Grace had said that, he had thought of the life growing inside her as a sort of thing, a responsibility he needed to shoulder. Now the reality of it had hit him, with all the accompanying excitement.

He was going to have a boy.

Going inside the house, Brant hardly noticed his sister standing in the hallway staring at him. ''Did Grace have a change of heart? Or you?'' she asked.

Startled out of his daydream, he turned to look at his sister. ''What are you asking me?''

''Um, maybe why you've got that goofy smile on your face?''

Pausing, Brant didn't even bother to counteract his sister's crafty barb. ''I'm going to have a son,'' he told her.

"I'm going to be an aunt to a little boy?" Cami's grin was huge.

"Didn't Grace tell you?"

She shook her head. "Not that. I can't believe it. I'm going to start crocheting a blue baby afghan. With some white stripes running through it. Or maybe orange and white, for our high school spirit colors. I'll have to ask Grace what color the nursery is going to be."

Cami walked away, lost in her plans. Brant stared after her, still grinning. He felt lost between a desire to give a victory shout or rub his hands as if he were a little kid getting a favorite toy. In the end, he did both, thinking about how beautiful Grace looked in the lace and denim maternity dress that had flowed around her short boots.

Heckfire. She was having his son.

THE YELLOWJACKET was crowded, per usual for a Sunday lunch crowd. That suited Grace just fine. Her meeting with Tilly, Maggie and Cami would go much better if they didn't have a chance to talk too intimately. The last thing she wanted to be asked about was her pregnancy, or her lunch date yesterday with Kyle. Today should be Cami's day. After all, she was getting married in two short weeks.

Grace was not. She pushed aside the slight tingle of envy she felt for her unmarried state. It was a status she had chosen, by not telling Brant in the first place that she was pregnant. Oh, he might not have asked her to marry him even then. It had been a gamble on her part. Having taken a home pregnancy test—one that the pharmacist had sworn was as reliable as any test in a doctor's office—Grace had lightly questioned Brant about marriage. If he had responded positively to her question, she would have mentioned the pregnancy. His vehemently negative reaction had stunned her and she hadn't wanted to compound the error by telling him they were going to have a baby. He would only have resented her for feeling as if he had to marry her. She would always have known, in her heart.

Before she had begun to show, he had left Fairhaven for three long months. His desertion had forced her to realize their relationship was truly over. He didn't miss her, didn't plan on reuniting. She had been frightened, then, knowing her condition would soon make its own blatant announcement. So she had opted for a straightforward approach in telling her friends. To her surprise, her admission had sat very well with the folks she had known all her life: Maggie, Sheriff Farley, Buzz, Purvis, Tilly and others. It had all worked out for her.

But today was Cami's day. She couldn't help being glad that she and Cami would be forever connected to each other by blood, anyway, no matter that they would never be true in-laws.

Cami came in, her lustrous sable hair glowing in the afternoon sunlight. Grace waved her over to the table.

"You look better than you did this morning," she told her. "A shower really does do wonders, doesn't it?"

Cami laughed. "Yes. Early-morning cattle feeding doesn't do much for my looks."

"I believe I've felt that way after sitting up late a few nights making adjustments to wedding gowns for nervous brides." Grace smiled as Tilly and Maggie came over to sit with them.

"Thanks for coming, Cami. We've got to make this quick, because the kitchen won't last long without us, I'm afraid. We wanted to ask you in person, honey." Maggie paused, her brown eyes alight with friendly caring. "Would you let the three of us throw you a wedding shower? A real, honest-to-goodness wedding shower, catered by Tilly and me?"

"Oh." Cami's eyes misted over as she looked around the table at her friends. "That would be lovely. But you're already doing my wedding buffet, Maggie. Isn't that too much?''

"Nope. Believe me, some folks in this town have been awful glad to get the extra employment. We were so worried you'd take your business into Dallas, Cami.''

"No way. Everything I've always wanted is right here in Fairhaven.'' She smiled around the table.

That was a stark contrast to the wandering foot Cami's brother had. Everything Brant had ever wanted was certainly not in Fairhaven. She'd expected him to come home from college with a serious girlfriend. When he'd first asked her out, Grace had thought he was joking. The second time he asked her out, Grace wondered what he saw in her. By the time they started making love, she thought the best thing that could have happened to her was Brant being in her life.

*Not any more permanently than anything else in his life, though.* Grace forced herself to smile Cami's way. "We were hoping you'd let us. It was Maggie's idea to give you a shower of some kind. Traditionally I suppose we should give you a bachelorette shower, but a fancy wedding shower sounded so much more, I don't know, festive or something.''

"It does,'' Cami agreed.

"Or if you'd prefer, we could do a barbecue, and invite men and women.''

"Hmm. Would that keep the boys from dragging my fiancé into Dallas to hit the topless bars?''

"No.'' Maggie shook her head. "But at least we'd be together for one night with the menfolk.''

"Might not be as stuffy a party, either,'' Tilly added. "Men tend to look forward to a barbecue.''

"It's all that male-bonding as they stand around the grill.'' Grace's voice was wry. "But we'll be happy to do either one, Cami. We just want to do something for you.''

"They both sound wonderful," Cami said slowly. "But—"

"Grim-faced rancher at three o'clock," Maggie murmured. "Don't look, but Brant's coming our way."

Grace's gaze skittered toward the door before she could stop it. The calm she'd been feeling a moment ago evaporated.

Without asking, he pulled out a chair. "Howdy, ladies."

"Howdy, Brant. What's happening with you?" Maggie asked.

"Not much. What are you ladies cooking up?"

"A bridal shower," Tilly told him.

"A bridal shower?" His stare was directed at Grace.

"Yes. We thought we'd give Cami one, since she is getting married, Brant." Grace's tone was dry. Had he looked alarmed? As in, thinking *she* was getting married? She glanced at Cami, but the other woman's face was guiltless. Cami had said she wouldn't mention Kyle's proposal, and Grace knew she wouldn't.

"Oh. Don't guess that's much of my concern," Brant said. "But it's nice of you to do that for Cami."

"That makes up my mind. I want the barbecue," Cami said decisively.

"What makes up your mind? What did I say?" Brant asked.

The four women stared at him. "If I have a standard ladies-only shower, the menfolk won't be interested. They'll look at the china and place mats and bud vases I get and smile condescendingly. But a barbecue will be different." She leaned over to kiss her brother's cheek. "Thanks, Brant. You are good for something."

"Don't know what that's supposed to mean," he grumbled good-naturedly.

"Well, I guess I better get back to the kitchen." Maggie stood, with Tilly following suit. "Can I get you something to eat, Brant?"

"I wasn't going to eat, but—" He looked at Grace, her expression bland as she stared at him. "I guess I could sit here and make it a threesome."

"We haven't invited you," Cami said pointedly.

"May I please join you for lunch?" Brant growled. Grace enjoyed his humbled expression, though she wasn't buying it for a minute.

"Do you mind, Grace? My big, rather bearish brother wants to eat with us."

"I don't mind." She shook her head, but the truth was, her heart was beating inside her as if it were a big drum. It felt as if everyone in the Yellowjacket Cafe could see her emotions clearly written across her face.

"What are you doing here, anyway, Brant?"

"Looking for you. Fortunately you left a note telling me where you were going, because your fiancé called. He's not going to make it in tonight."

"Oh, no." Cami looked stricken. "I've been counting the minutes until he returned. What did he say was wrong?"

"Something about the horse buying trip not winding up the way he and his father had planned. He'll definitely be home tomorrow."

Grace noticed how Brant's eyes skimmed his sister's face. He was completely concerned for her happiness. She thought it was nice that he'd driven in to town to let her know. Cami would have been so disappointed if she had hurried home to get gussied up only to discover it was all for nothing.

"Well, he'll just have to hear about the barbecue tomorrow," Cami said, though she still sounded unhappy.

"He said he'd try to call you tonight."

Brant picked up a pretzel, his gaze swiveling to Grace's. She started, not expecting him to catch her watching him. Carefully she broke eye contact and looked around the room.

Purvis and Buzz were in their usual places, red and black checkers occupying various squares. Sheriff Farley was behind the short-order line, working a smile out of a busy Maggie. Tilly was hurrying from table to table with a tea pitcher. Everyone seemed to have a purpose in life in Fairhaven. Why did Brant find it so empty?

"Mind if I horn in?"

Grace glanced up at the sound of Kyle Macaffee's voice.

"Would it matter if we did?" Brant asked sourly.

Grace saw the dark look Cami shot her brother. "We'd be happy for someone to make a fourth," she said quickly. "Please sit down."

Tilly brought menus, though they all knew the fare by heart. They put in orders, then the conversation ceased at their table. Grace tried desperately to think of something to say. She felt very peculiar sitting between the man whose child she carried and the man whose marriage proposal she was considering.

"So, Macaffee," Brant said.

"Durning," Kyle said equitably.

Tilly set glasses of water and tea on the table. Grace caught Brant looking at her, and for a moment, she felt unreasonably jealous. Tilly was so attractive, and she was just like Brant. They had similar carefree, don't-tie-me-down outlooks on life. She envisioned Tilly in Brant's arms and felt a little queasy.

"Are you feeling all right, Grace?" Brant asked.

"I'm fine," she murmured. But she couldn't meet his eyes. Instead she looked at Kyle. "Did you get any sick-animal calls this weekend?"

"Would you believe I didn't get a one? This is the most quiet weekend I've had since last fall. It was kind of nice, actually." He patted Grace on the back, his hand lingering just a moment. "You know, you look a little peaked, Grace. Are you sure you're all right?"

With everyone's eyes at the table on her, Grace thought

she'd never felt more humiliated. "I'm just a little warm," she said, drinking from the cool tea glass. The truth was, sitting with Kyle and Brant was indescribable torture. The baby kicked, sending her hand to her abdomen in surprise. Was he feeling his mother's distress? Kyle's hand rubbed soothingly along her back, but Grace couldn't relax. How could she sit and pretend everything was fine and dandy when she felt so pulled sitting with two men who each had a claim of sorts on her?

"You know, I think I'll go on home." Slowly Grace stood, pulling her purse to her side. "I'll feel better after I change out of my clothes, I think."

"Grace, let me walk you home," Cami offered, quick to her feet.

Thankful it was Cami who was offering, Grace nodded. "If you don't mind having to leave lunch with these two gentlemen."

Cami sent a smile Kyle's way as he stood, along with Brant. "Maybe we can do this another time, Kyle."

"I'll call you later and check on you, Grace," Kyle said.

"Thank you." She sent a grateful look his way. "I'm sure I'll be fine." Hardly sparing a glance for Brant, Grace nodded a curt goodbye before walking outside. The May heat beating down from the sky felt like hot irons. She didn't say much to Cami, who was silent herself. Grace treasured that. Probably only another pregnant woman could understand the sudden twinges that twisted inside a body stretched out of shape by a baby.

But once she got to her street, Grace noted an instant lifting of her spirits. The tree-shrouded front yard always brought her a sense of comfort. Unlocking the front door, she went inside the house, with Cami on her heels.

"I'm going to go change," she murmured.

"I'll help myself to a glass of tea from the kitchen, and if you don't mind, I'm going to put my feet up on your sofa in the parlor," Cami told her. "Just call down to me if you need anything, or if you feel so much better you want me to take off.''

"Thanks, Cami.'' She offered her a wan smile before heading up the stairs. Slipping off her dress and boots, Grace put on a T-shirt that reached her knees. Just doing that made her feel like a new woman. The strange feeling that had assailed her was already gone.

"I'm okay, Cami. I just needed to get out of my panty hose, I guess," she called down the stairs.

"You're sure?"

"I'm sure. Thanks."

"Okay. I'm going to take my tea with me, but I'll put it in a plastic cup."

"That's fine. Sorry about lunch."

"No problem. I'll lock the door behind me so you don't have to come down."

Cami's voice filtered away. Grace went back into her room, seeking the comfort of her bed. Lying down, she wiggled her toes and tried not to lay on her back squarely. The doctor had said it was best in the later stages of pregnancy to rotate sides, thereby keeping pressure off the main artery in the back. He had also said she should get lots of rest, but Grace found it difficult to do that. No wonder she was feeling a bit run-down. It was her only day off, and all she had done today was keep busy.

But staying busy kept her from brooding, Grace thought as she closed her eyes. It wasn't healthy for the baby to have an unhappy mother; he would sense it. She would be happy and serene for her baby's sake—which meant staying out of Brant's path as much as possible.

DOWNSTAIRS, Cami and Brant were engaged in a heated, though whispered, argument.

"I can't leave you in here with her! Grace would kill me!''

Brant shook his head, determined. Placing the sack containing the lunch Grace had ordered in the refrigerator, he said, "I'll just watch TV until she awakens. She worried me with that sick look she had."

He had never thought it was possible for a person to go so white. Grace had done more than worry him. She had nearly gotten herself a trip over to the new doc's office.

"She's going to be furious with me," Cami moaned. "Don't touch her, or upset her at all!" she commanded. "I think the reason she looked so ill was having to sit between the two men in her life!"

Cami clapped a hand over her mouth. Brant's warning sensors picked up. "Are you hiding something from me?"

"No." Cami's face was stricken. "Brant, do not so much as say or do a thing to upset that poor woman up there. I really think she's been through enough." She gave him a narrow look. "In fact, I'm not sure I shouldn't stay with you in a chaperon capacity."

"I am only staying until I'm certain she's fine," Brant said. "I'm not the big bad wolf."

"I'm not so certain," Cami grumbled. "I'm also not certain Grace isn't going to have my head for this." She shot her brother a last suspicious glare. "You're not doing this to get one up on Kyle, are you?"

"Do I need to?" Brant eyed Cami. She definitely was hiding something.

"You might need to. Whether or not you can, I don't know." Cami stared up at the ceiling. "Grace is resting. She needs it. Please don't do anything to make me regret this."

"I won't. I swear."

Brant shooed his sister out the door. With one last uncertain look at him, Cami headed off. The house was quiet and still after he closed the door. From the dining room window, he watched her walk down the street, heading toward the Yellowjacket where she would pick up her truck.

Five minutes later, when he was very sure Cami wouldn't have second thoughts about his intentions, Brant locked the door.

Very quietly, he ascended the stairs.

# *Chapter Four*

Brant couldn't resist a small glance in on Grace. It couldn't hurt anything to check on her. He would look in her room so fast, it would really just be a blur to salve his concern.

Walking from the stairwell across to her bedroom, Brant's eyes riveted to Grace as she lay in the white canopied bed. She looked like an angel. His breath caught in his chest as his gaze slid from her blond hair ruffling gently across the pillow, to the one slender, bare leg she had curled up over the covers.

Her stomach wasn't obvious as she lay on her side, hidden by the blanket. Still, Brant was astonished by the over powering sensation of protectiveness that swamped him. Grace Barclay was going to be the mother of the only child he would ever have. Every man wanted to have the very best woman in the world be the mother to his child. It was the Madonna effect working on him; a psychologist would probably tell him he was operating under the survival of the fittest instinct. But as he stared at Grace's eyes closed in peaceful sleep, he knew the very best woman for him was growing his child.

Slowly he walked toward the bed. He took the edge of the blanket, pulling it carefully over Grace's leg so that she was covered. She didn't move, and Brant could tell by her deep breathing that she was thoroughly worn-out. Of course, he had cut into her sleep last night with his late visit. An urge to caress the tiny freckles sprinkled over her cheek possessed him, but he couldn't risk disturbing her sleep. Instead he went downstairs, kicked off his boots and made himself comfortable on the sofa. Grace looked fine to him now, but just in case, he wanted to be here for her if she needed anything.

*You need to think about how our parents' divorce affected you.* Cami's voice disturbed his relaxation.

"No, I don't," he said out loud. "I've got everything under control."

GRACE AWAKENED, stretching languorously. The sun no longer streamed in her window as it had when she'd gone to sleep. It was late Sunday afternoon, and she should be making plans for work tomorrow, but the rest had felt too wonderful. She'd needed it, and she knew why. Brant's intrusion in her life had exhausted her emotional state. With any luck, she wouldn't have to face him again—perhaps until the barbecue that was being planned for Cami.

Sighing with refreshed contentment, Grace went into the bathroom that adjoined her room, retrieving a glass of water. Putting it on the nightstand, she raised the window in her room about three inches to let in the soothing spring breeze. Of course, this was the very window Brant had thrown gravel at last night, but she shouldn't have to worry about a repeat episode.

She had made it perfectly clear to him that she didn't want to see him, except when she had to. They could be civil—for Cami's sake. After the baby was born, they would have to be a little more civil, but, Grace told herself as she sank into bed again, that gave her some time to forgive him for his outrageous, he-man approach to his rights where she was concerned.

BRANT BOLTED UPRIGHT on the sofa, alerted by a squeaking sound from upstairs. Instantly he wondered if Grace was okay. He listened intently, not hearing any further movement. The noise could have been a sound on the street as a car or truck went by, but maybe he should check on Grace again.

Quietly he went back up the stairs, allowing himself a fast peek over the stairwell. Grace was still in bed, though she had turned over, her back to him now. Frowning, he wondered what the noise might have been. Obviously she was still asleep, so she hadn't made the sound. Walking into her room, Brant glanced around, his gaze immediately caught by the barely moving lace hanging from the top of the canopy. The window was open now, and that meant—

"Brant Durning! What in blazes are you doing in my house?" Grace demanded, rolling in a cumbersome fashion as she tried to hoist herself out of the bed.

He backed up quickly, knowing he was in big trouble. She would have discovered his presence eventually, but her bedroom was a bad place to have been caught. "You didn't look well at lunch—"

"Lunch was over four hours ago! Don't tell me you've been in my house all this time! Did you pick one of my locks?"

"Now, Grace," Brant said soothingly. As she made it out of bed, her bare legs caught his attention. The huge T-shirt she wore rode up to the middle of her thighs, and he decided that, if anything, Grace filled out from pregnancy was an even more attractive woman than she'd been before. "I didn't break in. I had Cami—"

"I might have known! Poor Cami! How dare you manipulate her so you could get into my house?" She pointed menacingly toward the stairwell. "Get out, right now."

"Please, Grace, I—"

"I won't listen to anything you have to say, Brant, not while you've concealed yourself under the pretense of being concerned for me. Frankly, you're getting on my nerves.''

That hurt his feelings. All he wanted was to get on some kind of caring footing with Grace, and she wouldn't let him. ''I'm not trying to, honest. But Grace, you looked so green at lunch I was honestly worried.''

''Well, if you're that thin-skinned, you ought to be glad you missed out on the really fun parts of pregnancy.'' Grace ran a hand through her hair. ''Please, just go, Brant. This is my only day to relax. I can't if you're jumping out at me from the shadows.''

His gaze dropped instinctively to her belly. It pushed firm and round against the soft-looking T-shirt. ''You're making this mighty hard on me, Grace. How can I take care of you if you don't let me?''

*Don't want me* was what his mind really wondered. Brant couldn't imagine not taking care of Grace. She didn't know how much she needed him.

''Brant, go away. Your protective routine is tiresome, and way too late.''

''That's not my fault, Grace. I would have felt the same way I do now six months ago if you hadn't hidden this problem from me.''

Her stomach, large and distended, couldn't be hidden by a Mack truck at this point, Grace thought with great embarrassment. Of course Brant would rush in with his Sir Galahad ideas when she was at her most unattractive. ''Let's not rehash this,'' she snapped. ''I have a little time left before I have to allow you visitation rights.''

''Visitation rights?''

She couldn't help noticing the paling beneath his tanned skin. Instantly Grace felt sorry for her harsh words. ''Brant, all I mean is that I know you're going to be a good father. Since the minute you found out you were going to be one, you've been pestering me. All I'm saying is that there's no

baby here now, so can't you just wait three more months
to assert your fatherly rights?''

"You make it sound like my intentions are solely for the
sake of the baby, Grace. While I definitely want to care for
my child, I also want to take care of you.''

"Fine.'' Grace told herself to ignore how handsome
Brant looked, standing in the hallway with that pleading
look in his blue eyes. Jet-black hair only emphasized the
rugged planes of his face, the determined squareness of his
jaw. "Take care of me by leaving, please. I can't keep
fending you off.''

He was silent for a moment. "Maybe I don't want you
to.''

"I'm not going to allow you to waltz casually back into
my life as if you never left me,'' Grace said quietly.

"Do you want me to beg? Romance you? Send flowers?''

She shook her head. "No, Brant. I want none of the
above. I want peace and quiet and a chance to enjoy this
last part of my pregnancy without you haunting me at every
turn. I can't relax with you in Fairhaven. In fact, I almost
think it would be better if you took this time to take another
cattle-buying trip.'' She dropped her gaze at the hurt in his
eyes. "Fortunately I'm leaving tomorrow myself.''

Brant's gaze skittered in the direction of Grace's glance.
A closed suitcase and an overnight bag sat beside the entrance to her bathroom. His chest tightened at the implication of what she was saying. This time, she was the one
leaving. She had family in another state; surely she
wouldn't leave him—the same way he'd once left her?

Fear made his words cruel. "Grace, if you're hoping to
scare me into a marriage proposal, it isn't going to happen.'' The stunned widening of her eyes made him wish
he hadn't said it.

"Believe me, Brant, the last thing I want is to marry
you.''

"So where are you going?" He wanted desperately to hear her say she wasn't going to stay away until the baby was born. If that was her plan, he'd have to do something drastic to keep her in Fairhaven. He'd have to do something so drastic he couldn't even wrap his mind around what he knew would be required.

"It's none of your business, but I'll tell you, if you promise to leave once I do," Grace stated. "You're ruining my Sunday relaxation. I'm not above calling Sheriff John to haul you out of here, Brant."

He could tell she meant it. Exasperated, Brant knew she had him with that threat. The last thing he wanted was to bring more attention to their untimely situation. "You won't need to."

"All right. I'm going to New York on a buying trip."

"New York!" His voice contained the same amount of enthusiasm as if she'd said she was going to the other side of the world. "You can't fly in your condition!"

Grace's eyes shot flames. "I already have a good doctor, Brant. I don't need you butting in any more than you have. Now go." She pointed down the stairs.

Brant's insides had turned into a mass of Jell-O. He couldn't believe she meant it. Yet, her bags were packed and waiting. Anything could happen to the stubborn woman in New York! In her advanced state, she would be easy prey for petty thieves. She might go into labor on the airplane. For heaven's sake, she didn't even look as if she'd fit into an airplane lavatory comfortably!

"Grace," he began, but she shook her head.

"Five seconds and I call John. His number is on my speed-dial, by his own request. Go!"

He set his jaw. "I'm going."

"Thank you."

He hesitated on the stair another moment. Grace shook her head again. There wasn't anything else to say. Brant stomped down the stairs, stuffed his feet into the boots he'd shed earlier and was very careful not to let the door slam on his way out.

The lock shot home behind him. He jumped, terribly insulted by the sound. Grace was locking him out of her house and obviously her heart. Didn't the woman understand what torment she was putting him through? Now she was going off all by herself to New York City, when she couldn't even make it through a Sunday lunch at the Yellowjacket without turning pale and frightening him out of a day's worth of deodorant.

There was no help for it. Grace didn't know it yet, but as long as she had his baby in her body, she was stuck with him. It was a package deal.

She wasn't going anywhere without him.

GRACE ALLOWED HERSELF a sigh of relief as she finally ran Brant off. Those five more seconds she'd threatened him with hadn't been because she wanted him to leave as much as she needed him to leave. In all the time she had loved Brant Durning, she had prayed he would return her affection. It was too difficult to sternly turn away the strength of protection he was offering her.

She wandered into the kitchen for a snack. Opening the refrigerator, she found a sack containing the lunch she'd ordered at the Yellowjacket. Tears jumped into her eyes as she sniffled to herself somewhat piteously. Brant was determined to care for her. While that was extremely attractive, she just couldn't allow herself to get used to it. Without the baby, Brant wouldn't be thinking two thoughts about her, and the knowledge broke Grace's heart.

"Poor little baby," she whispered, stroking a loving hand around her rounded stomach. "Your daddy's a wonderful man. He's going to love you an awful lot."

She hoped the baby would understand the predicament he'd been born into. Two parents, both of whom would love him dearly, but who couldn't give him a family.

Grace lost her appetite. Shoving the food back inside the refrigerator, she hurried back up the stairs. Slamming her window shut so she wouldn't have to worry about Brant deciding to scale her house to check on her through the window, Grace busied herself making a list of things she wanted to look for while she was in New York City. While wedding gowns and accessories were the top priority for the trip, she also intended to look for a baby layette. She was going to enjoy her two days away from Fairhaven—and Brant.

THE NEXT MORNING, Grace settled herself into the airplane seat as best she could. She'd been assigned a middle seat, which annoyed her. She had tried without success to change it, but there had been a last-minute sell-out of seats. She was too darned big to fit comfortably in this tiny little chair, and who knew how many times she'd have to get up to use the bathroom?

Sighing, Grace closed her eyes. She should have checked her seat location when she'd bought the ticket. All she could hope for now was that maybe her aisle seat mate would have mercy on her. After all, it would be better to exchange seats than have to allow her to squeeze by every thirty minutes.

"Excuse me," a deep voice said.

Grace's eyes flew open. "Kyle!"

He handed her a dozen red roses wrapped in cellophane. "Would you believe I just happen to be going to New York City?"

"No, I wouldn't."

"That's my seat over there."

"When did you decide to do this?"

He showed her his boarding pass, so Grace maneuvered into the aisle so he could take the seat by the window. "Last week, when you told me you were planning a buying trip." He sat, moving the seat belt in her chair so she could sit comfortably. "I hope you don't mind, Grace. I just didn't like the idea of you being all alone in New York."

"I've done it before," she said wryly. Though she was touched by his concern, she had really been looking forward to some time to herself on this trip. But what could she say to this man who had offered to marry her? Go away?

"I know you have." Kyle's voice lacked any kind of condescension. "But you haven't gone to New York pregnant."

Grace stiffly held the roses in her lap. What was she going to do with these, anyway? Standing, she reached to put them in the overhead bin on top of her overnight bag. A large male hand closed over hers to help.

"Brant!" she exclaimed, glancing over her shoulder. Her heart started racing like mad. Neither man was going to be pleased to see the other. "What are you doing here?"

"I—" He halted his explanation, his gaze narrowing on Kyle. "I see I'm not necessary."

The last thing she wanted was for Brant to think she had planned a trip with Kyle. Grace's mind emptied of any possible explanation for Kyle's presence. The baby kicked inside her, and suddenly Grace felt a bit nauseated.

"Listen, both of you—"

"Good afternoon, and welcome to Flight 1211, bound for New York City," the flight attendant announced over the microphone.

Grace hadn't made it through lunch yesterday sitting between these two males. There was no way she could endure a long flight sandwiched between them.

"Please, I beg both of you to deplane." Pushing Brant aside in the aisle, much to the annoyance of passengers who wanted to get around them, Grace stood so that Kyle could get out. "I know you both have the best intentions, and I'm truly touched in an astonished sort of way, but it's just too much. Please."

Kyle and Brant eyed each other with hostility, neither moving. "Please," Grace said softly. "Both of you go now. I will call each of you when I return, I promise, but you're both making me crazy."

"I don't see why I should have to," Kyle stated reasonably. "After all, I've asked you to marry me. Brant is the one without a good reason for being here."

"Don't tell me I don't have a good reason for being here!" Brant roared. "And what do you mean, you asked Grace to marry you?"

Interested onlookers peered over the seat in front and back of them, while others had stopped in the aisle, watching the unfolding drama with interest.

*The pilot needs to flip on the air-conditioning,* Grace thought irrationally. She felt faint, and mortified.

"Is there a problem?" a flight attendant asked impatiently.

"Yes, there is," Grace said. "These two men are bothering me. I insist you change my seat at once. Let them sit together, since they so badly want to."

"Aw, lady, give them a break," a balding man said. "It's obvious you liked one of 'em," he said, with a pointed glance at her stomach.

Grace ripped the seat ticket from the man's fingers. "Thank you, sir, for offering to exchange seats with me. Help yourself."

"Wait, Grace," Kyle said, getting to his feet. "I don't want you to be angry with me. I'll get off the plane, if you promise to call me at once when you get to the hotel so I'll know you've arrived safely."

"Thank you," Grace said on a sigh of relief.

She waited while Kyle made his way into the aisle. "Thank you for the roses," she said, pressing a kiss to his cheek. "I will call you soon."

He looked vaguely uncomfortable. "I'm not going unless

he goes, too." It was clear Kyle was waiting for Brant to be as chivalrous as he was.

"Oh, for heaven's sake!" She felt pushed to the limit of her endurance. "I thought at least you, Kyle, were going to be reasonable."

"I'm trying to be, Grace, but he's no gentleman. I don't trust Brant as far as I can throw him."

"Why, you—" Brant reached over Grace's head to make a grab for Kyle's collar.

"Please!" Grace pushed Brant away, accidentally sending Kyle against the balding man.

"Lady, if I'm gonna take your seat, I don't want to be a party to fisticuffs," he complained. "I like to sleep on plane flights."

"Mind your own business!" she admonished him. Taking a deep breath, she was just about to grab her bags and leave the plane when Brant's deep voice halted her.

"All right, I'll go." He stared menacingly at Kyle. "But I'm out the price of a plane ticket. Don't expect me to bring any more of my animal practice your way."

Brant stalked past everyone in the aisle, glaring at Kyle as he went by.

"Fine! Expect me to boycott beef!" Kyle stuck out his chest, but Brant only shoved his cowboy hat down farther on his head and slunk off toward the exit.

Grace sighed in exasperation. "Thank heavens! Now, if you'll just—"

"I'm going, I'm going," Kyle said, his tone rueful.

"Good! I can get my seat back," the balding man exclaimed, snatching his boarding pass from Grace's hand. He lurched down the aisle toward the back of the plane.

"I appreciate it, Kyle. Thank you for being a good sport."

He touched her cheek softly. "Say yes when you come back, Grace."

Kyle turned around and walked away. Grace was so relieved she didn't know what to do.

"Quit staring," she said to everyone watching her. "The show's over."

Sliding into her seat, she realized with relief that the two seats on either side of her would now be free. She wouldn't have to worry about being cramped during the flight. "Ahh," she sighed, allowing herself to unwind in the space now afforded her by the exit of the men in her life.

What was she going to do about them? she wondered. On the one hand, she had to seriously consider Kyle's marriage proposal and the emotional security a whole family would mean for her baby. On the other hand, Brant was likely to be such an impediment to the happiness of any married life she tried to enjoy that she seriously doubted the wisdom of accepting Kyle's proposal.

*Besides which, Brant owns my heart.* Therein lay the biggest problem of all. The stubborn man was so bullheaded that he would do anything for her, except become her husband. He was determined to retain his protective intrusion into her life without the benefit of a marriage certificate.

Well, she would fix that with him as soon as she returned from New York City. With time, perhaps Brant's novelty with being a father would wear thin, but she couldn't count on that. She would just tell him, in no uncertain terms, and more firmly even than she had told him at her house, that he was not welcome to make himself at home in her life anymore. He was thoroughly disrupting it.

The flight attendant instructed the passengers to prepare for takeoff. The plane began taxiing down the runway. Grace closed her eyes, feeling her spirits lift even as the plane began gathering speed, lifting into a diagonal ascent.

*Whoosh!* She suddenly felt someone land in the seat next to her. Grace started, her eyes flying open to see Brant buckling the seat belt. Her mouth dropped open as everyone seated around them started clapping.

# Chapter Five

"What are you doing, Brant?" she snapped.

"Just act like I'm not here," he told her, his blue eyes alight with mischief.

"You were supposed to get off the plane!" She was furious with his deception.

"Aw, babe, say you're glad to see me."

Grace glared up over the seats, and the clapping subsided. "Guess we know now which one's the father!" the balding man called from the back of the plane.

"I had my money on the cowboy," an elderly woman said. "He looks like he knows how to get out of the chute."

"Honestly!" Grace wouldn't dignify that with a response. She lowered herself into the seat. "The last thing I am is glad to see you, Brant. How dare you deceive poor Kyle like that?"

"Wasn't very gentlemanly of me," he admitted. "'Course, he's not very intelligent if he expects you to carry a dozen roses all the way to New York."

She could tell by the devilish delight in his eyes that he didn't care at all about Kyle. "I suppose you expect me to be more impressed by your John Wayne sling-the-girl-over-the-saddle routine."

His eyes softened as he leaned his head against the seat. He patted her hand, then grabbed a magazine from the seat pocket in front of him. "How long is this flight, anyway? Four, five hours? Long enough for me to convince you of my earnest regret for deceiving Kyle, and for slinging you over my saddle."

He was laughing at her! Grace was so outraged she couldn't speak for a moment. "I'm going to sleep. Do not speak to me the entire time this plane is in the air, or I will be tempted to scream until they move you to another seat."

"Plane's full." His tone told her he still thought he was going to worm out of her wrath.

"I'll switch seats with the bald man," she threatened.

"Okay." He held up his hands. "I promise not to say a word the entire time the plane is in the air."

"Thank you." She put the armrest of the seat next to the window up, allotting herself the breadth of both chairs. Scooching over to the window, she snatched a pillow from a passing flight attendant, and made herself as comfortable as possible. When the seat belt light turned off, she removed her shoes and curled her legs up into the seat next to her. This way she was almost comfortable, and might sleep the entire way to New York. It would be wonderful relief from being reminded of Brant's presence in the seat next to her feet.

Almost as if he sensed her thoughts, Brant absently reached over, never taking his eyes from the magazine, and began rubbing her feet. Grace rolled her eyes, sighing. He would keep his word by not speaking, but he would assault her senses in other ways. The massaging motion of Brant's strong fingers felt heavenly to her sore, swollen feet. Surrendering for the moment, Grace closed her eyes and willed herself to sleep.

AT THE HOTEL a few hours later, Grace eyed the hotel clerk with disbelief. "What do you mean, I don't have a reservation? I have a confirmation number. I reserved a room over a month ago."

"I'm sorry." He made another run through his computer. "Some error was obviously made. Did you call the 1-800 number or this hotel specifically?"

"I made reservations using the 1-800 number, of course," Grace said through clenched teeth. "There wasn't any reason to pay for the call, and I've never had any trouble getting a room in this hotel for any of my business trips before." She was careful to emphasize trips in the plural so the clerk would know her future patronage was in jeopardy if he didn't locate a room for her pronto. It was frustrating that this situation had to develop with Brant looking over her shoulder. She could take care of this matter; she did not need him tagging along to take care of her, as he seemed to think.

"I'm terribly sorry, ma'am. Let me get the manager for you."

"Is there another problem?"

"Well, actually, yes." He looked terribly embarrassed. "There's a large convention in town—"

"And you're booked." Grace couldn't believe it.

"Yes. I think that's why I'm not showing anything with your reservation number on it. There must have been a computer glitch of some kind." His eyes briefly skimmed her stomach in a sympathetic way. "Please wait right here. Perhaps the manager can arrange for you to have a room at another hotel."

"I don't want to stay in another hotel! My appointments aren't far from here. This is convenient for me."

Brant stepped up beside her. "Check my reservation for me, please. Brant Durning."

The desk clerk quickly checked his computer. "Yes," he said with a sigh of relief. "I do show a room for you, sir."

"Give it to her," Brant said briskly. "I can find another hotel to stay in."

"Are you sure?" Grace hadn't counted on him coming

to her rescue in this way. "You don't mind going some-where else?"

"No, I don't. If there's no room at the inn, then there's no room. I don't want you traipsing around town trying to find a bed." His eyes roamed over her, concerned. "I'll get a bellcap to take your suitcase and overnight bag up."

"I'm terribly sorry for the inconvenience," the desk clerk offered. "In the future, please—"

Brant waved him off. Grace stared as Brant went to re-trieve her bags. She finished checking in, while Brant stood stoically to the side. His eyes narrowed as she approached. "I appreciate you giving up your room."

"Never mind. Do you have everything else you need?"

"I do." She hesitated for a moment, telling herself it served him right not to have a room. He shouldn't have followed her to New York in the first place! Yet, she would still be out a room. "Brant, the room has double beds."

"I'll ask for a king-size bed if you'd be more comfort-able."

"No!" She dropped her gaze. "I was going to say that I'll be out most of tomorrow. The room will be empty. It doesn't make much sense for you to have to find a room in another hotel when I won't be around anyway."

"Are you inviting me to bunk with you?"

She couldn't raise her eyes to meet his. "In a totally platonic way, yes, I am. If you understand that…"

Her voice trailed off. She wasn't sure how to say exactly what she wanted him to understand.

"If I understand that I get the bed by the window, and you get the bed nearest the bathroom."

"Exactly," she breathed out on a sigh of relief.

"Ah." He considered her words. "It's okay, Grace. I didn't come to New York to make love to you, though that would be nice. I came to spend time with you. I can do that from a bed three feet away from yours."

"Thanks for understanding, Brant." She was glad he understood she didn't want to be pushed into any new layer of their relationship. She just wasn't ready.

"Come on," he said, taking her arm. "Let's get these bags upstairs. If you'll allow me to, I'll buy you dinner in the hotel restaurant."

She hesitated for the slightest second.

"Don't worry, Grace. I know what the playing rules are. It'll be dinner, and nothing else."

"Okay," she said ungraciously, not certain how much time the two of them could spend together before things might turn accidentally and disastrously romantic. "Dinner, and nothing else."

THIRTY MINUTES LATER, Grace sat at a dinner table that was covered by a white tablecloth adorned by a glowing candle. It might be romantic, if her dinner companion wasn't Brant.

"Now that we're in New York, I want you to explain what Kyle meant when he said he'd asked you to marry him." Brant's eyebrows were thunderclouds of disapproval.

Grace shook her head. "Don't glower at me."

"When were you going to tell me?"

"What difference can it possibly make, Brant? You and I have resolved our situation to our mutual satisfaction. We are free to lead our separate lives outside of the baby."

"You are *not* free to marry Kyle Macaffee!" Brant's eyes revealed his contempt. "Grace, you're talking crazy."

She lost her appetite, though the food was wonderful and she'd skipped the airplane lunch. "I'm exhausted, Brant. I'm going up to the room, if you'll excuse me."

She got up and walked out of the restaurant. Never in her life had she ever done such a thing, but Brant's chauvinistic attitude was wearing her down. For her sake, and the baby's, she needed a stress-free environment. Being with Brant was more stressful than having a bride panic at the last minute that her dress wasn't quite right!

The hotel room was at least quiet, Grace thought with a sigh of relief. She went inside and closed the door, enjoying the silence and the peach and green decor. Getting out of her maternity outfit, she had a quick shower, making certain the bathroom door was locked securely. When she finished bathing, she peeped cautiously around the door, but Brant still hadn't returned. With a sigh of relief, Grace slipped on a huge T-shirt, crawled into bed and promptly fell asleep.

BRANT SAT AT THE TABLE trying to finish his meal after Grace left, but he was fighting a losing battle. He didn't have any desire to eat. The revelation that Macaffee had the nerve to propose to the mother of Brant's child had kept him simmering all afternoon. He'd waited for the best time to ask Grace about it. Apparently he hadn't picked the right time—but the time was never going to be right where Macaffee was concerned.

He threw the dinner roll he was eating back onto the plate. Grace couldn't possibly be considering the veterinarian's proposal! Didn't she know how that would make him, Brant, look? As if he wasn't man enough to take care of his own offspring!

*Would I propose to a woman who was carrying someone else's child?*

Not likely. He wouldn't even propose to the one who was carrying *his* child. And he loved Grace.

Brant bowed his head. Why couldn't she be satisfied with that? Didn't she know that the best of marriages didn't last forever? That marriage wasn't a guarantee there wouldn't be heartbreak down the road in twenty, thirty years?

A memory of his parents splitting up tried to edge into his mind, but Brant shoved it away. How could he convince Grace to see his point in this matter? What he was offering her was honest; it was from the heart. If he had to change his feelings to suit her, in the end, their relationship wouldn't be what either of them wanted.

*Grace Barclay Macaffee,* his errant brain reminded him. The obstinate woman might actually marry that veterinarian, just to spite Brant! Women in town were crazy over Kyle. Privately Brant knew Kyle was a good, fair man. He'd been throwing business Kyle's way almost exclusively since the man opened his practice. Kyle had a way with sick, injured things; many a case Brant had thought was going to end with a shotgun or a hypodermic had turned around nicely under Kyle's capable hands.

*Damn it,* Brant thought angrily as he signed the dinner tab. *This is one case Kyle Macaffee isn't going to be doing any doctorin' on.* He caught the elevator, striding to the hotel room he and Grace were occupying, fully prepared to have it out with her over this matter.

In one of the beds she lay, soundly and deeply asleep. All the righteous anger left Brant immediately. He looked at her, securely tucked under the covers, even to her chin. She had the air-conditioning unit in the room going full-blast, cold enough to chill Alaska. She appeared obliviously comfortable.

There was no help for it. He'd need an igloo to survive in this room tonight. Stripping off his clothes, he took a fast shower. Then he crawled into bed, careful not to disturb Grace, and molded himself against her back.

SOMEHOW, Grace wasn't surprised when she awakened to discover Brant wrapped around her as if he were a warm, furry bear. He hadn't played fair ever since he decided to weasel his way onto the airplane. Painful memories of how much she enjoyed snuggling with him assaulted her, so Grace got up and went into the bathroom to get dressed and put on her makeup. If she was very quiet, perhaps Brant wouldn't notice her leaving. It would be nice to start her day without having a verbal sparring match with him.

When she emerged from the bathroom, she found a bright-eyed Brant staring at her appreciatively, already dressed.

"Breakfast is over there." He pointed to a tray that had been delivered while she was in the bathroom.

Her stomach bottomed out. "I'm not hungry."

"There's orange juice and apple juice," he said, ignoring her comment, "and some breakfast stuff like cereal and bagels. I didn't know which was healthier to eat when a woman is expecting."

"Brant Durning," Grace said, putting her hands on her hips, "you listen to me, and listen good. I did just fine without you before. I very much resent you trying to take over my life." She turned to go, and opened the door.

He shot up from the bed, putting a hand just above her head to keep the door closed. "Wait a minute, Grace. I kinda thought I was being considerate. I thought you might prefer having something to eat first thing. Isn't that supposed to help morning sickness?"

"That passed in the first trimester," she said between clenched teeth. It was extremely difficult to ignore the pickup in her heart rate. If only the man wasn't so darned sexy!

"Oh."

To his credit, he did appear embarrassed by her reference to the morning sickness she had endured. Grace drew a deep breath, willing herself to sound more patient. "Please move, Brant. I have an early morning meeting with a vendor."

"Well, hang on a sec. I'll just follow along, you know, walk you there. Can't be too careful in New York."

"Brant, I'm going alone. I'll be fine."

He didn't pay any attention, heading into the bathroom to run a comb through his hair and quickly brush his teeth.

"Just let me walk you," he said around a mouthful of toothpaste.

Suddenly Grace knew how she could keep Brant from accompanying her. "You know, I just don't think you'll enjoy hanging around all day escorting me from place to place. I've got appointments in the market, then I'm planning to attend a show."

"A show? Hey, I'd love to take in a show with you. Hang on just another sec."

Slyly Grace said, "It's a wedding gown fashion show."

He stiffened, blowing mouthwash into the sink.

The discomfort on his face made Grace laugh. Of all the things in the world Brant wouldn't want to be faced with, it was wedding gowns. She decided to jab the needle in a little deeper. "Not very interesting to a man, I know. And my day only gets less exciting. After the show, I've made an appointment with a friend of mine to look at some of her baby layette samples."

"Okay." Brant brightened, immediately leaving the bathroom to retrieve his wallet. "I don't know what a baby layette is, but I'm game to learn."

She couldn't believe it. "Brant, baby layette is just a term for baby stuff! You don't want to pick out towels, clothes, washcloths—"

"Hey, little man, shopping for your first clothes in New York City." He grinned hugely and reached out to pat Grace's tummy. The grin disappeared from his face the second his hand made contact. His gaze held Grace's, a mixture of puzzlement and astonishment widening his eyes. "I didn't know that was how it felt," he said hoarsely.

Grace's blood thundered in her ears. After a second, Brant's palm spread slightly, exploring. The baby chose that moment to stick out an elbow or heel.

"Grace!" Brant yelped. His eyes got even wider at the movement under his hand. "It's alive!"

Grace laughed at his amazement. "Haven't you felt Cami's stomach?"

Shock jerked his hand away from the amazing feel of her stomach. "Why would I want to do that?"

"You're going to be an uncle, Brant, whether you like the idea or not. I just thought maybe you'd, I don't know, hugged your sister when you got back into town, at least…" Her words dwindled off.

Brant backed up a step, temporarily confused by what Grace was suggesting. Hug Cami? Heck, no, he'd been more disposed to give her a good solid whumping. "I…I didn't think about it," he said lamely. He eyed Grace's stomach again with some trepidation. "She's not as big as you are, and I guess it never occurred to me…"

"You were gone for three months and didn't hug your sister when you returned?"

He didn't like the accusatory expression on Grace's face. "If you're going to make your appointment, we'd better get going," he said abruptly. "Do you want any of this juice or not? I think my son ought to at least have a healthy snack before he starts his day."

It was diversionary tactics, and Grace was never fooled by those, but at least she walked over and took a glass of orange juice from the tray. He was relieved when she grabbed a muffin as well.

"I'll eat this on the way," she said, swishing past him.

Her perfume teased him as she swept by, her hair all gold and shiny as it fell in long, attractive curls over the top of her navy blouse.

"Fine." He closed the door behind them. "Let's go get some baby lingerie."

"Layette!" Grace called over her shoulder.

"Layette," he repeated, trying the new word on his tongue. Grace's disapproval hurt his feelings, because, deep inside, he knew she was right about his sister. Maybe if he

got the hang of this baby layette stuff, he'd pick up an extra
one for Cami as a peace offering.

Dang, but it had never occurred to him that, not only was
he going to be a father, he was going to be an uncle as
well.

IT WAS ANNOYING that Brant had to remember while Grace
was inside the market that he had not fully gotten it through
her head that she was not marrying Macaffee. Brant pushed
away from the wall he was leaning against, shooting an
impatient look at his watch. She was taking too long!

*What if she's picking something out for herself?*

He felt ill. Grace would love to wear a gown like she'd
been fitting other women into all these years. Like any
woman, she must dream of being a bride. Macaffee was
offering to make that dream come true. Brant was offering
her security, which she didn't seem too impressed by, and
he was offering her his steadfast companionship, but that
didn't seem to be enough, either.

That baby was *his*. The woman was his, too, though she
was acting as if she didn't know it. His son wasn't going
to ride on a tractor with anybody but his own father. A grin
spread over his face just thinking about holding a little boy
body between his legs as he steered a tractor over the family acreage. He would point out places he'd loved to explore as a child—

Feminine giggles jolted him out of his reverie. Two
young women, probably early twenties, were staring at him.

"You look like the Marlboro man without a mustache,"
one of them said.

They were kind of cute. Brant puffed up a little under
their admiration. "I don't smoke, though. Smoking's bad
for your health," he told them.

"He talks just like a real cowboy!" the other one cried
with delight. "Can we have our picture taken with you?"

Only in New York, Brant thought, would anyone think

his cowboy hat and boots were a fashion statement. ''Sure,'' he said easily.

One girl ran to stand beside him, while the other snapped a picture with her camera. They quickly traded places, and Brant smiled obligingly for the last shot.

''What is going *on?*''

Grace's astounded voice let the air out of Brant's pride. ''Just playing tourist,'' he said.

''You certainly are.'' She looked angrier than he'd ever seen her. Grace looked…hurt. Brant realized he had made an error the size of the Empire State Building and knew it was time to go into damage control.

The two girls stared at Grace bravely because Brant had allowed them to take his picture. ''Would you mind taking a picture so both of us can be in it with him?''

Before Brant could head off what he knew must be coming, Grace had dropped the package she'd been carrying and thrust the full width of her belly next to Brant. ''I'll be happy to, if you don't mind taking one of all *three* of us with my camera,'' she said too sweetly.

The girls' jaws dropped. ''Um, we um—''

Grace smiled, catlike. ''I understand.''

''We've gotta catch a bus. 'Bye!'' they called, hurriedly strolling away.

''Grace, I—''

''Don't say a word, Brant. I'm surprised, but not shocked.''

Grace picked up her package, turning on her heel to hurry off. Brant had to lengthen his stride to keep up. ''It was harmless, Grace. They were just girls, for heaven's sake!''

''And you just couldn't resist playing big, strong, cowboy.'' She didn't slow down.

He reached over to take her package from her. ''I'm not sure why you're so upset, babe.''

"Upset! Upset!" Grace halted, whirling to face him. "Who's upset?"

Brant watched her warily. "I think you are."

"Well, why would I be upset? Because while I'm inside working, you're outside playing urban cowboy for a couple of girls who are young enough to leave their bras at home?"

He hadn't given any consideration to their breasts. "Ah—"

"I mean, I know you were probably impressed by the fact that their bottoms were still so tight they could sit on a crack on this pavement and make perfectly perpendicular lines, but damn it—"

To Brant's utter disbelief, Grace burst into tears. "Hey, babe. Don't cry." He lowered the package to the concrete and wrapped his arms around her. "I'm sorry. I didn't mean to upset you."

She sniffled against his chest. He kind of liked holding her against him, feeling her need him, though he wanted her to quit crying.

"Is it a hormone thing?" he asked, looking for a reasonable explanation for Grace's distress. It just wasn't like her to fly off the handle.

"No, it's because you're a jackass." She kept her face hidden against him. "I'm all pushed out of shape, Brant! I'm like a straw with a watermelon inside it. My ankles are the size of your biceps, and you're letting two beautiful girls paw you. How am I supposed to feel?"

Ah. What she was feeling was suddenly clear to him. "You're just a little jealous, honey, but—"

She jerked away from him and went speeding down the sidewalk. "Grace, wait!" He snatched up the package and took after her. "What did I say?"

"You bigheaded baboon," she flung at him. "Naturally your preoccupation with yourself won't allow you to think of anything but how I must be eaten up with jealousy over you. You're just so wonderful, I'm not certain we can both fit inside this taxi.''

She hailed the one closest to the curb and hopped in, giving directions to the driver. Brant barely had time to close the door before the taxi zoomed away.

''What am I missing here, babe?''

''Your ego? You must have left it on the sidewalk since we're both occupying the same seat.''

Her eyes were large with sarcastic innocence. Brant wasn't sure how to deal with this fiery Grace.

''Please tell me, because I can't make it right if I don't know what I'm doing wrong.'' He hoped she would see how much he really wanted to make her happy.

She took her gaze from his and stared out the opposite window. ''I feel unattractive.''

His mouth fell open. She had never been more beautiful in her entire life! ''Like you couldn't sit on a crack and line up perpendicularly?'' he asked carefully.

''Exactly.''

He shook his head, reaching over to sweep her into his lap. ''I'm sorry. I shouldn't have been playing tourist with two babes.''

''Brant!''

He laughed, nuzzling her neck. ''Grace, you're beautiful. Maybe I should have told you sooner, but I've always been attracted to you.''

''I know *that*.'' Her freckles stood out a little with a rush of color to her skin. ''I wouldn't be in this condition otherwise.'' She sighed. ''I just didn't enjoy having to fight off the cover girls from hell.''

''Grace.'' He pressed a kiss against her temple. ''I—''

''Hey!'' the taxi driver called. ''No neckin' in my cab!''

She slid off Brant's lap. ''I'm paying you to watch the road, sir.'' To Brant, she said, ''I'm sorry I went hysterical. You were right. It probably was only hormonal imbalance.'' She looked away, obviously saving face.

"That's okay." Secretly Brant was a little amused, and maybe a little pleased that Grace still thought enough of him to let her hormones go awry. "Now where to?"

"My final appointment, then I'm finished for the day."

"Baby stuff?" Brant sat straighter, his attention caught. "So what's in this big box we've been lugging around?"

Grace didn't look his way. "A wedding gown."

## Chapter Six

Brant recoiled as if he were holding a boxed cobra. "Wedding gown?"

"Uh-huh."

Surely she hadn't picked out a dress for herself. Surely she wasn't giving consideration to Macaffee's proposal. "Can I ask why?" he demanded. Fear gave his voice a jealous, sharp edge.

"It really wouldn't be of interest to you, Brant. I'll hold the box if it's a problem." She looked out at the passing scenery, without giving him so much as a blink at her expression.

"No, I don't mind carrying it." He desperately wanted to know what its presence in the taxi meant.

The cab pulled to the curb. Grace paid the driver before Brant even realized they were at their destination. He wedged himself out the door with the large box, and saw Grace heading toward the glass doors of a building at a good clip. Obviously she was still out of sorts with him. Brant didn't think he could blame her, actually. He shouldn't have let those girls take his picture, but it wouldn't happen again.

Grace held the door open, and Brant squeezed past her, then tried to keep pace as she headed toward a door with no name on the outside. Once past the door, however, he could see hangers with all kinds of little baby things hanging from rolling racks and on the wall. "Wow," he said.

"These are lines of kids' clothing my friend is taking orders for. Usually she only works with department stores and boutiques, but she told me to come over and look at her samples."

A woman taller than Grace came out of the back of the showroom. "Grace! You made it."

The two women hugged. "I did, and I brought you something, Jana. First, let me introduce you to…" She hesitated, obviously not having considered how she would introduce Brant. "This is my friend, Brant Durning," she said slowly, "Brant, this is my friend, Jana Watkins."

"You must be a closer friend than me," Jana said with a meaningful smile at Grace's belly. "It's nice to meet you, Brant." He couldn't shake hands very well because of the package he held.

"Jana, here's something I think you'll want to see." Grace took the box from Brant's hands, completely avoiding eye contact with him.

Jana led them from the reception area into an office and put the box on a desk. "Oh!" she exclaimed, pulling the lid off, "It's beautiful, Grace! Absolutely beautiful!"

Jana held the gown against herself. The long slender style suited Jana's height, though Brant instinctively knew that nothing like that would fit on Grace in her condition. He wondered if there was such a thing as maternity bridal wear.

"Do you really like it?" Grace asked, watching anxiously as Jana hurried to examine her image in a mirror.

"I love it! I knew I could trust you to choose the perfect gown." She hurried over to hug Grace enthusiastically.

Brant's skin grew hot along his collar with embarrassment. Jana obviously knew he was the father of the child Grace was carrying. She had to wonder why Brant wasn't ponying up for a few yards of satin and lace for his woman.

"Thank you." Jana smiled luminously. "My fiancé is going to love you for picking this out. And you for carrying it all the way over here so I could see it, Brant." She smiled so widely, Brant forced a grim smile in return. "Now, come on, you two, and see if I've got anything you'd be interested in."

"I really appreciate this, Jana," Grace said, walking ahead with her friend. Brant followed along at a more calculatedly casual pace. This was women's business. He should have stayed outside on the sidewalk.

No. He'd gotten into more trouble when he'd tried to stay out of the way. Brant crammed his hands into his pockets, trying not to be too interested in the baby garments hanging here and there.

"What about this, Brant?" Jana called merrily.

She held up a bib that read Daddy Did It. It had lace all around its edges, and Brant's neck felt even hotter.

"I don't think it's quite what he had in mind, Jana."

"Well, that was just for starters. Let me show you some coming home outfits that are to die for."

Coming home outfits? Brant pondered that. Didn't babies just stay at home most of the time, anyway? Why did they need special outfits to come home in?

"Oh, this one's adorable," Grace murmured.

Brant eased over to see what she was admiring. It was the tiniest thing he'd ever seen: white, with a little satin giraffe on the chest area, and little snaps down the front.

"Isn't it sweet?" Grace asked him.

"I—yeah," Brant agreed. "Don't boys wear blue? And isn't that awfully small? I don't want him to be, you know, bound up."

Grace and Jana laughed. "It's a nine-month size, Brant," Jana explained.

"Yeah, well Grace is six months now. She'll be nine months when she delivers, I'm sure. You better get a larger size, Grace."

The women laughed again. Grace shook her head. "I'll take this one in the newborn size, if you've got it, Jana. It's too cute."

They spent an hour looking at outfits and washcloths and stuff Brant had never considered a baby might need. He watched the pile of Grace's selections grow with contentment, until she held up a lace and white dress.

"It's so beautiful! I've never seen anything like it."

Grace's gaze went up and down the dress as if she was looking at heaven. It was tiny, in Brant's eyes, and all that lace was an inexcusable mistake to put on anyone's baby. Any baby worth its salt would be irritated by the itching. He started when she put it in the pile.

"Hey! You're not putting a dress on my son!" he roared at once.

"It's a christening gown," Jana told him.

"I don't care what it is, it's not going home with us. My boy's wearing pants, as is meant to be."

"What's that supposed to mean?" Grace was bridling.

"I really don't know." Brant threw himself into the nearest chair in a huff. "Look, Grace, I'm all for women's lib and everything, but I'm not comfortable with my boy wearing skirts."

"Put the dress back, Jana," Grace said softly. "Brant's done pretty well getting up to speed so far. It'll take a little longer to explain some other things to him."

"Danged right," he muttered. "Hey!" He straightened, his attention caught by an outfit hanging on a display near the wall. "Now that's more what I had in mind."

It was blue jean material anyone could find in any state, connected by snaps to a red handkerchief print shirt he could have bought in Texas, but the outfit came with the requisite snaps down the legs. Brant was delighted he'd found something he could relate to. "I'll take that. Got any boots to go with it?"

"No." Jana laughed, and got the little Western outfit

down. "For the first few months, maybe a pair of white bootie socks will suffice."

Brant was disappointed. "Okay. Do you have another one of those Western outfits, then?"

"Brant, I hardly think I'll need two." Grace's eyebrows rose. "I mean, I've probably got enough for one trip, don't you think?"

"The second outfit's for Cami," he said gruffly, not looking at Grace. To Jana, he said, "I'll take a few bibs and washcloths, too, please, none that say anything about daddy doing it."

He felt Grace lightly touch his arm in approval, which Brant liked, but was careful not to acknowledge. His eyes caught on the white baby gown Grace had so admired. It *was* awfully pretty, but he was going to have to keep a close eye on her and make sure she didn't truss his son up like a mama's boy. Shoot, none of the neighboring rancher's kids would play with his child! "Jeez. How's he gonna look in Future Farmers of America with a dress on?" Brant grumbled.

Grace and Jana laughed, dismissing his complaint. Brant tried to grin, as if he'd meant the question to be funny, but he was serious about his boy not wearing that dress.

Christening gown or whatever, that dress looked suspiciously like a wedding gown.

ONE HOUR LATER, they had finished up and returned to the hotel. Grace said her back was hurting, so she went to take a shower. Brant threw himself on the bed and turned on CNN, but his thoughts weren't on the bickering broadcasters.

His thoughts were on what Grace looked like nude. He didn't have the right to know, of course, but his body responded just thinking about it. She'd gotten terribly upset over his antics with the female tourists, but it had never crossed his mind that she might be. Grace put those young things to shame.

Had he ever told her how beautiful he thought she was? During the months they'd gone out as a couple, he couldn't remember saying such to her. Something told him he hadn't—of course he hadn't. Romance wasn't his strong suit.

His gaze slid once again to Kyle's roses, now wilting in the ice bucket Grace had commandeered as a vase. What a dumb thing to do, anyway. If that was romance, Kyle Macaffee had thrown fifty dollars down the drain.

The shower quit, and Grace came out a moment later wearing a flowing caftan. "You look comfortable," he murmured, thinking she also looked gorgeous.

"Oh, I am." She sank onto the opposite bed with a pleased moan. "I'm sorry I can't accommodate you for dinner, Brant."

"It's fine. I'm a bit worn-out myself." Actually he'd been amazed by how much Grace could get done in a day. He wondered if she was pushing it by being so active. "We can order in something from room service."

"That sounds wonderful."

"Do you want me to toss those flowers so I can get you some ice and a soda?"

Grace turned to stare at him. "Toss my flowers? Why would I want you to do that?"

"Well, they're wilting," Brant said pointedly, trying to sound practical. Even he could hear the sheepish sound in his voice. "I didn't think you'd want them anymore."

"They're beautiful! Of course I don't want you to throw them out." Grace sat up.

Brant was tired of looking at the silly things. He supposed Grace would want to tote them back on the plane all the way back to the Dallas airport. "Are you planning on taking them back with you?"

"No."

"Then we can throw them away just a few hours early and be able to use the ice bucket."

"Kyle was sweet to buy those for me!"

"I'd say he was lacking good sense to spend that much money on something that's going in the trash."

"Oh, for heaven's sake, Brant! You wouldn't know romance if it was staring you in the face!"

He halted in the act of reaching for a room service menu. "Grace, if that's what you're looking for, I'm not going to be able to give it to you."

"I didn't ask you to," she said stiffly. "Just don't begrudge it to me if someone else does."

"Fair enough." He slapped the menu back onto the table between their beds and stared at the ceiling. *Mother left Daddy because she'd found a man who would treat her the way she deserved to be treated,* Cami's relentless voice reminded him. Two years after their parents had split up, while Brant was still wrestling with why it had happened, Cami had stated the reason for him in practical terms he had never accepted. Women didn't leave a good home with a solid roof and three square meals, and all the money she could spend on dresses, all for a romantic fling. It just didn't make sense to him.

That reminded him of another no-two-ways-about-it fact. He had to tell his parents that he was going to be a father. Cami had told them of her own predicament, of course, with all the joy and enthusiasm she had for discovering she was going to be a mother.

"Have you told your parents?" he asked with a sidelong glance at Grace.

"Yes." She didn't look at him.

"What did they say?"

"What could they?"

Her coyness wasn't helping him out. Suddenly he knew he didn't want the Barclays to think ill of him for not marrying their daughter. "Do they know the child is mine?"

"Until a few days ago, this child was only mine," Grace said stiffly. "But yes, they know you're the father, Brant."

"What did they say?"

She rolled her head to look at him. "That they were sure you'd do the right thing by me. They've always liked you." She sighed as if she didn't understand why they would.

Brant's collar felt a bit tight. He jerked one of the top buttons open on his shirt and tried to relax. In his own way, he was doing the very best by Grace that he could. Certainly his way wasn't the conventional way, but it was all he could offer.

"What about your folks? Do they know?"

"Not yet. I'll have to tell them soon."

They were silent for a moment. "Maybe you should wait until after Cami's wedding. Two pregnancies in the family out of wedlock might come as a shock to them."

Her voice held a tinge of amusement, but Brant saw nothing funny about any of it. "Don't you think they'll figure it out for themselves when they see you at the wedding, Grace?"

"Well, my maid of honor dress won't lie, that's true."

He closed his eyes, feeling an ominous tightening around the front of his skull.

"Kyle has offered to be my escort to the wedding. Maybe your parents will think—"

"Grace Barclay!" Brant was outraged. "Just pick out what you want me to order you for supper, okay?" The tightening was increasing to an intense viselike feeling. "I'm going to take some aspirin."

He got up to get one when Grace suddenly jumped. "Oh, my!" she exclaimed, rubbing her stomach. Her expression was somewhat pained.

"What is it?"

"I think…he kicked me. Not very gentlemanly of him, was it?" She tried to smile, but her eyes looked tired.

"Can I help?"

She shook her head. "It was probably just a stray—oh!"

"What?" Brant felt helpless.

"Nothing. Go get your aspirin. The little guy is probably in the mood for a little exercise."

"I don't know." Brant wondered how a baby could exercise all cooped up in there. Maybe Grace had pulled a muscle with all her running around today. "Let me look."

"No!" Grace's brows furrowed.

"Oh, come on, Grace. It's nothing I haven't seen before."

"Trust me. You haven't seen this. And you're not going to." She rolled onto her side, keeping her hand firmly on her abdomen, groaning slightly.

"Either you let me look under that thing you're wearing, or I call a doctor." Brant was adamant on this point.

"You're overreacting. It's probably gas."

"Let me look." He reached out and rolled her gently onto her back.

"Gas isn't visible to the naked eye, so there's no reason for you to look."

He reached for the telephone.

"Oh, Brant! For pity's sake. Let me pull a blanket up, then." She covered herself to the waist, then raised her caftan up just enough for him to see her stomach.

Her stomach didn't look so big when she was lying down. "Lucky for you it's only a small watermelon."

"Brant!"

She started to fling down the caftan but he wouldn't let her. "Did the pain go away?"

"It's not really pain. It's more like discomfort." She paused for a second. "There he goes! See!"

Brant knelt and leaned close, seeing a ridge appear to the left of Grace's navel. "What is that?" he demanded.

"Probably a foot. Give it a poke and see."

"A poke!" Brant wasn't going to touch it. He didn't want to hurt her or the baby.

"Like this."

She reached up and gently pressed with one finger. Instantly the ridge went away. Brant sucked in his breath. "How'd you do that?"

"I'm not sure what appendage that is, but if I poke him, he'll stick it back out in a minute. I say I'm playing tag with him."

"You're probably poking him in the eye," Brant said worriedly. "My son's going to have his eyes gouged out by his own mother."

Grace laughed, and the ridge reappeared. "You try."

Tentatively he reached out with a forefinger to touch her. Electricity shot through him as he felt the firmness of Grace's naked belly. He touched the ridge, and it went away like magic. The wonder of it made Brant spread his entire palm over the place where the ridge had been. Grace lay completely motionless as he experienced the first moment of awe. "Where did he go?" he whispered hoarsely.

"I don't know," Grace whispered back. "Maybe he was so comforted by the feel of your hand that he's going back to sleep."

Brant's mouth went dry. His throat felt as if it were tight elastic. Grace's huge hazel eyes watched him with the pride of her motherhood shining from them.

There was only one thing he could say through the thick cotton of his emotions. "Grace Barclay, I'm going to have to marry you, aren't I?"

## Chapter Seven

Grace pulled her caftan back over her stomach. Brant's expression was so stunned, so amazed and so afraid. She wished he hadn't said it, but it was best to head off the question he'd voiced. "No, Brant, you're not going to *have* to marry me."

He rocked back on his heels, then moved to sit on the other bed. "I don't see any other way around this, do you?"

"I told you on Sunday that the last thing I wanted was to marry you," she said quietly.

"Yeah, but—" He swept a hand through his dark hair, tousling it. "You didn't mean that."

"Why wouldn't I have meant it?"

His face held wary confusion. "Because that's why we broke up in the first place. Now, I'm willing to marry you."

"That was a long time ago, Brant. A lifetime ago for me." She held up a hand at the protest he was about to make. "I had a lot of time to think while you were gone, Brant. You had every chance in the world to ask me to marry you, but instead you left. You wouldn't have even called me or come to see me once you returned to Fairhaven. If you hadn't come in to get Cami's dress, you wouldn't be here right now." She met his hard blue stare. "There really isn't much left to say about this, Brant."

"I think there is." He got up, pacing the length of the room before turning. "Grace, it's not fair to the baby for us not to get married."

"It's not fair to the baby if we *do*." She leveled him with her eyes. "I simply don't see marriage as a reasonable alternative."

"How can you say that! Marrying Kyle Macaffee *is* a reasonable alternative?" His tone was thunderstruck.

"I'm not going to marry Kyle." Grace dropped her gaze to stare at the peach and green coverlet on the bed. "I...was considering it. Maybe I would have, but your intrusion into my life has basically ended that course of action."

"I should think so!"

"Not because of any feelings I might have for you," she said waspishly, "but mainly because you won't go away. It would be too hard on me to have divided loyalties between two men. For now, I think it's best that I tell Kyle you and I are going to have to see how our lives work together where this baby is concerned."

"Well, that's more like it," he said begrudgingly.

"But I'm not entertaining any thought of marrying you, either." She was definite on this point. "And none of your hard-driving, stubborn tactics will change my mind, so you can quit sneaking into my house and following me on business trips."

"I can't help being worried about you, Grace."

"You don't have the right. The baby is your concern, true, but I want it understood that as far as you and I go, there is no plan for anything more than what we've got at this moment. Which is a baby's future, and nothing else."

"I don't believe you mean this."

"I do. A bridal bouquet and a gold wedding band couldn't begin to fix what was wrong with our relationship, Brant. I had time to realize that while you were away. Plenty of time."

"You're bitter because I left. You're still angry, and keeping me hostage for my refusal to marry you before."

She shook her head emphatically. "No. You're still not proposing to me. You don't really want to marry me. It's the baby, essentially, that you're proposing to." Her gaze softened for a moment. "Believe me, Brant, one thing you have convinced me of in the past few days is your commitment to this child. You'll be a good father. For a man who's totally lost when it comes to the concept of baby supplies, baby clothes, whatever, you have made a good stab at trying to figure it all out. But it's all for the baby."

"It's not all for the baby. I want to help you, too."

"I know. I appreciate that. But it's not enough to build a marriage on."

"How do you know what's enough? How did you know that what you thought was enough before to build a marriage on would have been enough in twenty years?" His voice was strained, his expression haunted.

She had no good answer for him. "All I can tell you is what I feel. And I feel that you're not in love with me."

"I...I do love you, Grace."

He struggled to say the words, so she tried to be gentle with her response. "You're not *in* love with me, Brant. And while I have genuine feelings of love and affection for you, I don't think I can share anything of myself with you."

*Not anymore.* She didn't say it, but somehow, the words were clearer because she hadn't.

"You didn't used to feel that way. What's changed, Grace?"

Again, her eyes slid away from his. "My body, for one thing. I could never let you see me naked, and I'm assuming that's a part of being married."

"I'd love to see you naked! I mean, I'd have to."

He'd definitely perked up. Grace laughed, a little wistfully. "Brant, it's so hard to explain. When we...broke up, it was because you didn't see a future for us, a future with me. That's rejection, plain and simple. To a woman, it's like being told 'I don't want you enough to marry you,' or 'You're not the woman of my dreams.' If I wasn't what you wanted when I was slim and at a more attractive state, how do you honestly think I can feel comfortable letting you see me with overlarge, sagging breasts, stretch marks and cellulite I didn't know I had?''

He didn't say anything.

Grace shook her head. ''I don't feel beautiful, or desirable anymore. If I wasn't enough for you before, I surely can't be the way I am now. And rumor has it the bod goes downhill from here.''

''Grace, I—''

She waved him silent. ''Let me give you another thing that's changed. I'm not myself. I don't know who I am sometimes. One day, I was salting a tomato to eat, and for some reason, I burst into tears. I don't even know why. Tears just poured out of my eyes, and to this day, I don't know what upset me.''

''Jeez. If a tomato can make you cry, I'm in a boatload of trouble.''

Refusing to smile at him, she said, ''Exactly my point.''

He paced one more length, then crossed his arms over his chest. ''I can handle stretch marks, and I don't care about mood swings—as long as you quit crying eventually. That kind of stuff wouldn't make me not care about you. It's certainly no reason not to marry me.''

It was irritating that she couldn't make him see what was so clear to her. Sitting up and arranging a pillow behind her back, Grace shot him an impatient glare. ''It's two good reasons to me, but let me give you the third and most important. Your proposal, if one could call it that, was so begrudging, it felt like a donkey was straining to pull it out of you. 'I'm going to have to marry you, aren't I?' are not exactly the words of a man who wants to get married.'' She eyed him malevolently for a moment. ''I've dressed expectant brides who were thrilled to be going down the aisle because their man had finally proposed. They thought everything was going to work out just fine. Then that little baby comes along, bringing with it responsibility, and the men realize that past the initial 'doing the right thing,' they're in a place they didn't want to be.''

''I've never had a problem handling responsibility.''

''You left Cami to take care of the ranch for three months, Brant! And now you're here in New York, and who's taking care of the ranch again but your pregnant sister!''

''I believed the ranch could wait two days. This is more important to me.'' His gaze was angry, his voice indignant.

''The baby is, Brant.'' Grace sighed. ''I'm going to sleep now. I'm exhausted.'' She hesitated, uncomfortable, as he obviously was. ''Can we just forget we had this conversation?''

''Can *you?*''

''I don't know.'' She reached up to turn off her lamp. ''Good night, Brant.''

He didn't say anything. A moment later, his boots hit the floor with a thump. The covers were jerked off the other bed. Thick silence curtained the room. Grace closed her eyes tightly, refusing to let her heartbreak spill over.

''I DON'T EVEN WANT TO THINK about the return trip, Maggie.'' Grace sat in the Yellowjacket Cafe the next evening, appreciative of the sympathetic ears listening to her story. Tilly had put a plate of steamed vegetables and fried chicken in front of her, but Grace barely picked at the food. ''Brant and I hardly said a word to each other.''

''Well, I'm not sure if there was anything left for the two of you to talk about. It's clearly an impasse.''

''It's clearly *impossible*,'' Tilly said, defining the matter further.

Grace had walked over to the Cafe after the dinner rush,

so she could enjoy the luxury of having her two friends to herself for another moment. Buzz and Purvis were sitting in their customary places, but they were engrossed in checkers. "What am I going to do?"

"Wait it out, I guess," Maggie said slowly. "Seeing as how you feel the way you do, what else is there?"

Tilly nodded. "Marry in haste, divorce at leisure."

"Tilly!" Maggie exclaimed.

"No. It's all right." Grace sipped some tea. "Tilly has put her finger on exactly what's bothering me. Brant was certainly in no hurry to marry me before, when he had all the time in the world. What good can come out of rushing now? The ink would hardly be dry on the marriage certificate before he might realize being tied to me wasn't what he wanted for the rest of his life."

Maggie and Tilly were silent, gazing at her with distressed eyes.

"I don't want to get married impetuously, then have Brant want a divorce. Or worse yet, stay with me and hate me for it." She touched light fingers to her stomach. "What kind of a way is that for a child to grow up?"

"I don't know," Maggie said on a heavy exhalation of breath. She patted Grace's hand. "I'm not saying a child doesn't need a father, honey. But I am saying that he'll get plenty enough love with you to mother him. Maybe that's more than some kids ever get."

"That's right." Tilly cracked her gum resolutely. "You listen to Maggie. She's a pillar of salt."

Grace giggled. "Like Lot's wife who sneaked a peak at Gomorrah burning?"

"Yep," Maggie replied. "Except what I see is some good people who love each other, but maybe not at the right time, right place in their lives. Give it time, Grace. Everything may yet turn out for the best."

"I hope you're right."

The cowbell on the door handle jangled as it opened.

"Howdy, Kyle!" Maggie called.

"Hi, Maggie, Tilly." His eyes settled on Grace. "Hi, Grace."

"Hi, Kyle." She patted the seat next to her and he joined her.

"Hungry?" Maggie asked.

"I'd appreciate a glass of tea," he said, his eyes only for Grace.

"I'll get it," Tilly said softly, leaving the table. Maggie melted away, too, leaving Kyle and Grace alone together.

"How was your trip, Grace?"

She smiled into Kyle's brown eyes, flattered by the admiration she saw there. Yet it made her sad, too. "It was fine, I guess. I'm glad you stopped by. I...I need to talk to you."

It was hard to hold his gaze. Grace felt so awful. What she had to say to Kyle was going to hurt him.

He sighed heavily. "I think I know what the subject matter is." Hesitating as he searched her face, he said, "It's over, isn't it?"

She closed her eyes, turning away for a moment. "I'm sorry, Kyle." Forcing herself to look in his eyes again, she said, "I care about you a lot. Part of me really thought marrying you might be the best thing to do."

"But with Brant back in town..."

She hated every second of this conversation. "Yes. It does make matters more complex. Not that Brant and I are close to working anything out, but it's difficult for me to feel caught in the middle. I'm sorry." Gently she reached to cover his hand with hers. "I just need this time to gather my wits for being a single mother."

"I knew this was coming," Kyle said sorrowfully. "I went around to Brant's ranch to apologize for the altercation on the airplane." A slight smile turned up his mouth. "Brant and I have been agreeable friends over the years. I don't like to be on anybody's bad side unnecessarily, and

I figured I was as much at fault for what happened as he was."

"Oh, Kyle, that was nice of you," Grace murmured.

"Yeah." He chuckled disparagingly. "Only Cami told me Brant had gone to New York. That's when I knew the sneaky devil was determined to win you at all costs. I can't blame him for that."

She started to apologize, but he dismissed her with a wave. "It's okay, Grace. My pride was stung at first, but then I thought about it, and decided you're better off with Brant pursuing you if he aims to make everything right for you and the baby. A family should be together."

"Well, I'm not sure what's going to happen in the future, to be honest. We didn't get along so well in New York. Right now, we've left it at the fact that he can see the baby when he's born. In the meantime, I want peace in my life." She scrunched her face apologetically. "I hope you understand."

"I do." Kyle got to his feet, dropping a light kiss on her hair. "Tell Maggie I'll catch that glass of tea later. I'm gonna go home and lick my wounds."

"Oh, Kyle—"

"Teasing, Grace. I'm just teasing."

She could tell by the pain in his eyes that he wasn't. Sadly she watched Kyle say goodbye to Buzz and Purvis as he left the Cafe. The baby kicked, making Grace jump. She put a hand over him, disturbingly aware that he was the only man in her life right now.

"WHAT'S THIS?" Cami glanced at Brant suspiciously. She was sitting in the kitchen, adding up some totals with a calculator.

Brant had laid the box close to her arm, hoping she might not notice right away. Making his peace offering without having to offer any words of apology would have been the easy way out. Not admirable, of course, but he knew Cami was going to let him have it with both barrels loaded.

"It's a little something I picked up in New York. For the baby," he clarified.

"Oh?" Cami's eyebrows jumped to the top of her forehead.

"Can you just open the box without acting like it's a bomb?" he demanded testily.

"I'm sorry, Brant. I didn't realize you were interested in the baby. Did you have an epiphany in New York?"

"Cami," he growled.

"Okay." She reached for the box, taking the lid off. With an expression of amazement for his benefit, she lifted the outfit from the box. "My goodness, Brant, this is almost cute." She looked at the little denim jean and red bandanna shirt for a moment. "Grace picked this out, didn't she?"

"No," he said gruffly. "But she did point out that I haven't congratulated you on the baby, Cami. I apologize for what I said to you, and Dan."

"Well." Cami looked as if a brief wind might knock her over. "Apology accepted, as far as I'm concerned. You might smooth over the waters with Dan when you get a chance. Maybe even welcome him into the 'bosom' of the family."

"Cami!" Brant's tone was brisk. "Don't push me."

She laughed. "I couldn't resist picking at you."

"You've never held back before. I wouldn't expect you to start now." Brant sat at the table across from her, trying to wade his way through these deep waters. He really did want Cami to know that he'd rethought her situation. "By the way, do you know what you're having yet?"

"No. Dan and I want to be surprised."

"Isn't finding out you're having a baby enough of a surprise?"

She laughed merrily. "It certainly knocked you out of whack."

He thumped a palm on the table, unable to disagree. Brant couldn't remember the last time he'd been tied in this many knots.

"Were you and Grace able to come to any reasonable agreement?" she asked gently.

"No." He bit the inside of his mouth for a moment. "I'm not sure that I didn't manage to make everything worse."

"Uh-oh. You did work on your medieval thought processes, didn't you, brother?"

"I think so." He wasn't sure, but he knew he'd tried.

"And you did keep your foot out of your mouth? No smart aleck, chauvinistic remarks, right?"

"Cami, I really tried to be open to new suggestions. And I tried not to get into Grace's way. Too much, anyway."

"Sum this up for me. Give me the moment you realized the two of you weren't sharing the same vision."

That was easy. "When she wanted to put a dress on my son."

Cami laughed. "That doesn't sound like Grace. Was it pretty?"

"Yeah, I guess. Hey! You're not going to tell me that's the latest trend for boys, are you? 'Cause I can tell you, my son's not even going to get an earring when he's a teenager. Or a tattoo, either."

"Right. Your boy's gotta toe the line." Cami made her voice gruff on purpose, mimicking Brant.

"Yeah. Exactly."

"Okay, so you two disagreed over a dress. That's nothing major."

"It's not?"

"No way. You shout and rant and rave for a while, just to get the testosterone moving around, and Grace listens until she's sick of your idiocy, and then she puts the kid in the dress. That's how it works."

"Cami, does Dan know how you think?"

She giggled, then plain guffawed at him. "Dan wouldn't get all worked up over a christening gown. He's a traditional sort of guy."

"So am I!" Brant was completely lost in Cami's logic. "Let me give you another moment when I knew things weren't going to move into a straight line, then. Grace won't marry me."

"Oh. And that came as a huge shock to you?"

He didn't like the sarcasm in her tone. Raising a forbidding eyebrow at her, he said, "Is there a reason it shouldn't have?"

"Well, let me see. You disappear, then when another man is willing to take on your responsibilities—"

"Cami! Let me stop you right there. I don't want to hear one single word about responsibility, okay? I didn't know Grace was pregnant when I left. If she had told me, it might have changed things."

"Probably would have. You would have done the right thing by her, and made her miserable for the rest of her life because you didn't want to be married. Why does a baby change the equation?"

He stared at her in disbelief. "You sound just like Grace." In fact, it wasn't the first time he'd been struck by how alike the two women were.

"Brant," Cami sighed, "it's not that hard to figure out why she'd feel that way. If I were in her shoes, I'd feel the same."

"You *are* in her shoes, for crying out loud! Why are you beating a path to the altar, and I couldn't drag Grace there with a couple of Clydesdales?"

"I'm happy to be getting married because Dan loves me. And I love him."

"I love Grace."

"Well, *I* knew that." Cami managed to make his statement of love sound like poison. "*You* didn't know that before. So she didn't know it, because you didn't tell her.

Suddenly Grace discovers she's having a baby, and you're nowhere to be found. Why would she believe you when you tell her you love her now? Nobody develops true love in the space of a single second.'' She thought about that for a moment. ''Well, Dan and I did, but that's different. He's a forward thinker.''

''Oh, for—'' Brant glared at his sister. ''And I'm not.''

''No.'' Cami shot him a saucy grin. ''You're so backward, your face is looking at your—''

''Okay. I've had enough. Thank you kindly for your sisterly support.'' He shot up from the table, prepared to stalk from the room.

''I guess you'll be at the barbecue my friends are throwing for me on Saturday, brother?''

Pausing, Brant definitely heard the baited hook in Cami's words. ''Don't try to get me and Grace together, Cami. She and I have agreed that we'll wait until after the baby's born to see how we feel about anything more between us.''

''Oh, I wouldn't dream of trying to throw you two together.'' Her voice was sweet, her expression saucy. ''Thanks for the baby outfit, Brant. You're going to make a wonderful uncle.''

He puffed up a little. ''Of course I am. Everybody keeps acting like I've got bricks in my head or something, but I've got my good points, too.''

Cami laughed, looking back down at the figures she was adding. ''You do, Brant. And you're right. Pigheaded stubbornness can be an admirable trait in a man. Guaranteed to win a woman's heart every time.'' She paused to give him a gleeful grin. ''I'll see you in the morning.''

Brant wasn't sure what his sister's point was, but as he stomped off up the stairs, he knew her quirky little mind had been making one. Heck, Grace was stubborn, too, as stubborn as any woman he knew, so he wasn't suffering from some dreaded disorder of the personality no one else had.

In fact, now that he thought about it, Cami could be more obstinate than he could. Rubbing his chin thoughtfully, Brant had a lightning strike of disturbing intuition.

Cami and Grace were twins sometimes in the way they viewed life. If Cami could be contrary, Grace was right along with her. He'd kind of thought Grace might reconsider his proposal if he gave her a few days to cool off.

Now that he rethought that strategy—and a few of Cami's choice zingers—Brant realized Grace had no intention of changing her mind.

## Chapter Eight

Grace put out the final plate of hors d'oeuvres and glanced around her house. She was proud of the decorations she had thought up for Cami and Dan's bridal barbecue. Taking Cami's colors for the wedding—rose and white—Grace had adorned the dining-room table with a deep rose tablecloth, covering it with a white lace overlay. It draped nicely into the rose-colored bows she'd tied on each of the four corners. Soon, Tilly and Maggie would arrive with the food, and they could set all the serving dishes here. The coffee table in front of the fireplace would serve nicely as a place for guests to put their gifts. She had bought a lovely arrangement of Rubin and Calla lilies with some white roses mixed in for this table.

On the back patio, Grace had set up the portable barbecue grill, and decorated a rectangular table with a cabbage rose-patterned cloth in the same colors. She had set out several soda bottles and pitchers of tea, as well as some brightly colored plastic glasses. Sheriff John had volunteered to be in charge of the grill.

In spite of her organization, and how nice everything looked, Grace had nerves. Taking a deep breath, she stole one more look at herself in the oval mirror in the hallway. Brant had to attend his sister's barbecue. It would be awkward for her, and probably just as much for him. They hadn't left New York on the best of terms, nor had they talked since. To her knowledge, Brant hadn't even stopped in at the Cafe; Maggie hadn't mentioned it if he had.

The doorbell chimed, and Grace went to admit a smiling Maggie and Tilly. "Hi, everyone! I see you've put all our friends to work."

Buzz and Purvis stood behind the two women, loaded down with huge trays of barbecue that they'd unloaded from Maggie's truck. "Put everything in the kitchen, please. All the serving bowls are in there."

Tilly came in, wearing a long, slender dress that emphasized her height. "You've done the place up so nice, Grace."

"Mmm-hmm," Maggie agreed. She was wearing a yellow suit that Grace thought suited her dark skin perfectly. "I hope you haven't worn yourself out. We could have done this at the Cafe."

"I barely did anything. Since you two cooked, I had the fun of decorating. Please, make yourselves at home."

"Does that include this poor stray we found hanging out by your mailbox?" Tilly asked. She tugged Brant in by his arm. "He seems to be waiting for an invitation."

Grace's heart dropped to her Sunday boots. "Brant needs no invitation," she said crisply. "He can start warming the grill up for John."

"We went ahead and cooked the meat at the restaurant." Maggie cleared a place on the counter for Purvis to set down a large tray containing olives, pickles and purple onion rings. "Seemed like it would be easier that way."

"Okay. We'll still eat on the patio." Except that left nothing for Brant to do, and he was obviously as uncomfortable as she felt. He looked nice in black trousers that emphasized his height, and a dark green patterned shirt that somehow brightened the blue in his eyes. Why did she have to be so attracted to him? It wasn't just the fact that he was handsome, nor that the second he stepped into a room, he commanded attention. There was something more that kept this man from being just another good-looking guy.

Maybe it was just Brant. The way he was looking at her made the skin on her arms prickle, as if he was trying to figure out what she was thinking. "Since there's no grilling to be done, Brant, please just..." Well, not make himself at home, as she'd instructed everyone else. "Please, excuse me."

She hurried off to answer the doorbell. It was Sheriff John, along with Cami and Dan. Grace hugged Cami, and then Dan, and took the gift Sheriff John was holding to set on the coffee table. All the while she was conscious of Brant's eyes on her, watching her every move. Grace went to the refrigerator to get out the corsage she'd bought for Cami.

"Hold still a second, Cami," she said. Trying to pin the silly thing on with Brant standing so close by was nerve-racking. Maggie had come from the kitchen with Buzz and Purvis to greet Cami and Dan. Sheriff John and Tilly were standing around watching as well. "There. I think I managed not to put a huge hole in your blouse. You sure do look nice, Cami."

Cami smiled at Dan, then back at Grace. "You do, too, Grace. Doesn't she, Brant?"

He only nodded jerkily, to Grace's distress. Cami meant well, but it would be so much better if all of them wouldn't try so hard to help the situation along.

"DID YOU NOTICE the way those two keep sneaking looks at each other?" Purvis asked Buzz.

Buzz wiped some barbecue sauce from his mouth. "Yep. Everybody's noticed. It's only Grace and Brant that think nobody's noticed them doing it."

"We oughta do something about those two."

"Like what?"

"I don't know." Purvis glanced around the kitchen.

"Hard to get 'em in the same room to talk. Each time one of 'em walks near the other, that'n leaves the room. It's like watching Ping-Pong balls."

"We could tell 'em something needs their attention on the patio, then lock 'em out. They'd have to talk to each other then."

Purvis considered that for a moment. "Don't think it'd work. They'd just walk around the house and let theirselves in the front door. Has to be something more surreptitious."

He was proud of his fifty-cent word. Buzz didn't appear to notice, and Purvis was disappointed. "They're gonna have to sit in the same room while Cami and Dan open their presents."

"So?"

Buzz scratched his head. "I dunno. They'll be in the same room, at least."

"It's hard to believe you fought in World War II," Purvis said in disgust. "What kind of tactical maneuver is that?"

"Ground control. You gotta have the enemy close together in order to launch an appropriate attack. Same as in checkers, you know."

"I'm beginning to see your point." Purvis could relate to anything that involved checkers. "Get more jumps if the checkers are lined up just right."

"Exactly. Now, here's the plan…"


TEN MINUTES LATER, everyone was seated in the den area, ready to watch Cami and Dan open their shower gifts. Brant was especially uncomfortable with this part of the evening. It reminded him that if Grace would have accepted his proposal, she might be able to celebrate their wedding with her friends, too.

*Of course,* the plaguing voice mocked him, *if you'd asked her six months ago when she mentioned marriage to you, you wouldn't be feeling like a cowboy who's just been thrown.*

She looked gorgeous. He managed to get a glance every time it was safe to, and he didn't think she'd ever looked more beautiful in all the time he'd known her. The emerald green dress swayed around her ankles, skimming the top of the cream-colored slightly heeled boots she wore. The emerald brought out the silver highlights in her hair and emphasized the hazel of her eyes. The best part, though, was the pinpoint freckles dusted across her nose. They had always been one of his favorite features, and the deep, rich green of her dress brought those to the surface.

Since Grace was still in the kitchen, and he was the only other guest to venture into the den, there were only two seats left, one next to Purvis and one across the room next to Buzz. Brant headed for the one next to Purvis.

As soon as he sat down, the old guy moved across the room to sit in the other available chair. That left the spot next to Brant open, and he saw Grace eye it reluctantly as she came in from the kitchen. Everyone was looking at her innocently—too innocently. Purvis and Buzz sneaked a grin at each other and nodded. Instantly Brant knew he'd been shanghaied by those two checker-loving codgers.

Silently Grace took the chair without a glance at him, and Brant felt his palms begin to sweat. He hoped Cami and Dan would open the presents without delay so he could escape. Much more of pretending as if he and Grace were casual, when her stomach proclaimed they hadn't been in the past, and he was going into seclusion at his ranch until the baby was born.

"IT WAS A LOVELY PARTY, Grace. Thank you."

Cami hugged her, as did Dan. The happy couple left, their car overflowing with gifts. Maggie and Tilly were in the kitchen cleaning up. To Grace's relief, Brant had scooted out to help Dan pack the presents into the car, had waved goodbye at her from the street and promptly taken his truck out of her driveway.

"Well. That was easy with you two doing all the work." Grace came back into the kitchen to discover Maggie and Tilly were in the process of leaving. The sheriff had lingered on the pretext of helping them load up, but Grace knew better. When he could, the sheriff stuck to Maggie as if he were paste.

"I'm glad you let us have the shower here, Grace," Maggie said. "It made for such a cozy gathering. At the Cafe I think we would have all felt like it was just hanging out as usual."

"Well, I was happy to do it."

The three friends looked at each other silently for a moment. "Grace, there's something Maggie and I want to ask you. Actually Cami's in on it, too, but she asked us to go ahead and discuss it with you so she could go on home with Dan." Tilly waited for Grace's nod. "We're hoping you'll let us give you a baby shower."

"Oh." Grace stared at Maggie and Tilly for a second. "Well, that's awfully sweet of you, but—"

"Honey, think about it for a while. Then let us know," Maggie interrupted. "We'd really like to do something for you."

Because there wasn't going to be any wedding showers like the one they'd given Cami and Dan. For the first time, Grace was just a tiny bit envious of the fact that everything was going so well for them. Reprimanding herself, Grace shook her head. "You're both kind to offer. But I can't let you."

"Grace," Maggie said quietly, "that baby's coming in two months."

"Three." Grace corrected her quickly.

"Two." Maggie's tone was stern. "Your due date is August 1. This is the end of May. You've left an entire month off your countdown."

Grace remained silent.

"That baby's coming, no matter what you and Brant decide to do. It's not going to stay in your stomach until the two of you work things out."

Grace walked into the den and sank into a chair. "I don't suppose it will."

"It's time to start getting some things ready." Tilly sat on the chair arm and patted her back. "Have you decided where the baby's going to sleep?"

"In my room," Grace said automatically.

"That'll work for a while, especially if you're going to breast-feed, but what about after that?" Maggie asked.

"The guest bedroom." Grace stared up the stairs in bewilderment. The guest bedroom upstairs at least had a bathroom attached. She had her office in that room, but maybe that should be moved into the bedroom downstairs. She wanted her child close by—

"Okay. Do we need to paint? Wallpaper?" Maggie's approach was methodical.

"I...haven't thought about it." Grace stared down at her fingernails for a second. "I don't suppose the baby cares, do you?"

"Grace." Tilly squeezed her shoulders. "The baby doesn't care. But most new mothers do. We want to help you, if you'd like to decorate a nursery." She glanced at the pretty stuff Grace had set around to create the bridal shower atmosphere for Cami's party. "We know you'd like such, Grace. Let us help you with this."

Tears welled up in Grace's eyes. "I feel silly, leaning on you for help."

"Why?" Maggie demanded. "Grace, what you're facing is difficult. We're in a position to help."

Couldn't she enjoy this support from her friends without feeling guilty? Brant hadn't looked at her all night; he couldn't wait to leave her house. They'd agreed to keep any meetings between them to a minimum until an infant necessitated more contact. Decorating a nursery didn't have to involve Brant.

"I think I'd like that," Grace said softly.

"That's my girl," Maggie said with a quick pat on her hand. "Now, what we'd kinda been thinking on is a nursery shower."

"It sounds interesting," Grace said weakly. "You two always manage to cook up unconventional ideas." She sat up, liking the idea more and more. "I really appreciate you both for this. You'll just never know how much."

"How about Sunday afternoon after church?" Maggie asked.

"Tomorrow! Why so soon?"

"Because," Maggie said sensibly, "this won't take long. Cami, Tilly and I have got this all planned out. Next weekend's the wedding, and Cami and Dan'll be gone for their honeymoon. Then that next weekend already gets us to the middle of June. You haven't bought a crib, nor even enrolled in those classes we're supposed to be in. I'm still your labor coach, aren't I?"

"Yes." Grace hadn't cared to broach the subject to Brant. He was struggling so hard to catch up with basic baby concepts that the idea of trying to explain coaching to him seemed ludicrous.

"I figured as much." Maggie tapped her chin. "We gotta get settled into those classes. By then, it's coming to July, your last month. It'll be hotter than Hades, too hot to paint and such. Might as well do it while we can still let a breeze in."

"I suppose you have a point." Grace couldn't believe she hadn't figured out all of this herself. She was usually so organized, so precise! "I don't know why I haven't been thinking about all this."

"Because you've been busy with plans for Cami, Grace," Tilly said kindly. "Isn't it easier to think of what someone else needs rather than yourself?"

"I...guess." She had bought a few baby outfits in New York. More serious purchases, however, such as a crib, she had put off thinking about, spending all her emotional energy on her business instead. It was the busiest time of the year for her, and plus, she unconsciously avoided slowing down long enough to think out her situation. "The size my stomach's getting should have warned me it was time to start thinking about the baby. But tomorrow! I don't even know what color I want the nursery to be!" Grace was alarmed by the speed with which her friends were planning to convert her office into a real, can't-ignore-it-any-longer baby room.

"Well." Maggie's expression was sheepish. "We didn't think you'd have time, so Tilly and I went to Home Depot and spent an afternoon looking over paint chips and wallpaper borders. Do you mind if we take over this project?"

Grace considered briefly before shaking her head. "I think it would be best if you do. My head is whirling."

"Good." Maggie stood. "Plan on your nursery shower being tomorrow, then, directly after church and the lunch crowd. We've got lots to do."

"It's just going to be the four of us, right?" Grace asked. There wouldn't be time to ask anyone else.

"Not exactly." Tilly's grin was infectious with its slyness. "We were going to surprise you, but decided tonight maybe that wasn't the best idea. A week ago, we invited everybody to come over and get some paint in their hair."

"Everybody?" Grace couldn't imagine who all cared to paint on their Sunday afternoon off.

"Everybody who was here tonight."

Tears jumped into her eyes. "You're such good friends. What would I do without you?"

Tilly and Maggie glanced at each other hesitantly. "Well, that's that, then," Maggie said too quickly, heading for the door.

"Get your rest," Tilly called gaily. "We're bringing

munchies, so don't go shopping, Grace. Just rest, and we'll see you tomorrow.''

Tilly pulled the door closed behind her. ''Do you think Cami can pull off her part?''

''Of course,'' Maggie snorted, hopping into the truck and gunning the engine. ''When have you ever known Cami *not* to be able to wrap Brant around her little finger?''

# Chapter Nine

That night Brant awakened suddenly, his mind teeming with the aftereffects of the most disturbing dream he could ever remember having.

"Why didn't you and Mommy get married, Daddy?"

His eyes opened wide before he rolled over to try to get more comfortable. The question could go unanswered.

"Why, Daddy?"

The little boy voice bothered him again. A face he didn't know but might love one day stared at him inquisitively. Brant exhaled tiredly. "It's hard to explain, son. I'll tell you when you're older."

*Wait a minute.* Some things you were never old enough to hear—especially from your dad. His father had been his usual self as he unemotionally explained that his wife had left him and that they had decided to get a divorce. There had been no spark of indignation, or even shock. It was as if his mother had never existed for his father, so her absence wouldn't mean anything more than her presence had.

Brant hadn't handled the scene well. "Why?" he'd wanted to shout at his father. "Why don't you do something?"

"Why? Why?" the little boy voice mocked him. "Why don't you do something, Daddy?"

Brant shot upright in the bed. His heart pounded; his mind's eye saw Grace and her laughing hazel eyes.

How could he ever make his child understand what he didn't even understand himself?

CAMI GLARED AT BRANT mutinously. They had just gotten home from church. He was hungry, he was still tired for some reason and he had a lot to do today. Now his sister was suggesting he accompany her into town to see Grace, which was the last thing he was going to do today. She was the reason he was tired! He hadn't slept a wink last night from thinking about her.

"I am not going, Cami. Besides, Grace will be much happier if I'm not there."

Last night at the barbecue had proved to him that the ornery woman really didn't want to be in his company. She'd spoken two words to him, and no more.

"It's not going to kill you to move some furniture for us, Brant. In fact, it'll be good for you to do some painting. Let out some of the artistic, sensitive side you keep so well hidden."

"No. That's final. It's not open for discussion."

Cami sent an appraising look his way. Brant stiffened, recognizing his sister's churning brain cogs.

"Did you ever get around to calling Mom and breaking the good news?"

"I thought I might this afternoon. I've got a lot of chores, but it's not fair to wait until she and Grace run into each other at the wedding next weekend."

"True." Cami appeared to consider his words. "What about Dad?"

"What about him?" Brant demanded. This was a turn he definitely didn't want Cami's brain to take.

"When are you going to tell him?"

"Someday." Brant wasn't going to call his father anytime soon. He was a remote man, difficult to talk to. They hadn't shared many heart-to-hearts over the years. Brant saw no reason to start now.

"Of course," Cami began casually, "Mom will likely mention it to him this weekend when she and Dad are forced to acknowledge each other's presence."

"Each other's—" Brant broke off his words, feeling his gut tighten. It had never occurred to him that his parents might actually end up in the same room together after they'd divorced. "Dad is coming?"

"Yes!" Cami was indignant. "Who did you think was going to give me away?"

"Me, damn it!"

"*Ohhh.* Brant, I'm sorry." Cami looked honestly distressed. "I mean, he is my father. He has to walk me down the aisle."

Brant crossed his arms, more hurt than he'd care to admit. "I suppose so. I just hadn't thought of it, is all." *For the love of heaven. Both of my parents are going to be here this weekend.* "Where are they staying?" he demanded.

"Here, of course." Cami looked at him as if he was crazy. "It *was* their house, once upon a time."

"Who invited them?"

"I did. Brant! What did you expect? That I'd make them stay in a Motel Six?"

"I don't give a damn! Mother can stay, but our father can stay somewhere else!" Brant's heart hammered in his chest. "Cami, do you think you could have included me in your plans?"

"You weren't here for three months." She bit off the words. "Why are you so upset?"

"Because." Brant stomped out of the room, but Cami followed at his heels. She wouldn't go away, not his sister, until she'd totally messed up his mind. "They got a divorce. They don't need to stay under this roof at the same time."

"Okay. I can tell them the house is full."

"Not Mom. You ought to have her around to help you get dressed or something." Brant didn't know. What he did know was that he was about to bust from what he was hearing.

"Brant." Cami put a soft hand on his arm. He halted, turning slowly to face her. "Let go of it."

"I can't. I can't! They were married nearly thirty years and threw it away just like it never happened." He snorted. "In all that time, the old man couldn't figure out how to be a husband to Mom?"

"Uh, some men are slower than others."

Cami's eyes were trained on him with an expression so intense Brant realized she was lumping him in with his father. "I'm not like him." Just a little, but it wasn't the same at all. "Maybe I am somewhat. But I'll figure it out when the time comes."

"Brother," Cami said slowly, "the time was nearly seven months ago."

He stared at her, angry. Angry with everyone. Angry with himself.

"I've blown it, haven't I?"

"I'm not sure. You scared Grace pretty well when you left. She knew you didn't want to give her anything of yourself. Now the stakes are higher. She wants to be loved for herself, but the baby is what brought you back around to her. Without the baby, would you have ever called her again?"

Caring for her had been way too frightening. How could anyone make a lifetime commitment? "I don't know," he murmured. "I never got over Grace. She is the only woman I've ever cared about."

"But you didn't want to get hurt. I understand, Brant." Cami's eyes clouded. "It hurt when Mom left Dad. It was painful seeing her hurt all those years Dad pretty much left her out of his life. But, Brant, you don't have to be the man Dad is." Her eyes pleaded with him. "Don't you see that? You can let yourself care for Grace. You can show her you do.''

''I feel like my brain's dissolving,'' Brant complained. ''Once you start working on me, I actually think you make sense, little sister.''

''Good.'' Cami gave him a playful smack upside the head.

''Where would you suggest I start in my wooing of Grace?'' He held his hands up in surrender. ''I'm only asking because you seem to have all the answers.''

Cami snorted at his sarcasm. ''Let's go slap a little paint on her walls and see where that gets you.''

He eyed her in disgust. ''You did it again. You little she-devil.''

She laughed out loud and tweaked his cheek. ''You're going to miss me when I'm gone. Don't say I didn't warn you.''

He already missed her. In fact, he missed a lot of things. After the soul-wrecking dream he'd had last night, Brant was beginning to fear missing even more.

GRACE CAME HOME from church, where she'd missed most of the sermon while she was cautiously sliding her vision to Brant, who sat about ten pews away. Her feelings were a little bruised, and she realized she had wanted him to sit with her. She wanted to see him—in spite of all her protestations otherwise.

It had felt so awkward sitting in church, but not being together. Somehow, Grace felt as if they were cheating the baby.

Afterward, she had not seen him. Though they'd agreed to this arrangement, it was still difficult. Grace skipped going to the Cafe for Sunday brunch and hurried home instead. Taking off her dress and Sunday shoes, she changed into some maternity shorts and a loose top. Catching sight of herself in the mirror, Grace thought, *The fewer clothes*

*I have on, the less attractive I am.* Definitely her belly protruded more in shorts than when she wore a dress.

No matter, she decided. For painting a room, shorts were a must. Grace yawned, curling up on the bed to indulge in a short catnap.

Two hours later, the doorbell chimed, startling her awake. "Maggie!" she exclaimed, aghast that she hadn't been getting anything ready for her guests. Flying down the stairs, Grace opened the door. Her apologies died on her lips at the sight of Cami and Brant standing on the porch.

"Hi. Come in," she told them, her eyes fastened to Brant's face. Why was Brant here? She ran a hand through sleep-tangled hair, dismayed.

"Are you all right, Grace?" Cami peered at her closely. Brant's gaze was just as concerned.

"I'm fine. I fell asleep for a while," she said sheepishly. "You two sit down and make yourselves comfortable."

Brant's eyes were pinned to her stomach. Grace backed away, mortified. "I'm going to run upstairs for a minute. Cami, please play hostess if anyone else arrives."

She flew to her room and snatched up a hairbrush. Maggie hadn't mentioned that Brant was going to help decorate the nursery. What did Brant know about wallpaper and curtains?

Quickly she brushed her hair, teeth and washed sleep from her eyes. She dabbed the slightest bit of perfume under her hair, before realizing it was too hot to work without her hair in a ponytail. Swiftly she pulled her hair back.

Her gaze dropped to her stomach. No doubt about it: The baby was definitely announcing his presence now. All this beautifying for Brant couldn't disguise her condition. If she was hoping to make Brant aware of her as a woman, she was dreaming. He couldn't be aware of anything but her pregnancy. Downhearted, Grace rejoined her guests.

"Are you sure you're up to this, Grace?" Cami asked.

"Yes. I don't know why I fell asleep like that. I was just

going to close my eyes for twenty minutes." She couldn't look at Brant.

"I've been tired more myself," Cami replied. "The baby makes me want naps in the afternoon." She shot Brant an impish grin. "I'll be glad to go on my honeymoon so I can leave all the ranch chores to Brant."

The doorbell chimed, saving Brant from his sister's teasing. Grace noted he seemed distinctly surprised to hear Cami say she was tired more lately.

On the porch, she found Sheriff John and Maggie. Buzz and Purvis lurked behind them, while Tilly was walking up the sidewalk with what appeared to be bags from the grocery store.

"Come on in, everybody," Grace called, trying to let them know by the sound of her voice how much she appreciated them coming to help her with the nursery. The last thing she wanted was for anyone to know how much seeing Brant had unsettled her. Her gaze narrowed on the giant box John was carrying. "Party supplies?"

"Nope." He carried the box inside and sat it in front of Brant.

"Open it, Grace," Maggie told her. "It's just a little something for the baby."

"I thought decorating the nursery was for the baby." Grace tried to make her voice stern, but she could feel tears tickling the back of her eyes. Her friends were too good to her.

"Honey, it isn't a baby shower without a present. Go ahead and open it. Brant, you take one end and Grace, you get the other."

Grace eyed the pink giraffe and blue elephant wrapping paper with some trepidation. The box was too large to contain a bib. She forced herself to meet Brant's eyes over the box. Her heart was pounding uncomfortably; she felt herself perspiring. The last thing she'd ever envisioned was opening baby gifts with Brant Durning. All their friends were looking on with indulgent smiles, so Grace swallowed her uneasiness. "On the count of three," she told him with her brightest, let's-get-this-over-with smile. "One, two, three!"

He pulled one end, she pulled the other to reveal a brown box. Brant slit the tape on the box, and gestured for her to look. Grace peered into the box.

A jumbo-size, white-woven bassinet basket lay inside.

Grace burst into tears.

"What is it, Grace, honey?" Maggie asked, glancing at Brant in bewilderment.

Tears slid down Grace's cheeks as she shook her head. Buzz and Purvis shifted uncomfortably.

Brant took a quick look inside the box. "I think this is a tomato kind of moment. Grace is just surprised."

"Oh," Cami murmured, as if she understood.

"I don't know why I'm crying. I'm happy!" Grace wailed. "You're all doing too much for me. I just don't know how to say thank you. This is the most beautiful thing I've ever seen."

Tilly pulled a tissue off a table and handed it to her. "We're glad you like it. We weren't sure what to get. We figured you'd want to pick out your own crib and baby furniture."

"Why don't you take it upstairs so we can get the boys working?" Maggie suggested.

Grace wiped her eyes and stood. "Are you sure you want to do this? The bassinet is more than enough."

"We've come to fix a nursery and that's what we're gonna do," John said. "This may be the only time you've got five strong men here to move stuff, Grace. Point the way."

IN THIRTY MINUTES, the men had Grace's office moved downstairs. It occurred to Brant that she was having to do an awful lot of changing in a lot of different ways. Other than trying to get his feelings sorted out, Brant was just trying to get up to speed with this baby business, but he hadn't been inconvenienced in any way. He intensely disliked the sensation that Grace was doing this pregnancy all by herself.

He hated feeling remote, absolutely detested it. Yet, there didn't seem to be any way for him to be more included.

"All right. Now we're down to the tacks," Maggie said with satisfaction. "Guys, unscrew the light plates, et cetera. Tilly, start stirring the paint. Brant and Grace, go find yourselves something to do."

"Do!" Grace glanced at Brant sharply. "I've got to help with the painting."

"Uh-uh. Ain't good for a pregnant woman to smell paint fumes."

"Oh, for heaven's sake! You said we had to do this project this weekend so the window could be open to let in a breeze. I'll be fine."

"Nope." Sheriff John took her by the shoulder and gently showed her to the door. "Not taking any chances. Besides, we got too many people in here, and you two'll be underfoot. And Maggie and Tilly's wanting their decorating to be a surprise, so no peeking till we're finished. Brant, why don't you help Grace set up the bassinet?"

He realized he'd been outmaneuvered again. Sourly Brant hoped Grace didn't think he'd been a party to this plan. What was there to putting together a bassinet, for crying out loud? "All right," he replied, disgruntled, "though my painting skills would come in handy."

He'd left the box with the bassinet in it in Grace's bedroom to get it out of the way. Following her down the hall, Brant eyed her. "I think we're victims of well-meaning friends."

"Let's just make the best of it." Her voice was so crisp, Brant knew Grace was as uncomfortable as he was.

"Fine." Carefully he pulled the basket from the box and

set it on Grace's double bed. "Looks small laying there like that." He squinted at the print on the box. "Says it's jumbo-size, though."

Grace couldn't take her eyes off the basket. "I love the wicker look," she said softly. "I bet it cost a fortune."

He glanced inside the box again. "Well, here's the wheels so baby can go coasting at his option." Pulling the rest of the contraption out, Brant put the basket on top of the frame, assembling the screws that held it together. "What're you going to do with this thing, anyway?"

"I guess I'll keep it by my bed, so that when the baby gets up in the night to breast-feed, I'll have him close by."

Brant paused. "Breast...feed?"

A pink blush crept up Grace's neck. "Well, yes. What did you think?"

Brant wasn't sure. "That he'd drink out of a bottle?" How in the hell was he going to be a part of any of his baby's life if he couldn't even hold him in his arms to give him a bottle?

"I'd like to give breast-feeding a try. It's better for the baby."

He kept his eyes on the screw he was attaching. "I'm sure it is." Breasts were great for males of any age. Wisely he refrained from offering any assistance in that department. It sounded as if the baby would have his own efficient, self-serve operation.

"What's that supposed to mean?"

Brant barely glanced up, but he saw that Grace had her hands on her hips. "Nothing. Don't get all heated up with me, Grace, because I hardly know what you're talking about. I guess I just thought I'd be able to help out with the baby some." He couldn't look at her. The screw was well in place, so Brant abandoned trying to act busy.

"Well, there'll be something you can do, Brant. I promised not to leave you out, and I meant it." She looked to make sure they hadn't left any pieces that went with the bassinet inside the box. "Oh, my goodness," she murmured.

"What?" What else could Maggie and Tilly and crew have put in the treasure chest Grace was digging through?

"Look." She pulled out a lacy cloth bumper, a tiny pillow and a package of sheets. "Oh, it's going to be so darling!"

Brant watched as Grace began tying the bumper inside the bassinet. Little white satin bows appeared through the wicker. He swallowed, seeing how happy all this made her. What could he do that would bring that same smile to Grace's face?

"Cami and Dan signed up for some baby classes," he said hesitantly. "He's going to be her labor coach. I can only guess at what all that entails, but..." He paused as Grace's head came up, her eyes wary as her fingers stilled on the ribbons. "Would you like for me to be your labor coach?"

By the astonished, rather unhappy expression on her face, Brant knew the answer was no. Immediately confusion swept him.

"Maggie's going to be my labor coach." Grace got busy with the bows again. "Thank you for offering."

Her voice was crisp again, and Brant knew there was no sincere gratitude behind her polite thank-you. He stared down at his hands, seeing the cracks and chapped skin of a working man. What was there to give Grace that she didn't already have?

How was he ever going to show her that he cared?

# Chapter Ten

Grace shot Brant a nervous glance. She could feel him struggle with their situation. Offering him a tentative smile, she suddenly froze when his hands wrapped around her wrists and gently tugged her closer, a move she in no way resisted.

"Grace," he whispered, "you're shutting me out."

She hesitated, staring up into his eyes. "Maybe a little."

He gave a small grunt. "Maybe a lot. I know you had to do a lot of thinking about this baby on your own, but it's not that way anymore. We said we'd wait until after the baby's born to see how we feel about getting married, but I can't wait any longer to do this." Without hesitation, he molded his mouth to hers.

Grace closed her eyes on a sigh at the feel of Brant's lips on hers. A million old-new emotions sizzled through her. He felt so good! This man she loved, how could she tell him no about anything?

The next second, he'd sat on the bed, pulling her onto his lap. His palms captured the side of her face, his lips meeting hers, pressing, demanding, again and again. Grace sighed with sublime happiness and wrapped her arms around his neck. It was sheer heaven to be in his arms again. She had dreamed of this moment for the six months she'd known it to be impossible. Her eyes closed, she let her other senses work: Her fingers told her his skin was just as rough at the neckline as ever, his hair just as soft, his shoulders just as broad. She could smell aftershave and soap and clean-washed shirt. The taste of him as their tongues met reminded her forcefully that only this man had ever made her want to drown in his love.

The past slid away for the moment, until suddenly, unfortunately, they were both out of breath. Pulling away, Grace tried to avoid meeting Brant's eyes. She succeeded, for a moment.

"Grace," he said huskily, "you're beautiful."

No, she wasn't, but she was shaking like crazy at what she'd just done. "You're awfully proud of your handiwork."

He laughed a little. "I am at that. Amazed, to be honest. The fact that there's a little person growing inside of you— well, it leaves me without words. But Cami's pointed out that I'm without words most of the time." He took her chin in his fingers and pulled it up so that she had to look into his eyes. "I've always thought you were beautiful, ravishing, sexy. I wish I'd told you before."

"Just because you're getting out of wallpapering and painting doesn't mean you should go overboard." She gave him a mock stern look. "You might say something you'll regret later."

"I hope not. I don't want to hurt you ever again."

She smiled at him, a hopeful, trying-to-be-brave smile, before he lay back on the bed, pulling her with him. Snuggling her head in the crook of his shoulder and enjoying the small circles he was smoothing over her back, Grace wondered if this could really be happening. The white lace canopy hung overhead, as it had many other afternoons they'd lain together, and Grace told herself not to expect too much. This moment together was just a beginning.

BUZZ PEEKED into the bedroom, his mouth agape at the sight of Grace and Brant entwined in each other's arms. He sped back into the nursery.

"I don't think Grace cares to bring us any munchies and drinks right now." His chest bunched out with pride when he caught everyone's immediate attention. "Her and Brant's sound asleep on the bed."

A delighted gasp erupted in the room. Tilly clapped her hands together. "Our plan is working!"

Maggie held up a hand. "Are they asleep on the same side of the bed?"

Buzz nodded importantly. "Wrapped around each other like cotton on a swab."

"Guess putting together a baby bassinet's hard work," Purvis interjected.

Sheriff John laid down his paintbrush. "Well, now what?"

"You take Buzz and Purvis downstairs and help them set up a tray if you can find one. Bring some sodas and chips and whatever else Tilly had, and we'll have us a celebration!" Maggie picked up her paintbrush again, giving the wall under her supervision an approving glance. "This is going very well, if I do say so myself."

BRANT SHIFTED AWAY from Grace, as much as he hated doing it. The way she'd been sleeping, ever so trustingly, against his shoulder had given him hope for their relationship. Memories of the way things had been before...before the marriage question.

The question was no longer a point, of course. His bachelor brain had not been able to bear thinking about getting married last fall. Now, he knew it was something that had to be done, for many reasons. He might have taken down the first chunk in Grace's wall of resistance, but how to get past it altogether?

Somehow, he knew she'd be uncomfortable to wake up and find him still sleeping with her. They hadn't meant to fall asleep together, and the fact that it had happened so innocently was wonderful. Still, at this point on the game board, he didn't want to be told to return to square one. She could be mighty determined, and if she said she wasn't marrying him, then she meant just that. He wasn't going to push.

Touching his finger softly to her cheek and pulling a quilt over her legs, Brant said softly, "It ain't over till it's over, Grace Barclay." It was a vow of a different kind, and he could be just as determined as she could.

He walked into the nursery, surprising Maggie so badly she dropped her paintbrush. "Dang it, Brant! It's a good thing we put down a drop cloth, or there'd be white paint on this ice blue rug. What are you doing in here, anyway?"

Brant eyeballed the seven pairs of eyes sternly reproving him. "We finished putting the basket together." He jammed his hands into his jeans and tried not to give away what he'd really been doing.

"Looked like you quit on the basket and started in on the bed," Buzz said offhandedly. His near-toothless grin told Brant that everyone knew he'd been napping with Grace.

"Grace was tired," he lied, but everyone booed him. He laughed at their good-natured teasing. "Shh! Don't tell anyone, but she might be thawing on me." His antennae quivered as he darted a nervous glance over his shoulder. If Grace ever heard him say something like that, she'd stay at the south end of the thermometer with him!

"Sunday naps just get better once you're married," Maggie teased.

"How the hell would you know?" Brant shot back.

Her eyes widened, but she didn't look John's way. "I...I reckon I just heard that somewhere." She cleared her throat.

"As a matter of fact," Brant said, allowing his eyes to

slowly rove the room face by face, "there isn't a married soul in here."

"Been married, though," Buzz offered.

"Yeah? How was it?" Brant demanded.

"Sunday naps get ya through the rest of the week." He grinned hugely.

Buzz's wife—and Purvis's, too—had passed away many years ago, which was, Brant supposed, how the two happened to have so much in common with each other. Neither seemed interested in finding another woman, and they had to be getting on to seventy, or older—

His speculative eye lit on his sister and Dan. "I don't want to hear about your Sunday naps. Somehow, I think that's why I'll be standing at the altar next weekend."

"You must like those naps, too, brother," Cami snapped back. "And apparently, you learned to like 'em a lot sooner than I did."

Laughter exploded. He could feel the back of his neck burning. "That leaves you, John."

"Don't drag me into this. Maggie and me, we don't take naps. We're too young and full of energy."

The sheriff grinned at the round owner of the Cafe. Maggie sniffed and slapped a roll of wallpaper boarder into his hand. "See if you have enough energy to start prepasting that." To Brant, she said, "We might none of us be married...yet—" she nodded toward Cami and Dan "—but we've got plenty of good advice for you."

"Such as?"

"You got lipstick on your mouth."

A red flush burned his face. Brant rubbed his mouth impatiently, unable to meet any of their interested faces. Every last one of them was holding back a snicker, and if they weren't people he'd known forever, he'd feel more stupid than he already did. "That's the best advice you've got?" he demanded.

"Nah. That ain't advice. It's a fact," Maggie said placidly. "The advice is to take your butt into a jewelry store, Brant, and get Grace something she can't tell you no over." Maggie's eyes trained on him with pointed amusement. "Ain't that your problem? She won't make an honest man of ya?"

The laughter was back in the room. Brant bit the inside of his cheek. A jewelry store! He'd rather walk barefoot over bamboo shoots.

"Now, if you're shy, Dan oughta be able to show you the ropes." Maggie pointed with another roll of wallpaper to a glass that was sitting on the makeshift worktable. "There, in that glass so it won't get paint on it, is the token of her lover's esteem."

"Maggie," Brant growled. He didn't want to be reminded too much of how Dan had gotten Cami the way she was. Glancing at his sister, he saw the crestfallen expression on her face and realized she wanted him to go look. Whatever was in that damn glass meant an awful lot to her. Trying not to feel as if he was about to examine an insect in a bottle, Brant advanced on the glass.

"Wow!" he said, pulling the ring from its resting place. "Must be good money in horses, Dan." The diamond in it was huge! Brant couldn't imagine putting so much money into—instantly, he warned himself to slow down. Dan appeared to be doing everything right for Cami. She was having a—what had Purvis called it?—a hoedown? at the Double D. Grace had specifically helped Cami select a gown and veil—no cutting corners on the dream-come-true stuff there. And a honeymoon to a romantic destination was topping the whole marriage off...maybe he'd better change his way of thinking. If Grace ever relented on having him, he'd need something like the sparkly thing he was gingerly holding between his fingers to give her.

"It's nice, Cami," he said, dropping it back into the glass. He couldn't force the question he wanted to ask onto his tongue.

"Thanks, Brant," Cami said softly, something akin to sisterly pity in her eyes.

"I got it at the jewelry store on the square," Dan said kindly. "Mr. Carpenter won't gouge you like the city stores try to."

"Oh." Brant acted nonchalant, as if he wasn't filing away where the ring had come from for future reference. "Well, what do you want me to help with, Maggie?"

She looked suspicious at his abrupt change of subject. "Well, since you and John are the tallest, you can start slappin' up that border. But you ain't supposed to be in here," she reminded him. "This is part of your wedding—I mean, baby gift from us."

He ignored her slip, which he felt was halfway on purpose, and got up on the stepladder. "I know nothing about putting up border," he complained.

"And you know nothing about women, either," Maggie replied, sticking a brush and a flat-edged piece of plastic into his hand. "By this time next week, you'll have gone through a crash course. I hope you survive it."

Brant laughed at Maggie's ribbing, because he had to be a good sport. He thought about Grace asleep and soft and warm down the hall. So much was changing so fast, for now all he could do was hang on and try to pass the course.

GRACE AWAKENED, hearing voices carrying down to her room. She stretched, then halted immediately as she remembered how she'd gotten where she was. Brant had been kissing her as if there was no tomorrow. Somewhat chagrined, she remembered that the feel of being in his arms again had been more like there had only been yesterdays between them. The yesterdays before they'd broken up...she reflexively touched her lips in wonder. Her heart aching, Grace knew that she still loved Brant with all her soul. The baby bassinet stood white and beribboned in the waning afternoon sunlight, and Grace pushed herself to her feet. It was humiliating enough that she'd fallen asleep when she should be acting the part of a good hostess. No point in cowering in her bedroom, even if it was going to be awfully hard to look into Brant's eyes.

He couldn't be fooled by her coolness anymore. Brant Durning knew he had her heart, body and soul—which was a dangerous position for her to be in.

"I'm awake!" she called down the hall, loud enough to startle someone into slamming the nursery door closed.

"Don't come in!" someone shrieked.

Grace grinned. That panicked yell sounded like Maggie. "Anybody thirsty, or hungry?" Grace called through the door.

"No, but we're sleepy!" Cami called back.

Grace laughed. "Since I'm awake now, I can play hostess like I should have been doing all along."

"Just cool your jets, Grace!" Maggie's tone had Grace smiling. "Stay right where you are. We'll be out in a sec."

Whispering erupted on the other side of the door. Grace ran a hand through her hair, satisfied that the ponytail holder was still on. A quick glance at herself in the mirror was in order, however, especially since Brant had kissed her. She wanted to look nice, in case the opportunity presented itself again.

Five minutes later, Maggie bellowed down the hall. "Grace! You can come in now!"

Grace flew to the nursery, putting a hand over her heart in astonishment. "It looks like something out of _Southern Living_ magazine!"

Lace drapes hung from the window, highlighting a wallpaper border that had been pasted in the middle of the walls. The paper was decorated with blue trains and rocking horses. Grace gasped, realizing the same border had been hung at the top of the ceiling. On one wall, a mural had been painted of a train chugging through a field where horses grazed. "Tilly," she murmured. "You talented thing. However did you do that?"

"I had lots of good help." Tilly beamed with pride. "I'm so glad you like it."

"Like it! This is a dream come true!" She hugged Tilly's neck, then Cami's, then gave Maggie an especially huge hug. Then she made the rounds of the men, stopping only long enough to try to wipe the paint off of Buzz's nose. "Thank you all so—where's Brant?"

She turned and looked at Maggie. "Is he downstairs?"

Her heart crumbled as Maggie shook her head. "He had to get on home," she explained. "He said he'd call you later."

"Oh," Grace murmured, before smiling brightly for her guests. She was determined to act as if his absence didn't affect her, even if it hurt her beyond words that he wasn't here to see the unveiling of their baby's nursery. "Well, let's pull this bassinet in here, just for starters, so I can get the full effect." She hurried down the hall, wiping a tear that had nothing to do with hormones from her eyes. Rolling the basket into the nursery, where all her friends gathered around to admire it, Grace realized that the baby bumper fabric matched the wallpaper border. She bit her lip, reminding herself that these people had done an awful lot for her, and that she owed them a happy face. Who cared if Brant had bailed out on her?

She shouldn't be one bit surprised that he would kiss and run.

BRANT HATED TO LEAVE Grace without saying goodbye. He would have liked to see the look on her face when she saw the nursery. As far as he could tell, the duded-up room was everything a mom could want for her child. When Grace saw all the love and thought that had gone into what her friends had done, Brant had a feeling the woman was going to tear up and bawl far worse than she had over the bassinet.

He should be there to hold her. Maybe even sneak in a kiss or two under the guise of concern.

His truck rumbled into the town square, past one of the four stoplights Fairhaven possessed. As usual, he scanned the sidewalks looking for faces he recognized. Carpenter's Fine Jewelry was emblazoned in gold letters above a gold crown on a shop window. Brant winced. He wasn't quite ready for that, though it was good to know where Dan had gotten the ring for Cami. All in all, Brant thought the gentle horse breeder seemed to adore his little sister. It was a thought that made it a little easier to give her away.

*Dad's giving her away.* Brant pulled his mind back from the reminder, at the same time jerking his gaze away from Carpenter's window. His eyes lit on Kyle Macaffee, who was talking to an elderly woman. He knelt to examine the dog she had on a short, pink leash even as he appeared to be listening to the old woman.

Brant didn't slow the truck to wave the way he might once have. He regretted the words he and Kyle had spoken to each other. The man was a fine vet, and an honest one. If he couldn't fix what was ailing your livestock, he told you so without false hope. One day, Brant hoped to recharge that business relationship based on mutual trust. He hadn't meant his threat that he'd take his business elsewhere, and he sincerely wished he hadn't said it.

Kyle and Dan were similar men, he realized with a sudden flash of discomfort. Gentle, kind, sensitive to people. He, Brant, was more given to the brisk approach—and if Cami could be believed, some underdeveloped ideas where women were concerned.

That sad notion brought him back around to the most brisk, emotionally underdeveloped, insensitive man he knew: his father. Brant hadn't left Grace's house to go home and take care of the livestock, as he'd said, as much as he had a chore to take care of he was completely dreading.

He could no longer put off calling his folks to tell them they were going to be grandparents—twice.

## Chapter Eleven

Forty minutes later, Brant was treated to Elsa Durning's sharp gasp of dismay. "Not you, too, Brant! What is going on with you and Cami?"

Very well that his mother might ask, Brant thought wryly. He hadn't expected his news to be anything less than a shock. "I couldn't tell you, Mother. Bad timing, I guess."

"I...just don't know what to say." She was quiet for a few moments. "Does this have anything to do with us getting a divorce?"

He knew what she was referring to. "No, Mom." He sighed heavily. "I wish I could blame this on someone. Unfortunately I have no one to blame but myself. The laugh's on me, to be honest. I was all set to yell Cami's ears pink for being careless, and then discovered myself in a similar predicament."

"Yes, but Cami's getting married." His mother's voice was perplexed. "And well before the baby's born. Can I expect like news from you?"

He scrubbed his neck sharply. "I don't think so, Mom."

The silence on the line was so long he wondered if she'd fainted. "Can I ask who the mother of your child is?"

Rolling his eyes at the reaction he knew he was about to receive, he said, "Grace Barclay."

"Grace Barclay!" his mother shrieked. "You...we...

son, listen, I don't mean to interfere, but Grace is from a fine family, one we've known for years. You just can't get her in the family way and then not marry her.''

"She won't marry me.''

"I don't care what you say, Brant, this generation's got to start living up to its responsibilities. This is no roadside trollop you've impregnated like a troublesome mare, this is a girl from a good family.''

"Mom, did you hear me? She won't marry me.''

He heard a sniff at the other end. ''Maybe you haven't asked properly. Brant, it's none of my business, but I doubt you know how to...well, I'm sure you knew well enough how to take care of the, um, part of the relationship that requires the least verbal communication, but talking to a woman is what requires the most finesse. Trust me.''

Brant closed his eyes and shook his head. This was a hard conversation to have with his mother. ''I've done my best.''

"Try harder,'' she snapped. ''You have the future of a baby hanging in the balance. Put your energy into telling that woman what she wants to hear, and do it soon. You're not going to like some other man raising your child, Brant Durning. And if Grace doesn't marry you, she will marry someone, someday.''

Cami had said the same thing. A vision of kind Kyle Macaffee patting an old lady's dog loomed in his mind. Brant grimaced, knowing that his mother was speaking from the voice of experience. If he didn't like the fact that his parents had divorced, he would have liked it a lot less if his father had been in Brant's situation and never married her.

"I hope you'll have this remedied by the wedding next weekend, Brant. I'm sorry for the harsh words,'' she said, her voice softening. ''I just hate for you to suffer because of the mistakes your father and I made.''

Brant bit his lip, forcing his emotions back. "I have to call Dad and tell him."

She was silent for a long time. "Good luck."

He snorted, his stomach in knots. "Mother," he said quietly, "I don't suppose you have any suggestions?"

They both knew what he was asking. His mother sighed heavily. "I wouldn't like to suggest anything that might make your problem worse, Brant."

"Can't." He couldn't say anymore for the choking sensation in his throat.

"Do you love her, son?"

"I always have. She doesn't believe that, though. With good reason."

"I see." He thought he heard her sniffle again. Then she said, "I'm not a good person to ask for advice."

Brant had to know. "What would have changed your mind? What would have made you stay, Mom?"

She hesitated. "Well, it was much different for me. You and Cami were grown. You didn't need us, anymore."

*We did, Mom,* he wanted to shout. But he didn't.

"I just needed more, Brant. And your father couldn't give it to me. I couldn't face the thought of all those years ahead of us on that huge ranch with no love in the house. No feeling of companionship." She started crying in earnest. "I hate to say it, but once my mind was made up, there wasn't anything your father could have done to change it. I sincerely hope that's not the position you're in, Brant. What really concerns me, though I mean this in a positive sense, is that you and your father are mirror images in many ways. Just as Cami and I are."

His throat dried out. A few moments later, he said goodbye and hung up, feeling torn, racked. Staring at the phone, Brant wondered how he was going to call his father. Still, he had to do it.

One minute later, he dialed his father's number.

"Hello?" a gruff voice said, though the greeting sounded more like a demand.

"It's me, Dad."

"Oh. Hello, Brant."

"Did I catch you at a bad time?"

"No."

The master of the understatement, he thought bitterly. No "Surprised to hear from you," no "How are you doing, son?"

"Haven't heard from you in a while, Dad." He was detouring from what he needed to say, but his throat closed.

"How is everything at the ranch?" Michael Durning asked.

"Fine."

Brant didn't know what else to say, and by the clearing of his father's throat, he knew he was just as uncomfortable. There was nothing to do but get it over with. "Guess you're coming to Cami's wedding."

"Yes."

"Well, I have a small announcement of my own." Now who was understating? "I...I." He steadied his voice and started over. "I'm going to be a father."

Lord! It sounded terrible having to say that to his own father! Brant cringed inside, feeling all at once as if he were an overactive teenager. He really was going to be a father—and how in the heck was he going to keep from messing up what he could hardly comprehend?

*This is the biggest thing I've ever done in my whole life,* Brant realized with sudden and overpowering gut instinct. A father was someone a kid looked up to, respected, trusted—

"You and Cami...are you okay out there?"

"Yes, Dad." Brant sighed and rubbed a weary hand over his eyes.

"Does your mother know?"

"As of about five minutes ago, yes."

Michael Durning coughed. "So, is there a double wedding next weekend?"

"No. So far, there isn't going to be another wedding."

"Ah."

Brant waited for about twenty seconds.

"Damned irresponsible of you, son."

"Yeah." Actually, more than his father knew. "Well, that's all I called to say."

More silence. "I don't suppose I can help you in any way."

"No." Brant pushed away the bitter thoughts in · his mind. One fought back before he could stop it. *You can tell me how to keep from losing my woman the way you lost Mom.* But he didn't say it, the same way he hadn't told his mother that he and Cami had needed her, that they still did, though perhaps in a more adult-to-adult role.

Then he knew. He never said anything that might expose him emotionally. Words that might cost his heart went unsaid.

Shock made him shy away from the truth. He couldn't be like his father.

He just couldn't.

THURSDAY NIGHT before Cami and Dan's rehearsal dinner, Cami was holed up at the Yellowjacket Café. Grace couldn't say the bride was having second thoughts; it was more like she was suffering jitters.

"Cami, can I get you a glass of soda?" Grace asked.

The bride-to-be shook her head. "I don't know what I want. I think I want this whole thing to be over."

"I thought you were looking forward to it!" Grace couldn't believe the stalwart Cami she knew was acting this way.

"I am. I want to marry Dan more than anything!" She lowered her voice confidentially, though no one could hear them. Tilly and Maggie were in the kitchen, where Sheriff

John was bothering the broadly smiling owner. Buzz and Purvis were glued to their barrel seats, and other than a few customers eating dinner, no one was around who cared to listen to Cami's onset of nerves. "It's just that my folks are coming in tomorrow night. It's got me in a dither, I guess."

Grace frowned. "They're not arriving together, are they?"

"No. Mom's taking a plane in from Florida, and Dad's flying in from his place in Montana. But they'll arrive within an hour of each other at the airport, and Brant and I are going out to pick them up. At least he'll be with me."

Grace cast her eyes toward the table. She'd heard barely a word from Brant since he'd kissed her at the baby shower. He'd called once to see how she was doing, but that was it. His no-show behavior hurt her feelings, though this was exactly the relationship they'd agreed to. Somehow, after they'd kissed, Grace supposed she had begun hoping that…well, that pigs would fly. Nothing really had changed between them, except that they'd given in to the attraction they'd always felt for each other.

"I'm sure everything will go fine," she murmured. "It's your big weekend. Your parents will be on their best behavior."

"I know." Cami sighed, and for the first time, Grace noticed the dark smudges under her eyes. "It's just hard. I mean, I've given Brant the very devil for letting our parents' divorce bother him so much. The truth is, I haven't let myself think too much about it. Taking over the ranch has kept Brant and I so busy, I just didn't allow myself to dwell on it. But they're going to be here in Fairhaven, together again, and I'm expecting a baby…oh, I don't know," she sighed. "It's going to be so awkward."

Grace had been suffering from the same kind of twinges. Spending the weekend around Brant at a marriage ceremony was going to be tough. She reached over to pat

Cami's hand. "In three days, you'll be cruising in the Mediterranean. I hope you've chosen appropriate sunbathing wear."

Cami laughed, some of the fatigue disappearing from her eyes. "I can't wait for that." She nodded her head in the direction of the kitchen.

John had sneaked a hand around Maggie's waist. She moved away swiftly, rapping his hand with a wooden spatula. Grace laughed as he shrugged and walked their way.

"Don't you know Maggie's kitchen is a dangerous place to be, John?"

"I do know it." He took a seat at their table. "Guess I'll take refuge over here with you two."

"It's a little safer here," Cami began. "Uh-oh. Here comes my brother. Brant! Over here!"

Grace wanted to shrink into her chair. Did Cami have to be so exuberant with her holler to Brant? Her stomach suddenly constricting, she forced a smile to her face.

"Brant Durning! Haven't seen you all week." John pulled a chair out for him. "Thought maybe you were avoiding us."

"Nah." Brant nodded at Grace and his sister. "I'm still picking wallpaper paste out of my eyelids," he groused.

His eyes looked tired and red, as if he was telling the truth, Grace thought. Actually he was wearing the same pensive expression Cami'd had on her face thirty minutes ago.

"So. What's new?" John asked him.

"Not much. Just catching up with some spring chores. Trying to get the place spruced up some, too. Guests start arriving tomorrow."

"Yep." John nodded, his eyes lighting as Maggie neared.

"Can I get you something, Brant?"

"A cola and a turkey sandwich. Split it with me?" he asked Grace.

Her heart rate accelerated. "I just ate. Thanks, though."

"You look good."

His comment was the same as if he were looking over one of his steers, Grace warned herself. He hadn't said anything special. She nodded warily in thanks for his compliment but didn't reply.

"Mom just called," Brant told Cami.

"Has she got mother-of-the-bride nerves?" she asked.

"Don't think so. She wanted to remind us that she's bringing Dr. Nelson with her."

Cami's jaw dropped. Grace looked away in embarrassment. Dr. Nelson was Mrs. Durning's new husband, though neither Cami nor Brant ever mentioned him. To them, she was still Elsa Durning.

"Well, that only edges the discomfort level up a notch," Cami commented. "I don't think Dad's going to enjoy this wedding very much."

"None of us are." Brant jerked his eyes up as everyone at the table gasped. "I didn't mean that, Cami! I meant— oh, heck."

John shook his head at him. Brant put his hands up in a warning gesture. "Hey! I'm sorry. I'm glad Cami's getting married. It's all the other stuff that's going along with it that's a pain." To John, he said caustically, "I hope you're taking notes. One day it's gonna be you sitting in the hot seat."

John's eyes darted toward Maggie, who was putting up an order, her dark hands flying competently. "Uh-uh. You'll have to find someone else to feel sorry for you. Maggie knew what I was about before she got involved with me."

"Yeah, well." Brant glanced at Grace. Instantly her heart shrank at the look in his eyes. If she didn't know better, she would think his expression was saying, "So did Grace. And look at the position I'm in now."

Stunned, she sipped at her drink. Was that why Brant

had only eked out a cursory phone call to check on her?
Had the nursery decorating been more than his bachelor
heart could stand? Or had he suddenly realized what she
had feared he would all along—that the commitment growing in her belly was more than a wedding ring could make
up for?

"I think I'll go on home." She rose from the table, unable to meet Brant's eyes. Nodding to John, Grace gave
Cami a quick hug. "Good luck tomorrow night. Call me
when you get in from the airport if you want to talk."

She waved to Maggie and Tilly, and said good-night to
Buzz and Purvis as she sailed past them. Once on the sidewalk, Grace hurried toward her house, her feelings hurt and
frightened.

"Don't think you'll have to eat that turkey sandwich,
Brant," Cami said mildly as Tilly put the plate in front of
him. "You can't possibly be hungry after putting your foot
in your mouth."

"What'd I say?" Grace's swift exit had alerted him that
something had gone awry, but he hadn't even spoken to
her! In fact, he was trying very hard not to say anything to
make matters worse between them. He'd spent most of the
week trying to figure out what he should say to Grace. He
loved her; she knew that. She just didn't believe he loved
her for her. How was a man supposed to get around that
roadblock?

"I don't know if it's what you say so much as what you
don't say." Cami sighed, reaching over to grab the half of
the sandwich he'd offered Grace. "And when you talk
about my wedding, the look on your face spells panic."

"Well, damn it! I am!"

"I know." She bit into the sandwich. "I am, too. But
Grace read it as something else, I think. What do you think,
John?"

"I think it's time for Maggie to close up shop," he said,

watching the owner of the Yellowjacket Cafe with a gleam in his dark eyes. "She's supposed to cut my hair tonight."

Cami stared at him, then at Brant. "You know, you two are frighteningly similar."

"What's that supposed to mean?" Brant demanded.

His sister shook her head, a maddeningly knowing look on her face. "You both are suffering from macho, barbaric personalities." She ignored the heated denials from both men. "In your case, John, you have a little more time to work out the kinks. But, brother, if I was you, I'd at least put a quarter in the phone and call Grace to whisper goodnight in her ear. I'm thinking it's going to be an awfully long weekend for you if you don't."

Cami got up and left the table abruptly. Brant stared after her.

"What was that all about?" John wanted to know.

"I'm not sure," Brant murmured. "Ever since my little sister got pregnant, she's been an irritating fountain of knowledge."

"Mmm," John grunted. "Bad side effect."

"I don't know," Brant said thoughtfully. "What's irritating about it is that so far, she's been right on the bull's-eye." He bit the inside of his jaw before getting to his feet. "John, I'm going to have to call it a night."

The sheriff sighed. "You losing a quarter or throwing gravel tonight?"

"I think I'll try ringing the doorbell this time." Brant shook his head. "Though if Cami's right, Grace isn't going to open the door."

"Well, don't make me have to come after you for disturbing the peace."

Brant waved John's comment off and beat a hasty retreat. He'd spent all week grappling with the conversation between him and his father, and trying to figure out a way to convince Grace that he wasn't in this thing simply because of the baby.

Ringing the doorbell at Grace's house, he waited impatiently on the porch. There was no answer, and belatedly Brant realized there were no lights on inside. That had to mean she was at her shop. Striding back up the sidewalk, he headed toward the Wedding Wonderland. If he'd been smart, he would have checked there first, since it was right across the street from the Yellowjacket.

Peering through the window, he saw a light on inside a stockroom. He tried the door handle, but it barely moved. Pushing at it more firmly, Brant felt the door move inward.

Instantly the security system wailed its announcement of a break-in at the Wedding Wonderland.

# Chapter Twelve

Brant practically jumped out of his skin. Reflexively he jerked the door shut, but the alarm continued shrieking. Glancing over his shoulder, he saw the regulars peering out the window at him. He could practically hear the laughter.

The door gave way in front of him. "What in the world are you doing, Brant?" Grace demanded. She looked as if he'd scared her badly. That was the last thing he'd wanted to do.

She touched some numbers into the alarm panel in a box by the door. Welcome—yet strained—silence fell between them.

He needed to explain his behavior. "I was going to—"

Behind him, he heard Sheriff John's lazy whistling. Brant cringed.

"I see you got Grace to open the door, Brant," he called. "Maybe next time the Fairhaven High School band could help you get Grace's attention. The police don't like having to come out for false alarms."

"I'll keep that in mind, John." In the Cafe window, Brant could see Cami shaking her head at him. He felt a momentary strike of annoyance that his private life was always so public in this town. But wasn't that what Grace had tried to explain to him? She'd said he was so worried about what other people thought that he didn't show any expression at all. She'd said these people were their friends. Glancing back at Grace, he felt a larger fear that he might have turned into the cardboard man that his father was.

"I'm sorry, Grace," he said, throwing caution to the wind. "I stopped by your house, but you weren't there. I took a chance that you were here."

"I'm catching up on some book work." Her eyes were huge in her face, the lines around them tired, from what he could see in the light of the lamp hanging above the door.

"I didn't mean to frighten you out of your wits." He paused, glancing down at her stomach. "Hope the little guy's okay."

A tiny smile floated onto her face. "It didn't disturb him in the least."

His boy was brave! Brant liked that idea. "Grace, the reason I was trying to find you is because I think I owe you an apology."

Her gaze dropped, but at least she didn't slam the door shut. He forged ahead. "I'm not sure what I said in the Cafe, but what is clear to me is that somehow I upset you. Grace, that's the last thing I want to do." He reached out to smooth a curl behind her ear, and Grace's eyes jumped up to meet his.

"It's okay," she said softly.

"No, it's not. Tell me what I said."

She shrugged. "You didn't say anything. I think...I think I feel that you resent me for this."

She touched her stomach, which Brant couldn't help noticing seemed larger than when he'd seen her last Sunday. He eyed it curiously. "I don't resent you at all. I just don't know how to make it right."

"What do you mean?" The overhead lamp sent a soft glow onto her face, and Brant thought she'd never looked so beautiful, so alluring.

"I'm not sure myself, but I'm going to give it a try." One last backward glance over his shoulder sent the regulars skittering from the window. "You're beautiful, babe. I know I never said it while we were dating, but you were the only woman I could ever spend an entire night thinking about. I don't mean just the hours before I went to bed. I mean the entire night. I spent months trying to figure out how I was going to…to, well, get you to let me make love to you."

Grace's mouth dropped open. "What is the matter with you?"

He frowned. "What do you mean?"

"You sound like you've got an extra dose of pregnancy hormones or something! I've never heard you so… emotional."

Brant decided to take Grace's astonishment in stride. What was she supposed to think, with him doing a one-hundred-eighty-degree turn on her? "I've had a lot of time to think in the last week," he began, not able to tell her that talking to his father had convinced him that he didn't want to always keep his feelings under tight rein. "I've had a lot of time to think about us. I want you to know that I'm sorry for everything."

Grace hesitated before shaking her head. "I'm not."

"No, I don't mean that. Anxiety made him rush his next words. "I wish I hadn't been so paranoid about loving you, Grace. That's all I'm going to say right now, because I don't want to rush you. I want you to have time to think about what I've said. But think about this—I spent the last three months trying to get you out of my system. I couldn't."

He dropped a last kiss on Grace's lips. "Can I walk you home, or do you still have work to finish?"

"I have about another hour's worth." The confusion in Grace's eyes told Brant that what he'd said was long overdue.

"Will you be careful walking home?" he asked her. "I worry about you."

"John and Maggie will walk me home, after she finishes closing up the Cafe." She stepped back inside the door. "Thank you for coming by, Brant."

He jammed the Western hat he was carrying back on his head. "You think about what I've said."

"I will. Good night."

She closed the door softly, and Brant headed toward his truck. Somehow, he felt as if he'd made headway. In the next couple of months, he ought to be able to manage some more.

Maybe he could even get Grace to the altar before his son was born.

GRACE HELD WONDERING fingertips over her mouth as she covertly watched Brant through the lace curtains. What had gotten into him? All this sudden rush to spill his heart out to her had something to do with his parents' arrival tomorrow night, Grace felt sure. She'd never seen Cami as upset as she was, either. One minute Cami had been a blushing bride-to-be; tonight she was more nervous than a mare around a stallion.

She backed away from the window, her hand falling to caress her stomach. Maybe his folks had put the pressure on him to marry her. Grace shook her head at that notion. Nobody pressured Brant Durning to do anything. He and Cami were alike in few ways, but they did share that trait.

Could it be that he actually wanted to marry her? She thought about the regretful look she'd seen in his eyes as John was proclaiming his intention to stay single. Possibly she'd misread what she'd seen in his eyes.

Sighing, Grace walked to stand in front of a three-way mirror. Her stomach protruded without any lack of restraint now. She decided to wait until after this weekend was over—and Cami and Brant's parents had gone home—to ponder his words. In all likelihood, everyone was simply suffering from an advanced case of wedding overexcitement. She didn't want to read too much into Brant's words in case he had been propelled into them by something other than a real desire to marry her.

All the same, Grace couldn't help thinking as she eyed her stomach in the three-way mirror that she hoped Brant meant what he was saying. Time was running out.

"SOMETHING'S WRONG," Maggie proclaimed darkly. "I don't know what, but it is." She reached over and smacked John's roving hand with the wooden spatula for the eighth time that evening.

"Ouch!" he cried. "Maggie, that hurt!"

She never smacked him hard enough to cause him pain, but she was plain out of patience tonight. "Quit trying to pat my behind, John. I've got a lot on my mind."

Comforting fingers massaged into her shoulders. "I'm sorry, Maggie. Guess I was thinking about getting you alone."

"I know. But I'm too upset." Maggie sighed and turned to face John. "Did you get an eyeful of Grace's stomach tonight?"

He rubbed his face thoughtfully. "I reckon it looked like she's growing a bun in her oven, same as she has for a few months now."

Tilly glanced up from where she was cleaning off the counter. It was past closing time, and they were doing the nightly cleanup. They were alone, the three of them. Even Buzz and Purvis got shooed off when the doors locked. "What's going around in that mind of yours, Maggie?"

"It's something I can hardly explain." She attacked a dirty pot with gusto. "For the last couple of weeks, I've been having this notion that Grace is bigger than she oughta be. Now, I know she had a sonogram, and those things are s'posed to be reliable, but my gut's telling me an error's been rung up somewhere."

Tilly gasped. "Don't you think Brig Delancey knows what he's about?"

Maggie nodded. "That's what's bothering me. Now, if it was the old doc, I mighta been more worried, 'cause Lord knows he was getting feeble. But Doc Brig knows his stuff." She tossed down the pot and picked up another, scrubbing at the caked beans around the rim. "And I know that Grace goes regularly for her prenatal checkups. So she's getting measured, and weighed...I know there ain't no way of what I'm thinking to be right, but all the same, something's not right."

John scratched his head. "Mistakes are made all the time with those sonograms. Could be the due date was miscalculated?"

"Could be, but Doc Brig's seen her since then, so he would know by her measurements if she wasn't on track." Maggie shook her head, completely puzzled. "What do I know anyway? I ain't a doctor."

"No, but if you're worrying, there's probably a reason," John said, his statement borne out of knowing Maggie Mason for years.

"I was worried enough to rush decorating that nursery."

Tilly turned. "Is that why you got all fired-up to do that? You said something about it being cooler in May, and a bunch of other nonsense, but I just figured you were in the mood to decorate."

"No." Maggie shook her head decisively. "Either Grace Barclay is cooking twins, or she's carrying the biggest baby known to man, or—" She sighed heavily, knowing no good could come of her next suggestion. "Or Grace is further along than she knows."

"How far?"

Maggie squinted toward the Wedding Wonderland. "I left my crystal ball at home, but judging by the way she's filled out in the last week, and dropped in the middle, too,

I'd say we're looking at a run to the hospital in a couple of weeks."

"Weeks!" Tilly dropped her sponge. "Do you think you better mention to Grace what you're thinking? She might need to make another trip in to see Dr. Delancey. She hasn't had time to go to breast-feeding classes, or coaching classes, or anything!"

Maggie raised her brows at John in question. He held up his hands. "Don't ask me. We all agreed when Brant came back into town that the less that got said about their situation, the better they'd probably both be. We've kept our interfering to a minimum so far, and nature seems to be taking its course."

The three of them stared at each other for a moment. "'Course, if you're honestly having misgivings, Maggie, and I've known you too long to think you're just whistling Dixie, somebody might at least mention it to her. She's going to need more than paint and wallpaper if that baby's gonna put in an appearance soon."

Maggie bit her lip. "Go get her, John."

He nodded once, considering, then left the Cafe. A moment later, he'd returned with Grace.

She sank gratefully into a chair. "I was ready to call it a night," she said, putting her feet out in front of her. "I've got all this energy during the day, but tonight, I'm unusually tired."

Maggie was eyeing her curiously. Grace raised her brows. "What?"

Maggie came over to sit across the table from her. Tilly and John grabbed a seat as well. He reached over and lit the candle with his lighter, and the four of them sat in silence watching until the flame caught.

"I don't know how to say what's on my mind, Grace," Maggie began. "I sure don't want to upset you. But I—we were wondering when the last time you saw Dr. Delancey was."

Grace looked around the table at each of them. "I'm seeing him next week. Why?"

"Well, I don't exactly know."

Maggie's gaze skimmed her stomach, which just rose over the top of the table. Grace sat a little straighter, so the roundness was a little more hidden.

"You have discussed your due date with Doc Brig, right? It wasn't a date you arbitrarily selected based on the last cycle you had?" Maggie watched her closely.

"Where are all these questions leading, Maggie?" Grace suddenly felt nervous. "I've discussed everything with Dr. Delancey. You know I listen closely to whatever he has to say."

"Hmm." Maggie leaned back in the chair. "You've changed in the last few weeks, Grace. There isn't any chance—" She broke off her words. "I don't want to worry you, honey, but you sure don't look like you've got two more months left in you."

Grace clasped her fingers into her skirt to keep them from trembling. "I—I don't know what to say. I'll mention it to Dr. Delancey when I see him." She jumped up from the table, prepared to flee, but John's hand shot out, capturing her wrist.

"I'll walk you home, Grace, if you're of a mind to go." Gently he pulled her down into the seat. "'Course, I gotta tell you something else. I've known Miss Maggie a long time, and ain't many times I've known her to be wrong about something. We're not trying to upset you. We're worried about you."

"I know you are." Grace sank into the chair, braving a glance around the table at her friends. The candlelight showed the concern in their eyes, and she was truly ashamed. "I'm sorry," she whispered. "I couldn't tell you the truth. I couldn't tell anyone the truth."

"You mean…you mean I'm right? You are due sooner than you said you were?" Maggie looked shocked.

"Yes." Grace couldn't meet her eyes. "We'll probably have a Brant Durning, Junior, in a couple of weeks."

"Oh, Grace!" Maggie and Tilly jumped up to come around the table and throw their arms around her. "Why didn't you tell us?" Maggie demanded.

Tears began flowing down her cheeks. "I didn't want anyone to know! And after Brant came back, I didn't want him to feel pressured to marry me. I wanted him to have as much time as possible to think about being a father." She began sobbing in earnest, unable to help the tears that wouldn't stop.

Her back was being rubbed soothingly, but Grace couldn't be soothed. "The truth is, I knew I was pregnant when I mentioned marriage to Brant back in the fall. I told you I found out after he left, but I was already at the end of the first trimester when we broke up. I spent three months hiding out, hiding my stomach, hoping he was going to change his mind and come back to me. But then, he flat-out left Fairhaven, and there I was, six months pregnant."

Grace blew into the tissue Maggie had pressed into her hand. "Of course, Dr. Delancey wasn't going to give me away. I should have told you," she said with an apologetic glance around at her friends, "but I guess I was trying to put off the inevitable as long as possible."

"You sure had us fooled," Maggie said, her voice awed. "I guess it's because you're tall that you kept it hidden so well, but you surely only started looking full of baby this month." She blew out a heavy breath. "Grace Barclay, we don't have time for those coaching classes!"

She smiled ruefully. "I figured they weren't going to tell us anything you didn't already know, Maggie." Reaching out, she touched her fingers to her friend's. "I don't think they can teach you anything."

Maggie straightened, nodding with pride. "We'll do fine, Grace." Her eyes suddenly filled with tears, too. Tilly sniffled, and John glanced away. "Great day in the morning," Maggie said, her voice breaking, "that baby's already in the home stretch, John! We're gonna have us a baby before we know it!"

They all laughed, and then shed a few more happy tears. Grace looked around at her friends who so obviously shared her elation. It felt wonderful to get her secret off her chest.

Almost off her chest. Sooner or later, she was going to have to tell Brant the truth. This was not the weekend to disrupt what little equilibrium he had left.

"You just gonna let that little baby make a surprise announcement on the daddy," Tilly asked, putting a name to the thoughts in Grace's head, "or are you going to give him some advance warning?"

Grace hesitated the slightest second. "If you will all keep my secret a while longer, I promise I'll tell him right after Cami's wedding."

"Right after, as in once the rice is thrown?" Maggie demanded suspiciously. "Or right after, as in sometime in the next two weeks, and preferably after John and I've run you up to the hospital?"

"Right after his parents have gone home, I'll tell him." Grace tried to control the sudden racing of her heart. "I promise."

## Chapter Thirteen

Brant could honestly say he'd never been more nervous in his life as he waited for his parents' planes to arrive. Beside him, Cami was silent, which glaringly announced her own nervousness. He couldn't remember the last time his sister hadn't been boiling over with delirious excitement since he'd returned home.

"Brant! Cami! Yoo-hoo!" a cheery voice called.

His mother ran toward them, bags and packages askew, and followed by a tall, distinguished man. She threw her arms around Cami first, giving her a tight squeeze. "Cami! I can't believe my little girl is getting married." She pulled away briefly, staring at her stomach before pulling her close again. "You look wonderful!"

Brant felt his mother's hand reach out to pull him into the embrace. He went willingly into the whimsical circle of his mother's love and perfumed scent and exuberance. She was like Cami that way, a delightful whirlwind bringing pleasure to everyone around her. Brant tried not to think about the man standing behind her, patiently waiting for the awkward mumblings of welcome that he had probably come to expect from the Durning clan. A part of him had to admire that Dr. Nelson would go through this for his mother's sake. Dr. Nelson, fossil finder and archaeological authority, who took his mother to fascinating places in his hunt for the history of life, Brant thought sourly.

He forced himself to break away from his mother to face Dr. Nelson. Putting out a hand, he said, "Welcome. Let me help you with some of those packages Mother's loaded you down with."

The man smiled, his expression appreciative at Brant's overture, but not overeager. Cami remembered her manners at the same time.

"Thank you for coming, Dr. Nelson," she said, her voice only slightly cool for the Cami Brant knew. "I...I—"

Brant was horrified when his sister burst into tears. Cami never cried!

"I'm sorry," she moaned, "I don't know why I'm crying."

"Maybe I shouldn't have come," kindly Dr. Nelson said, his voice distressed.

"No, no!" Cami waved her hand and scrubbed her eyes. "I honestly don't know what's come over me."

"Ah." Brant had experience with this. Cami was having a tomato moment extraordinaire. Thanks to Grace, he knew what he was dealing with. He pulled his sister to him to support her, and jerked his head in the direction of the luggage carousel. "Dr. Nelson, if you'll get your suitcases, Cami and I'll get the car."

"Fine, fine, Brant. Call me Bob, if you would. Hate to stand on formality," he said, glancing at Cami in some alarm. "Can I get you a glass of water?"

"Cami, are you all right?" Elsa Durning Nelson asked.

"She's fine." Brant pulled his sister to the sliding doors with him. "We'll be right back with the car."

Once in the bright sunshine, Cami pulled away and dabbed at her nose. "I wish I hadn't done that!"

"It doesn't matter," Brant said curtly, watching the traffic before they stepped out. "If you hadn't, I probably would have."

"Really?" Cami stared up at him in astonishment.

"Hell, yeah. I feel like bawling like a baby. It doesn't help that Bob is so nice, either. I'd like to hate him. But all I can do is...face the facts, Cam. Mom's happier than I've ever seen her."

His sister halted right in the middle of the street. Brant tugged her to safety. "You're right. You know, you're really right, Brant. For once."

Airplanes whined overhead, and taxis whizzed past impatiently. He shrugged at her teasing. "Miracles happen, I guess."

"I thought I was the smart one in the family." Cami's nose was red and her burnished curls looked forlorn somehow. Brant reached out to give her a swift hug.

"I might have had some catching up to do, but I'm getting there." Of course, he needed a lot more coaching.

"Well, the prospect of being a father certainly seems to agree with you."

Brant took off in the direction of the car. "Maybe."

It wasn't that, but he wasn't going to tell his wiseacre sister all his secrets. He had a few more months to think about being a father. That wasn't what was shifting his thought process into high, enlightened gear.

It was trying to figure out how to get his reluctant woman to the altar that was forcing him to think on a higher plane. He had a goal. He wanted a "yes" out of Grace Barclay—and he wanted it soon.

No baby of his was going to think that his father hadn't wanted him.

WHEN HE AND CAMI had pulled the car around, Brant was dismayed to see his father waiting on the sidewalk with Bob and Elsa. "Oh, boy, oh, boy," he said sarcastically to Cami. "Isn't this going to be a fun ride home."

He got out of the car, walking to shake hands briskly

with his father. Cami managed a hug and a fast kiss on the cheek for him.

"Plane get in early, Dad?" he asked. If his mother had looked dazzlingly happy ten minutes ago, she looked downright unhappy right now.

"Actually it was right on schedule. I must have gotten the flight times mixed up."

"Oh." Brant tossed his father's suitcase into the trunk. That wasn't too hard to envision happening. Elsa Durning had been the anchor that held his father in place for nearly thirty years.

Silently they all got into the car, Michael Durning up front beside Brant who was driving. Bob, Elsa and Cami squeezed in the back. Brant ground his jaw as he maneuvered the car into traffic.

Grace was going to marry him, he decided obstinately, and when she said yes, she wasn't ever going to go flying off with some archaeological fossil finder who could give her what he couldn't. Or some kindhearted veterinarian, either.

Brant might have been slow in catching up, but he was about to make up for lost time.

GRACE DOUBLED OVER at the sudden pain in her stomach. The baby's kicks had grown more insistent in the past few weeks, making it much harder to ignore them. She'd been beset by aches and pains that she'd never dreamed pregnancy would bring her. Lying on the bed, Grace told herself all she had to do was get through the rehearsal dinner tonight, then the wedding tomorrow night. Then she could put on sweatpants and big tops and be comfortable for the next two weeks. Her sister, Hope, a high school teacher, was coming into town to oversee the shop for her, and that was the biggest relief of all to Grace. Now that it was the end of May, Hope was on break, and was planning to spend the summer helping Grace with the new baby.

Sighing, she couldn't help thinking that she was lucky to have all the help she was getting. She was better prepared for single motherhood than most women in her position might be. The most surprising event was Brant trying harder to woo her, which was nice, in a way.

In another way, it was unsettling. She'd seen the determined glint in his eye, saw it blossom and take shape last night when he'd set off the alarm at the Wedding Wonderland. When he found out that he was going to be a father a lot sooner than he expected, Grace had no doubts that Brant was going to insist on getting married immediately. Well, first he was going to be mad as the dickens that she'd deceived him. But as soon as that passed, Brant's let's-get-this-thing-done personality was going to dictate a quick solution.

Grace meant to stick to her guns on this matter. She wasn't going to marry a man who had run out the door at the first wind of permanent commitment. She'd spent too many months alone, frightened into planning for a future for her and her baby. That future hadn't included Brant, and she saw no reason to change the picture, when she had everything so well organized. Brant was only putting forth this extreme effort toward marriage because of the baby—as his grudging marriage proposal in the hotel in New York attested.

For days, she'd watched Cami and Brant suffer over having to see their parents in the same house but no longer together. Grace wasn't going to give her baby the same future. After all, Brant had picked up and left her once.

Who was to say he wouldn't do it again?

THE REHEARSAL DINNER was true to its name, Brant thought grimly, sitting at a table in a fancy restaurant in Fairhaven. They were rehearsing parts they all were going to play at the altar tomorrow night. He felt sorry for Cami and Dan.

They were supposed to be the happy bridal couple, and he didn't think he'd ever seen more miserable people.

The rehearsal itself had gone just fine, perhaps because the minister and a few support staff from the church were looking on. But now he, Grace—as Cami's maid of honor—his parents and the bridal couple were alone, trying to figure out what to say to each other. Dr. Nelson of the exquisite manners wouldn't intrude on a private family matter and had taken himself off to Glen Rose to see the dinosaur footprints. Despite his absence, nobody was comfortable.

Though Grace looked beautiful, she also looked heavy with her pregnancy. Brant wondered how she could get much bigger than she was, and felt a momentary surge of pride in his son. Obviously the boy was going to be a linebacker! The pride somewhat deteriorated when he realized his mother was staring at Grace, though trying not to be too obvious about the direction of her gaze. Cami was nowhere near showing.

"Is your food all right, Grace?" his mother asked. She had been in the process of making overly polite conversation with Cami's fiancé, but had taken a moment out to shoot a worried look Grace's way.

"It's delicious, thank you." Grace smiled, but it wasn't her usual bright smile. Brant felt a moment's worry that she was overtired. After this weekend was over, he would insist that she get plenty of rest. Under the table, he reached over to rub the top of her leg soothingly. Grace started, before actually seeming to draw some comfort from his gesture.

"Are you all right?" he leaned over to whisper in her ear.

"I'm fine. Don't worry about me," she whispered back.

He patted her leg, before glancing up to catch his father's stern eye on him. "More bread, Dad?" he asked, passing the rolls to that end of the table.

"No, thank you." He hesitated for a moment. "Well, Dan, I guess you and Cami are looking forward to your honeymoon."

"Yes, we are."

Dan appeared to be blushing, and Brant felt momentary pity for him. No doubt he was remembering the hell Brant had raised on him when he'd discovered Cami was pregnant, and assumed any moment Michael Durning was going to blow. Brant snorted to himself. If his dad blew at anyone, he'd be shocked.

"Well, I must say, this isn't the way I envisioned things happening for my children," Elsa said brightly. "Two grandchildren, for heaven's sake. I'll have to join a frequent flyer program so I can see my grandbabies often."

Nobody had much to say to that. Brant thought that was probably the quickest rehearsal dinner anyone had ever had in history. They vacated the restaurant, and thirty minutes later, he was putting Grace into her truck.

"I wish you had let me pick you up," he said. "Will you at least let me drive you to the church tomorrow, and then up to the Double D? You're going to have a lot to carry, Grace, with your dress and all."

"I'll be all right." She started the engine.

"Grace, I'm going to pick you up tomorrow night," he stated, his tone no-nonsense. "If you don't need me, I sure as hell need you. This weekend is just about the biggest fiasco I've ever seen."

"I know." She paused to look up at him. "Poor Cami!"

"Maybe the champagne tomorrow night will loosen everyone up. Besides, there'll be so many guests at the D that it'll feel less awkward."

"I hope you're right." Grace's expression softened. "Cami's going to be such a beautiful bride."

"Yeah." Grace would be one, too. He planned on telling her that very thing tomorrow night. Tonight had not been the night to ask her to become a limb on his family tree.

After the wedding, he was sure his folks would unbend enough to appear less intimidating to Grace.

"Well, good night, Brant." Grace smiled, but he was once again struck by how tired she looked.

"Are you sure this wedding isn't too much? I don't want you shaking anything loose too soon," he tried to tease. It fell flat, by the look on Grace's face. "Tilly could stand in for you, you know, if you're not feeling up to it."

"We'll only be throwing birdseed tomorrow night, and I can get plenty of rest after that. Besides, I've let all the seams out of my maid of honor dress. Tilly couldn't fit into it unless there were two of her." She sighed heavily. "I haven't been sleeping well is all."

He leaned through the truck window and gave her a lingering kiss on the mouth before she could pull away. "Sleep better tonight, Grace Barclay. I may need you to hold me up at the altar."

"Not sleeping well, either?"

"I don't think I will tonight. We've got to take Dan out for his bachelor party."

"Oh! I'd forgotten about that." The look on Grace's face turned distinctly unhappy, but Brant wasn't sure why.

He reached out to run a hand along her cheek, and one finger along the tiny freckles there. "Did I tell you that you look beautiful tonight?"

"No, but you don't have to tell me every single night, Brant."

Still, Grace perked up a little. Brant gave her a devilish grin. "I noticed my boy's pushing you out of shape quite a bit. You don't let him keep you up all night playing tag, okay?"

Her gaze slid away from his. "I won't."

"Well, I'll pick you up tomorrow afternoon, about five?"

She nodded slowly. "I'll be ready."

Brant stepped away from the truck so she could drive

away. He watched the taillights disappear in the dark, the strangest notion hitting him that Grace hadn't once smiled, or laughed, all evening.

Maybe it was worth putting a call in to Dr. Delancey. Then again, the doctor wouldn't discuss Grace's pregnancy with him, particularly as they weren't married.

That was a situation that could be remedied sooner than later.

WHEN BRANT RETURNED to the Double D to meet Dan, who insisted on dropping Cami off at home, he found a pair of unsmiling parents waiting for him in the den.

"We'd like to have a word with you, Brant." His father's voice was stern. His mother's posture was stiff.

"Sure." Brant threw himself into a chair across from them. "What's up?"

"What's up with you?" his mother demanded tartly. "When are you going to marry Grace?"

"As soon as she'll have me." Brant shrugged at them. "I already told you that on the phone."

"You didn't tell us you were running out of time!" his mother nearly shrieked. "You said she was pregnant. You didn't say she was due any minute!"

"Now, wait a second." Brant held up a conciliatory hand. "Grace isn't due for another couple of months. I think her due date's in August. I still have time to change her mind."

His father shook his head. Elsa stared at him. "Son, you have lived on a ranch too long not to know a female who's in the extremely advanced stages of pregnancy."

Something discomforting began edging into Brant's brain. He gave his mother a suspicious, sideways glance. "Are we calling six or seven months advanced?"

"No," she snapped. "We're calling a full nine months of gestation and about-to-deliver-any-day-now advanced."

"Mom, you're just surprised. Grace has only filled out in the last week. She didn't look like that a few days ago."

Elsa got up and began pacing the room at breakneck speed. "I think you need to have a long heart-to-heart with Grace. Someone's misread their calendar—or someone isn't telling every detail of the story. But if she gets through the wedding tomorrow night, it'll be a miracle."

"I think it's just a big baby," Brant said. "I swear, she just popped out this week."

His father had been silent up till now. "Brant, listen to your mother. She was a nurse for most of her life."

"I am listening! I can only tell you what I know." He slammed his palm on his knee in disgust. "I have to drive Dan into Dallas for his bachelor party now. Will you feel better if I tell you I had planned on asking Grace to marry me tomorrow night?"

"I thought you said you already had, and that she'd turned you down."

"Yeah, well." Brant's collar got warm. "I think I need to ask her again."

"Well, it might make us feel better, son." His father looked out a window. "Your mother doesn't think there's a whole lot of time left for you to convince Grace that you're suitable husband material."

He appreciated their concern. Yet, he resented it as well. Of all people to be lecturing him on a dash to the altar! "I've got it under control." He gave Elsa a kiss, and his father a brief nod. "Good night, Mother. Father."

"Oh, dear," Elsa moaned as Brant left the room. "This is the kind of predicament I can envision Cami in. But she's been so levelheaded about her situation, while my son is out in left field."

Michael didn't reply. The two of them sat in the den, among the possessions that used to be theirs, until they heard Dan and Brant run down the stairs. Cami shouted something out the upstairs window at the departing men, evoking much laughter.

"Elsa." Michael stood, and she stared at her ex-husband with raised brows. "Sooner or later, Brant will work this out. He may be his father's son, and a bit on the reticent side, but he is also your son, which means that if Grace Barclay thinks she's going to be a single mother forever, she is underestimating Brant. He will love his child with such ferocity that Grace will know she is loved, by the very fact that Brant's heart will never, ever belong to anyone else. I watched you over the years love your children that way, and I think it always frightened me that you could love so much. I know now what a gift that kind of love is. Brant and Cami will have that same love for their spouses, and their children. Tomorrow night, I can leave this house happy, because I know that your legacy is firmly ingrained in those kids."

Elsa's eyes filled with tears. "That's the sweetest thing you've ever said to me."

He nodded, turning to leave the room. "I have no doubt of that. Losing what you love is a hard way to learn that you should have been more caring of that love all along."

Elsa stared out the window for a long time after her ex-husband left to go to the hotel where he was staying. She hoped Brant knew what he was doing. Grace hadn't looked at him more than twice all night—and that couldn't bode well for Brant.

Michael might think Brant was a lot like her, but he contained plenty of Michael's traits. If Brant had spent nine months and more giving Grace the cool side of his heart, she didn't think Grace would be too easily convinced to become Mrs. Brant Durning. Michael had spoken his heart far too long after their relationship was over for it to have changed anything for Elsa. She could only pray Grace still wanted Brant.

GRACE TRIED NOT TO THINK about the bachelor party very much. It was just so hard to know that Brant would be looking at a bunch of skinny, dancing women—no doubt minus pertinent pieces of their clothing—while she looked like a dirigible had taken up residence inside her!

She got into bed, telling herself she needed to sleep well for tomorrow. Her conscience would be a lot lighter after she told Brant the truth, even though she knew what his reaction would be. It would be easier to handle Brant in marriage overdrive than continuing to keep this secret. She closed her eyes, almost looking forward to the next twenty-four hours.

For Cami's sake, she hoped the wedding would be a dream come true.

## Chapter Fourteen

As Dan's best man, Brant stood at the altar, his gaze moving over Cami's face, and then Grace's. Whatever had been bothering Grace last night appeared to have dissipated. She looked soft and lovely in a pink dress. It was long and beaded, and had a short jacket over it, which for some reason, did an excellent job of concealing her pregnancy. The wedding in the chapel was a private family affair, and Brant couldn't help being glad about that for Grace's sake. Though about twenty-five people were in the chapel, he felt as if the situation was less awkward for Grace this way. By the glow on Cami's and Dan's faces, he suspected they enjoyed saying their vows with only their family and closest friends surrounding them.

Grace took Cami's bouquet from her, so that Dan could slide the ring on her finger. Brant's heart swelled with pride as he watched. His little sister had chosen a fine man to be her husband. Brant hoped that any lingering doubt Dan might have had about his welcome into the family had been dispelled last night at the bachelor party. Though he hadn't been exactly slobbering drunk, Brant had gotten loose enough to apologize for his shotgun approach to making certain Dan intended to marry his sister. He thought Dan had received the apology very well.

After the bachelor party, Brant had slowly driven home,

lost in his thoughts. In the lonely, dark streets of Fairhaven, he'd stopped his truck in front of Carpenter's Jewelry Store, his gaze tired but focused. After a moment, he'd circled back around the square, past the Wedding Wonderland, to Grace's house. He'd let his truck idle a moment as he stared up at her darkened windows. Everything had been quiet, and he'd hoped she was getting plenty of rest.

The minister's voice jerked him out of his reverie. With a start, he realized the couple had just been announced as husband and wife. Cami and Dan turned, so Grace bent to straighten the train as the bridal couple walked back up the aisle. Brant winced. The sight of Grace bending over that way looked painful. Gently he took her arm and helped her up before escorting her behind Cami and Dan.

And then it was over. Brant breathed a deep sigh of relief out in the May twilight. Well-wishers thronged around Cami and Dan. Somebody gave Brant a good pounding between his shoulder blades.

"Hey!" Sheriff John exclaimed. "Your feet didn't catch on fire at the altar, Brant! That has to be a good sign."

"Shut up, John," Brant groused. "If I was you, I'd be careful about what I was dishing out. One of these days, you might find yourself in a monkey suit like this and listening to the organ-grinder."

"Uh-uh." He gave Brant a sly nudge. "I did see you giving Grace the look-see a bunch. Maybe going through a marriage ceremony'll get her warmed up for one of her own."

Brant shifted his gaze over to where Grace was being helped into a waiting limo. "Hey, there goes my ride." He pulled at the stiff collar once before thumping John on the back. "You're going to be my best man, John, when I get Grace up there. If anybody needs a warming up, it's you." He pointed a good-natured finger at the sheriff before he jogged to the limo and jumped in next to Grace.

"Hey, gorgeous," he said.

She laughed outright. "Oh, Brant. Don't lay it on so thick."

"I meant it. Have we got this ride all to ourselves?" He gave her a meaningful look. "'Cause if we do, I've got a good mind to give the limo driver something to listen to." Before Grace could react, he blew disgusting, noisy raspberries against her neck.

"Ugh!" She playfully pushed Brant away. "You are in way too good a mood, Brant. What did you get into last night?"

"A little too much beer and nothing else." He leaned his head against the seat, eyeing the partition between them and the driver. "Would you believe I'm getting old? Dan holds more beer than I do."

"Yuck. That's not a product of being old. That's a typical reaction to a man who's getting married in twenty-four hours. They're looking for a comatose state so they can endure the fact that they're actually saying a willing 'yes' to lifelong imprisonment."

The smile slid right off Brant's face as he turned to look at her. "Grace, I wouldn't need a comatose state."

She stared at him before dropping her eyelashes to hide her thoughts. The seat across from them was suddenly filled with yards of white satin and laughing bridal couple.

"We're going to have to ride up to the ranch with you two," Cami informed them. "Sorry, but the wedding limo has broken down. Is that bad luck?"

Grace shook her head. "I think the only bad luck that affects a wedding day is if the groom doesn't show up for the ceremony."

Instinctively her gaze met Brant's startled one.

Dan banged on the glass partition. "Get this buggy hauling, driver! I got a garter to get off my wife's leg!"

"Oh, for heaven's sake," Cami laughed. "Use the speaker, honey." She shook her head patiently at her new husband's antics.

Brant leaned back as the limo pulled away from the church. Out the window, Cami yelled happily that she'd see all the guests at the Double D. Dan pressed a wildly rambunctious kiss against Cami's cheek.

"Be careful of my veil, honey!" Cami admonished him, but he completely ignored her, pulling her into his lap for a smacking kiss that she seemed only too happy to participate in.

Brant turned to roll his eyes at Grace, but she was looking out the other window. It made him wonder if she was enjoying this wedding circus. He expected her to look wistful, maybe even envious.

Actually, though she obviously was happy for Cami, she seemed plainly immune to the event itself.

More to the point, she seemed completely immune to *him.*

THE GUESTS MILLED through the Durning house and over the grounds, apparently thrilled with the wedding buffet goodies the Yellowjacket Cafe had provided. Grace wasn't sure how Maggie had managed to do this much. She wandered over to her friend to compliment her.

"This is delicious, Maggie," she told her, gesturing with the plate she'd emptied. "You did a wonderful job." Her gaze swept the outdoor buffet tables, which were draped with tulle and flowers and lots of steaming food.

"Thanks, Grace. You just remember that when it's time to put out some calls for bids on your wedding." Maggie gave her a playful smile.

Grace's stomach pitched. "I think you're safe for a long time, Maggie. But I wouldn't dream of not throwing my business your way. After all, one day I'll probably be fitting *you* for a wedding gown, won't I?"

"Touché." Her friend looked pensive for a moment. "I'll tell you a secret, if you promise not to tell a soul. *Not a soul.*"

"I promise." She turned curious eyes on Maggie.

"I mean it, because this would really hurt John's feelings." At Grace's reassuring nod, Maggie said, "John asked me to marry him a long time ago. He's always wanted to get married."

Grace's jaw dropped. "What's all this macho posturing about never getting to the altar all about?"

Maggie shrugged. "Saving face, I guess. You tell a man no, and what're they supposed to do? Tell all his friends you turned him down?" She turned over some fruit on the buffet, making sure it was chilling evenly. "I don't mind his blustering, anyway. It suits me for folks to think he's the one who doesn't want to get hitched." She met Grace's eyes. "It ain't good to have a man's pride beat down."

Grace hardly knew what to say. "Maggie Mason! I can't believe you've kept this a secret from me all this time."

"I bet you'll be hearing that yourself from Brant before the night's over." Maggie's gaze slid meaningfully toward Brant, who was introducing his mother and her new husband to some guests.

Grace didn't want to think about that right now. Her stomach turned again, painfully. "How did you get all this done, Maggie? The ice sculptures are stunning, the decorations are perfect—"

"I leased out for the ice sculptures, and I hired extra help for the food and decorations. I intended to be mostly a guest tonight, and enjoy being with my friends. Don't change the subject." At Grace's guilty expression, she said, "I just want you to be prepared, Grace. I think Brant's going to be a bit hot that you kept the truth from him."

"I had my reasons." She felt like crying. It was true, but she dreaded the moment.

"Don't let it go any longer than this weekend, Grace." Maggie rubbed her back soothingly. "I'm sure I'll hear the blowup clean over at my place."

"I hope I'm not interrupting anything, ladies." Brant

came to stand beside Grace, and she instantly stiffened with dread. "You two look so serious, I wanted to remind you that this is a joyous occasion. Maggie, the guests are raving about the food. I appreciate you doing this on short notice for us."

"You're welcome, Brant." Maggie shot Grace a warning glance as she moved away, saying, "I was happy to do it. Anytime."

Maggie's absence left Grace standing with a handsome Brant. She couldn't have imagined he would look so attractive in a formal tux, but the dark color set off the blackness of his hair and the deep blue of his eyes. Why had this man always been the only one who could set her heart to thundering?

"Let's take a walk, Grace." Brant took her arm gently, leading her away from the wedding party. "It's such a nice night, and I haven't spent two seconds alone with you."

Her guilty conscience sent prickles throughout her stomach, though she allowed him to lead her toward a paddock. "Cami lucked into wonderful weather for an outdoor wedding," she remarked, telling herself to keep her voice slow and steady.

He drew her to him as he leaned against a split rail fence. Tucking a strand of hair behind her ear that a mischievous May breeze was tugging at, Brant looked into her eyes. Grace's heart rate picked up enough that it was hard to breathe.

"Grace, I couldn't help thinking about us while we were standing at the altar tonight. I don't want to wait any longer to marry you." He hesitated, before saying, "The longer we wait, the more gossip it's going to cause. And I really believe that our place is with each other."

Putting a finger over her lips to stop her protest, Brant said, "You have every right to be sore at me for what I said in the hotel in New York. I didn't mean that I was going to have to marry you, but my mouth spoke before my brain had a chance to operate. And I know I'm not saying all this as pretty as it should be, but Grace, I want you.''

Before she could react, he'd leaned his head forward, touching his lips to hers. Grace could do nothing but close her eyes and enjoy the kiss. It felt so good when he slid his arms around her, deepening the kiss. The sun was going down, sending gentle rays of heat upon them, and she could hear distant birds cawing at each other—and ringing in her ears. Sighing, she leaned into him, her hands automatically reaching to hold him closer to her.

Far-off laughter from the party guests floated their way. Brant gently broke off the kiss, his smile reluctant as he stared down at her. ''Sounds like somebody else has decided to find a moment alone together.''

She could barely nod as she ever so slightly separated herself from him.

''So, what's it going to be, Grace?''

Keeping her eyes trained on the starched shirt of his tux, Grace shook her head. ''Brant, I'm sorry. I can't even think about anything like marriage right now.''

Taking her chin between his fingers, Brant tipped her head to look into her eyes. ''When do you think you will be able to? We don't have a whole lot of time, Grace.''

They had less than he knew. Unhappily she stepped away from him, brushing at her skirt. ''I've done a lot of thinking about it this week, Brant. I don't know why. Maybe it was seeing you and Cami so upset about your folks. It might have been...other things going through my mind. But I know that I can't marry you. Not now.''

She shook her head at him before he could interrupt. ''It's not a matter anymore of whether or not you would have ever asked me. It's knowing that it would hurt me too much when you decide you can't handle being tied down. Wait. Hear me out,'' she said in defense of the explosion she could feel he was about to have. ''You and Cami have been the most miserable people this week because your parents were coming, and they weren't arriving as a couple. It hurt *me* just to watch the two of you suffer so much, Brant!''

She cast pleading eyes on him, seeing the mutinous look growing there. "Please, Brant. Think ahead. If you feel it's going to be hard on the baby if his parents don't get married, think about how much worse it's going to be if we don't *stay* married." Taking a deep breath, she said, "In light of the fact that you just recently found out you are going to be a father, my gut feeling is that you're rushing to make things right, and that you might regret it later." She backed away from him slowly. "Let's take a little more time to think about this, okay? A little more time to smooth over some of the rough spots."

He advanced on her. "How much time?"

Thinking guiltily of her due date, Grace turned her head and began heading toward the house. He caught up, grabbing her arm to slow her down. "How much time?"

"I'm...not sure. We'll know when the time is right," she stammered.

He pulled her to a complete stop. "I'm going to have to think about this, Grace Barclay. I have the strangest feeling you're putting me off. For the life of me, I can't figure out why."

"I told you," she insisted.

His eyes narrowed and he released her. "Don't forget I'm driving you home tonight, Grace. Don't you dare find a way to disappear on me. You and I are not through talking."

He tapped her lips lightly with a finger, before slipping an arm through hers to escort her back to the party. Grace pasted a happy smile on her face, but the truth was, she felt ill. Near the buffet tables, Maggie sent her a questioning look. Grace shook her head, receiving a you-gotta-tell-him eyebrow raise from her friend.

She'd had all she could stand. Depositing Brant near guests she knew he would have to speak to, she headed into the house. Running up the stairs to the room where she had dressed for the wedding that afternoon, she closed the door and threw herself on the bed.

Cheerful voices floated in through the window, but Grace closed her eyes. She'd had all the wedding euphoria she could stand for tonight. She was delighted for Cami's sake, but Grace knew her moment of reckoning would arrive with the tossing of the birdseed on the departing bride and groom.

GRACE MUST HAVE SLEPT, because all of sudden Cami was shaking her awake.

"Grace! Are you all right?" Cami's distressed face was so at odds with the beauty of the wedding veil above it that Grace felt terrible for upsetting her friend.

"I'm fine." She pushed herself to a sitting position. "I just got tired and came up here for a nap."

"It's a good thing you did, but you missed out on the cake! Oh, well, there's lots left." Cami gave her a playful pat on the arm. "Are you up to getting me out of this dress? It's time."

"Time!" She lumbered off the bed. "Goodness! Turn around so I can unbutton your dress."

While Grace worked on the back, Elsa Durning entered the room, going without a word to unpin the veil from Cami's hair. "I don't think I've ever seen a prettier veil, Cami," she murmured. "You are a lovely bride."

"Thanks, Mom." In the mirror, Grace could see Cami's eyes glowing with happiness. "Grace insisted on this veil."

Elsa met Grace's eyes without hesitation. Unspoken thoughts lay in Elsa's eyes, which Grace could read very well. Now was not the time, but she realized Elsa was not leaving Fairhaven without having a talk with her. Grace sighed, knowing she would do no less if she were in Elsa's shoes.

"It's lovely, Grace," Elsa commented without any inflection. "Thank you for helping my daughter."

Between them, they wiggled Cami out of her dress and undergarments. "That reminds me!" she exclaimed. "I have something for you, Grace."

Cami hurried over to her dresser and took a small, silver-wrapped box out of a drawer. "Here," she said, handing the tiny package to Grace. "For the world's greatest maid of honor."

Tears sprang into Grace's eyes. "I didn't do that much, Cami."

"Well, open it!"

Grace met Elsa's eyes over the box. Though Grace felt that they should be dressing Cami for her no doubt impatient groom, Elsa seemed to be waiting to see what the box contained. Hurriedly she unwrapped the box and gasped.

"Oh, Cami! You shouldn't have." Grace adored the gold circle pin, surrounded with tiny pearls. "I love it!" She leaned to give Cami a hug, careful of both their stomachs. The women laughed, and Cami took the pin from her to attach it to Grace's dress.

"There." She shrugged at Grace. "I hope it brings you good luck and the same happiness I've found."

It was plain that Cami was wishing Grace good luck with working everything out with Brant. Considering her condition, Grace blushed a little under Elsa's watchful eyes. "Thank you, Cami."

Quickly Elsa and Grace finished dressing Cami. Without further delay, the bride hugged them both, then ran down the stairs to meet her groom. Laughing, the other two women followed. Cami ran to kiss her father, and then Brant. Someone pressed a tulle birdseed bag into Grace's hand, and she joined in throwing it on the departing couple. For the first time, sentimental tears jumped into Grace's eyes as the limo pulled away, with Cami and Dan waving goodbye.

"That's that, I guess," she murmured to herself.

A gentle, but determined hand closed around her upper arm. "Not quite," said Elsa Durning.

## Chapter Fifteen

"If you have a moment, Grace, I would like to speak with you."

Grace sighed inwardly, recognizing Durning determination in Elsa's eyes. "All right."

Elsa took her into a parlor room off the hall, motioning her to take a seat. Reluctantly Grace complied.

"Grace, I guess I feel that before I go, I should welcome you into the family. Whether or not you and Brant ever marry is a personal decision the two of you will have to deal with, but married or not, you are still carrying my grandchild.

She paused, giving Grace a chance to register her words. "If there is anything I can do to help you, I hope that you'll feel free to ask me."

"There isn't, but I appreciate your offer." She couldn't meet the older woman's eyes with comfort.

"I see. Well, I suppose I'm not far off the mark to suggest that I'll be returning to Fairhaven in a few weeks."

She directed a pointed stare at Grace's stomach, telling her silently that she might have fooled Brant, but his mother wasn't as gullible. Grace didn't offer a denial of Elsa's statement. "Will you have help of any kind with the baby?"

"My sister, Hope, is coming to stay with me."

"For a few days?"

"For the summer. I'll need help running the shop for a while, and also taking care of the baby."

"Hmm." Elsa's eyebrows raised. "If you have Hope living with you, obviously you and Brant are not planning on a household arrangement other than the one you have right now."

She was asking, basically, if the two of them were planning to live together. Grace couldn't blame Brant's mother for being curious, especially as the two of them weren't planning the same sentimental wedding Cami and Dan had chosen.

"No. I'm sure Brant has his hands full with the ranch, and I like where I live."

"Well." Mrs. Durning stood. "Certainly things have changed since I was a girl. I don't know what to make of everything, to be honest." Her gray-blue eyes, a more faded version of Brant's, looked at Grace without a hint of disapproval. "Expecting two grandbabies in the same year has me flustered, not to mention the unusual circumstances. But," she said with a shake of her head, "maybe it's better for you young people to be sure you know your mind. Divorce is difficult. If you honestly feel that you and Brant are not meant to be together, then perhaps you are being wise and mature." She pursed her lips before looking steadfastly at Grace. "However, the fact that you will not join the Durning family in name doesn't mean that I will think less of, nor spend less time with, this particular grandchild. I hope you will understand when I return in, what, two weeks?"

Her guess was a calculated question. "Yes," Grace replied, knowing she had to be truthful with Elsa.

"I will want to see my grandchild. I will probably be underfoot. If the mountain will not come to Mohammed, I will be at your house every day with a burp cloth in my hand. It will not be to press you about Brant, because I intend to stay out of your business. But please," she said softly, her eyes earnest, "let me know my grandchild."

Tears sprang into Grace's eyes. "You're welcome at my house anytime."

"Thank you," Elsa whispered. Without warning, she drew Grace into a hug, startling her. "I've known your family for a long time, Grace. I'd love to treat you like a daughter now."

"I'd like that." More than anything, Grace appreciated Elsa's kindness. She had been so afraid of the unknown; now she could relax knowing that no matter what, she and her baby wouldn't be outcasts for not making a desperate dash to the altar.

"Elsa!" Dr. Nelson entered the room, knocking on the wood paneling to announce his arrival. "I've been looking all over for you. I was afraid you'd holed up somewhere, crying sentimental tears over Cami leaving."

"No." Elsa sniffled, but offered him a smile. "What's to cry about that?"

"I don't know." He looked from Grace to Elsa. "I thought perhaps because your only daughter just left the nest."

"Oh, but she didn't," Elsa said with a meaningful look at Grace. "Come on, Bob. It's time to say good-night to the guests."

AN HOUR LATER, Grace stood waiting in the hallway for Brant to take her home. She had helped Maggie put trays and food away, despite her protests. Finally Brant told her in no uncertain terms to go get her things. Grace had been glad to acquiesce, realizing that the euphoria of a lovely wedding was wearing off and she simply needed to get home.

"I think that's everyone," Brant said, coming to join her in the hallway. Bob and Elsa had made their way upstairs, the last guest was gone and it was just the two of them standing under the foyer chandelier. "Mission accomplished."

"Yes." She offered him a tentative smile.

"You know," he said, cocking his head to listen, "this house already sounds different."

"What do you mean?"

"It's...silent."

"It is after midnight," Grace said softly.

"No, it's not that. I think—" Brant hesitated, looking over his shoulder. "I'm used to listening for Cami. She's usually got the TV running, or a radio going full-blast on a country and western station, or something mixing in the kitchen. But it's...quiet now."

"You're going to miss her, aren't you?" Grace felt a sympathetic twinge for this big macho man who had just watched his sister leave.

"Well, it won't be the Double D Ranch anymore," he said, trying to sound matter-of-fact. She heard the strain in his voice, and knew he was trying to underplay his feelings. "It'll be just a single D. One Durning. No plural, unless, of course, you've changed your mind?"

"I don't think so, Brant." Her eyes lowered to the marble floor beneath her feet.

"Come on, then," he said gruffly. "I'll take you home."

They were silent on the return drive. She couldn't help thinking that life had changed very fast for Brant; he was going to have a lot to get used to very soon. Without his sister around to poke at him, he was going to have way too much time to brood. He was probably too keyed up after the wedding to be able to sleep tonight. She certainly was.

As he pulled in the driveway in back of her house, Grace took a deep breath and a plunge she hadn't planned on. "Would you like to come in for a nightcap?"

Surprise lifted his brows. "Really?"

"Yes, really." Grace smiled at him. "I can't bear to think of you all alone at your house tonight."

"I won't be alone," he grumbled. "It's hard as hell to think about Bob and Mom sleeping upstairs together."

She had forgotten all about that. "Well, come on in. I'll get you a fortifying beer."

Sliding out of the truck, she heard him following behind her. They went inside her house, and Grace flipped on a few lights as she walked through to the kitchen. "Oh, I'm glad to be home," she murmured. Grabbing him a beer out of the fridge that had been left from the previous weekend's barbecue, she said, "Make yourself comfortable. I'm going to change out of this dress, if you don't mind."

"Take your time." Brant accepted the beer and walked into the den where they'd unwrapped the bassinet last weekend. "I was sure glad to get out of my monkey suit."

"Brant." Grace laughed. "How could you call that exquisite tuxedo such a thing? Cami worked hard choosing an outfit that would complement your masculine image."

"What's that supposed to mean?"

She laughed again as she headed up the stairs. "Originally she picked out baby blue for her wedding colors. You would have worn a silver suit—"

"Over my dead body," Brant yelled up after her.

"She said that would be your reaction." Grace grinned as she unzipped her dress. Slipping into an oversize shirt and baggy shorts, she breathed a deep sigh of relief. It wasn't true, of course, about the silver tux, but she and Cami had enjoyed a good laugh over austere Brant wearing one. Brushing the hair spray from her hair, Grace let it fall soft and loose around her face, not even wanting a rubber band pulling at her after being in panty hose all day.

"Maternity panty hose is a cruel and unusual punishment," she muttered as she went downstairs. Getting a cold glass of water from the tap, she joined Brant in the living room. "Sausage casings would be more comfortable."

She hadn't sat close to him, so he scooted closer to her. Grace leaned into him, suddenly too tired and too needful of his strength to pull away. "Your mother and I had a nice talk tonight."

"Hmm. I should have warned you. I got mine last night. Grace," he said, tipping her head back so he could look into her eyes, "this is our decision. Mom means well, but I'm willing to go at your pace for a while longer, if need be."

"Really?"

"Yes. Really." He leaned to drop a soft kiss against her lips. "I'm not happy about it," he murmured. "I'm old-fashioned enough to believe that being a father means I ought to be a husband, too. But I'm not going anywhere, Grace. Not this time."

She moaned under his lips as he kissed her again. He traveled from her lips over to her cheeks, and down her neck. One hand pressed at her back to support her, the other pushed her hair gently from her face. The kiss left her breathless, and wanting. She had wanted this man for so long. "Stay the night," she whispered.

Hesitating, Brant checked her expression. "I can sleep on the sofa, if you just don't want to be alone tonight."

"You'll like my bed better."

"I know, but—" Brant took her hand and pressed it to his lips. "Are you sure?"

"I'm sure." Grace rose, pulling him with her. "This feels very right to me."

He allowed her to pull him up the stairs into the bedroom, where only the small nightstand lamp sent comforting light into the darkness. She leaned against him, this time wrapping her arms around his neck to join them together for a long kiss.

"Oh, Grace," he murmured against her mouth. "Won't I hurt you? Or the baby?"

"Not if we're careful."

He glanced at the double bed doubtfully. "I'm not sure

this is a good idea. There isn't room for three in that bed. We might squash him.''

She laughed softly, her fingers nimbly unbuttoning the casual Western shirt he wore. Guiding his hands to her T-shirt, Grace silently showed him that everything was going to be fine. Very carefully, he removed her top, running his hands along the smoothness of her back.

''Grace, you feel so good,'' he said on a husky whisper. ''As crazy as it sounds, I remember your skin being this silky. You feel just the same.''

''Just bigger,'' she murmured.

He chuckled, undoing her bra and sliding that off, too. Taking his time, he kissed his way down to her breasts. ''Maybe.''

''Maybe!'' Grace laughed, giving him a gentle push onto the bed. ''Brant Durning, I'm a lot bigger up top.''

''It's kind of...interesting,'' he said, catching her to him.

She felt her skin heating wherever he kissed her. Without worry that he wouldn't find her attractive, Grace slid out of her shorts, and helped him take off the rest of his clothes.

''So that's the baby,'' he said, his eyes wide as he ran one hand over her stomach. ''Made himself right at home, little dickens. I don't believe there's another spare inch in there.''

Reality swiftly intruded. She opened her mouth to tell him the truth, but he was putting sweet kisses on her stomach before kissing her lips again. Sighing with happiness, she gave herself up into the wonder of being in Brant's arms again.

Pleasure cascaded over her as they joined together. ''I've missed you so much,'' she whispered.

''I was wrong, Grace.'' He moved inside her, burying his face in her hair. ''I shouldn't have acted the way I did.''

''Shh. Let's not think about that right now.'' She couldn't. She didn't want to. Spasms built inside her, and she clung to Brant's strong-muscled back in wonder.

"Oh, Brant..."

Her moan was against his mouth as he took her lips with fast, passionate kisses. "Oh, Brant!"

It just about killed him, but he stopped. "Am I hurting you?"

She shook her head wildly. "Don't stop," she begged.

He allowed himself to relax at her words. Stunned by the force building inside him, he felt Grace's climax, and that was all it took to send him over the edge into her arms.

They lay together, enjoying the feeling of being entwined.

"I've missed you," he told her, rolling gently to one side so he wouldn't crush her or the baby. "I never forgot how wonderful you feel when we make love."

Unease tugged at Grace. It had been more than wonderful; there had been an emotional power in their lovemaking that had been stronger than anything she'd ever felt. Maybe it was the baby making her sentimental. Maybe it was the joy of being with Brant again. But for now, she couldn't bear to spoil the beauty of the moment.

In the morning, she would tell him the truth.

IN THE MORNING, Grace rose and got dressed, admiring Brant as he slept in her canopied bed. She went downstairs and fixed some breakfast, still glowing from last night. If only...if only there wasn't one major problem in their way.

"Good morning," a voice said, just as warm arms encircled her. She squealed, jumping.

"Brant! I didn't hear you come down."

He grinned, more handsome than ever with his black hair tousled from sleep and his blue eyes lit with playful laughter. "You were obviously somewhere else."

Handing him a glass of orange juice and a plate of toast, she ushered him into the living room.

"Hey, I peeked into the nursery. Looks great. Maggie and Tilly can do just about anything, can't they?"

"Yes." They could, but nobody could help her with what needed to be done now. "Brant, we have to talk."

"Talk?" His expression was instantly wary. "It's not the baby—"

"It isn't anything to do with the baby. Well, it is, a little," she added hastily.

"Why don't you just say what's on your mind?" he asked quietly. "Obviously this is delicate subject matter. I'm listening."

"Brant, I didn't tell you the truth about my due date." Uncomfortably she watched his expression change to disbelief as his gaze ricocheted from her face to her stomach.

"Was my mother right?"

She nodded. "If she told you I'm due sooner than later, she was right."

He put the glass of orange juice back on the table. "How soon?"

"Maybe two weeks."

"Two weeks! Grace Barclay, what about last night?"

"Last night was wonderful."

"I know that, but we could have put the baby at risk!"

"Dr. Delancey said making love was fine as long as I felt good."

"I just got back last month! Why would he have been discussing sex with you?"

"It's probably something all doctors mention to their pregnant patients, along with the rest of the laundry list they have."

Jumping to his feet, he paced the room. "Why didn't you tell me the truth?"

Grace rubbed her hands over her wrists nervously. "I didn't want you to feel pressured. Not any more than you did."

"Pressured! Who feels pressured?" He paced a few more times. "I do. I feel pressured! You said we had a couple of months."

"I know. I'm sorry."

"And I said—" Brant ignored her "—I said I was willing to go at your pace."

"That's right. I didn't want to have to speed anything up."

"I don't think we have to worry about that, Grace. If you're going to have that baby any day now, the time for pacing ourselves is past."

"No, it's not. That's exactly what I wanted to avoid. Brant, my feelings haven't changed."

His jaw jutted, his expression turning stubborn. "I can't believe I'm hearing this."

"Look." A defensive streak hit her out of nowhere. "I waited for you to ask me to marry you. I knew I was pregnant. By the third month, when I knew I couldn't wait much longer before I started showing, I mentioned marriage. I got a good look at your backside rushing from my bedroom for my trouble. Six months later you resurface, discover you're going to be a father, and expect me to gladly march down the aisle."

"Grace! It wasn't the way it's done. The man is supposed to ask the woman!"

"Oh, pardon me if I intruded on some medieval tenet of the Chauvinist Bylaws," she spat. "I didn't realize I was intruding on your sense of correctness by inquiring as to whether your intentions were honorable, Brant Durning. Of course, if we're going to reach that far back into etiquette past, you should have asked me to marry you *before* you made love to me."

"My intentions were always honorable!"

"Oh, I see. You intended to marry me all the time. You just didn't want to talk about it."

"I—I," he sputtered. "I hadn't thought about it, Grace. But my intentions were honorable!"

She hurt, just as much as she had when he'd walked out several months ago. He wasn't about to see her point at all, which was why she couldn't just fall in with what he wanted now. "You have something very basic confused here, Brant, but it doesn't matter. I'm sorry if it's inconvenient that our baby is coming a few weeks earlier than you'd gotten used to—"

"A few weeks!"

She ignored the interruption. "But you have just proved my case all over again. Instantly you want to leap into the courthouse to buy a marriage license, because you've discovered Junior's on the way. Well, I'm not going." With a taut sob, she instinctively covered her stomach with her hand, as if to apologize to the life inside her for having to hear its parents argue so bitterly. "What you're asking me is to take you back, Brant. The problem is, we can't go backward."

"I don't like any of this, Grace." He grabbed his keys, which he'd thrown on the coffee table last night. "I'm going to have to think about this. Obviously I wasn't prepared to be lied to. You'd already deceived me, Lord only knows when you'd intended to tell me about my child. I'm sorry, but all I know is, I gotta have some fresh air."

He jogged upstairs to get the rest of his clothes, hurrying back down to stalk to the door. "I'll pick you up for dinner tonight, when your shop closes. You and I have a lot to talk about, I think it's safe to say."

"Fine!" Hurt, anxious, self-righteous tears stung her eyes.

"Fine." He shot her a hard look, one that contained disbelief and betrayal, and closed the door behind him.

It was too much for Grace. She hurried up the stairs and flung herself onto the bed. The sound of his truck engine being gunned flooded through her window, before she heard it pull down the driveway.

Brant was furious. She had known he would be. Between now and dinnertime, she needed to think of a way to salvage this mess.

She still couldn't say yes, though right now, she doubted very much if Brant would be interested in restating his offer.

"THAT COTTON-PICKIN' WOMAN," Brant grumbled to a sympathetic Maggie and John. "She's got me tied in so many knots, I feel like a lariat."

"Love's a many-splendored thing," Maggie said sympathetically, "but only if it's working out for ya."

"It hasn't ever worked out for me where Grace is concerned."

That bothered him. It really did. He wasn't the kind, sensitive type of individual she seemed to want. Self-pity filled him. "Heckfire! Grace knew what I was about when she got involved with me. I asked her out, you know, but she didn't have to say yes."

"Probably shouldn't have," Maggie told him.

"I'll tell you something." He looked up to meet the warm acceptance in his friends' eyes. "I'm glad about the baby. I'm real glad about it. I may not be beans as a date, but I'll be a great father. I've decided to." He might make some mistakes along the parenting line, but he wasn't going to struggle with it the way his father had. When the boy needed a pat on the back, Brant was going to give it to him. Then an extra one, just in case there was any misunderstanding of how proud he was of his child.

"Don't say that, Brant." Maggie squeezed his arm. "You're a good man. You and Grace just went at this a little crossways. It'll all work out, I'm sure it will."

"Yeah. Well, I'm not so sure." He got heavily to his feet. "I'm off. I just wanted to stop in and thank you for all your help with Cami's wedding before I got on home to my chores."

John and Maggie nodded as he walked to the door. "See ya, Purvis, Buzz."

The men mumbled a goodbye at him without their customary enthusiasm. They barely glanced up from their checkerboard. Brant's heart sank. Nobody seemed to know what to say to him. Even he didn't know what to say about the problem he had on his hands.

SOMETIME BETWEEN the time Brant was picking up litter that had floated down from the party into the pastures, and the time he was making his bed, he discerned one important thing. Grace wanted him in her life, that was clear from last night. They were going to be together forever, whether they were married or not, though he didn't think that should be the case. But with the baby coming, she would need help.

She was going to need *him*. That necessitated a gift, a practical gift, that a woman like Grace clearly would understand was a peace offering. She would clearly know that, for now, he was still trying to be utmost patient with her.

That was one thing he knew he had to be. Brant had gone to the bookstore this morning after he'd stopped at the Yellowjacket, and bought out half the titles on expecting a baby. Each and every one of the first chapters of those books preached the rewards a man could reap if he was patient and sensitive to his partner's needs. Apparently a pregnant woman had so many different changes going on inside her body that the rest of her life needed to stay on as even a keel as possible.

That sounded reasonable to Brant. Though patience wasn't his strong suit—especially now that the window of opportunity had closed up on him significantly, he could be supportive. He could be helpful.

To Brant, the way was clear. Grace needed a bigger bed.

## Chapter Sixteen

Brant made sure he picked Grace up on time at the Wedding Wonderland. She didn't seem pleased to see him as he poked his head in the shop, but he told himself that within the next half hour, everything would be smoothed over between them.

"Ready?" he asked her.

"Let me lock up." Her back was stiff, her eyes unwelcoming.

"Are you hungry?"

She didn't turn to look at him. "A little, but I'd like to change before we go out. If that's all right with you."

"I'm in no rush." Actually, it might even work in with his plans.

They drove in silence to Grace's house. She hopped out and went to the back door. "That's strange," she murmured. "I know I locked this door when I left."

He shrugged, his expression innocent. "I read that pregnant women can start getting forgetful, they've got so much on their minds thinking about the baby and all."

She gave him a narrow glance but said nothing as she went inside.

"Do you want me to check around and make sure there's no burglars?"

"No, thanks. I must have just forgotten to lock the

door," she called, heading up the stairs. "I'll just be a second."

Exactly one second later a blood-curdling shriek resounded from upstairs. Brant shot up the staircase and hurried to Grace.

She was staring at a California king-size bed. It took up nearly every inch of her bedroom, which meant there'd be plenty of room for him, Grace and Brant Junior.

He glanced at Grace. Her mouth twitched spasmodically, but no sound was coming out. Of course, the bed was completely bare of sheets. Brant hadn't had time to make it. By the horrified look on Grace's face, he wondered belatedly if he should have taken the time to do so. "Do you like it?"

Grace leaned against the wall, her eyes riveted to the bed. "What in the world is that awful thing? Did you do this, Brant Wyndford Durning?"

"Yes." His heart sank at her adjective. "You don't like it."

"Where is my bed?" Those hazel eyes of hers looked like chips of uncrackable ice.

"In the nursery," he said practically. "The baby can sleep in it when he's bigger."

"This is the ugliest thing I ever saw!" she said between gritted teeth. "What could possibly have possessed you to think I would want such a monstrosity?"

"Grace, you're going to need help with the baby." His tone was reasoning, placating, as he might speak to a mare gone wild. "Now, I understand that you're not ready to come to terms with getting to the altar, and in your condition, I can see why you'd want to wait. But I need to be here to help you."

"My sister will be here," Grace hissed.

Brant didn't see that as a problem at all. "She'll need someplace to sleep, then. Might as well be close to the baby."

"I don't think you're hearing me, Brant Durning," Grace said, her hands on her hips. "You can't just move in here. Making love last night was not an invitation to move your boots under my bed permanently."

"Wait a minute, Grace." Brant tried to control the anger that wanted to surface, but the woman was confusing him. "We're having a baby. That means our lives are connected for the rest of our days. Now, I'm trying to understand your reasons for not wanting to marry me. I'm really trying to be patient." He drew in a deep, calming breath. "I *really* am. But you cannot expect me to jump in the sack with you every time the urge hits you, then kick me out every morning. We need more of a relationship than that. *I* need more."

"How dare you?" Grace advanced on him to jab a finger against his shoulder in feminine rage. "You sneak into my house without my permission to have the most atrocious bed I've ever seen delivered so we can have a relationship? This bed," she shrieked, gathering steam, "no doubt, was trundled past the Yellowjacket and parked outside my house for everyone in Fairhaven *to see what the father of my child thinks enough of me to consider a gift?*"

The last words sounded like a near-scream. Brant reminded himself that the books called for patience. Trying again, he said, "I thought you didn't care about gossip." She had reprimanded him for caring too much about what people thought several times. "Besides, when the baby is born, I'm afraid I'll roll over on him."

"I hadn't planned on three of us sleeping in a bed!" Grace retorted.

His mouth fell open as the implication of her words sank in. "You don't want me to help you at night with the baby?" He couldn't comprehend that. All the baby books said the first month could be rough with extra feedings and diaper changing, and maybe even colic. Brant knew all about colic from having horses. You had to walk those suckers, and keep walking 'em, even when you were dead-tired and the horse wanted to quit. He'd figured on doing the same with his boy.

"I will have Hope to help me." Grace bit off the words. Her expression was taut and drawn, implacable.

Full realization of what she was saying dawned unpleasantly for Brant. "You haven't planned much on me being around, have you? You've got everything taken care of."

Hurt feelings forced him to hope that Grace would smile now and say there was something in his baby's life she was counting on him helping with. When she said nothing, keeping her furious gaze locked with his, indignation blew up his pride. "All right. If that's the way you want it, Grace. Obviously this is my punishment for being unable to meet your previous timetable for a wedding." He shot her a disbelieving look over his shoulder as he headed down the stairs. "I'll call the furniture store and have the bed taken back. But I won't be calling you again. If you're determined to have this baby without me, there's not much I can do except stay out of your way."

He hurried to his truck, unable to ignore the burning in his eyes. The only place he knew to go where he could sit and be among people who at least had a kind word for him was the Yellowjacket. Parking his truck out front, he went inside, throwing himself into a booth in the back.

Maggie came over at once, closing the red wooden blinds against the last rays of afternoon summer sun. "Howdy, Brant. How's life treating you?"

"So good I'll take a glass of your tea to celebrate."

By the uh-uh rise in her eyebrows, Brant figured Maggie had heard the sarcasm in his voice. Giving him a la-di-da shake of her head, she went off to get his tea.

Sheriff John Farley cruised in the door a second later, while Brant was morosely examining the cracks in the old wooden table. He spied Brant in the back of the Cafe.

"Hey!" he shouted, taking off his hat. "Hell of an engagement ring you had delivered to Grace, Brant."

Brant let his head sink onto his palm. He refused to reply, especially with Buzz and Purvis and everyone else in the restaurant looking up at John's ribbing.

"I came here to be amongst friends," he replied sternly, "not amateur comedians."

"Naw." John slid into the booth across from him. "You came here because Grace gave you a good, swift kick in the pants. Man, are you confused." He laughed heartily at Brant's scowl. "Did it ever occur to you to buy the woman an engagement ring instead of a place to park your butt?"

"I bought one of those, too," Brant said, morosely flipping out a ring box. "The woman hasn't been in the mood to accept it, yet. Keeps telling me that she won't marry me." He set the velvet ring box on the table between them and sighed deeply, running a hand through his hair in agitation. "The baby books say I need to be patient. I'm trying, I really am. It's just so hard."

Maggie walked over with the tea, instantly snatching the box up the second her eyes lit on it. Flipping it open, she gasped at what lay inside. John craned to look at it, too.

"Damn, Brant," he said, "there's a difference between patience and idiocy. That diamond would have got you a yes out of Grace for sure."

He shook his head. "You don't know Grace. Once she makes up her mind, it's made up. There aren't any if, ands or buts. And if the woman says she's not saying yes, I could give her Queen Elizabeth's tiara and she'd slap it on my head, instead."

"I don't know." Maggie closed the box with a snap and put it back on the table. "Sure is a pretty ring, Brant. Gotta say you picked out a beauty, though I can't say I would have expected you to ante up for such a big one."

"Didn't want her to have less than Cami got." He scowled at the table, not seeing the cracks anymore. "Three months ago, I probably wouldn't have bought it. But I thought Dan probably knew a little bit better at romancing a woman than I did. After all, he managed to end up at the altar while I'm still wearing egg on my face.''

Maggie slid into the seat next to him. "There's no egg on your face," she said softly. "All of us around here, we think you're doing the right thing. We think you've tried awful hard to make inroads, Brant, even if your methods are a bit screwy at times.''

"Tell that to Grace. Where she's concerned, I can't do anything right.''

"No, now I can't tell Grace anything, hon. We happen to think she's done her best to cope with what she had, what she thought she was gonna have. All I'm saying," Maggie said, reaching to put a comforting hand over Brant's, "is that neither of you is wearing egg. It's gotten a little rocky for the two of you, but ain't nothing worth having if you don't have to work for it.''

Brant snorted. "Having Grace say yes without bucking me anymore would be just fine.''

Maggie patted his hand silently. John opened the box again, shaking his head as he stared at the ring. Nobody said anything, and Brant figured everything that could be said, had been.

Except yes.

MUCH TO GRACE'S DISMAY, Brant was at the Yellowjacket. She'd seen his truck parked outside. After a moment's indecision, she hurried in the door. She needed to talk to Maggie, urgently.

The Cafe owner greeted her, taking her to a booth at the front to sit. "Darn big crib Brant had delivered to your house today," she said softly.

"It's not funny, Maggie." Grace could feel Brant staring at her. She wasn't about to turn around. "Don't you even mention that horrible thing to me.''

"Aw, honey, maybe it isn't so bad."

"You haven't seen it!" Grace shook her head. "I didn't come to talk about that. I have a question."

"Coulda called me over the phone, Grace." Maggie cast worried eyes on her.

"I...knew you'd be getting busy with supper rush." Besides, Grace had desperately wanted to discuss the situation privately, where she knew kitchen help wouldn't be running around bothering Maggie.

"Maggie," she whispered, "I've got a stomachache."

Her friend pinned laser-intense eyes on her. "What kind of stomachache?"

"Just a strange...unusual stomach. I didn't think anything of it...particularly as I'd just seen Brant's delivery." Grace drew a deep breath. "I think I'm having contractions."

Maggie nodded at her struggle for definition. "That's normal. Have your waters broke?"

"No."

"All right." Maggie leaned back in the booth, her gaze flicking to the back of the Cafe. "This could be the beginning, but it still could be a day or two before anything significant starts happening."

"You don't think...I mean, Brant and I...we—"

"No." Maggie waved a hand at her dismissively. "Doubtful. Did anything hurt at the time?"

Grace shook her head. To the contrary, it had been exquisite.

"If you're real worried, you should put in a call to Dr. Delancey. It's probably a good idea, anyway, as he might want to examine you."

"Okay." Grace wasn't all that worried, now that she'd had a dose of Maggie's common sense. Excitement and anticipation had flooded her to the point that she had to talk to her friend. Now, with more rational reasoning to work with, Grace could slow down enough to think straight.

"Phone's in the kitchen," Maggie said unnecessarily.

"Thanks." Grace got up and headed to the kitchen. She caught the doctor's office just before they closed. After a moment, Dr. Delancey came on the line.

"Think you're having some signals, Grace?" he asked kindly.

"I'm not sure." Her heart was fluttering. "I've had some off and on contractions for a few days, but this started out as a stomachache, and feels like it's progressing."

"Well, calm down," he told her, much in the same tone of voice Maggie had used with her. "You're probably just at the start of things. You could come in and let me check you, but frankly, with a first child, you could still have some time. You probably want to get poked at as little as possible."

"Yes." Grace could agree to that with ease.

"It's a nice evening. Why don't you go take a nice slow walk around the square, or do something else that might take your mind off of it? Sitting and worrying's not the best thing to do right now."

"That's a good idea." Grace couldn't imagine sitting. Suddenly she realized one thousand items that had to be crossed off her to-do list before this baby could be born. "Thank you, Dr. Delancey."

"You're welcome. I'll have my pager if you have any further questions. No matter the hour, Grace, if you get concerned about anything, you just call."

"Thank you," she repeated, hanging up.

Maggie came to stand at her side. "So?"

"I'm supposed to go take my mind off of it. How in the world can I do that? I've got a million things to do!"

Maggie laughed. "First thing you better do is tell the father not to leave town."

"Oh, my gosh!" Grace had forgotten about Brant glowering in the back of the Cafe. "I guess I'd better." She glanced his way, only to snag on his gaze. "Maybe not right now," she murmured. "I'll call him later. Bye, Maggie." Hurrying to the door, she called, "Thank you!"

"You want me to come by later?"

"What for?"

"Just to check on you?" Maggie's grin was broad.

"I'm fine," Grace called. "I'll call you when I start feeling like it's getting close. Dr. Delancey said this baby might take his sweet time about getting here."

She waved and hurried out the door. Not that she didn't appreciate Maggie's offer, but there was a lot Grace wanted to think about if Brant Junior was fixing to change her world around.

First, she had to alert Hope that she might be needed sooner than later. Brant's red truck caught her eye, slowing her feet. Brant had offered to be there for her. Did it really matter whether he was in her life just because of the baby?

Wasn't it more important that he wanted to be there?

"I DON'T KNOW what to do about those two," Maggie confessed to John. "They've got themselves tied up so well they can't find a way out of the knot."

"Not our place to do anything probably." John rubbed Maggie's shoulders as she walked him out to his cruiser. "Maybe we've meddled as much as we should."

"I suppose you're right. The horses have been led to water. Goodness knows, nobody can make them drink."

"You going up to Grace's later?"

Maggie squinted that direction. "I have a feeling she won't need my coaching until the morning. She said she would call me later. I expect she just wants some time to herself."

John got into the cruiser, rolling down the window. "Did she tell Brant?"

"Nope."

He scratched the back of his neck. "Well, I'll never figure women as long as I live."

She gave him a gentle slap on the arm. "Quit trying. We don't want to be figured."

Sighing, he said, "I don't guess anybody thinks the father would be interested in knowing he better wash up tonight and get some clothes ready and all, if his baby's fixing to come looking for him?"

"Grace didn't seem disposed to say anything to him."

"One part of me says we've meddled enough, Maggie Mason. The other part says those two are so stubborn, the only thing that would keep them together long enough to talk this out would be a locked jail cell."

She gasped. "You wouldn't!"

"I could." He sighed heavily. "But I won't. Call me if you need anything." He pooched his lips out for his kiss goodbye. Maggie dropped a swift one on his mouth and hurried back inside, the idea of a jail cell intriguing her once she got past her initial shock.

"Maggie!" an insistent male voice called from the back. Brant waved at her, so with a glance at the kitchen to make sure everything was proceeding as it should be, she headed to his table.

"What was that all about?" he demanded. "And don't tell me nothing, because I've got eyes in my head."

"Really?" she retorted. "Then how come you're so blind?"

"What's that supposed to mean?" He narrowed his gaze on her. The woman was keeping something from him, that was certain. Grace had likely put her up to it.

"I can't say. I shouldn't have said that. I think I've got nerves," Maggie replied, sounding shocked at the thought. "I can't remember the last time I was nervous."

"Is my baby on the way?"

She glanced at him in surprise. "Why would you think that?"

"Grace came running in here like a wind had pushed her through the door, takes a few seconds to talk to you, then heads to the phone. Shortly thereafter, she's out of here like a shot." He wanted her to know he was paying attention. "Not a word does she say to me, the father of the child and the last person she wants to be bothered with at this moment."

"Brant, can I see you for a sec?" Grace asked, appearing from behind Maggie's broad back.

Maggie and Brant both jumped guiltily. He had never even heard the Cafe door open.

"Uh, if Miss Maggie's through bending my ear," he said, trying to save face.

Maggie backed up. "I think our discussion's finished." She headed back to the kitchen, saying, "I'll get you a glass of water, Grace. It's getting mighty warm in here."

"I'm sorry, Brant," Grace said without acknowledging Maggie's comment, nor sitting down. "I overreacted a little when I saw the bed. You're right. I can't expect you to sleep on the sofa after the baby comes. Nor should you and I be making love if I don't intend to marry you. I shouldn't have done it."

Brant's heart had soared when he realized he was the willing recipient of an apology. But it had shattered at the rest of Grace's words. Now, he could only stare at her as he tried to understand what she was truly telling him.

"That's all I have to say." Whirling around, Grace started to hurry back on her way.

Brant grabbed her wrist before she could take two steps. "Oh, no, you don't, Grace Barclay. I didn't like the sound of that. Your behavior is making me very suspicious. You have two choices. Either you tell me what's going on right here, right now, or I take you home and you tell me there. It's your choice, but either way, I'm stuck to you like glue until I know."

# Chapter Seventeen

Grace leveled Brant with her eyes, secretly pleased that he even wanted to talk to her after she'd yelled at him this afternoon. The bed had come as such a shock, she knew she hadn't been gracious in the least. She should have thanked him, before telling him to send the crazy thing back to the store.

Of course, in her heart of hearts, it hadn't been what she had been hoping Brant would one day want to give her. She dreamed of a proper proposal, a heartfelt proposal, after waiting so long to hear one from him. Now, of course, the door was about to bang shut. She was about to have their baby—and everything else would have to be incidental.

"I will let you walk me home." Delight flooded her as Brant immediately stood.

"I should drive you."

"Walking's good for me." Her stomach muscles twisted around strangely, whether from the baby or Brant's presence, Grace couldn't be sure. "Maybe I will let you drive me."

"Are you okay?" His face was concerned as they left the Cafe. Brant waved absently to all the regulars as they got into his truck, but his mind was on Grace. She hadn't answered him. She was so silent and pale that he was worried. Pulling into the driveway, he got out, walking around to help her down. "You look a bit peaked, or something. It's because I upset you, isn't it? I should have asked you, Grace. I should have—"

"I've got a little bit of an upset stomach." Grace interrupted, stopping on the sidewalk under the full, spreading limbs of an ancient oak tree. "I could be at the beginning of my labor."

"What?" Brant's face paled to match hers.

"Or I could not be," she said, turning to hurry toward her house.

"Wait just a cotton-pickin' minute here! How can you be at the beginning of labor?" He followed her breakneck pace easily.

"I'm not sure. It could be nothing."

"Grace, stop!" he roared. "Either it's labor, or it's nothing, but it can't be both. Which is it?"

"Most likely labor." She let them in the front door, running a hand over her forehead. "Whew! It's hot out there."

"You need to sit down. You need to rest. You need a glass of something cold to drink." Brant began pacing through the den after he situated her on the floral-printed divan in the den. "We need diapers. Have you gotten diapers?" At the shake of her head, he began pacing again, "We need formula. No. We're breast-feeding."

"The baby is breast-feeding," Grace reminded him wryly.

He stopped his pacing for only a split second to glance her way. Totally ignoring her attempt to tease him, he kept right on going. "Did we buy enough clothes for the baby when we were in New York?"

"I think a little pack of T-shirts in the beginning will do fine." She had to grin at Brant's lack of composure. "Brant, could you sit down for a moment? You're making me feel like I need to get up and clean out a bookcase or scrub shower walls with a toothbrush."

"You're not doing anything." He sank into a chair next

to her. "Jeez. I don't think I can do anything. My brain's just gone on the blink."

She laughed, amazed by the sight of strong, stubborn Brant completely undone by the advent of a baby. "Maybe you should go home and rest."

"I'm not leaving." He looked out a window, then crossed to another window. "Listen, you make me a list, and I'll go get whatever's needed. I'll leave long enough to do that. But I'm spending the night with you, Grace, whether it's in the big bed, the guest room, or the sofa. You might need me."

Cramps hit in the middle of her belly, and Grace shifted a bit to ease them. "Maggie's coming over."

"Fine. The whole damn cafe can come over. But I'm staying."

"I think I'd like that." Grace smiled, a trifle uneasy from the sudden shifting of a baby inside her. "This baby has usually been so active, always doing flips in my belly. He's been so still today, it had me worried. But he's right back on track now."

"That's it! You're going to Doc Delancey's. No point in worrying if there's nothing to worry about."

"No!" She leaned back into the sofa, stretching a bit. "Now, listen, Brant. These are the ground rules. Only one of us is going through delivery, and that's me. So, your job is to be strong, to be a guide, and let me be the nervous one, okay? I've already talked to the doctor, and he thinks I'm fine. I was just voicing a bit of woman worry out loud, but you're not supposed to get all wound up."

"You want reassurance." From his baby guide research, he remembered that was part of his job. And patience. He'd been very short of that.

"Yes, I do."

"Reassurance." He adopted a gruff persona. "Everything's gonna be fine, Grace. That little baby's just taking a breather before he comes squalling into the world."

"That's better." She laughed. "Ooh, I don't want to laugh."

"What is it?" He leapt to her side.

Grace took a deep breath. "It's time I sent you to the store for baby stuff, I think."

He looked at her carefully. "I think I've changed my mind about leaving you. Let me go check what all they stuck up in the nursery, and then I'll make up a list of what's needed for John and Maggie to go pick up at the store. I know you'll do just fine, Grace, but I don't want to leave you."

She sighed happily, feeling the gathering of new hope mixed with new life inside her. "Oh, that sounds so nice, Brant."

"What does?" He wasn't paying attention as he rooted around for a pencil and paper.

"What you just said." Grace closed her eyes with contentment.

"I said I didn't want to leave…hey, lady," he said, putting the pencil and paper down immediately. He crossed the room to sit on the sofa next to her, pulling her close. "Haven't I said that?"

"I don't think so." She met his dark blue eyes. "Maybe I've been so hurt that you left that I haven't heard you if you did say it."

"Maybe I should just add convincing to the list of patience and reassurance a pregnant woman needs. Grace, honey," he said, burying his face in her neck, "I goofed when I moved the bed in here, I'll admit. What I was trying to say was that I don't want to ever leave you again. I shouldn't have the first time. But I did, and doing it taught me one thing." He looked up to gaze into her eyes. "I couldn't ever forget you."

"Really?"

"Really." He put his hand over hers, which rested on her belly. "I'm just glad you had this little guy waiting around to knock some sense into my head. Being a father has forced me to reprioritize. You come first, babe.''

"Oh, Brant.'' Sentimental tears jumped into her eyes. "That's so sweet.''

"It's true. I want to take good care of you and the little man.'' He sat up straight. "Hey, what are you going to name him?''

"Brant.''

"That's good for a start.''

"Mmm. Brant Wyndford Barclay.''

"I don't like that!''

"Wyndford *is* a bit stuffy,'' Grace agreed.

He cocked his eyebrow at her. "That's not what I mean!''

"I know.'' Grace gave him a gentle smile. "But I can't do anything about the Barclay part right now.''

"Will you ever?''

She knew what he was asking. "Maybe. I think so. Right now, I'm so scared, I'm not sure. Can we have this discussion again when my stomach isn't upset?''

Brant jumped to his feet. "Can I get you something?''

"Some more of those wonderful words you were whispering in my ear a minute ago?''

He dropped next to her, wrapping his arms around her. "You should go upstairs and get changed into something extremely comfortable. I'll find an old movie on TV for us to watch, and root around in your refrigerator for some snacks. Then we'll just wait out the countdown.''

"Okay.'' She started to get up from the sofa, but he clasped her to him for one last hug. "Grace, I intend to tell you for the rest of my life how much I care about you. In the back of my mind, I can't forget that I'm a product of my environment. If I ever slip up and forget, will you give me a small reminder?''

"Like a frying pan upside the head?''

"I don't think it will ever take that much,'' he replied,

his expression very serious. "There was never anyone for me but you, Grace. I took you for granted. That's all there is to it, the long and the short. I expected you to go along with my vision of our relationship. I didn't want to get married, but I didn't expect you to leave me. In my mind, it was always me and you, together, forever. When you asked about marriage, my only reaction was to run. I've worked through what I was running from, but it wasn't you." He touched her hair, tenderly brushing it away from her face so he could see all of her features. "I wasn't running from you. I was running from me."

"Oh, Brant." She snuggled close for an enfolding hug.

"You have another commitment from me," he said huskily against her hair. "I'll teach my son how special his mother is. I will help him to see the difference between giving, and being afraid to give. I have to, you know." He put his head against hers. "I want my son to know that there's nothing to be afraid of when it comes to love."

BRANT JERKED AWAKE, glancing at his watch in the darkness. Four o'clock in the morning. He'd heard a moan, and it wasn't coming from the bed he was in.

"Grace!" he called, jumping from the bed. They'd fallen asleep in the California king size bed so that both of them could stretch out comfortably. "Where are you?"

"In here."

Her reply was more of a moan, and Brant hurried into the connecting washroom. "What is it?"

"Plain old labor pains," she told him.

"What are you doing in here? Why didn't you wake me up?"

She looked as pale as the white ceramic tiles in the bathroom. "I wanted you to get some rest. There's nothing you can do about labor pains, Brant. Go back to sleep." Her face pinched alarmingly.

"Come on in here," he told her. "Let me see if I can find you a position where you can relax."

She in no way looked relaxed to him. There were no socks or slippers on her feet, and her hair was tangled. He wondered if she was cold.

He drew her to him. "Maybe you'll be happier in the nursery in your old bed." At least it had the white lace canopy and sheets and all the trimmings. He hadn't had the chance to buy the accoutrements for this one. They'd merely pulled out a few blankets and pillows and made do. Obviously he'd slept great in the enormous, hardly made bed, while she'd been miserable.

"I'm doing fine." She moaned slightly, rubbing her stomach. "Maggie called after she closed the Cafe and suggested I rock." She bent her knees a little in a slight lunge and shifted back and forth on her feet. "Like that. It does seem to help. So, I've been rocking and walking."

"What can I do?"

She shook her head. "Just be here for me."

Fat lot of good he was doing her. He hadn't even heard the phone ring. "Come here," he said, helping her to the bed. Leaning against the wall where a headboard should have been, Brant pulled her up against him so that her back was facing him and he could support her stomach with his palms.

"That feels better," she sighed.

They sat like that for a while. Grace tried to doze in between contractions. After an hour, when another particularly agonizing spell hit her, he frowned at his watch in the dimness. The contractions seemed to be coming faster, maybe ten minutes apart. He wished greatly that he'd spent more time going over the baby manuals.

This baby seemed determined to be on the early introduction course.

"*Oh-h-h,*" Grace moaned.

"That's it. I'm calling Doc Delancey. Roll over here and

lay on your side, babe.'' He helped Grace curl up, covered her with one of the mismatched blankets and headed for the phone. ''Where's the number?'' he muttered, finally resorting to calling information. Brant felt the taste of panic in his mouth. He didn't know the first thing about what he was supposed to be doing, and Grace wanted him to be patient, reassuring and convincing.

He'd read the page in the book that said women in the throes of delivery sometimes yelled at, perhaps even cursed, the man who'd gotten them into this predicament. He hoped Grace would go easy on him. It was probably best if he got her on to the hospital where she could have trained physicians and nurses helping her instead of him.

''Please page Dr. Delancey,'' he commanded the answering service who took his call.

''Is there an emergency?'' the irritating woman asked.

''No. Yes! My wife's—my baby's having a baby. Wait. I'm having a baby. Jeez!'' Brant exploded. ''Will you just page the damn doctor!''

''Right away, sir,'' the clipped tones came back at him, ''if you'll give me the phone number where the patient can be reached.''

Brant gave her the number before slamming the phone back on the cradle. He cast a guilty glance at the ceiling. Hopefully he hadn't awakened Grace if she'd been managing two minutes of sleep. The phone shrilled, and he pounced on it.

''Hello?''

''This is Dr. Delancey.''

At the calm voice, Brant told himself to slow down. Women had babies every day, and he could make it through his woman doing it. ''Doctor, this is Brant Durning.''

''Hello, Brant. How are you?''

He was fine except for the sweat soaking the underarms of his T-shirt. ''I'm holding up. I think.''

''Ah. How is Grace?''

"Better than me."

"It's normal for you to feel this way." Dr. Delancey laughed. "Do we have contractions?"

"Best as I can tell, they're about ten minutes apart and getting more intense. Although I was asleep for most of them."

"They weren't that bad if you slept through them. Grace is probably just now getting warmed up. This isn't false labor to have continued this long, so why don't you put her overnight bag in the car and come on down to the hospital?"

"Overnight bag?" Had Grace packed one?

"Well, really she'll need very little, and as the hospital is close, you—"

"I can handle an overnight bag, Dr. Delancey. Anything else?"

"No, just don't forget Grace. And you'll need a car seat eventually. The hospital won't let you go home without the baby in a proper car seat."

"Okay." His mind was so frantic he hoped he could remember.

"Now, don't rush to the hospital and have a wreck. She's still got some time to go. Proceed at a calm pace."

"Okay." Brant took a deep breath. "Thanks, Doctor. Proceed at a clam place."

Brig Delancey chuckled. "See you in a bit."

Brant vaulted the stairs. Grace was still rolled into a ball. "How are you doing?"

She tried to smile. "Same."

"Do you have an overnight bag packed?"

"It's in the closet."

Great. That was the hard part, because he sure wouldn't have known what to put in it. "Let's try to get you dressed."

"I don't think so. I'm going as is." Grace jumped from the bed and began a frantic rocking to and fro, breathing deeply until the pain passed. "I'll worry about being pretty some other time, but no one's going to see me at five o'clock in the morning."

He liked her practical attitude. "Now, is there anything else you want me to get you?" he asked, helping her to the stairwell.

"Call Maggie."

"Now?"

"Now." Grace slowly walked down the stairs. "She's my labor coach."

"Labor coach." Brant frowned but picked up the phone and called Maggie. After talking for a brief moment, he went outside, seeing Grace already huddled in his truck. Locking the door behind him, he hurried to the driver's side. "Rats! I forgot the overnight bag!"

"I got it." Grace's lips looked stiff with pain as she talked. "It's in the truck bed."

"Oh. Good thing you're handling this so well, because I'm sure not."

A bloodcurdling howl emitted from the woman he loved. He stared at her in astonishment.

"Great day! What's happening?"

Grace panted wildly as she arched against the seat. "I'm having a baby, what do you think? Get me to the hospital!"

Brant jammed the pedal to the floor, flying out of the driveway. Behind him he saw cruiser lights flare in the night. Slowing down, loud honking sounded as the car swept around him. Maggie's arm fluttered outside the passenger window.

"Your police escort just arrived, babe. I'll have you at the hospital in no time."

Following John at a decent speed, Brant let his mind go on autopilot. He didn't worry about what entrance to the hospital to go to. He didn't worry about how he was going to get her from the truck to the safe, helping hands of trained personnel. He just put Grace's head in his lap.

"Squeeze my arm if you get another pain. And I'm ready for another shriek if you need to. In fact, don't be surprised if I yell along with you."

"Shut up, Brant."

"Okay, babe." Trailing behind the cruiser, he pulled up outside the emergency entrance. In an instant, Maggie was at Grace's door, opening it and carefully helping her out.

"John'll park your truck," she called to Brant. "Let's get her inside."

"You guys act like I'm dying. I'm just having a baby." Grace gritted between teeth she couldn't unlock for the pain.

"You let us engage in hysteria, you focus on the baby," Maggie instructed her.

"If I'd said that to her, it wouldn't have made her feel better." Brant shot Maggie a glance over Grace's bowed head. "I'm glad you're here."

"You're the man that got her into this, honey. Me, I had nothing to do with it." Maggie laughed heartily. "Come on, Grace, step up here and we'll have you inside in a jiff."

"Oh, Maggie!" Grace's voice sounded torn. "There's an alien inside my body."

"I know," the other woman said soothingly. "And he's trying to land his spaceship. Breathe. Breathe."

Brant hurried to the desk to announce Grace's presence. A nurse with a face that looked as if it had seen one too many birthing mothers said, "Are you the labor coach?"

"No. She is." He pointed to Maggie.

"Only immediate family and her labor coach are allowed in the labor room with the patient."

The nurse began leading Grace away. "Maggie!" he shouted. "I just pulled rank on you. I'm the man who got her here, I go in the labor room. You sit in the waiting room with John."

Maggie grinned. "Whatever you say. Call me if you need a break."

"I thought she was the labor coach," the old nurse mentioned.

Brant shook his head. "It was a misunderstanding. I'm doing the coaching around here."

"Are you sure, Brant?" Grace looked wan. "I didn't think you'd want to—"

"I want to. Now shh-shh." He allowed the battleaxe nurse to take her to a table. "Relax if you can. Squeeze my hand if it helps."

"I'm going to check you now," the nurse said.

Brant closed his eyes, feeling squeamish. The woman didn't look near as gentle as he'd want her to be, but Grace never batted an eyelash.

"She's at eight," the nurse announced. "We're going to have to get down to business fast."

Brant stayed out of the way while Grace was prepped. Dr. Brig Delancey strode in, taking command. "Good job, Grace," he said.

"I don't feel like I'm doing a good job. I want to quit now," she moaned.

"Hang in there. The epidural will start working fast." He gave Brant a shrewd eyeing as the anaesthetist arrived. "You going to be all right, Brant?"

"I'm fine," Brant replied indignantly. He couldn't pay too much attention to the doctor as he was closely watching the anaesthetist approach Grace's back. "For crying out loud, I've seen plenty of cows calve. I think I can handle—"

He lost his voice when the anaesthetist pierced a wicked looking needle into the area around Grace's spine.

"Whoa! Dad going down!" Dr. Delancey called.

Grace watched them gather around the man who had fathered her child. The nurse with the stern face continued to hold Grace's hand, patting it.

"You know he'll get paid back for that comment in his

next life," she told the nurse. "He'll come back as a woman."

Together they watched Brant being helped to his feet.

"Oh, God, no," he moaned, overhearing Grace's prediction. "Anything but that."

Dr. Delancey propped him into a chair. "Stay there until you catch your breath."

He already felt immensely better now that they'd finished with Grace's back. She was lying down, already looking a lot more comfortable. "There's your baby," she said, pointing to the monitor.

Waves moved across the monitor. Amazement filled Brant at what he could see. An instant connection to his child jolted him.

He couldn't wait to hold the tiny person who was going to change their lives. New emotion for Grace, something he'd always felt, magnified a hundred percent at the sight of those waves. Unable to speak, he hurried off to get Grace a cup of ice chips. "I know what I'm supposed to be doing," he told her, kissing her on the forehead when he returned. "Hope I didn't worry you when I hit the ground."

"No." Her voice was calm. "We're in a hospital if you concuss yourself."

He chuckled, then sat in a chair nearby to hold her hand and wait for the arrival.


IT COULDN'T HAVE BEEN more than an hour later that Grace was wheeled to the delivery room. Brant had gone out once to give John and Maggie an update, but now as he tagged along behind Grace's gurney, he felt a peculiar churning in his stomach. The big moment was at hand.

"You wait outside a minute, Brant," Dr. Delancey told him. "We'll get you shortly."

Immediately the operating room doors closed in his face. "What the—"

Glancing to each end of the hall, he saw no one to tell

him what was going on inside the OR that he couldn't participate in. "Why, why—"

In the operating room, the nurse rolled her eyes as she glanced at Dr. Delancey. "I figure you've got about thirty seconds to give her that last injection before Mr. Durning—"

"I'm sorry," Brant huffed, coming to stand alongside Grace, "I can't wait outside, Dr. Delancey. You'll have to call security—"

"It's all right, Brant." The doctor grinned. "We're all finished. Let's get to delivering a baby."

Sweat popped out on Brant's forehead. He desperately chanted his mantra of ice chips and patience. Grace pushed, and he supported her back.

Suddenly baby cries filled the room.

"Oh! Oh!" Grace cried, her face alight with joy.

"Oh, my Lord." Brant's tone was thunderstruck as he stared at the infant. "I can't believe I just saw that."

He reached out to touch the baby, but it was whisked away before he got a good look. Nurses quickly measured, wiped clean and weighed the squalling infant. Planting a tearful kiss on Grace, Brant kept a watchful eye on what they were doing with his child. "I can't believe it, I can't believe it," he repeated. "You're so brave. You did such a good job. You're amazing."

Grace's eyes sparkled under his praise.

"Everything's all there, all fingers and toes," the doctor announced. "Perfect health."

"Here you go, Dad," the wizened nurse said, handing the wailing baby to Brant, "isn't she beautiful?"

"She!" Grace and Brant glanced at each other, astonished.

"It's a girl?" Brant asked, astonished.

"Yep. Guess it was her thumb they saw on the sonogram." Brig Delancey grinned hugely, but Grace and Brant never saw it, never heard his quip. Brant took the baby from the nurse, holding her in his hands as if she were most fragile crystal. As if he were holding a miracle he'd waited for all his life.

He was transfixed by her rosy mouth, by her waving little fists.

"Grace Barclay," he said quietly but firmly, "if you don't agree to marry me right this instant, I'm going to cry right here in front of my little girl."

Their eyes met over the squirming bundle. Grace was exhausted, but she smiled at him. "That baby appeals to you, does she?" she asked, falling even more deeply in love at the marveling expression on Brant's face.

"This baby's a tractor rider if I ever saw one." He glanced down quickly, but not before Grace saw the tears in his eyes. "She's strong." He let one of the minuscule fingers wrap around his.

Grace's doubts suddenly washed away. "I'll marry you, Brant," she said softly, but with conviction. It was the only thing she could say. She loved the man far too much to hold out any longer.

The nurse took the baby from Brant. He bent over to press a lingering kiss against Grace's lips. "I love you."

Though Grace had dreamed of hearing Brant say just those words, it still startled her into her own admission. "I love you, too."

"I'm not saying this just because of the baby," he said huskily, "though watching you give birth was the most incredible, beautiful, frightening thing I have ever seen." He took a deep breath. "I have always loved you, Grace. I always will."

He enfolded her into as much of a hug as he could manage with nurses cleaning her up. The nurses and doctor were acting as if they weren't listening, but several smiles lit the operating room.

Happy tears seeped from Grace's eyes. "This is the happiest day of my life."

"It's the happiest day of mine. It's a good thing you didn't get over me."

"How could I? You wouldn't let me."

"I couldn't." Brant closed his eyes for just a moment. "I never told you this before, but you are the only woman I have ever loved."

"I knew that. I knew it all along."

"How?" Brant met Grace's warm gaze.

"Cami told me."

"Cami! I'm going to have a talk with that sister of mine."

"Oh? And what are you going to say to her?"

Nearby, their little daughter was raising a ruckus, and Brant smiled tolerantly. He touched his lips to Grace's. "I'm going to tell her that she can't keep a secret...and then I'm going to kiss her for sending me to the Wedding Wonderland for her dress."

Another wail went up from the baby, who appeared to dislike being charted or weighed or graphed. Grace shot Brant a teasing grin. "She'll want you to buy her a wedding dress one day."

"I know." He chuckled. "But since her mother owns the shop, I can look forward to that day."

# Epilogue

Three weeks after the birth of Margaret Elise, a wedding party was in full swing at the Double D ranch.

"I'd like to toast the lady who's putting the double back in the D around here," Brant said loudly to the assembled guests, lifting a champagne glass. "Grace, you've made me the happiest man alive. It isn't often a man gets two women for the price of one."

Hoots of laughter followed his comment. Grace raised her glass in a silent toast to her new husband. For a man who had been marriage-shy, he seemed to be taking to it with gusto. He made a tall, handsome groom, dressed in a formal evening tux as black as his hair. She admired the way he looked, knowing that this man who made her heart thunder was happy to be hers.

Tearing her gaze away, Grace glanced around the lawn. Maggie, as usual, had outdone herself on the catering and decorating and everything else. Sheriff John had given Grace away, whispering to her as he stood beside her at the altar that Brant hadn't taken his eyes off of her since the moment she began her walk down the aisle. Brant's eyes had indeed been on her, protectively, possessively, and Grace had known complete joy in finally wearing one of the dream-come-true gowns from the Wedding Wonderland.

''Isn't she adorable?''

Grace glanced toward Brant's parents. Though her own parents were traveling on another continent and hadn't been able to rearrange their tickets fast enough to get home for the wedding, Elsa had certainly kept her word. Right now, she and Michael Durning were staring down at baby Margaret. Already way too spoiled, and dressed in the lovely gown Grace had admired in New York. Brant had called her friend, Jana, a few days after Margaret was born to have the gown sent to Texas as a surprise for Grace. He teasingly referred to it as the baby bridal gown, which never failed to make Grace laugh. She was delighted, and even a little humbled by his instant, awestruck attachment to his little girl.

Behind Elsa and Michael, Dr. Nelson stood a discreet distance away, happy, it seemed, to be wherever Elsa was. Texas agreed with him. While Elsa helped Grace give a bridesmaids' luncheon today, he'd roamed off to Waxahachie to see the infamous courthouse where, long ago, a sculptor had carved fascinating feelings about a woman into the stone.

Michael Durning would always be odd-man-out, but he appeared to lavish attention on Margaret—maybe the way he hadn't on Brant and Cami.

Grace's glance flicked to Brant's sister. Cami was a lovely matron of honor, and now beginning to show. Grace grinned at her new sister-in-law. There was a lot the two of them would get to share....

Happy-go-lucky Tilly had been the recipient of Dr. Delancey's conversation for the last half hour, Grace noticed. Kyle Macaffee had come, too, a bit bashful and very brave, she thought gratefully, since he might have preferred staying away. She would certainly have understood. Her sister, Hope, serving as her other wedding attendant, had asked the handsome veterinarian for assistance with something, and the two had been engaged in conversation ever since.

Somehow, Kyle didn't look bashful anymore. Since Hope was staying in Grace's house for the summer so the baby could be close by the shop, who knew?

"Time to throw the bouquet, Grace!" Cami helped her up the stairwell far enough to toss the flowers backward. "All you single women line up for a chance!"

Some women moved forward readily, others balked but were shoved close by friends. Grace closed her eyes and tossed.

"Tilly!" Cami exclaimed as the waitress caught the flying bouquet of whites roses and satin ribbons. "You're next!"

The whole room erupted in laughter as Brant needed no urging to come take the garter from Grace's leg. He did a bit of a rooster dance as he got closer, strutting while the men got into place.

"Stop, Brant!" Grace laughed, somewhat embarrassed by her new husband's antics.

Ignoring her, he refused to give the crowd much of a glimpse of her leg, instead snaking his hand up to find the garter, all the while wiggling his eyebrows at the onlookers. Suddenly he snatched it off and fired it from the tip of his finger.

The little piece of blue and white satin flew across the room—and hit Sheriff John squarely in the face even though he tried to duck.

"Sheriff John!" Brant called. "The next man to find himself at the altar."

"Not me!" he called good-naturedly, though Grace noticed he glanced Maggie's way. She shook her head at the sheriff. Grace hoped that wouldn't be the case forever.

Brant leaned over, kissing her and stealing all thoughts of her guests from her mind. "Mrs. Brant Durning, Mrs. Grace Barclay Durning, other half of the Double D, your overlarge bed awaits you upstairs. It has been properly short-sheeted by some pranksters, because I heard them complaining greatly about the difficulties in trying to short-sheet a California king-size bed. Shall we inspect their handiwork?''

Grace laughed, getting to her feet. Out of the corner of her eye, she saw Buzz and Purvis doing an excellent job of passing out birdseed. ''Did you arrange for the limo driver to drive us around long enough for our guests to leave?'' she asked. ''When I get you back home, I want you all to myself.''

''Not near as much as I want you all to myself,'' Brant told her, tucking her close as they prepared to run through the shower of falling birdseed. ''The chase is over, Mrs. Durning, but the best part has just begun.''

THE NEXT DAY was considerably quieter around the Yellowjacket Cafe. In the kitchen, Maggie gave Sheriff John's hand a solid whack with her wooden spatula. Buzz could hear the resounding crack at his checkerboard, but he barely noticed it. He had something far greater on his mind.

''Playing checkers isn't as much fun as it used to be,'' he told Purvis Brown.

''I know.'' Purvis looked around the cafe. He didn't have to ask his friend what he meant. With Grace and Brant honeymooning, and Cami and Dan busy combining ranches, it was going to be too slow for at least a little while. ''Still, it's better than this crazy contraption of my grandkid's.'' He pulled a Nintendo computer game from his pocket.

''Gimme that!'' Buzz said, impatient to see what the buttons could do. After a moment, he sorrowfully shook his head, giving it back to Purvis. ''This generation's gonna grow up without knowing the benefits of a thinking man's game like checkers.''

''Yep,'' Purvis agreed. ''Strategizing. That's what makes men succeed on the battlefield, the football field, and everywhere else.'' Purvis put the game away, glancing at his friend shrewdly. "So, who can we work on now?''

Buzz sidled his gaze across to the kitchen where Tilly was picking up short orders. "There's Maggie and Sheriff John.''

"That'd be like sifting sand through the eye of a needle,'' Purvis commented. "Impossible.'' He thought for a moment. "What about the new doc? Dr. Delancey? Last I checked, he ain't got nobody.''

"Maybe.'' Buzz rubbed his chin. "Tilly ain't, either.''

Purvis pulled his gaze away from the kitchen and the long-legged waitress. He shook his head. "Naw. Ain't nobody been able to stay with her long enough to hear the bell.''

It was a many-told rumor about the waitress. Men said that trying to date Tilly Channing was like trying to stay on a bronc for eight seconds.

Buzz rubbed his palms together, his eyes lit with sudden excitement. "Then again, finding Tilly a man just might be fun. And there's our good-hearted veterinarian, Dr. Kyle Macaffee, who's still on the loose....''

Purvis nodded his satisfied agreement. "Your move, old friend.''

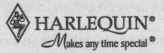

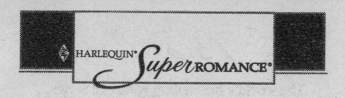

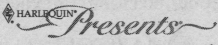

# HARLEQUIN®
# INTRIGUE

## WE'LL LEAVE YOU BREATHLESS!

If you've been looking for thrilling tales of
contemporary passion and sensuous love stories
with taut, edge-of-the-seat suspense—then
you'll love Harlequin Intrigue!

Every month, you'll meet four new heroes
who are guaranteed to make your spine tingle
and your pulse pound. With them you'll enter
into the exciting world of Harlequin Intrigue—
where your life is on the line
and so is your heart!

## THAT'S INTRIGUE—
## ROMANTIC SUSPENSE
## AT ITS BEST!

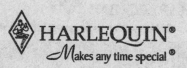

HARLEQUIN®
*Makes any time special* ®